THE
WAKING
ENGINE

THE WAKING ENGINE

David Edison

TOR®

A TOM DOHERTY ASSOCIATES BOOK

NEW YORK

This is a work of fiction. All of the characters, organizations, and events portrayed in this novel are either products of the author's imagination or are used fictitiously.

THE WAKING ENGINE

Copyright © 2014 by David Edison

A Tor Book
Published by Tom Doherty Associates, LLC
175 Fifth Avenue
New York, NY 10010

www.tor-forge.com

Tor® is a registered trademark of Tom Doherty Associates, LLC.

Library of Congress Cataloging-in-Publication Data

Edison, David.
    The waking engine / David Edison.
        p. cm.
    "A Tom Doherty Associates Book."
    ISBN 978-0-7653-3486-2 (hardcover)
    ISBN 978-1-4668-1677-0 (e-book)
    1. Future life—Fiction.   I. Title.
  PS3605.D557W35 2014
  813'.6—dc23
                        2013028407

Tor books may be purchased for educational, business, or promotional use. For information on bulk purchases, please contact Macmillan Corporate and Premium Sales Department at 1-800-221-7945, extension 5442, or write specialmarkets@macmillan.com.

First Edition: February 2014

Printed in the United States of America

0 9 8 7 6 5 4 3 2 1

For Marilyn Sue and Bunny

ACKNOWLEDGMENTS

There are more people to thank than there are pages for thanking. Every friend, every teacher, every obstacle, every encouragement: thank you.

In general, thanks to the patience and understanding of my family and friends, who let me be a gregarious hermit without (much) complaint.

In particular, I would not have written this book without the support of my agent, Loretta Barrett, who signed a madman with three chapters and told him to come back when he'd written a book. Or without Jennifer Didik, who fought for me and did her best to keep me sane. Or without Paul Stevens, my editor at Tor, who bought, midwifed, and championed the manuscript. Or without Christopher Michaud, who read so many versions of this book that he became a part of it. You are all partners.

Susan Grode and Nancy Cushing-Jones, thank you for connecting the dots that led to this wonderful career.

I reserve an enduring gratitude for the teachers in my life, and there are many: Bernard and Marilyn Edison, my first and best teachers; Carol Frericks, my second mother; Stacie Lents, dearest friend and first critic; Evelyn Pronko, who was right to tell me to pull myself together in fifth grade; Rebecca Richardson, Madelyn Gray, Carolyn "Lyn" Thomas, Charles Derleth (I didn't forget), and Joanna Collins, alongside every other teacher at the John Burroughs School, the best high school in the galaxy; Lowry Marshall, who taught me to write on my feet; Ellen Kushner and Delia Sherman, wise friends and fairy godmothers; and my beautiful Lena, who needs no words to teach.

THE
WAKING
ENGINE

PROLOGUE

The room was empty except for the smell of disuse and a small woman with a heart-shaped face and a cloud of flaming red hair. She wore a thin dress that had once been a color, and no shoes. Her bright brown eyes blinked at the knives of light that cut through the slatted windows. Alouette is as good a name for her as any of the others she's used, and Alouette began to smile when she looked at the crumbled molding around the ceiling. Thick fluid had begun to seep from beneath the plaster and flow in dark curtains down the walls; she stifled a laugh.

"Oh," she said. "The walls are weeping. It must be Tuesday."

Alouette paced the room, tracing its boundary with her toes in the dust that lay heavy on the floor; she tested the wall with a finger but was unsurprised when it came away dry.

"The tears like to run down, don't they? But don't stay to play. Would ruin the effect, I suppose." Alouette sighed and ran bloodless fingers through her bloodred curls. "You are so pretentious," she said to the gurgling walls.

She shivered, but not from cold, and looked down at the circle she had traced on the floor, its smooth curve marred only a little by her foot-printed meanderings—she walked on the balls of her feet and her step was light, and besides, the circle was a thing she'd *intended* to make, which made it more real somehow. Where Alouette was concerned, intent was everything.

Except for Tuesdays.

"Oh, oh," she said, pulling a demitasse from behind her back. A thimbleful of bright green tea steamed within. "I do not want to do this. I do not mean for this to happen, but it will, and so I must cause it. I have to make a thing, because the thing will be made. Oh, oh, everything runs wrong on days like this." She tossed the tiny cup out the window, spilt tea catching the light like brilliant-cut citrine.

Alouette rubbed her bare arms, feeling their softness and noticing without pride or dismay the whiteness of her skin; like the dress, it too had probably held color, once upon a time. A poppy-red ribbon tied around one ankle caught her eye, and she lifted her foot off the dusty floorboards, admiring the curl of satin. It was the only brightness in the room.

Yes, she liked this shape, and the feel and look of it. She liked the skin and the light bones; *loved* the hair, but then she almost always wore red up there. Alouette nodded, letting a little vanity into the room—she was only delaying the inevitable, but a strict discipline had never really been her style. She nodded: yes, she liked this shape for many reasons, but mostly because it felt the truest. If she'd ever been a true woman, she might have looked like this.

Squaring her shoulders to bring herself to attention, Alouette let them slump again as she studied the circle of clean nothing drawn in the dust of dirty nothing. She wished she knew why it was that great things, beautiful or terrible or both, so often stepped out of nothing to shake the worlds and raze the heavens only to creep back into nothing at the end of their day.

"I'm so sorry," she said to the circle as she embellished it with more empty spaces, twirling blank lines into the dust with her toes like a broken ballerina. "I am so sorry, stranger, to cause this thing to be done to you. You deserve a better Tuesday."

And as she moved, the worlds moved; or rather, something moved *through* the worlds. The strings were invisible and the call inaudible but somewhere, somehow, a thing moved in an impossible way. *Not a thing*, Alouette reminded herself, deliberating on that descriptor; *it's a human being that moves*. As Alouette spun almost drunkenly, someone moved from *here* to *there*. Someone ignorant and innocent and, now, someone lost.

The lost were Alouette's specialty. They were province, her provenance, and on awful days like this—her creation. Her *byproduct*.

She held the lost things of the worlds closest to her heart: lost men and women, lost kingdoms, worlds, and civilizations—lost ribbons and empty rooms. She held back the tide of loss and losing that described the arc of the metaverse in all its tragic iterations, on tiny scales and on scopes for which only gods and powers could grieve. In the foreign sharpness of her mind, the being who called herself Alouette saw that this forgotten room cried ropes of snot and salt for her occasional betrayals. The walls wept for the circle she danced into the dusty emptiness. The walls bawled because she never, would never *cause* a thing to become lost. Loss was her defining hate, her passion, sacrifice, her ruin.

She never intended loss.

Except on Tuesdays.

1

My braying heart continues in spite of itself: I am. I am. I am.

I do not know why I am here, but it is clearly not to Die. I see them, the Dying people, spiritually aged, faces bleached of all color by worlds of weekdays; I see them stumbling through the cathedral forest beneath the Dome. My God, I think they are like birds. Piloted by instinct.

I'll spend hours birdwatching there, watching them Die—their bodies evaporate like smoke and the last look on their faces is peace, the first true peace they have known in dozens or hundreds or thousands of lives. Peace comes like a broken clock.

I hate them for that, the idiot birds who get to Die. If it were within my power to deny the Dying their Deaths, I would. Why should they find peace while I find none?

—Sylvia Plath, *Empty Skies & Dying Arts*

Cooper opened his eyes to see a spirit shaped like a woman, who cradled his head in her hands, her hair a halo of pink light that fell over his face. Angel eyes the color of wet straw looked down on him, and she smelled of parchment and old leather. As his eyes adjusted to the light, he saw that her freckled skin was tan, nearly brown, and for a long moment Cooper waited for her to speak. *This is heaven*, she would say. *You will find peace here, and oblivion. We will heal your hurts, friend. Welcome home*, she would say. *You have been away too long.* Cooper would smile, and submit, and she would guide him somewhere radiant.

He did not expect the slap to his cheek. Nor the second that followed, stinging.

He did not expect the angel to drop his head onto the hard ground and declaim, "I can do nothing with this turd."

"My friend was not wrong, Sesstri," a man said, cursing. "That is what makes him my friend and not my dinner."

The woman pulled away and light came pouring over Cooper's eyes, almost as blinding as before. Struggling, he could see that it wasn't the light of heaven needling through his pupils—the sky above was jaundiced and cloud-dappled, and he lay in the rain on an odd little hillock that bristled with yellow grass. Above him, the two strangers just stood there, glaring down at his body.

And suddenly his body was all Cooper could feel: lit up with pain, scalded. How had he thought himself dead, let alone at peace? His bones ached and his bowels shuddered, and an abrupt crack of lightning overhead seemed to pierce his skull and live there, screeching agony between his temples. He tried to sit up but couldn't. He couldn't even roll onto his side, and when Cooper opened his mouth no words came out—he jawed like a fish in air, and flopped as helplessly. Flocks of birds pinwheeled across the sky. Bells rang and rang.

What happened? Cooper scrambled inside his head to reassemble some kind of continuity of experience. The last thing he could recall was drifting through a borderless sleep into a half-dream of lightless depths. He recalled sensing bodies in motion, masses larger than planets drifting through the murk below his dream-self. He could not see them, but somehow—he *knew* them. And maybe then he had passed beyond shadows. Maybe then he'd seen a city. . . .

"Bells for the abiding dead, what a waste of my time!" The man standing above Cooper cursed again and raised his boot. Cooper had time to blink once before the crunch of boot-heel slammed him back into darkness.

When he next opened his eyes, Cooper could tell by the quality of the light that he'd been moved indoors. He heard voices, the same man and woman from earlier, still arguing. He'd been dropped onto something hard but covered in padding, and when the wood creaked beneath his weight and a pillow found his cheek, he realized it was a sofa. Something about creaking wood and narrow cushions felt instantly recognizable; for half a second, Cooper worried that he'd broken the furniture, an old, familiar thought. He closed his eyes before anyone could see he'd come around, playing detective with his senses as rapidly as his addled mind could muster. He smelled kitchen smells—soap and old food—and something pleasant, like flowers or potpourri. Peeking out from between his lashes, Cooper saw a blurry image of his saviors—captors?—the man and woman who'd taken him home.

"I've finished examining him, Asher. You can come back in." The woman, who sounded annoyed, smoothed strawberry-blond hair so pale it fell past her shoulders like a bolt of pink silk. "I cannot help you with this. Anything your friend said you'd find on that hill is between you and the sheep guts, or whatever absurd claptrap he employs to disabuse you of your coin. I'm not going to rifle through every corpse that wakes up south of Displacement and Rind for you, anyway, so you'll have to do the dirty work yourself."

"Fine, forfeit your fee, Sesstri," said Asher, and Cooper noticed that the tall man, broad-shouldered but gaunt, had skin and hair the pale gray of old bones or nearly pregnant clouds. "I'd pay you for examining his body, but since I carried him back to your house, I think we're even."

Cooper squeezed his eyes shut again and *felt* them approach, felt them hover over him.

"He's as heavy as he looks," said the gray man.

Sesstri made an unhappy noise. Cooper didn't need eyes to feel her scrutiny. He kept still when she jabbed his chest with her finger.

When she spoke, Cooper could tell that Sesstri had turned away. "He is just a person. He's just like everyone else." She hesitated. "A little green to wake up here, but nothing unheard of—I only died twice before I came here myself. Whoever he may have been, he is not the 'something special' you are looking for. He will heal no wounds, diagnose no conditions, and answer no questions." She left the room, seeming more interested in the singing teakettle than the men defiling her home. "Muck up the place all you like," she called out, "I haven't seen the landlady since the day she handed me the keys."

Asher knelt close and brushed Cooper's face with his hand. "You can open your eyes now, friend. We don't need her." He whispered, tobacco on his breath, and Cooper peeked through his eyelids. The face so close to his own was a silver mask that smiled: "Welcome to the City Unspoken, where the dead come to Die. In my city, everything old is made new again, and anything new is devoured like sweet eel candy."

Cooper looked at Asher's ghostlike hair as he pulled away and turned to stir something at the sink beneath the window. Over his shoulder, the window showed a square of lemony sky and an unfamiliar, pale green sun. When Cooper sat up, head throbbing, Asher turned to him holding a tray piled with buttered toast and two steaming mugs. His gray skin was smooth and his eyes flickered like strange candles, red and blue and green together. He was handsome and repulsive at the same time, like a great beauty embalmed. Something wriggled inside Cooper's head, an instinct trying to name itself. It didn't come.

Nothing came, Cooper realized—no panic, no outrage, no bewilderment or dispossession at waking to find himself . . . well . . . wherever he'd found himself. Nothing came but fog in his mind and an empty-headed sense of confusion.

Asher smirked when he saw Cooper awake, but said nothing, content to lean on his hip and observe the new arrival. The moment stretched. Then it snapped. "What . . ." Cooper blurted, then faltered, unable to pick one question from the dozens that crowded his tongue. "Why is the sun green?"

The last thing Cooper remembered was lying down fully clothed on his own bed after another long day of work and text messages. But these weren't his friends, this wasn't his apartment, and he certainly hadn't been sending texts to any ash-skinned thugs. All he knew for certain—this was no dream. It hurt too much, and the logic didn't follow itself moment-to-moment as in a dream.

"Welcome to the waking," Asher said with a smile. "Drink this." His long-fingered hands were huge.

"Sesstri's taking notes." He handed Cooper a mug steaming with the scent of jasmine and spice. "I left the room while she strip-searched you, though, if that spares your ego any."

Cooper looked down at the mug shaking in his hands and fought the urge to throw it in the stranger's face. His gut, as always, told him to say "fuck you," and, as always, he said nothing. He grimaced, though the tea and buttered bread smelled like heaven.

"Drink it," Asher commanded.

Jasmine and pepper filled his mouth, hot and real. And it did bring Cooper back, clearing some of the fog from his head. He began looking at his surroundings in earnest while rolling sips of tea across his dry tongue. They sat alone in a room, the wallpaper calligraphed with un-familiar symbols. On a wooden table against one wall spun an odd-looking Victrola, its mouthpiece carved from a huge spiral horn, and a low table piled with books. In fact, every available surface seemed piled with books. Asher handed him a plate and this time Cooper accepted it eagerly.

"This is a living room," Cooper said before filling his mouth with toast. It was bliss.

"Ah, yes. It is. I'm Asher." The gray stranger introduced himself, nodding.

Cooper reciprocated through a mouthful of buttery ecstasy. "Maybe you could . . . tell me . . . where I am?" he added.

Asher watched Cooper scarf down the toast and drain the spicy tea, then held out a hand. "Can you stand? Come upstairs with me, and I will show you."

Of course I can stand, Cooper thought before trying—and falling back onto the couch. He frowned and grabbed another slice of toast as Asher lugged him to his feet, but a few steps later his legs weren't so wobbly after all.

He followed Asher up a narrow stairway that turned at odd angles and led higher than Cooper felt it ought to. At one pinched landing stood an end table where an armful of foxglove shoots wilted from a china vase. "She can't be bothered with flowers . . . ," Asher half muttered, shaking his head.

At the top of the stairs, the gray man opened a splintered door with a kind of reverence. Sweeping one smoky hand, he ushered Cooper through the portal.

As he stepped out onto the wooden widow's walk nailed to the roof, a chill passed through Cooper's body. A city lay spread out before him. More than a city—a comment on a city, on all cities, a sprawling orgy of architectural imagination and urban decay. Buildings and blocks stretched to the horizon, and Cooper's head reeled to take it in, from the spired heights that pierced the distance to the crusts of abandoned blocks, smoldering and dark where they lay. He turned and turned, but the city was all he could see, opening itself to him. There were wards that seemed to bustle with life, but there were also dead zones—whole precincts left to rot within the girding chaos. What he saw seemed to be the very idea of a city, barnacled and thick with itself.

Veils of fog hung at various altitudes within the air, draped over the city in colors of rock crystal—smoky quartz, amethyst, and citrine. The wind was strangely warm, and Cooper smelled a dozen different flavors of incense on its shifting gusts. A song of competing bells tolled point and counterpoint across the metropolis, sending flocks of birds wheeling into the air at intervals.

And competing skies. The pale yellow sky that Cooper had seen through the window downstairs seemed to have slid off to one side of the heavens, following its tiny green star. In the east, heavy clouds played peekaboo with a bluer firmament, and a yellow sun seemed to emerge, fading into and out of existence as he watched.

The skies, he marveled, watching them change.

Asher led Cooper, dumbfounded, to a weathered spyglass mounted upon a pipe at the edge of the walkway. Cooper hesitated—did he want to see? Did he want to accept the reality of this fever-dream? But he put his face to the glass and opened his eye to the city, despite suspecting that once he saw the details of this nightmare, once he knew its shape and aspect, it would be irreversibly real. The city would be real and he would be well and truly lost within it, unhinged, a ghost among ghost-men.

Through the telescope he saw snapshots of the whole: monuments and mausoleums pitted and scarred with age lay tilted, stone and gilt akimbo as the growth of the city slowly devoured them. Mansions hid behind walls that sheltered riotous gardens and skeletal gazebos. To the west, a sculpture of a weeping woman worked entirely in silver sat buried up to her massive head in newer stonework—a garland of exhaust pipes about her neck belched bruise-purple smoke into the air from below. Not far from that, an alabaster angel blew his shofar before a ramshackle square that brimmed with black oil, summoning a host that would clearly never come. And chains, everywhere chains—thick as houses, exposed by canals, or pulled up from belowground and winched like steeples over bridges and buildings, draped across districts, erupting from the tiled floors of public squares.

Panning, Cooper saw wide boulevards lined with sycamores, elms, and less familiar trees, avenues that glittered darkly or pulsed with traffic. The larger thoroughfares led from a shadowy axis that reminded him of an orb spider's web. At the center of the web, near the horizon, a vast plaza yawned. The plaza itself must have been huge to be so visible from this distance, but what lay beyond was bigger still: was it a structure, or a mountain, or something still more bizarre?

Above the central space loomed a dome that would dwarf a hundred arenas, a hemisphere worked in copper and glass that looked like lacework but whose struts must have been the thickness of a city block. It commanded the horizon like a fallen moon, and was strung with banners and limned from within by a green-gold glow. The great dome sat at the heart of a cluster of smaller spheres, bubbles of stone and metal that adhered to the central structure, bristling with arched bridges and needle-thin towers.

"Who lives there?" Cooper asked, pointing to the dome that dwarfed everything.

"In the Dome?" Asher wrinkled his nose. "Fflaen the Fair—at least, he used to. The Prince."

"Oh," Cooper said.

"He rules here." Asher bobbed his head and said no more, gaze lost in his city.

"Where *is* here?" Cooper asked at length, trying to keep the welling terror from his voice. The gray man didn't answer his question. Instead, his eyes drifted to the distance. Fires flickered out there, in the towers of the city. Towers that burned but never fell.

That was a sight that made Cooper's gut twist. Could he hear crying? He looked to his acquaintance. *"Where is here?"* he asked again.

Asher's eyelashes were the color of smoke, and the silence stretched until it became an answer of its own.

Cooper made it back down to the living room in a blur, where Sesstri explained matters more thoroughly. "Listen to me very carefully. This may sound complicated, but it's not: the life you lived, in the world you called home, was just the first step. A short step. Less than a step. It's the walk from your house to the barn, and what you think of as death is nothing more than the leap up into the saddle of your trusty pony. When you die *there,* you wake up, well, not *here* usually—but someplace else. In your flesh, in your clothes, older or younger than you remember being, but *you*, always you."

Cooper nodded because it was all he could do.

"There are a thousand thousand worlds, each more unlike your home than the last. Where you end up, or how you get there, nobody really knows. You just do. And you go on. Dying and living, sleeping and waking, resting and walking. That's how living works. It's a surprise for most of us, at first. We think our first years of life are all we'll ever see." She paused, her thoughts turning inward. "We are wrong."

Cooper said nothing. He was dead *and* he was going to live forever?

Sesstri considered him and drew a long breath, raked her fingernails through her morning-colored hair. "Life is a very, very, *very* long journey. Sometimes you go by boat, sometimes by horse. Sometimes you walk for what seems like forever, until you find a place to rest."

"So . . ." Cooper drawled, deliberately obtuse because humor seemed the only way he could go on breathing. "I have a pony?"

Asher chuckled. Sesstri didn't.

"There is no pony!" she snapped. "The pony was a mere device. In the country of my origin, we smother our idiots and mongoloids at birth. You are fortunate to have been born into a more forgiving culture." Asher's chuckle grew into laughter.

Sesstri rested her palms on her knees and made an obvious show of being patient. "Let me say this as plainly as possible. There are a nearly uncountable number of universes—*universes*; mind you, when we speak of 'the worlds' we speak of whole realities—most of which are populated to a greater or lesser extent with *people*. Universes with planets that are round, or flat, or toroid—and others with space that conforms to no geometry or cosmology you or I would recognize from home. On most of these worlds, people are born, and live, and die. When we die, we don't cease to exist or turn into shimmering motes of ectoplasm or purple angels or anything else you may have been brought up to believe. We just . . . go on living. Someplace else."

"People call it the 'dance of lives,'" Asher interjected, miming a jig.

Sesstri cocked her head for a moment as if tucking away a fact, then widened her eyes to ask if Cooper followed her so far. He nodded, hungry for Sesstri to continue even though he had already swallowed a bellyful of follow-up questions. Toroid? Which was it, worlds or universes—or was that distinction itself subject to variation? She was a much better instructor than Asher, and Cooper's only option was to learn.

"There's little logic behind where we go, although a great many thinkers have spent a great deal of time failing to prove otherwise. I might have succeeded. We live and die, then wake somewhere new. We live on, die again, then wake once more. In a sense you're right—it is a kind of prison sentence, and life will exhaust you at every opportunity. It's a slow and painful way to travel, but that's life: painful and slow. And very, *very* long." When she finished, she looked at Cooper with a mixture of doubt and expectancy, waiting for the inevitable reaction of shock and confusion, but it did not come.

"Welcome to the Guiselaine!" Asher sang out, his arms spread wide. "The best worst district in the whole nameless sprawl." He and Cooper stood atop a brick bridge that straddled a foaming brown canal. Foot traffic, rickshaws, and carts of every design pushed past them toward the warren of crooked alleys and side streets that comprised the Guiselaine, and Asher grabbed Cooper's wrist, pulling them into the crush. Cooper resisted, but Asher dragged him along anyway; the man was strong. The crowd eddied around a small fountain square at the far side of the bridge before swarming into a tangle of shadowy lanes where the walls tilted overhead, hiding the sky behind half-tunnels of stone and wood and daub.

The two men waded through a river of dirty faces, citizens of a dozen flavors—the rich mixed with the poor mingled with the alien, all distracted by conversation or the challenge of a swarming market at noon. Asher steered through the crowd expertly, his gray face and white-crowned head breaking above the rabble like the prow of a ghost ship, fey and proud—a ship of bones, a ship of doves.

"The City Unspoken has many quarters, but for my money, the Guiselaine is the one to see," Asher confided to Cooper as they ducked onto one of the broader thoroughfares. "A most deplorable gem of a borough." He waved a gray hello to friendly faces Cooper was too distracted to make out. "All tangled streets and hidden treasures. Harmless fun during the day, quite another story after dark. Which is, of course, when I like it most." Asher spread his hands in a mock-spooky gesture, and Cooper grinned in spite of himself. He took Asher's hand and gripped it tightly as they darted through the busy world. Whatever had happened to him had dispossessed him wholly, and Cooper found his head full of odd whispers. The crowd didn't seem to help.

They stopped to stare into the window of a shop that displayed an array of the strangest stemware Cooper had ever seen: scrimshawed goblets carved from human skulls, pale leather wineskins that bore the sewn-up eyes and mouths of human faces, and a ghastly masterpiece that dominated the display—a silver decanter set within the corpse of a toddler boy, plasticized by some grim process, whose split skull and abdomen cradled the silver vial while shining filigree slithered around its chubby limbs. It looked like some metal parasite had emerged to gorge itself upon the child, slipping silver tentacles around every spare feature of flesh. Looking at the decanter, Cooper felt detached from the horror, somehow, his head running a line of practical questions. How do you cleave a child so cleanly from crown to belly? How do you work silver so intricately, without burning the flesh or ruining the composition? How do you get a child to make such a beatific expression as you bisect the front of his face? There was no life here to sense, no sensitivity. Just art, artifice, and commerce.

Those were things he could understand, at least. He'd spent most of his life thus far as a consumer—why should life change, wherever it went? Wasn't that the gist of Sesstri's lecture?

"Come on, Cooper," Asher complained, tugging at the newcomer's wrist. "Bells, but you're slow."

A man with black skin—not brown, black—knelt over the body of a child, a boy, who stared at the sky with an uncomfortable intensity. *ComeOnSabbiComeOn,* the man said, except he didn't. Cooper wasn't close enough to hear and, in any event, the man hadn't moved his lips. *SabbiSabbiLookAtDaddy,* Cooper heard again as they neared—the man felt terrified.

How do I know what that man feels? Cooper asked himself. But he did.

Cooper looked to Asher to see if he'd heard, too, but Asher appeared oblivious. Cooper looked to the black man as they passed him, but the man did not even see them, cupping his son's cheeks in his carbon-dark skin. *SabbiComeBackAround! DaddyNeedsYou!*

The passersby did not hear, either. Cooper thought he would have known if they heard the man but ignored his suffering, because he saw that every day in New York. No, he'd heard words that hadn't been spoken. Him, and only him.

"Asher," Cooper began, beginning to freak out as they turned a corner into a ramshackle courtyard where a dusk-skinned woman in a tattered dress leaned against the wall by an alleyway, pressed by a rat-faced man with bulging eyes and shaky hands. Her hair was curled and coiled atop her head but was caked with dust—like a wig left out of its box for a decade or two.

Something stopped Cooper in his tracks. Asher looked back, impatient, but Cooper stared in horror at the woman and her accoster, distracted from his own thoughts.

She had a sad face painted brightly to obscure the truth, and she laughed like a schoolgirl every time the small man spoke, flashing a smile that never touched her eyes. He cupped a hand to her breast and she held it there, whispering encouragement. He drew a lazy line across her throat with one finger and dripped words into her ear. She licked her lips and pressed against him, but inside she was screaming. Cooper knew, because he could *hear* it.

NoNoPleaseNotAgain. He could hear it. Words that weren't spoken. Fear.

NoNoNeverICan'tBreathe ICan'tBreatheKillMePleaseKillMe, KillMe-Dead, AndMakeItStickThisTime, MakeItStickThisTimeICan'tBearToWake-UpAgain.

"Stop it!" Cooper yelled, dashing forward. "Stop! Asher, help, he's going to kill her!"

Asher barked a laugh, and caught Cooper's arm as he shot by. "Of course he is, Cooper." He waved an apology to the woman and the rat-faced little man. "Apologies, do carry on." They did.

Asher pulled Cooper close and growled, "Please don't do that. You neither know our customs nor have the moral authority to intervene. And you make me look bad."

"What *is* she?" Cooper asked, aghast, as the woman and her paramour withdrew into the gloom of the alley.

"She's a bloodslut," Asher said coldly, but his eyes were downcast. "A life-whore. A stupid girl who signed the wrong contract somewhere along the way, and now she's stuck here. She can't die, so she sells her body and life to any jack with two dirties to rub together. He ruts her, guts her, then fills her mouth with coins."

"Wait, *what*?" Cooper's brain couldn't quite gear itself up for the question of death. That poor woman didn't *seem* dead, merely exhausted. But her thoughts, if that's what he had heard . . . her fears . . .

"She can't die," Asher said, pointing to a pair of figures picking each other up from the dirt. One kept her gaze low, the other leaned against the bricks trying to catch his breath. Both looked too thin, too worn. "Not properly, anyway."

"That's horrible." Cooper was shivering. "Her job is to let dirty little men kill her for money?" He couldn't keep the disgust from his voice— what pathetic creature could survive that way, let alone turn a profit? Then again, if she couldn't die, he supposed she had no choice *but* to survive. If that were the case, maybe it was no wonder her brutalized thoughts scraped the inside of his head.

Asher nodded. "Kill her, and whatever else they want to do to her. For money. Why else? Hurry up." Asher nearly dragged Cooper down the street as bells began to toll in the distance. Bells and bells and bells, a city of them.

But Cooper's thoughts were back in the alley with the woman who looked more . . . *used* than should have been possible. Here that seemed to be normal. What other nightmares were normal, here, that should be awful? Was hearing the fears of strangers as inconsequential as screaming inside, screaming for peace? He'd *heard her,* heard her panic inside his head. What did that make him? Deathlessness aside, Cooper couldn't figure out what unnerved him more: the contents of her head, or the fact that he'd been exposed to them.

A few moments later came a brain-piercing scream that trailed off wetly. No one on the street seemed to notice. Asher saw Cooper's discomfort, flashed his winning corpse smile, and pinched Cooper's arm. "Don't worry, really. A few hours from now her body will jerk upright, skin whole if not new—she'll spit out her wad and be open for business again."

"Oh." Cooper's stomach convulsed and he nearly tossed his toast. "No wonder she was screaming." He smelled fried bread and crispy fish from a hawker they passed, and swallowed hard.

Asher gave him a funny look. "It's just a little death, Cooper."

"So death means absolutely nothing." His body felt numb.

Asher shook his head. "No, that's not at all what I—"

"—All my life, all *everyone's* life, we're so scared of—what, a travel-ogue? Death is a game, just part of the economy, and my life means— meant—*means* nothing?" Cooper bit out the words accusingly, like the City Unspoken and its deathlessness were all Asher's fault.

Asher put his hand on Cooper's chest and pressed him into the brick wall of the lane. His force was controlled and guided, just this side of dangerous. "*Don't say that.* Don't say that; death is the worst thing that can happen, so don't ever say that." This, too, passersby ignored; these were a people inured to every kind of disturbance. Had any of them been New Yorkers, once?

Cooper let that fuel his indignation. This metropolis was worlds worse than ignoring indigents and stealing taxis. "The worst thing that can happen is a nap and a brand-new body, are you *kidding* me?"

Anger clouded Asher's gray face. "Every time we die, a whole world dies. What do you think they're saying about you right now, Cooper?" Asher shook his head in disbelief. "Is it 'Oh, Cooper stepped off to an- other universe for a brief visit but we expect him to return shortly. Can- apé?' Or do you think there's a funeral somewhere with your fucking name on it?" Asher was livid, but his skin showed not a pulse of blush. He let Cooper go, who doubled over at the thought of what his family and friends must be feeling.

Now came the fear and confusion that Sesstri had expected earlier. Cooper pictured his mother, obliterated by losing her only son. His fa- ther, cracked in half with grief. Life had been dull, but it had *been*. Coo- per's head reeled. *How could I forget that?* he screamed inside. *How could I, for one single moment, doubt the totality of my death, back in the world where I lived?*

"I apologize," Asher nearly stammered, "I associate honesty with anger. It . . . explains a lot. Are you crying?"

Cooper couldn't breathe. His family and friends—what nightmare must they be enduring? Sheila and Tammy would be screaming when they found his body in the apartment they shared. Mom would be turning in place, trying to put right something that could never be fixed and was the heart of her world. His dog, Astrid—would she sit by the door, waiting for him, wondering why he never came back to her? She wouldn't understand, just *ache*. The same went for Cooper as for those he'd left behind. No understanding, just pain and loss and a false promise of peace at the end.

"This is sickness," he choked from his knees, "how could they not be my first thought? This is sick, sick, sick." He looked up at Asher, stringy-haired and chisel-faced, the piss-colored sky going blue behind him. Quicksilver clouds gathered, not minding the schizophrenic heavens above them. "Can't you see how sick this is, or are you too dead to notice?"

The colorless man closed his eyes and took a breath. "There are sicknesses. Living is not one of them." He fixed Cooper with a tight-jawed expression. Asher's false levity had fled.

Cooper stood up, wiped his eyes, and crossed his arms like an obstinate child. Despite the death and deathlessness, despite the bloodslut's impermanent murder, he found himself. Despite the background noise of fears murmuring in his head as people passed. "Explain. Now. I can deal, if I *know*." Cooper leaned against a wall so ancient its bricks had crumbled into little pockets for weeds and moss. "Am I really dead or only dreaming? I feel awake, but . . . Am I in a coma? Is this some kind of fucked up comaland? Sesstri says I'm dead. Are *you* dead? What's with the urban purgatory? What's with the—"

"Okay, okay." Asher held up his hands in defeat as a meatmonger glared at them, two jackadays blocking her passage through the narrow lane. "Walk with me, and let this nice woman get on with her deliveries." Cooper thought Asher wanted to flee.

A cart filled with wrapped bundles dripped watery blood as it trundled past. Its minder cleared her throat in disapproval. He looked at the butchered meat and considered his body, lifeless and cold somewhere so far away that distance wasn't even the proper metric.

"On . . . on Earth we don't . . . we don't wake up after we die." It sounded so stupid, so utterly unhelpful.

"*Earth?*" Asher crowed. "You named your home after *dirt*?"

"Hey, fuck you." Cooper frowned. "You're supposed to be filling me in, not attacking my cultural heritage. The afterlife is hard enough as it is."

"What's after life?" Asher asked, sincerely, indicating a trio of passing shoppers laden with brightly colored bags, who turned up their noses. "There's *only* life."

"That doesn't make any sense," said Cooper, his bewilderment starting to burn into anger. That was good—anger he could handle, anger was familiar. "If I lived, and I died, then this place—whatever it is—must be the afterlife. It's *after* my *life,* isn't it?"

"No! Blessed batshit bells, it's just the beginning; that's what I'm trying to show you." Asher screwed up his face as if choosing his next words carefully. "You live and you live and you live, and one day, maybe, if you're lucky, you get to stop."

"I just don't believe it. I can't. You and Sesstri, you say that whenever someone dies, they just . . . wake up somewhere else?" Cooper grimaced and imagined a hundred wakings like he'd had today. A thousand. "Are . . . are you dead too?"

Asher scoffed. "I'm older than dirt."

How could Asher be so cavalier about something so revelatory, Cooper tried to understand. Then again, if what he said was true, who wouldn't be jaded by a thousand thousand weekdays?

"And then they die again and wake up somewhere new, again and again and again?"

"Most of 'em. Most of the time." Asher's face flickered with a frown before his mask of gray cool reassembled itself. He held his arms against his ribs in an uncomfortable-looking way for just a moment longer, taking deep breaths. Cooper realized that this was hard for him, too.

"Right." Cooper scrubbed his face with his palms. "Except the blood-slut, she stays here."

Asher nodded. "Correct."

The dam burst and Cooper's questions erupted without pause: "Do we all go to the same places? What happens if we don't want to start all over again? Why did I wake up with my clothes on? Do people just . . . wake up on hillsides like that? Where do our new bodies come from? How did you know to find me there? Are you some kind of social worker? And why me, why are you helping *me*, when millions of people must be—"

"*Breathe.*" Asher put his hands on Cooper's shoulders, but the instructions were useless.

Cooper's mind had initiated a kind of cascade of possible weirdnesses: accepting that he wasn't dreaming or comatose and that he most definitely *was* strolling down a cobbled road where a prostitute had just been murdered as part of a routine transaction, *was* holding the arm of a madman, *was* hearing whispers inside his head—what possible flavors of the bizarre should he be preparing for? Dragons? Zombies? Dark Lords or Evil Empires? Mind control? Trickster gods or elaborately plotting aliens? The options fell away one by one, rendered inadequate by the chrome-colored clouds and the spirit of the bloodslut still shuddering inside her body. Cooper realized that despite his lifetime of escapist education, a tacit understanding of his own ignorance would be the only benefit for which he could possibly hope.

Asher seemed oblivious to Cooper's internal cataclysm. "You'll learn everything about it soon enough. No, we don't all follow the same path of lives—we go where our spirits are drawn, so one life is rarely too different from the next. We are who we are, forever. Often we wake up younger, sometimes much younger, but also sometimes older. There's a certain amount of chance to everything, Cooper."

"What's this 'each life not too different from the next' load?" Cooper pushed Asher away and threw his arms out wide. "I'd say this is pretty fucking different from what I'm used to!"

Asher paused. "With exceptions, obviously: the brave, ambitious, or"—here he gestured at Cooper—"the unlucky witless." Then, changing the course of the conversation, "But there are other kinds of exceptions, like the body-bound, for instance, including the bloodsluts and most members of city government. They're bound by contracts to this world, this city, and their own inescapable bodies."

Cooper felt aghast and relieved at the same time—relief that the small-town fictions of god and heaven from his childhood were as imaginary as the space ninjas and Japanese *manga* of his young adulthood, and aghast that not one single experience of his life before could possibly have prepared him for this day. Even his acid tongue was useless.

"And all this living, then, Sesstri said it wasn't endless? That this city . . . that the City Unspoken is where people come to *actually* die, for real?"

"Yes." Asher explained as kindly as he dared. "People live as long as they need to live, whether they want to or not. Toward the end, there is a . . . a kind of pilgrimage. There are different ways to end yourself, if that's what you really want, but only True Death offers complete oblivion. And there are only a handful of places in the worlds where True Death is possible for those in need, although it can be a difficult blessing to obtain." And then, "More so, lately."

"Why?" Cooper felt his questions drying up in his throat. This was too much; he didn't remember dying, and he couldn't imagine . . . what he couldn't imagine. The fears of others that murmured inside his head were drowned out by his own.

"True Death is only granted to the deserving few. You can't just be suicidal, you have to have *earned* oblivion. And there are very few places where the gates to True Death are open. This city is one of those places. The oldest, if you believe the state propaganda, but certainly the most infamous. We are the crown jewel of ultimate obliteration."

"Oh," said Cooper, listening to his fears.

They walked in silence after that, and Cooper reassembled his self-possession by trying to orient himself geographically. He soon realized that tangled as the Guiselaine was, it had a certain logic to its construction. Each street seemed to be dedicated to one specific purpose—he and Asher darted down a lane lined with shops that sold only women's shoes. Boots of every shape and condition were displayed below razor-toed heels, beside fur-lined moccasins, rusted metal clogs, and sling-back fantasies. The street after that held birds of all conceivable varieties perched on wire stands, bound by chains, or within cages. The air shimmered with clicks and caws and the cries of the falconers, swarthy brutes in leather greatcoats who held their most prized beasts on gloved wrists.

"How can you find your way through this termite's nest?" Cooper broke the silence as they took another shortcut. They'd taken so many turns in such a short span that Cooper thought for certain they must have doubled back on their path at least half a dozen times, but he'd seen no repeated intersections or blocks he recognized.

"Sense of smell," Asher answered, then reached into his pockets. "That reminds me. Take these." He filled Cooper's hand with octagonal coins of several sizes. "For later." Cooper heard a finality in Asher's voice that made him uneasy.

"Money. Thanks."

"The big ones are dirty silvers, the smaller ones are nickeldimes. One dirty will get you a cheap meal. A nickeldime buys a rickshaw ride to just about anywhere. Don't pay more than five dirties for a room or you're being robbed blind."

"Thank you, Asher," Cooper said, bemused by the generosity. "But I think I'll stick close to you for the time being." He poured the coins into his empty pocket; when he'd lain down on his bed back home he'd had a stick of lip balm in his jeans, but discovered now that he'd lost it. Which was just great—Cooper was dead with the papery lips to prove it.

A man with liver-yellow skin and bloodshot eyes stumbled out of a storefront, screaming incoherently. Beneath his matted hair his face was wild, twisted, and he wore a strange kind of suit that looked far too new to be as filthy as it was. A woman in culottes and a faded t-shirt was shouting at the rabid-looking man. "Get out, you crazy pilgrim, your Dying insanity is bad for business!" She shooed him away. "Bells! What do you want with bridal veils, anyway?"

The stranger lurched first in one direction and then another, taking a strange tack-and-jibe approach to walking. When he saw Asher, he winced, and his eyes slid sideways to Cooper with a kind of relieved hatred. He threw himself forward, hands reaching for Cooper's throat.

Asher acted several beats more quickly. He pivoted on one foot and planted the other between Cooper and the madman, while reaching out with one long arm to wrap his hand around the man's neck—tripping and choking the lunatic at the same time. It happened so fast that Cooper saw Asher as a blur of smoke, moving more swiftly than any normal man. His assailant came to a full stop with a sickening popping sound from inside his neck. With Asher supporting most of his weight from his gullet, the man made a choking sound and began to claw at the air—although the length of Asher's arms kept him at a safe distance.

The deranged fellow glared at Cooper and raged, trying to shout through a half-crushed windpipe. "You have one!" he rasped. "Oh, oh, you should not be here. The darkness . . . you see the darkness, you hear the fright! The darkness in the depths can never be held to light. We Die, we live! Exult, extinguish!"

Asher threw the man—by the throat—across the street, into a row of trash cans. "Fuck off, pilgrim, or I will carve you into pieces."

The man lay there amidst the trash, moaning. *SisterWhereAreYou?* Cooper heard the man clear as day. *ICan'tHearYouAndItHurtsMe, Sister!* His fear was an alarm bell. *AstarnaxMySister ItHurtsToLiveWithoutYou IAmSoAlone.*

"I lost my sister," the man whimpered, aloud, to his trash-can pillows.

Cooper remembered Asher's admonitions and held his tongue.

"I did not lose my sister!" he screamed, suddenly incensed again. "She was stolen from me! Or she . . . she Died. Did I? I didn't Die, I couldn't Die. Nothing happened but *more heartbeats inside my haunted chest.* Where did my sister go? Astarnax? Astarnax, *where are you*?" He was laughing now, looking around blindly like he was losing a game of hide-and-seek. "Why did you steal my sister? Why?" *Cooper-OmphaleIBlameYouBlameYou!*

Cooper was dumbstruck. *How does he know my name?* "I . . . I . . . I didn't do anything to your sister," he stammered.

"Liar!" the man screeched, a raptor's cry. Window glass shuddered in its casements along the length of the street, a ripple of pain. The flow of the crowd juddered; everyone had felt *that*.

A moment of wretched silence passed before Asher pulled Cooper away, instantly lost in the crowd and hurrying from the crazy, too-knowing man. Cooper tried to gather himself, but his self did not want to obey. Too much, too fast, too *wrong*.

He grasped for a thought to ground him. A memory. Something green. He tried to remember his parents' home in the summer, tried to picture the gardenias that grew so big and waxy, the heirloom irises from his mother's childhood home, their purple flowers faded almost white. He tried to see the light through the windows as it fell on the desk in his father's study. *Yes. He had a green leather blotter with brass studs, and if you wrote on it you had to press very softly with the pen because he didn't want to score the leather.* Cooper knew these things still existed, but they were no longer his.

"What was wrong with that man?" he asked, walking in the lee of Asher's arm down the street. *How did he know my name? And what was that other thing he called me? Alm Fail? What does that mean?*

"Ignore it." Asher's tone was clipped. "It's nothing you need to worry about. The man was a con artist. He tailed us, or something. Whatever you do, don't let crazy people on the street make you question your own sanity. In all likelihood that's how *they* got that way."

"Why does everyone seem to want to die?"

Asher merely shook his head. His eyes darted around as if looking for an escape. "Watch out for the crazies." They passed two grimy men playing cards on a rubbish bin. Asher dipped his head in their direction and added, "And watch out for the swindlers. Don't be a fool with your money."

Cooper snorted. "I'm not an idiot—money is money. But what are they playing?"

"Three Whores. It's a scam, can't be won."

"Okay," said Cooper as they turned down yet another side street. "Then why would anyone play?"

"Why does anyone ever gamble?" He gave Cooper a sideways look. "Don't your people enjoy things that are bad for them?"

When Cooper didn't answer, Asher gave him another, more searching look. Cooper couldn't help but notice the perfect proportions of Asher's gray face, or the squared lope of his shoulders.

"What *happened* to you, Cooper?" Asher asked with an edge of intensity.

"How the fuck should I know?" Cooper threw up his arms. "Am I not the clueless one here? Wherever *here* is?"

All of a sudden, a clamor of wheels sounded from behind them. Asher threw Cooper face-first against the stone wall and held him flat as something big and fast and loud rushed down the cobbled lane at their backs. Startled, Cooper strained his neck to see a massive black-lacquered carriage bearing down the street like an angry bull made of gilt and teakwood—scattering hawkers and hausfraus alike lest they be crushed by its cherry-red wheels. As the carriage rushed by, Cooper saw a woman's hand with blue-green nails dangle from a red-curtained window. The hand twitched as the vehicle passed, and for an instant a finger pointed directly at Cooper's heart.

He stared at the receding, accusatory finger while Asher narrowed his eyes in distaste. A tattooed rickshaw driver stood drenched in sodden filth, shaking his fist and hurling unintelligible curses after the carriage. Across the street, a matronly woman held her hands to her head and despaired at an overturned bushel of bright green apples, gemlike fruit spilled into the mud.

"Dead gods fucked, fed, and flattered!" Asher cursed with a sneer.

"What the fuck was that?" Cooper demanded.

"There goes Lallowë Thyu, second wife of the Marquis Oxnard Terenz-de-Guises, who 'governs' this precinct." His eyes flickered red with hate and he stood motionless, glaring at the bulk of black opulence as it careened around the corner. "*Sic transit* pure evil."

"Uh-huh," Cooper mumbled, not really in the mood for local politics. "Well, your pure evil just pointed a finger at me as she hurtled past." The finger *had* pointed at him, he'd felt it.

Asher paused and gave Cooper a curious look, half-accusatory, half-hopeful.

"You didn't see that?" Cooper asked.

"Of course I saw it, but you're imagining your own significance." Asher scooped up an armful of apples and returned them to the grumbling woman, who handed one back with a nod. "Thyu has no reason to know you exist, and if you're lucky she never will."

"Then what was she pointing at—you?"

Asher hid his face behind the apple.

"Of course not. She has no reason to know I exist, either." He didn't sound convincing. "Apple?"

"What then?" Cooper caught the green fruit as Asher tossed it in the air and spun around, continuing down the lane.

Asher snapped, "She's a greedy bitch who'd grind her heel into half the city if she could. Lallowë Thyu is the worst kind of aristocrat. The kind whose foreign beginnings—which ought to make her a gentler citizen—only fuel her insane hunger for status, power, and *things*." His fists were clenched and he looked very much like he wanted to make a run for it. "I hate *things*."

"Not much of a materialist, are you?" Cooper teased the gray man's back as he walked away, then crunched off a bite of apple. "Or a royalist?" It tasted just like an apple should taste, which somehow put him at ease.

"Royalist?" Asher spat. He did not sound friendly now, not at all. "No! No, I am not." He paused as another carriage came tumbling down the alley, this one a windowless commercial lorry. His eyes lit up. "Bells. I'm not a lot of things, Cooper. For instance, I am not your friend."

"What does that mean?" Cooper asked, feeling a stab of fear and a lonely realization, but Asher only shook his head.

"Sesstri's right—you're not what I'm looking for, Cooper. I'm sorry. I have other failures to fix. I hope I gave you a bit of a head start, kid, but you're on your own. Just like everyone else."

Asher reached out and grabbed the corner of the lorry as it rolled by, stepping up onto the footman's perch. Cooper just stood there, gaping as wordlessly—as he had earlier that morning on the hill above Displacement—watching the carriage speed away with the tall gray-skinned man who had been Cooper's only hope.

"Don't forget all we talked about," Asher called out. "You'll need it."

2

My friend Lao-tzu says, "Darkness within darkness. The gateway to all understanding."

Of course Lao doesn't mean the absence of light, you'll see that. No, all of his friends appreciate that Lao-tzu finds freedom in that ultimate ignorance we all must face eventually: death. But I was raised to believe in a god who died for my sins. Of course I never believed in sin, and when death never came I had nothing left to pretend to believe.

It is like that everywhere, you'll discover. Names for gods that never existed or who lied about what they were, or disappeared ages and ages ago. Tedious ends to tedious pedagoguery, but there you have it.

My friend Lao-tzu also says, and I think him terrifically wise for pointing it out, that names are a waste of time. "The unnamable is the eternally real," he tells me, and I do think he's right about that. "Naming is the origin of all particular things." This means something a little profound, obviously, because it suggests that "things" can never be real.

Was that ever truer than in the case of worship?

Who is Christ on the cross to me now? I haven't seen him at any of the parties.

—Truman Capote, *Better Birds*

Sesstri Manfrix sat at her desk, watching the ink dry on another page of another journal and holding her quill in her hand like a poisonous spider. Everything was so different here. The City Unspoken was like nowhere she'd ever lived, and as much as the filth and decay offended her senses, she knew she'd make more discoveries here than in any library she'd ever scoured. There was enough history and unspeakable *age* here to fill a thousand ruined cities and still have mystery to spare.

It was a historian's nirvana. Or her nightmare.

And then there was Asher.

When she met him, murdering books in a library, he'd been awkwardly formal, and Sesstri had been too keen to work out the etiology of his colorless skin to notice the intensity of Asher's gaze. *Yes*, she would accept payment to help him with his research. *Yes*, she would be interested in knowing the subject matter. *Yes*, she was well versed in any number of disciplines pertaining to metaversial anthropology, *and* panspermic linguistics, and no, she did not mind legwork. She *would* like to hear about what concerned him, and no she felt *very* safe in the company of a strange man—though those last had been a lie and a lie of omission, respectively. Of course Sesstri felt safe; she bristled with hidden knives, razors, pins.

Sesstri had learned to mistrust reactions based upon her beauty. In her last life, she'd discovered old age with a kind of relieved exhaustion. When she'd walked into this house, shaky on the arm of the curly redhead who'd found her, who'd rented her the home, and she had gotten a look at herself in the mirror, she'd almost screamed. In the weeks she'd worked with Asher, poring over worm-eaten texts that all but crumbled in their fingers, Sesstri had caught glimpses of that infatuated look in the gray man's eyes, and knew that it would only be a matter of time until he—and by extension, she—had to deal with it.

But he'd trusted her, enough to finally relent and show her what frightened him so. Asher took her to Godsmiths, crossing one of the city's ever-present gargantuan chains, secured as a catenary bridge across the sundered earth of the gloomy district, and Sesstri wondered what the ramshackle ruin of a neighborhood contained that could possibly animate Asher with such fervor.

In Godsmiths they found the *svarning.* Just the smallest, lightest touch of it, but enough for proof-of-concept. The day had been sunless, a bright white sky empty except for the constant moonrise of the Dome to the east, its inner glow dimmed by the day.

"There is a word for this." He pointed to the emaciated women, standing rigid at their doors, staring toward the Dome. The stains on their trousers or beneath their skirts hinted at the length of time they'd been standing there. Many had milky eyes because of dead corneal tissue; they hadn't blinked in days.

"There is no word for this." Sesstri stood by the circle of dancing girls, scribbling notes on her pad as fast as she could. There was no point trying to intervene; that was not their purpose. But it was difficult for her to see the page; although the air was clear, her vision wavered, as with tears or intense emotion, though she had neither.

Asher told her the word.

The little girls' hands bled where their nails dug into one another's palms. They skipped with an exhausted gait, but their eyes were full of cheer. Horrible, agonizing cheer. They had moved beyond joy and pain into an extremity of feeling that conjured its own toxic magic. That was the *svarning*. Little girls who danced to the point of death and beyond, and beyond, and beyond.

But those were not the stakes. Braided tits of the horsemother, those were an example of the bare minimum casualties, not even a full outbreak. Asher promised that the *svarning* would evolve, not just from person to person but changing in aspect as it grew. When or if that mania seized the city, if it spread throughout the worlds . . . would the metaverse detonate in some kind of psychic supernova? Or would the cogs of existence run ever hotter, ever faster, and its fevered inhabitants spin on in an ever-more-tortured eternal life?

The plan was that Cooper was supposed to be someone special. The plan involved someone special leading them to a solution, somehow, somewhere. That's what Asher had promised her, however he knew, and she had promised to find and identify this special someone.

So why had she lied?

Sesstri stared out the window, over papers and books, to the towers of abandoned districts that burned like candles of stone, glass, and steel. Though they burned night and day, they never fell, and were held by undead masters who manifested as clouds of roiling darkness streaked through with red lightning, an ever-brewing storm above ever-burning skyscrapers. The gangs that worshiped undeath like a god had run those districts even before the government withdrew into the Dome—but now whole sections of the city seethed with black-clad youths engaged in constant battle against one another and the City Unspoken. Despite the untapped trove of history she knew lay within those impossible towers, Sesstri hadn't ventured anywhere near them, yet.

She'd learned from her contacts in Amelia Heights, from the artists and the artisans who still clung to their homes there, about the power of the forces martialing around those towers. The gangs, collectively called the Undertow, had acquired something since the prince's absence, some power or leverage that allowed their influence to grow: the liches, undead spellcasters with human intelligence and ambition, had either grown in number or flocked to the City Unspoken from elsewhere, filling a power vacuum. Their thralls—well, the youths had swelled in numbers to an even greater degree, and while the Death Boys and Charnel Girls weren't undead themselves, they'd tasted something of it, and it gave them power. The names they'd given themselves along rudimentary gender lines, Death Boys and Charnel Girls, they seemed silly names to her, but as a collective the thugs posed a real threat to the declining stability of the city.

And yet, the Undertow were only a symptom. The Dome, which dwarfed even the flaming towers and smoldered with a different light— gold and green, full of life—it worried her far more than a little army of children and monsters. Armies were finite. The damage to the City Unspoken, decapitated from its leadership, was much harder to quantify. Anarchy during crisis yielded nothing good.

She didn't quite trust Asher, despite wanting to. And she wanted him, despite not trusting herself one bit.

If only she hadn't lied about Cooper. If only Asher had possessed the good sense not to trust her, or the kindness not to take the boy to the Guiselaine and leave her to ponder her error. She didn't understand the pallid man—maybe that was why she felt so odd in his presence, as if she weren't quite as brilliant as usual—more spiteful, less gracious.

She'd told Asher everything but the crucial fact. She'd identified from the construction and branding of Cooper's clothing alone that his entire culture was childborn. There was a certain solipsistic air about civilizations that were illiterate to their larger metaversial context—her homeworld had been no different in that regard.

But if Asher knew that Cooper had a *navel* ... He'd be furious, but she'd been certain she would think of an answer before they returned. Nobody who'd died had a navel, only the childborn, for as long as they lived in their first flesh—*only* they had that scar, that connection to their mother and their first, only, literal birth. Sesstri put her hand to her own belly, flat and hard and perfectly smooth. She didn't like to think about her navel, or how she'd lost it.

But the more Sesstri considered the question, the less certain she grew that there *was* an answer to Cooper's arrival—or at least, no answer that she could uncover with mere perspicacity. No, the more she considered it, the less sense Cooper made. *A navel.* He was an erratum, to be sure, growing ever more erratic, and Sesstri's conviction that Cooper was worthless faltered.

What would she have done if Asher hadn't left the room before she'd stripped the foundling? How could she admit to him that she had *no idea* how such a thing was possible? To commute between worlds without death as your oarsman was impossible for lesser beings. For a godlike being—one of the First People—or an incredibly powerful mortal, certainly, but for a childborn young man like Cooper to wake up intact in his original body, the body of his childbirth? Sesstri couldn't explain that.

And she had no intention of telling Asher the truth until she could.

She walked the empty house, worried. Sesstri never worried. And she never lied to a client. So she was doubly distressed as she climbed the stairs of her little house south of Ruin and the Boulevard of Wings, staring at the vase of wilted foxgloves that sat by the landing's small oriel window. Her day had devoured itself this way, aimlessly, and nothing could be less typical of Sesstri Manfrix than *aimlessness*.

Of course it was more than Cooper—there was the *svarning*, which she could feel prickling at her skin and getting stronger every day. The Dying pilgrims were growing in number; they found it harder and harder to Die, and that worried Asher. As it should—the mass Deathlessness brought on a malaise that was partly psychological and partly paranormal, and entirely unpredictable. It infected the young as easily as the old, as if the air itself were tainted by the rotting souls of those who should be Dead. *Svarning:* a word from a language with no known descendants that was either ancient beyond reckoning or entirely fictional. If the word was real, Sesstri had translated its meaning as lying somewhere between "heartsick" and "drowning," and occasionally "illuminated," although the degree to which those interpretations were valid would be open to debate.

Death. Undeath. Power. *Svarning.* Sesstri wasn't disturbed by any of that—it was all grist for the mill of her mind. All part of her work. Like many of the metaverse's persevering geniuses, Sesstri Manfrix hadn't let the interruptions of death disrupt her studies. Instead she'd expanded the scope of her investigations to include an existence punctuated by periodic transmigration—through death—and found that what she lost in continuity she more than recouped through longevity. Her second life had been fortuitous: peaceful and providing access to many notes and records of the larger metaverse of which she had been so ignorant throughout her first life. In the reality that called itself Desmond's Pike, Sesstri had raised a family and researched the metaverse and its primary method of transportation: dying.

What's death to a historian who never dies? What's history to an eternal woman? Even after apocalyptic war came to Desmond's Pike, with gold machines that fell from the sky and disassembled the world one atom at a time, Sesstri knew that she'd have the luxury to answer her questions at her own pace. Now her limitless learning appeared threatened by the rise of the *svarning.* So she'd solve it. One woman against a metaphysical illness that threatened all universes? Of course she could solve it.

Other questions were less forgiving. What's love to a woman who'd never met her equal? What, for that matter, *is* love? The browning foxgloves didn't answer; they only raised further questions. Why hadn't she refilled the water in the vase?

Oh, Asher.

She'd lied because Asher frightened her, and Sesstri had decided at a young age never to be frightened of a man. Her father the Horselord had taught her that much, at least. She would solve the problem of Asher after she'd unraveled the threat to the metaverse.

The matter at hand: Cooper hadn't traveled here by himself; he smelled of no grand magics and heralded no invading army or technological superiority. He was as mundane as it got. That left few options, all of which pointed to the one subject that made Sesstri uncomfortable: the First People. *Gods,* the ignorant called them. She had no use for such charlatanism, and while there was no arguing the existence of any number of beings who were—or chose to remain—unfathomable to humankind and the other races of the Third People, there were no true *gods* in the absolute sense of the word, merely players of a larger game, with a wider reach and deeper pockets. They might be beyond mortal ken, but that was due to mortal limitations rather than a MacGuffin called divinity. Name them what you will, Sesstri felt, but worship was a waste of good incense.

She packed her satchel. She might as well get some work done, and as long as she had worship on her mind, she could catalog some more of antidogmatic stories told in and about the City Unspoken. She could sort through drivel about gods and goddesses and find truth there, somehow.

What truly irritated Sesstri was the idea that any knowledge might be barred to her because she was somehow *lesser,* and this struck her as the ultimate copout. Not to mention insulting. *Give me a week in the library of a goddess,* she knew, *and I'll come out with conclusions. Give me an hour with a demiurge and I'll return with citations and cross-references that are perfectly analogous to any other quarter of historical or empirical study.*

What's a god but a man behind a curtain?

Curtains *burn.*

For a while after Asher left him in the Guiselaine, Cooper didn't really pay attention to where he wandered. Dead, abandoned, alone, and lost— it made his chest tight and his eyes too watery to see well. By the time he could breathe, he'd found himself hassled on a dusty thoroughfare where everyone seemed to be in a hurry and nowhere seemed an acceptable place to *be.* He found an exception in a clearing at the side of the road, where pedestrians went out of their way to avoid what looked like a wounded airman from the First World War, hiding in a barrel of beer.

"Hi there," Cooper said, peering down into the beer. "Are you, by any chance, from a place called Earth?"

"Nerp," the pilot bubbled.

Cooper nodded, aiming for sanguinity and missing. "So you're not a fighter pilot from the First World War? The Great War, I guess you would have called it, only you wouldn't have, since you're not from it. From there. From Earth."

"Nerp."

"Ah. I see." He tried again. "It's just that you're dressed a lot like a fighter pilot."

The man lifted his head out of the beer enough to shake his head. "Oh, I'm a fighter pilot. That's why I'm dressed like one. I've just never been to Erp."

"Earth."

"Sky!" the pilot cheered. "I like this game. Your turn."

"Um." Cooper nodded again. "Why are you hiding in a barrel of beer?"

"I'm not hiding."

"You're not?"

"Nerp. I'm drowning myself in beer. It's the thing to do."

Cooper almost pointed out that drowning oneself in drink was not supposed to be a literal thing, but he remembered Asher's admonitions and checked himself. Perhaps, in the City Unspoken, death by beer was perfectly acceptable. That wouldn't be the weirdest thing Cooper had learned today.

"Where do the lost go?" Cooper asked the pilot, not intending to sound like a confused fortune cookie. The man sank a little, and his answer was not intelligible.

"I'm sorry, I don't quite follow." Cooper squinted his face and squeaked out an imposition: "Might you be willing to stop drowning for just another moment? I really am very, very lost."

With a sigh of superheroic effort, the pilot stood up in his barrel, raining lager onto the cobbled gutter, pointed down the road, and said: "Bridge. Music. Mountain." And then, as if to clarify: "Over bridge, through music, under mountain."

Then the pilot replaced his aviator's goggles, tugged at the red beads clustered at his suntanned throat, and submerged himself in beer again. One hand emerged from the pale yellow foam like a parody of the Lady of the Lake, holding an oversized beer stein brimming with ale. Cooper didn't stand on ceremony—he took the proffered pint and walked away as swiftly as his feet would carry him. He had the pint half-drained by the time he rounded the bend. Afterlife beer was stronger than he'd expected.

So when he stumbled, drunk, from the bridge built of giants' bones and reinforced concrete, Cooper hoped he saw what the beer-marinated fighter pilot with the red beads had described. He faced a pointed hill, odd and steep, where the crust of the city had been pushed up like an anthill or a volcano, wrinkling the weft of the architecture around it.

A road led down into a park, then continued on below and through the tall hill, which Cooper supposed might be the mountain in question. In the distance the Dome loomed, a planetoid moments away from collision.

Cooper stumbled toward the park, a nestled vale of cypress and stranger trees, rangy blue-tipped eucalyptus, curly willows whose curls spilled upward. Beyond the park, the road dipped beneath the mountain, dark as a funnel spider's web.

An overgrown drum circle seemed to have set up semipermanent camp in the park—dominated by a profusion of musicians and singers who sat atop or leaned against a length of massive chain that seemed more or less draped across the park. The tolling of bells that had followed him all day grew louder, but didn't seem to dampen the orchestral spirit of the gatherers. An odd little musical collective played a dozen tunes at once and each drew its own audience, using the oversize chain links as performance spaces and stages, or for seating.

Away from the tidal force of the streets of the Guiselaine, Cooper found the presence of mind to closely examine the throng for the first time. The people who arranged themselves according to the links of huge chain seemed plucked from a dozen countries and eras. A dozen worlds. A mule-eared busker juggled pomegranates in one hand while playing a brass horn with the other, and he winked at Cooper with overlarge eyes as he passed. A few chain links down, a trio of women with bared breasts and faces painted like Chinese princesses arranged sheaves of music on the shelves of a kiosk, singing in three-part harmony.

What are those chains for? Cooper mused. He'd seen them from Sesstri's rooftop running through canals and alleyways. They cut through the city, but whatever purpose they might once have served seemed forgotten, or at least buried.

Cooper burped loudly and tasted beer—a shaven-headed man with a chest scrimshawed in scars clapped and gave him a thumbs-up before going back to pounding out rhythm on the skin of his drum. Cooper gawped at the muscles dancing in the man's torso; in his stupor the scars seemed to wink like the faces in the bark of an ancient tree. One of the painted princesses broke away from her sisters to rest her hand upon the scrimshawed man's shoulder, leaning over from behind to kiss his cheek. The rough-looking man leered at her appreciatively, still drumming, and rubbed his beard against her peach nipple, inhaling the perfume of her breasts with a familiar relish.

"Beautiful, ain't she?" he asked when he saw Cooper look a moment too long.

"Oh. Yes." Cooper scratched his head. "Absolutely, yes."

Taking in his surroundings with an equanimity only the inebriated can command, Cooper made his way through the crowd of listeners and performers. Once he would have given an arm to step through a doorway into an otherworldly carnival, but now all he could do was look for an ATM sign. It was a compulsive reflex in a head not quite as prepared for total world-upheaval as it might once have fancied itself.

Shaking off his ghosts, Cooper thought that he hadn't intended to get drunk, but couldn't convince himself that he wished he were sober. It was that damn fighter pilot's fault, anyway.

Under mountain. Cooper looked up to see the rise of tilted buildings climbing up the near distance. It seemed that all the houses and rookeries could come sliding down on all their heads at any moment. The lane dipped at an easy angle, and as he left the music behind, Cooper smelled incense and dinner being fixed within nearby homes. Garlic, onion, meat—and from the descending path he followed, sandalwood, cedar, amber.

The steps were carved in a shallow decline on either side of a wide ramp intended for handcarts and rickshaws, and Cooper stumbled past townhouses and tenements in a succession of levels until the narrow ribbon of the sky was crisscrossed by a web of supports and rafters. Light spilled from open windows and the air chimed with the sounds of domesticity; he heard women argue with their husbands and children— *children,* of all things, the first sign of any recognizable natural order he'd seen in the City Unspecified. Cooper had assumed the city to be filled with old souls and death-seekers, but of course that wasn't true. Not entirely. Life and death, side by side, formed the meat and sinew of the city, and gave rise to all sorts of things, grisly and familiar— mule-eared buskers, screaming toddlers, and bread dough rising in the oven of a top-heavy house on an avenue that dipped down, toward the buried center of this cone-shaped urban mountain.

And it was buried thoroughly, that center. Cooper soon left the upper layer of habitations behind, passing through a stretch of abandoned buildings with empty windows and no smell at all except for dust, and dust, and dust. Here updrafts whistled over broken glass and murky casements; if he'd been sober, Cooper might have turned back, but drink had given him a measure of courage.

Eventually the way overhead closed entirely and the street became a tunnel of rough bedrock that had been hewn and re-hewn over the years as the strange mountain grew. Daylight faded and was replaced by burning torches. Cooper no longer felt that he was in a city—he felt a hundred miles from anything, a lone intruder in a desert tomb, guided down, down, down into darkness. Water trickled from the walls, filtered by strata of history, sliming wet stripes of calciferous deposits onto the stone.

When he'd walked down for so long that he feared the ground must soon swallow him up entirely, the tunnel opened via a cataract of stairs onto a broad courtyard. Looking up, Cooper realized he had hit the center of the mountain, and stood at the bottom of a deep cylindrical pit, a small circle of sky providing light from far above. Cobbled with smooth marble, the courtyard seemed far too clean and tidy to belong to the archeological layer cake through which he'd just descended. At the exact center of the courtyard was set a large metal crest, but the image it might have borne had been worn away entirely.

What he saw next defied possibility. The circular wall of the courtyard was lined with archways, packed next to and atop one another: hundreds of façades, porticos, and gaping mouths of stone or brick were scrawled across the towering shaft, packed in one beside the other like books on a helical shelf. Cooper craned his neck to capture the scope of the place; drunken vertigo pulled at his gut as his eyes spiraled upward and he struggled to stay standing. Each darkened threshold stood starkly different from its neighbors—some were supported by massive columns, tattooed with scrollwork or crawling demons or formed from slabs of raw metal, while others were little more than clay bricks covered with paint and thatch.

Cooper decided that the archways looked most like the gaping edifices of religious monuments: countless temples, churches, and shrines. The doorways—of all sizes, from mouths of humble driftwood to the Brobdingnagian gates of pillared cathedrals—were stacked together tightly and coiled up the walls of the cylindrical shaft. Many of the entrances bore what looked to be some sign of divinity: a fat stone woman holding her own engorged breasts, the baleful glare of a steel mask, the branches of a bone-carved world tree; on and on it wound, a small infinity of architecture. Stacked one atop the other in no apparent order, the walls crawled with portals and doorways and thresholds, yawning empty and black. His head spun faster as he moved into the center of the space, standing on the worn metal plaque at its middle, like a navel.

The circle of sky hung distant, darkened but cloudless, a deep royal blue that seemed worlds away from the brooding umber sunset of the music fair he'd passed through to get here. Fragrant smoke of a dozen flavors poured from the many openings, scrolling upward toward the promise of starlight far above like a pilgrimage of ghosts. But Cooper could see that the darkened doorways were mere façades and nothing more—no vaulted tombs or flame-wreathed altars lay beyond their gaping doors. Cooper realized with nervous awe that he was standing at the bottom of an immense well lined with the faces of a hundred religions, scalped and mounted.

From above sounded the tolling of a bell, quickly joined by another, and another, until the whole sinkhole was ringing with the tolling of countless bells, an infinity of church towers converging above Cooper's ears. He hiccupped and sat down hard on one of the wide steps that led into the well, bruising his tailbone. Even with his hands flattened against his ears Cooper's head still pounded with the army of bells, while his vision swam and he felt he would soon be ill. On and on they rang, and even when the tolling began to cease the well vibrated with painful echoes.

Cooper held himself as still as possible until he could stand to hear again, the bells a second heartbeat in his chest.

"Welcome to the Apostery," said a voice. "Where we bury our faith."

The Apostery.

The name rang in Cooper's head like a silver bell—the final note of the cacophony of the tolling he'd just endured—and he turned to see who had spoken. Something moved in the shadows. More than one thing, or one thing that made the sounds of many—a footstep to his left; the scuffle of gravel quickly silenced to the right; the quick sniffing sound of Cooper's scent being tasted on the air. Something circled him.

Cooper saw it as it spoke again, a figure in black lurking beneath the lintel stone of a nearby archway. He tried to position himself with his back to a wall, but stumbled and half fell against a column while his vision spun. Cooper fought down panic.

"The Apostatic Cemetery," the voice explained. "You came to hear the story?"

Then he slunk out from the dark, angling toward Cooper with predatory speed. His kohl-rimmed eyes were hungry and as black as the plugs in his earlobes, his body slant-ribbed and white where it showed through his tattered clothes. Despite Cooper's fear, he was trapped, rapt, unable to move. The youth stepped close and drew back his arm as if to gut Cooper with a dagger—but when his hand sprang forward the light from above struck no naked blade but a poppy, sepia red and fresh.

Cooper blinked at the young man's face, wondering if he could smell spilled beer. The stranger simply stood there, transfixing Cooper with his eyes.

He was a birthday magician, and Cooper the rabbit in his hat.

"For you," he said with a smile. White teeth crooked at the center and a shy blush made his handsome face lovely. Beneath the slits in his shirt blue stars spread across his chest and arms, buffeted by tattooed winds and waves.

Iamthesailorsstarstoguideyouhome. Iamtwinstorms of airandwaterto- drownandfreezeyou. Iwillhelpyou breathe when the sky has broken. Fear me, Cooper.

Cooper heard the words in his head but paid them no mind. His attention was focused on the pair of agate eyes gazing deeply into his own, as though the two of them were not standing beneath the glare of countless dispossessed religions, but were alone in a corner somewhere loud and smoky where nothing existed but two pairs of eyes and two pairs of lips, getting closer.

"I'm Marvin," said the stranger as Cooper took the poppy from his hand. Their fingers touched; Marvin's skin was warm and dry and felt for all the world like the most amazing thing Cooper had encountered since he arrived in this doomed city.

"I'm Cooper."

Silence. Comfortable silence, Cooper had half a mind to notice. For lack of an alternative, he tucked the flower behind his ear. Marvin had another tattoo inside his lower lip, but Cooper couldn't make it out.

"You came for the story?" Marvin asked again, more shyly, his earlier aggressiveness now evaporated in the face of, what? Something mutual. Something unexpected.

"Why are you talking to me?" Cooper asked, immediately wishing he hadn't sounded so defensive.

Marvin looked as uncertain as Cooper felt, and Cooper wondered if maybe he wasn't the only lost boy in this city. "I . . . I thought you looked like you could use a friend." It didn't sound very convincing, but it had the desired effect.

"Oh." Cooper hung his head, now wishing he hadn't taken the stein of ale and drained it so quickly. "I'm sorry. I just got here—"

"—I can tell—"

"—and I'm a little on guard, to say the least. I'm also a little bit tipsy. You said something about a story?"

Marvin nodded. "It's all they do down here, tell stories. Since you're new you wouldn't know it, but the Apostery is one of the oldest places in the city. It grows all the time. Whenever a faith dies out, so they say. The pilgrims and locals both come here to remember the songs they used to sing, back when they had something to sing about." Marvin thought about what he'd said, and made a face. "It's kind of fascinatingly pathetic, I think."

"Pilgrims?" Cooper asked as Marvin led him across the cobbled floor of the city's navel, toward the only archway that was more than a shallow front.

"The Dying," Marvin answered simply, as if that were obvious.

"That place is amazing." Cooper marveled as Marvin led him past the opening of plain rock into another passageway, a darkened progress that led on beyond the well of faiths.

"That?" Marvin said. "That was just the courtyard."

* * *

Nixon ran along the canal even though the edge was barely as wide as one of his feet. The other children wouldn't dare, but it was the fastest way between Rind and Ruin south of Lindenstrasse, and Nixon couldn't go into Lindenstrasse until the shops closed or he'd find himself hanging upside down from a thievespole. One too many apples snatched too boldly from the greengrocers' tony displays had earned him a bad reputation in the neighborhood.

Nixon could cope with a bad reputation. Most of the other street children avoided him like the plague. Some were afraid of kids who did business, and that was probably for the best. The others, the ones like him . . . they ran their own rackets. If he'd learned one thing since he'd come to the city, it was to keep his nose out of other people's games: impossible things happened here every day, and few of them were anything but awful.

And yet, the City Unspoken had given Nixon a golden opportunity for what he considered quite possibly the finest grift the metaverse had to offer: juvenile reincarnation.

It was true that without intervention of some kind, the soul of a person who died would transmigrate elsewhere, guided more by its own incurable nature than any cosmic plan, and would clothe itself in flesh that reflected the spirit's own self-image. Nixon represented one of the variant incarnations. Not the kind of folk who were just young at heart and tended to incarnate very young—no, Nixon and his fellow juvenile-incarnated anomalies were sick jokes: murderers and rapists and thieves of every caliber—generals, popes, and greedy opportunists. In a way, Nixon suspected that the young bodies into which they'd been incarnated represented an ultimate deviance of the soul—they may not see themselves as children, but each and every member of his loosely aligned group of reborn unboys and nongirls intuitively grasped the advantage of starting new lives dressed in the bodies of cherubs: it was the perfect scam. Less ambitious pseudochildren found employment between the sheets, but to Nixon's eye that was a life better suited to the city's three kinds of whores—the possibilities presented to a canny mind in a child's body knew no limit.

Take his current errand, for instance. The job was simple enough, but no regular kid could handle the employer. . . . Nixon scampered a little faster along the canal wall. It would not do to be late returning to the abandoned room, and the meeting should be over quickly enough—the ass end of a spy job rarely took long. All he'd need to do was nod. "Yes ma'am, miss crazy hair, I saw him, ma'am, clear as cut crystal." Then grab the money and *run*.

It was true, Nixon conceded, that there might be more glamorous or powerful lives to live—the endless bloody deaths of a Coffinstepper, for instance, hunting dangerous quarry across dozens of realities at once. Or the days of a plutocrat noble ruling a city with a stranglehold on the ultimate commodity. Those might be thrilling lives, but they weren't his. Not yet.

Nixon leaped over the boundary fence at the end of the canal and landed on Ruin Street without a sound. He dropped into a patch of sunshine, the street around him empty. The sun still shone overhead—the sky wasn't sane yet, but it was on its way, and Nixon took a few seconds to enjoy the heat on his face and chest. That green sun would go away, he could feel it, and an honest sky would take its place. From Nixon's vantage, the strangest thing about the City Unspoken—which was saying something—was its variable sky. Depending on the mood of the firmament, you'd wake up to any number of possible skies, and if it hadn't changed by lunchtime, you counted yourself lucky.

He patted his tan little belly and pictured the meal he'd buy himself with the coin he'd earn today. He pictured the sun he'd eat it under. Imagine that, Nixon marveled: honest coin, a yellow sun in a blue sky, and meat in a bowl at the end of the day. Life was *good*.

He passed the building with the blue door and shimmied up its gutter to the second-story window, where the red ribbon was tied around a bent nail sticking out of the casement. The window was still open, and Nixon pulled himself into the abandoned room with a brave face. He wouldn't let his legs shake this time, he promised himself as he felt his way through the boarded-up room and into the deeper darkness beyond, no matter how pretty the lady was, or how she burned the air just by standing in it.

When the sudden flare of a lantern splintered the darkness, Nixon barely suppressed a squeal.

In the hallway stood a small woman with a sweet face and red curls, who hung the lantern on the wall and smiled at Nixon. She wasn't wearing any shoes, just a faded shift, and there were far more curves exposed than Nixon was usually allowed to see. A ribbon as red as the one on the windowsill adorned her ankle, and she lifted a lovely foot off the floor just slightly.

"Did he come?" she asked. Her red hair moved like clouds across the sky, though the air was still.

"Who *are* you?" He asked the question before he could stop himself. *And what do you care about the gray hippie picking up some portly stiff?*

"Did he come?" she asked again. Nixon had the feeling this woman possessed extraordinary patience, but he couldn't say why. She felt *too real,* was all he could think—the hairs on her forearm, the pucker of her lips, it was as if the rest of the world were a grainy film reel and she, a true woman, had stepped in front of the screen. Thing was, Nixon was pretty sure she was anything but a true woman. There were things that looked like people, he'd learned, but weren't. Things that might even convince you they were gods—but they weren't that, either.

"I mean it," he insisted, "I really need to know who you are." He didn't, but he wanted to be able to lord this story over the other gutter rats, and how could he do that if he never found out the identity of the slight little thing who brimmed with power?

"If you're worried about the rest of your money . . . don't be." The woman handed Nixon a little wooden box, and he peeked beneath the lid. It brimmed with nickeldimes, easily twice as much as he'd been promised.

"He came!" The words were out of Nixon's mouth before he could stop himself. He held the box behind his back and retreated a step toward the exit; his curiosity evaporated in the face of cash.

A Cheshire grin lit the barefoot woman's face, brightening even the abandoned building that decayed around them. She did a little dance and held her hand out in an invitation, one eye shining in the torchlight, the other dark. Nixon hesitated, then tentatively put his small brown hand in hers. Her skin felt feverish-hot and cold as the vacuum of space, and for half a moment her bright eye blinded him as the darkness in the other yawned vertiginously.

She pulled the length of red ribbon from her ankle and tied it around Nixon's thumb. "When you see him again, I want you to do me one little itty-bitty favor. I want you to give him this. He'll be new and untrusting, but I want you to do it anyway. Use that disarming smile of yours." Dropping his hand, the being shaped like a redhead stood back and admired the boy as she might admire a puppy in a shop. "Will you do that for me?"

Nixon wasn't listening, which was nothing new. Then he snapped himself out of it and nodded with an earnest grin even though he didn't follow her logic—any newcomer should be untrusting, and what would he want with ribbons?

"You're a spicy one, aren't you?" she asked with a trill of a laugh. Nixon didn't know what she meant by that, either, so he looked at his feet. When he raised his eyes, he was alone in the hallway with a lantern and a ribbon and a boxful of dinner.

The Apostery was as vast inside as it was outside. For a long minute the only thing Cooper could process was the hugeness of the space: a vaulted cathedral ceiling soaring higher than any he could recall seeing before; massive support columns the girth of small houses rising into the darkness above, etched with names and signs, inlaid with silver and steel; smoke-stained wheels of candelabra dangling from chains as thick as his torso; and the light—the light that came streaming from all angles ahead, slanted on an angle that caught in the air, veiling the enormity of the space in serene curtains of dust and smoke that wafted through the air, unlike the barometric fumes that billowed up the well of the courtyard. Any bishop would give his favorite catamite for a place of worship like this. But this, Cooper began to understand, was no cathedral—rather a mausoleum. A grave for buried gods and the stories they told.

He and Marvin walked toward the light, their footsteps the only discernible sound in the enormous space. As they grew nearer, he saw past the columns to the source of the light, and that was the real glory. As the Apostery's courtyard was a vault of doorways, here was a court of windows—stained glass portraits ringed about the walls and rising in layers to the ceiling. It appeared that the mountain was hollow. Each picture captured the likeness of some being—gods, it could only be—of every sort imaginable and more. A blue woman with severed breasts and eyes like sapphires glared down from a throne of ice; a man with stag's horns crouched half-hidden behind a mask of leaves; a gray sword, point down, with garnet eyes staring impassively from the quillon. Panes of gold glass as tall as sequoias stretched upward beyond sight. On and on the windows shone, each more artfully worked than the next, and each was lit from behind as if by perfect afternoon sunlight, although it was evening already, they were far underground and, in any case, the sun could not possibly be in so many places at once. The light filled the air now, shading its smoke-strata a hundred colors.

"Apostery." Cooper repeated the name like an invocation. "Apostatic? You said? Like an apostle?"

Marvin shook his head. "Like an apostate. I told you, these people have nothing left to believe." Marvin indicated the visitors who sat with their own thoughts or strolled from window to window. "Atheism is the traditional faith of the City Unspoken. When your own persistence disproves the truth of every religion you've ever encountered, churches lose their punch. Hence the Apostery—the Apostatic Cemetery, where we mourn our lost gods, whether they were real or not."

Marvin steered them to an alcove off to the side, beneath a clerestory where a small group of people milled about. They joined the others and Cooper smelled the familiar scent of a campfire. He craned his neck and saw the reason for the gathering.

An old woman sat on a broken column, warming her toes over a fire tended by those gathered around her. The crowd bore many faces, and Marvin whispered to Cooper that he might even recognize some; they hovered near the fire pit—there were eyes faceted like gemstones, antennae and feelers and protuberances aplenty; jawless tongue-flapping faces; viridian and scarlet and mauve faces; fey-touched and bedeviled faces.

"The usual stuff, if you get around," Marvin explained, nodding at the more unusual-looking people. "Which, of course, you will. Eventually."

One feature every face shared was a certain flavor of anticipation, a kind of lonely hunger. And patience. Patience, because many of them had heard the old woman tell her stories before and knew it would bring them a measure of peace; those who had not heard the story had traveled far and long to hear it, which was why the faces of this gathering were stranger than those Cooper remembered seeing in the city above, and although they might not know that it was this particular story for which they had come, they had all learned patience along the way and gained the knack of sensing *important* when it was near.

Are these the Dying, then? They seemed nothing like the crazed man who'd assailed him earlier on the streets of the Guiselaine.

Only a hooded woman at the other end of the gathering seemed impatient. She tapped a pencil against a pad of paper, insistently, and pursed her lips. Pursed lips were all of her face that Cooper could see, obscured as she was by others, but he wished she'd stop tapping that pencil.

The old woman looked something of a scoundrel. Something about her seemed different than the others, as diverse as they were—a smile that lived in her eyes, a kind mischief crouched in her wrinkled mouth. Her sparse white hair braided with beads and bolts and bottle-caps, she smiled at the pencil-tapper. Cooper imagined that she would draw this one out, just because she could.

Eventually, after much tapping of the pencil, the old woman gave a conciliatory nod and began speaking. Her voice was strong and clear, not at all what he'd expected.

"Sataswarhi, hear me; be my midwife in the birthing of these words."

Marvin leaned in close to Cooper and whispered, "She is Dorcas, an elder of the Winnowed, a tribe that live beneath the city. They're rarely seen aboveground, but they send elders to the Apostery to tell a version of this story from time to time. It's never even remotely the same." Cooper heard the words and drunkenly processed something about an underground tribe and stories of debunked deities, but all he could focus on was Marvin's clove-scented breath hot against his neck. He wished it would move closer.

The elder Winnowed continued:

"Sataswarhi, heed me; I call you up from the depths beneath the crust of the worlds."

The hooded woman had stopped tapping her pencil and was hunched over her pad, scribbling. Cooper's head spun.

"Sataswarhi, help me; there is more weight in this story than my voice can carry without your touch upon my work." For a moment the old woman hesitated, looking up at the towering windows as if they were old friends; she smiled at her stained glass family. Then she explained herself:

"Storytelling is my contribution to the Great Work in which we are all instruments. This is a story our people tell about the origin of our city, not a tale of gods and goddesses. It is not a real story, but it carries some truth. Perhaps.

"Sataswarhi. Clear Star of the First People, the origin and namesake of the celestial river that flows from above down through every land, from the most distant dim heaven through every isolated cosmos until it spills, here, beneath our feet. Far below the source of the river lies its mouth, where the waters empty into the void beyond creation. *Here.*" The old woman, Dorcas, pounded her perch with a shriveled fist.

"*Here* did a tribe of the First People build a city. They named it, as it has been named and renamed ever since, again and again—until, like the snake that swallows its own tail, there was nothing left to hold a name. Today it is simply a city, and we call it as we like; we curse it or praise it according to our mood, but we know better than to ask its name. It is sometimes easier to live with a thing when you do not know its name, especially if you *do* know its nature.

"However, this is not a story of the nature of the City Unspoken as it sprawls and oozes today. This is not a story of our time, the time of the Third People, we who comprise what the shortsighted call *history*." A careful flick of the eyes to the woman with the notepad. Would the notetaker know that the tale was only one version among many, crumbs scattered for the faithless flock? "Nor is it a story of the Second People, whose crime was so great that nothing remains of them, as everyone knows, neither bones nor stones nor names. This is a story of the First People, the bright and dark ones who were born in the crucible of creation, who are the direct children of the Mother and the Father, born of Their destruction. They who are the children of the dawn.

"We only ever had two Gods, and They murdered Themselves to give us life, and it was terrible. A thing to shatter galaxies, if there had been matter or gravity then. When the storm of shadow and light had passed into mere turbulence, when the worlds first coalesced from the divine fallout of the Apostatic Union, then did the First People open their eyes. They rose from the dust and glitter of the worlds, or they gasped their first breaths in the ether between universes, that starless stuff which is empty yet always full. Wherever they stirred, the First People shaped the worlds around them. Some were great, and pulled the fabric of existence behind them like a heavy cape as they moved; it is true that some few of these still persist today in one form or another, disguised at the edges of our lives as gods or demons or half-whispered nothings that caress our hearts in the darkness. Many of the First People were not great, however, but lived much as we do, which is to say they depended upon one another. Community. They came together for shelter and solace, for survival, and so they laid down the foundations for everything.

"They built the first cities."

Marvin elbowed Cooper. *This is the good part, so listen up.* Cooper might have wondered why Marvin's voice in his head was clearer than before, or how he knew to think at Cooper rather than whisper, but Cooper's attention was so finely divided between following the story and trying to resist the further-intoxicating scent of his new guide that these arguably more important considerations were, for the moment, beyond him. He thought he might need another drink soon.

"Now of the great ones, there were many who found no interest in their minor siblings, and those who took interest often did so for less than generous reasons. The smaller children of the dawn could be fed upon, or manipulated and amassed into armies of soldiers or servants, or simply toyed with for the amusement of their more powerful kin. Still, there were a handful who were both great and kind, and it is to these—where they have endured—that the most lasting monuments, mythologies, and blood-memories are dedicated. There is Chesmarul, the red thread, who is called first-among-the-lost, who others claim was the first daughter of the Mother and Father and witnessed Their destruction with her own new-wrought, tear-stung eyes. There is the Watcher at Night-Tide, who does not condescend to speak his own name but bequeaths knowledge to those with the mind to seek it and the fortitude to withstand it. Another is his father, Avverith, inscriber of the first triangle and all that sprang from it—all things which come in threes, including architecture, which is idea written in three dimensions.

"This is not a story about Chesmarul, although we suspect she is always with us, after her fashion. Neither is it a story of the Watcher, even though it is his nature to observe all things. Avvverith Sum-of-Square gifted the lesser First People with the tools they used to build their cities, but has ever since been absent, so this cannot be his story.

"Instead we turn to Sataswarhi, the Clear Star, who made her home atop the ceiling of the heavens where she could look down upon all the worlds, all the baby universes exploding and expanding in their own pockets of space. She is said to be the source of all art, the inspiration behind inspiration. Not a muse as some consider the notion, not a passive beauty that turns men into dreamers—Sataswarhi is the active catalyst that turns dreamers into doers, poets into bards, wonderers into wanderers. From her home at the apex of creation a river flows, it is said, that touches upon every world in every little universe at least once. How it winds and where it turns are unknown quantities, and the legend tells us that in these days of the Third People, the river Sataswarhi flows still but is buried beneath aeons of rock and ruin.

"Of one thing we are certain, both then and now, that the river Sataswarhi begins at the highest point and ends at the lowest, the nadir, that land which sits like a drain at the bottom of creation, where all things must eventually find themselves before they pass out of existence and into oblivion. It was at this sacred but troubled place that the First People built the original incarnation of our city, fashioning a series of great gates encircling one another, a maze of concentricity crafted of diamond and gold, something bright to raise the spirits of the Dying as they made their pilgrimage. Here the First People built a fortress around a threshold, beyond which lay True Death.

"Now, listen closely; this is *important*. Although if you are here, you must know it already. It bears repeating."

Now. Marvin thought fiercely. Magic voices sound louder when you're a little fucked up, Cooper noted.

"There are many deaths, some larger than others. We are born only once but die many times. Each death is followed by an awakening on a distant world, where one lives again until another death comes to ferry the spirit across the void toward the next step of one's own journey. This is life; this is what it means to *live*. We are born, and we live. We find ourselves and lose one another only to be reunited somewhere most unlikely, for although the worlds are finite they are of nearly infinite variety—

some are cold and lifeless; some are bright but blind to the teeming others which surround them; many are rich in magic or invention, or both.

"There is only one common destination shared by everything that is born, and that is the City of the Gates, which we inhabit today like squatters in an abandoned mansion—eventually, all things that *are* must come to this place so that they can attain *iriit* and cease to be. It is the cloaca of the metaverse, the Pit, the Great Drain, the Exit."

"Iriit?" Cooper whispered, but Marvin shushed him. Cooper tried something new—he flexed a muscle in his head and thought, somehow, loudly: *What is that?*

An older word for True Death. Marvin thought back. *What makes this city famous.* For the first time, Cooper became conscious of the fact that he did not hear any fear in any of Marvin's thoughts. What made Marvin different?

"You may believe the river Sataswarhi is the blood of the Father-god, or the spirit of the Mother-goddess; you may believe it is only a metaphor for the processes of life and death; you may even doubt its existence entirely, and choose to believe that it is a myth cultivated to aggrandize the City Unspoken and its cash crop, True Death. My people, who live beneath the city where the old waters still flow, share these opinions and more besides, even though it is the river—well, *a* river—that sustains our troglodyte lives.

"And while the Winnowed venerate diversity of belief and nonbelief, living far beneath the streets of the city has given us an unusual education regarding its long-forgotten beginning. We make our beds beside the cornerstones of the founders, architecture long ago buried but still recognizable as the handiwork of the group of First People who built here—not the scattered poseurs of this era who masquerade as deities, or ply their petty schemes, or find refuge in distant worlds—but a people who lived as we do.

"We recognize the authority of no gods, but we approach worship in the reverence with which we see the footprints of the founders of the city. What stone survives tells us only enough about them to appreciate the depth of our own ignorance. They named their tribe 'aesr,' and appeared as brilliant-skinned people whose flesh was made of white light; they had only one eye, or perhaps four; proud crests topped their scintillating heads that might have been ornamentation or part of their anatomy; their limbs were arms and wings, and they tended to a grove at the heart of their city-maze that, I believe, was itself the remains of a primeval forest that covered the land during an even earlier age."

Cooper tried to picture the creature the Winnowed woman had described. What would he say to such a thing?

"The First People of the city—the aesr—had no king, but were governed by a prince; this much alone seems to have survived although the rest of their lives have been overwritten a thousand thousand times by the palimpsest feet that have walked the streets of this city throughout its history.

"What became of our founders remains one of the city's greatest mysteries. If the scale of time were less vast, we might know their fate—did they vanish or perish, did they file through the Last Gate? Did they Die at once or did they slowly become extinct? Did they travel elsewhere? What we can say for sure is this: they are gone, save one. He who ruled this place, the monster of light who locked up the nobility inside the Dome, and then fled.

"All that is left aboveground, tangibly, of the greatest of the cities of the First People now sits within a Dome half as big as the sky itself, the seat of our prince, last of his kind, who until recently maintained his lonely vigil over oblivion, as his kind have done since before we acquired memory. *This* is why we must have faith in the face of recent events: it is the prince's charge to protect True Death, for it is essential to the cycle of life on all worlds. What is born must die. What is here today must be gone tomorrow, or the next morrow, or the next. Like the river Sataswarhi, our lives must eventually empty into nothingness to create room for the waters that rush behind us. Otherwise comes the *svarning*."

The hooded woman gasped at the word. Cooper looked at her more closely now, and noticed the unmistakably pink hair she'd begun twisting around her pencil. *Fuck*. Why was Sesstri here, and had she seen him? Why had she gasped? He took a half a step behind Marvin, hiding. It was unwise, he knew, not to run to Sesstri and beg her for help, but he held back. She'd probably ordered Asher to get rid of him, for one thing. And then there was Marvin, who smelled like rum and smoke.

Old Dorcas faltered, looked confused, as though she'd forgotten where she was or why she was surrounded by her audience. Then she shook her head and finished abruptly.

"If the Last Gate closes, then we will all drown."

The barest hint of a susurration passed through those who stood listening. There were glances of acknowledgment tinged with something that resembled alarm. From his perch behind Marvin's shoulder, Cooper saw that neither Sesstri nor the Winnowed elder failed to notice the crowd's reaction. They held each other's eyes for a moment, and both looked haunted.

Marvin cocked his head back and rubbed his scalp against Cooper's ear, then craned his neck until their lips almost touched. Again, he spoke without words: *Don't you believe that, because it's a lie. The end of True Death would mean freedom for us all.*

Twirling a piece of red string knotted around a loose dreadlock, the crone continued with her story. Marvin snaked his arm around the small of Cooper's back, leading him away from the gathering. The old woman's story vanished from his thoughts with Marvin's touch, and it was all Cooper could do to keep his knees locked and his body upright. They walked toward the courtyard in a lusty haze, and through the drunkenness he felt electric fingers on his spine, testosterone sweat perfuming his thoughts with sailor tattoos and black gutta-percha earplugs, the promise of full lips and two bodies crushing together.

Then talons tore into his shoulder and spun Cooper around like a puppet. Sesstri's other hand yanked his wrist and pulled him away from Marvin.

"What. Are. You. *Doing*?" she hissed. "Don't you know what he is? And where the hell is Asher?"

The bitchiness in her tone brought out something that had lain dormant in Cooper throughout the whole day. He withdrew from her touch and lifted his chin, remembering her words that morning, when she'd been an angel cradling his head in her hands.

"What the fuck do you think I know? How could I know anything?" He spat—actually spat—in her face. "I'm a *turd*, remember?"

Sesstri had the good sense to hold back her anger but gave no sign of remorse or sympathy. She left the spittle to dry on her cheek.

"This animal," she pointed at Marvin, "will drag you back to his cohorts, who will rape you until you cannot remember your own name, force you to pollute your soul and offer it up to their masters. Know *that*, when your lips have been bitten off and you can't spit in any more faces."

She's lying. Marvin thought at Cooper. *And you know it.*

"You're wrong." Cooper didn't know it, but he knew he was furious and he let the rage speak for him. "You insult me and abandon me and then assault me when someone gives me a moment of basic human decency? Who do you think you are?"

Sesstri grabbed him by the arm and stalked toward the exit. "I'm the only chance you have at saving yourself, Cooper, and if you'd stop behaving like a brat who needs a spanking you might even understand when I explain why." Light from the courtyard streamed in through the incense smoke, and Marvin followed at a clip.

"And if you weren't such a stuck-up cunt I might even listen. Fuck off and *die,* if you can, and wake up somewhere far away from me." Cooper threw off her hand and stumbled into the starlight—overhead, the sky lit the well of faiths with a blue glow. He ran a few yards and tripped over the metal crest set in the center of the courtyard floor. Milling apostates looked at the commotion with annoyance.

"If I can?" Sesstri laughed, a bellyful of sound that didn't belong in her wasp-waisted frame. "Cooper, you bumbling disappointment, you have no idea how close to the mark you've hit. And unless you calm down and listen to me you will wish you could die and wake up anywhere else but here." She reached into her satchel and brought out her notepad, as if to read from it.

Cooper smacked it out of her hands.

Sesstri let the paper flap in the incense and stared at Cooper hard. "Have you even looked at your stomach yet, Cooper?"

"Have I *what*?"

"Are you drunk?" Sesstri asked with an escalation of incredulity. "I mean, honestly, Cooper, button your pants and open your *eyes.* You need my help, not a cuddle."

Cooper turned from her and saw Marvin's lip tattoo clearly for the first time—just inside his lower lip a black coin had been inked, with a stylized snake of negative space slithering forward as if wriggling out of Marvin's mouth. The light was far too dim for Cooper to have seen, and anyway the inkwork was a rough job, but somehow Cooper's eyes picked up the detail, and he did not question why. For a moment Cooper saw the tattoo more clearly than could have been possible—he saw that Marvin held a coin in his mouth, and a tiny green snake crept over it, a forked tongue darting out like an extension of Marvin's own. Then the overlaid image vanished.

What was that? he wondered, passingly.

"Your lip," Cooper said, scowling at the coin and snake. The tattoo hardly looked friendly. "I don't . . . I don't think I like that."

"It's his slave brand," Sesstri sneered. "The symbol of his masters and the sign of his enslavement to them. He's a *goon,* Cooper, stationed here to cull the unwary and those enchanted by the promise of True Death."

"That's a lie!" Marvin challenged her.

"Oh really?" Sesstri was smug. "I suppose you'll tell me that tattoo on your lip, whatever it is, is *not* the symbol of your bondage to the Undertow, and you *aren't* a runner for a gang that worships lich-lords who swarm unseen above your burning towers? You *aren't* in thrall to undead remnants who steal souls from the dance of lives and bind them in torment? Who rape children to taste purity?"

Marvin cursed beneath his breath and took a step back. Cooper stood bewildered.

"That's not right," Marvin began, but his protest sounded feeble. "It isn't torment to be free."

As he pleaded, other figures emerged from the shadows above. Black bodies like boomerangs jackknifed overhead, whooping, flipping from portal to portal and swarming the air. Landing like maleficent dancers, young men and women wearing dark clothes hit the pavement stones rolling, tumbling, screaming laughter and manic smiles. They all looked like Marvin. A thin girl rose like smoke out of the shadows behind Cooper; two boys leapt over his head, caterwauling, and pushed off from each other, spiraling to the ground bare of chest and foot, wearing only silk trousers. Around him, devout apostates scattered inside while casting dire glances over their shoulders. Cooper heard chirrups of their fear as the pious impious flapped away: *UndertowOverheadUnderfoot NoPeaceNoPeace . . .*

"Oh for fuck's sake," Marvin groaned, reaching for the wrist of the thin girl. "Couldn't you have held back for a few more seconds, Killilly?"

But the girl spun out of range and grimaced. "Shove off, Marvin. Can't you see it's not going to happen? Slake your lust with Hestor as usual, and leave the thighs of this full-figured insect alone."

Marvin looked away.

"Do you still feel like fondling strangers, Cooper?" Sesstri sneered at Marvin, who narrowed his eyes but said nothing. "This boy works for the *undead.* Do you want to discover yourself trapped in the lair of skeleton wizards who drink innocence like wine? Do you want to be their slave? Their meal?"

"Don't listen to her," Marvin said to Cooper. "Come with me and you'll see freedom."

"Or don't, and save yourself from mutilation." Sesstri's tone was casual. "Asher and I can help, Cooper. You don't need to resort to trash. Don't be stupid."

"Come with me," Marvin begged. *Now.*

Marvin's sad eyes and full lips were a siren song, and Cooper wanted so desperately to make himself inseparable from those lips, the smooth skin of that body, muscle and hair and spit. But Sesstri's warning was hard to ignore, and she wouldn't warn him if she cared as little for Cooper as he'd thought. And where did sirens lead you, but the rocks? He didn't have enough information to make the choice. Cooper didn't make a decision so much as follow an instinct he usually ignored:

"*No,*" he said. It was his word, and it felt good to finally say it.

He turned on his heel and ran, the blood in his head already pounding out a rhythm of escape. He pelted out beyond the courtyard and was sprinting up the tunnel to the surface before either Sesstri or Marvin could say another word. He felt bells ringing in his head like a thousand sermons, urging him to run faster, faster, away from the—the what? For a moment the chaos of bells and tears buzzed into a kind of white noise, which in turn collapsed into a high-pitched hum, then fell quiet. Cooper ran from Sesstri and from Marvin and from their dueling falsehoods, and he could feel their focus on him like raptor eyes.

Don't leave! and *Not yet!* cried their unconscious fears. And from Marvin a second, deliberate whisper into the language centers of Cooper's brain: *I'm not what she says I am.* Cooper sobbed and ran faster, bells still tolling all around him.

Through a haze of tears, he ran out from under the mountain, through the music, and back across the bridge of titan bones and rebar. He fled the bells, past the wet spot where the fighter pilot's barrel had been, and past the footpaths that led over the canals into the Guiselaine, where Asher had abandoned him—he wouldn't go in there, it was dark now and looked ominous. So Cooper darted down unknown streets, barely drawing notice from the jaded citizens of the City Unspoken, until at last he collapsed outside a three-story tenement in a filthy square, where the only sound was children playing cruel games, and all he could think about was home.

3

I've come to understand only one thing: that there's no country in a
dozen heavens so beautiful as Missouri. Excepting Arkansas.
　　　　　—Sam Clemens, in a posthumous letter to Gertrude Stein

Nixon sauntered into Maw's boardinghouse like he'd scored a table gra-
tis at Lutèce on Saturday night, ignoring the clamor of semi-feral street
kids and the smell of boiled dandelion greens. Husks of brown vegetables
bobbed like long-dead things in the pots by the kitchen, but Nixon turned
up his stub nose at the ever-brewing daily pot: he'd filled himself with
roast meat and clean potatoes, and for once he hadn't had to eat on the run.
He'd bought himself a proper dinner and had eaten it like a gentleman—
or as close as could be, sitting behind the Guile & Gullet, balancing his
bowl on his knees while taking great swallows of yellow beer from a
cracked stein.

The other children shied away from Nixon as he walked through the
common room into the smoking room behind it, revealing the secret divide that set Mother Maw's Minorarium apart from the rest of the gangs,
houses, and work programs for the children of the City Unspoken. Maw's
children—*real* children, born in the city but abandoned, orphaned, or
just plain unlucky—were camouflage for the kids like Nixon—unboys
and ungirls blessed with juvenile reincarnation.

Nixon heard shouting, shouting of a dialect and timbre that sounded
promisingly familiar. Memories flickered through his little head. School-
boy days in short pants and long ties, steno paper copies, the roar of heli-
copter blades. So much came rushing back at the sound of a simple voice,
it almost touched his heart. He heard a voice plump with the confidence
that all its problems had a simple—and swift—solution. He heard a shrill
disbelief that the shouter's concerns might not merit sufficient attention.
He heard the certainty that came only from being the golden child of the
most gluttonous opportunity: in other words, Nixon heard America.

His housemistress, the amphibious Mother Maw, stood in confrontation with a bewildered young man in jeans and a black t-shirt. If Maw had gotten to her feet, it spelled trouble for the round-faced American, who was *pointing his finger* at Mother Maw. Disastrous. Worse? The American was the chubby guy Asher picked up that morning, the one he'd been paid to tail. Not a good sign. The American insisted:

"Listen, somebody must have been through this before, you've got to—"

"—I don't, and I won't. Never mind that I can't. I've never heard of—"

"—*everybody's* heard of traveler's checks, it's the only reason they're any use at all. There must be a bank nearby—I can't be the first real person to get lost here. Could you at least—"

"—Out, out, and *out!*" Mother Maw was livid, her fat froggy neck shaking in leathery agitation. She was standing, and for the first time Nixon saw the feet that protruded from Maw's stained orange housecoat—and he almost lost his dinner. "You're too old, too new, and too full of questions to be of any use to me. *Get out!*"

She lifted a fat but powerful leg and kicked the American in the shins, sending him to the floor. She saw Nixon watching at the threshold and pointed a webbed finger.

"Clean out the trash, *boy.*"

Outside, the American sobbed into his hands like a child, pumping snot from his face in volumes. He looked like he'd lost his only friend or something.

"American, eh?" Nixon crossed his arms and sucked on a piece of candied eel. The idiot sat dejected on the doorstep with his face in his palms, and appeared not to have heard.

"I am so *stupid!*" he wailed. "I just thought, maybe . . ." and then he seemed to deflate. The American let out a sigh that went on until Nixon was sure the man's lungs would collapse.

Nixon cleared his throat and repeated himself in a wooden tone: "American, eh?"

Still nothing. *Fucking moron,* Nixon thought, afraid he might miss out on the grift because his mark was too stupid to bite the bait. *YouAmericanMoron.*

Cooper sat up and looked at the boy properly for the first time. Dirty brown hair covered a pug-nosed face with big dark eyes, and a filthy shirt pulled over a belly that stuck out with a bit of defiance. What now, a child to taunt him?

"What did you say?" Cooper asked, more skeptical than hopeful. He shook his head to clear it of the bird-scratch feeling of Nixon's thoughts against the hull of his mind. "You know America?"

Nixon held his arms out wide in an exaggerated shrug. "Can anybody really *know* America?" he asked philosophically, playing at uninterest by turning away from the stranger to look at the starless night sky. "I've seen the amber waves, sure. Never did find a majestic purple mountain, but then, I was awful busy."

"Can you help me?" The fool took the bait.

"Maybe." Nixon looked him up and down appraisingly but didn't seem impressed. "What's help, and what's it worth to you?"

"I don't have any money," the American said, and Nixon saw it for a lie but let it slide.

"Gimme your shirt, then." Nixon's goals were immediate, not grand.

"My shirt?" The stranger felt his black t-shirt like it was the only thing he owned. He looked like he'd been asked to give away a kidney.

"It's cold," Nixon explained. It wasn't, but he needed a better shirt to pull over the dead giveaway of his smooth belly, or what good was being prepubescent?

"I don't think I'm your size," said the stranger with suspicion.

"Suit yourself." Nixon turned to leave, his line baited. "Good luck, *Americano!*"

"Wait!" The American reached out to stop him. "What will I get for my shirt? And I'm not giving it to you until I'm satisfied."

Nixon rolled his eyes. *Whatever happened to trust?* he wondered.

"Follow me." He led the teary-eyed stranger toward the rundown square's only exit.

"But isn't there a place where people go when they're lost?"

"Of course there is. We're living in it." Nixon waved his arms.

"This shithole hostel?" The American looked behind them doubtfully. He could still hear Mother Maw excoriating children inside, the occasional cry from a web-fisted beating.

"No—this shithole city, stupid."

* * *

Asher won his fourth toss in a row and collected a pile of chips from his opponent, the Marquis Oxnard Terenz-de-Guises, who for all anyone could tell was ignorant of his own wretched luck. The lantern-jawed marquis reached for the dice cup to begin another round, but Asher laid a gray hand atop the marquis' ring-bedecked pink one and shook his head. Nobody could lose so much coin so quickly without being totally unfamiliar with the rules of the game—or perhaps too drunk to care. Neither the staff nor the patrons of the Guile & Gullet saw fit to correct the fault, whichever it may be.

"I threatened to make you into dinner, you know," Asher said, aware that the marquis was only half listening.

Oxnard spilled more drink on his fine red coat and was trying to lick it off, so Asher took enormous pleasure raking in the marquis' chips. Relieving Terenz-de-Guises of this much coin was a delight, no matter how badly he'd bungled things. The man had been winningly handsome before he'd married, and even five years of excess had merely cushioned his good looks. He always wore a red footman's jacket when he went carousing—it was nominally a disguise, except that everyone knew the marquis by sight and he didn't help matters by using his actual given name as an alias and letting everyone address him as "milord."

For all his faults, the marquis did possess a fabulous memory of the conversations he'd had, sober or otherwise. And since he drank frequently and with company both great and inconsequential, Asher had found he made for an excellent source of information. More so, the marquis was that rarest of creatures: a *willing* source of information. If he'd been more self-aware, he might have been termed a gossip, but in his dissipation Oxnard embodied something that resembled a revolving door for idle chatter.

"My friend," the marquis repeated, "I still do not understand why you are cross with me. I had a spot of news, heard from a wee bird about a package arriving today, and so I passed the news along. Is the erroneous chatter of birds the birdwatcher's fault, my good man? I think that it is not."

"My friend"—Asher's good mood hid a dangerous undercurrent—"is this wee bird a faerie bitch you regret marrying?"

"On the contrary, she's been an enabler *par exemple,* even if she is a little evil. I only mentioned whatever-it-was to you because I hoped you'd get there before she could." Oxnard rolled his eyes. "And why is it always about my wife? I could never regret my ruthless angel. Her skin like porcelain, her ears like pointed daggers, her hair that falls so straight and black . . . and though she *does* loathe you, *mi amor* is not responsible for every ill that befalls you, certainly."

"But she's responsible for this one." Asher pushed the matter. "What was it, a divination? A scrying bowl? Sheep guts? How did you—she—know what we would find?"

Oxnard set aside the dice and rested his palms flat on the table. His eyes didn't glitter now. "My mother-in-law," he said, "is a creature I make every effort to avoid, even on a conversational level. *Hai?*"

Reluctantly, Asher nodded. "*Hai.*" Best not to push a nobleman when he pushes back, but his thoughts spun: Lallowë's *mother?* Asher knew the marchioness was fey, but could confirm little else. Bells, were faeries involved with this?

Oxnard continued as if the matter had never arisen. "My father, the late marquis, was ever fond of reminding his friends and relations not to seek answers from the astral planes, and I for one have always followed that advice. To wit: you'll marvel at my entirely *terrestrial* source of information from no less a place than within the Dome, where my kind are imprisoned. But me? Not only am I free of the wretched place, I get *regular updates.*"

Asher looked doubtful. "The Dome is sealed. It's impossible to get word in or out."

Oxnard chuckled. "You sound so certain, my friend, as if you'd sealed it up yourself. But it's a big glass bubble—who's to stop a well-placed informant from jotting down notes and holding the paper up to the windows for anyone to read?"

"Is that how you operate, Terenz-de-Guises?"

"Of course not, *mon ami,* but you see my point. Nothing that big is *secure,* man. Why, a good Coffinstepper could crack the vault all by herself. Would you like to hear the latest?" Oxnard toyed with the rings on his fingers.

"You know I do."

"My comrades from the Circle Unsung, it seems, have started to *Kill* one another." His smile was deep and self-satisfied. "Capital K. Gone, obliterated."

"That's not possible." Asher waved away the notion. "True Death is a gift granted only to those who have lived enough to earn it. No man can Kill."

Oxnard raised his brows and stared at Asher for a long moment, a moment pregnant with an unspoken challenge. Then he looked away, brushing crumbs from his fingers. "I'm afraid that's old news and no longer true if, indeed, it ever was. The Circle seems to have found a way . . . They uncovered a Weapon that Kills. Locked up for five years in the seat of True Death has, apparently, spurred my fellows toward ingenuity. I can't say more, of course, without forsaking my own oaths to the Circle, but yes— the governing council of nobles has, twice now, Killed their own members in rather egregious waves."

"How disturbing." Asher did not sound disturbed.

The marquis smirked. "The Circle engaging in group Murder isn't disturbing, it's an extension of their basic nature. The bastards hate each other, but they're incapable of acting independently. No, what's *really* disturbing is the fact that someone inside the Dome has taken it upon themselves to become a vigilante. There's a Killer, now—a single man or woman with access to this Weapon and the tenacity to use it."

Asher rolled his eyes. "Now you're just telling stories . . . milord."

Oxnard waggled his finger. "Just this week, two Tsengs and a dozen stableboys were Killed by a single attacker. My informant witnessed the Murder firsthand. Here, have a quince, man, they're altogether too delectable to avoid. Some nutrition will put the color back in your skin."

"My skin never had any color, milord," Asher reminded the nobleman.

"How interesting." The marquis did not sound interested.

"I'm impressed with your resourcefulness, but tales from the Dome are hardly relevant to those of us on the outside. Where are you taking this?" Asher asked. Madness inside the Dome—that no longer concerned him. Let them destroy each other. The madness outside threatened far more than the status quo.

"You and I, pale vagrant, we are an odd pair to be friends, wouldn't you say?"

Asher nodded.

"And friends love nothing more than to help one another, *non*? I have helped you, I think you'll see. And in return I ask nothing. However . . ."

Asher cursed.

"*However,* there *is* something of sentimental value I seemed to have mislaid. A bauble, an heirloom—a box of red metal, about the size of a jewel box, open along one side, but otherwise unremarkable."

"You want a jewel box?"

"I want nothing. But if ever a friend should come across my lost jewel box, why, nothing would make me gladder than to see it again."

Asher shrugged. "Fine. I'll keep an eye out."

"Just the one eye?" Oxnard hailed some of the staff and waved at the tabletop. "I suppose that will do."

Asher pinched the bridge of his nose as two barmaids hurried over. He felt a headache coming on. The marquis continued.

"Now let me ask you this—girl, more wine—what would you have done—girl, no, other-girl, bring us a second platter of cheeses, the quince is rather woodsy all by itself—if you *had* found whatever it was that you thought I promised you? Your cup is empty, by the way—other-girl, never mind the cheese, just find the first one and hurry her up, we've two empty glasses now, *two.*"

"I'm sorry?" Asher asked, genuinely confused.

"I asked," sighed the Marquis with exaggerated patience, "what you would have done if you'd found anything where I sent you?"

"I didn't say I found nothing," Asher muttered. "It just wasn't helpful."

"Are you certain?"

"About as certain as can be, yes, milord."

"Well"—the marquis flashed his pretty blue eyes and reached unsuccessfully for the rear end of a nearby serving girl—"that's not terribly certain, is it?"

"What do you mean?"

"Only that portents are notoriously vague, eh? Isn't that rather the point of saying sooth—that the answer will somehow make sense to someone, and therefore be validated? 'A red door and a house on fire!' Now that could mean any number of things, for instance."

"I suppose . . ." Asher didn't suppose any such thing. Cooper was *not* what he'd been promised.

"If that's the case"—the marquis smiled at his own reasoning—"why not take whatever it is you *did* find and *do* something with it. Whatever you intended your next step to be." He waved his hands in mock secrecy. "Not that I'm remotely curious about the details, of course. Your business is your own, I'm sure."

Asher frowned.

Oxnard rolled a broken chip across his knuckles. "I can only imagine what my wife must be feeling now, to have her prize snatched from beneath her watchful, exotic brows. A lady like *ma cherie* would never mope and whine and gamble. Why, she'd be planning . . . something painful, I'm sure."

Asher's frown deepened.

The marquis pushed the remainder of his losses to Asher's side of the table, almost spilling his beer in the process. Every eye in the room was on that pile of chips, and Asher discreetly swept them into his satchel.

"Don't forget the broken one, friend." The marquis tossed the broken chip he'd been toying with onto the table and smiled dismissively. On the chip, someone had drawn a crude profile, a long-haired woman with an overlarge nose. Terenz-de-Guises stood to leave the Guile & Gullet for fresher meadows. "I've told you my heart's desire and given you all my chips, what's left to say? And if you've got nowhere else to start on your little project, then any old hole is as good as the next, eh? You'll excuse me for needing to relocate, but the dinner hour has passed. Other wenches to grope, you know."

Lallowë Thyu twitched an eyebrow in consternation at her empty wineglass. She sat in a solarium paned with glass and black lead, filled to capacity with lush plants. Leaves like slabs of green steak dripped water into sluice-runs carved into the stone floor, and exposed root systems that crept over stone pots and the moss-stained feet of statues set among the hothouse blooms. Surrounded at her table by an immensity of white pet-als, the Marchioness Terenz-de-Guises looked the picture of courtly fem-ininity: petite, dark of eye and hair, primped to apparent helplessness.

But upon closer inspection, Lallowë Thyu's delicacy was an illusion. She was thin but whip-strong, and her copper-oxide eyes simmered with a cruel tenacity. She wore a sleeveless blouse of gray-green silk that matched her eyes, and her feet were bare except for a coat of clear lacquer upon the filed turquoise chips that grew from her toes in place of nails.

She exhaled a string of birdsong curses in her native tongue that could have stripped the lead from the windows and pondered for the hun-dredth time why she'd bothered to marry rich in the first place. Oxnard, the Marquis Terenz-de-Guises, had been the perfect patsy, but it was not as simple to master life as a married woman as it was to master the man. Now she had a household to run, a district to govern, and cryptic orders from her mother to obey. Cryptic, and increasingly disturbing. And the bloody eyeball atop the ice cream sundae was—she'd missed the boy. And then seen him with *Asher.*

A queen of faerie made for an odd parent under normal circumstances, and these were anything but. Air and darkness were one thing; madness and monsters were part of their culture, but what her mother had be-come . . . and the new name she'd taken: the Cicatrix, Queen of Scars. Scabbed with metal and plastic. Lallowë shuddered, and obeyed.

Past the archway that exited the solarium, down the parquet hall and through a series of dressing rooms hung reams of expensive parchment paper. Several nights ago a message had appeared, as they did, upon one long sheet: a missive from the Cicatrix, containing orders.

They were odd orders. Brief and plainly written, which was itself un-usual, they mentioned a location and the description of a man, and a single untranslatable word. *Svarning.*

Setting the word aside, Lallowë had considered what to do. Mother provided the details of the human's arrival, but had given not so much as a hint as to what to do with it. Him. She *had* to stop doing that.

For once, Lallowë erred on the side of caution. To be certain, she would enjoy ripping the guts out of the meaty childborn that seemed so abruptly important, but without knowing why he was important, she risked her *own* evisceration. The Cicatrix was not a forgiving parent—or, at least, she was forgiving no longer. Lallowë's sister had taken care of that.

So Lallowë had waited in her carriage, idling at the corner of Dismemberment and Ruin. Tam had tried to catch her attention, but was Lallowë really expected to pay attention to every corpse that woke up in that beige, lifeless neighborhood? She'd expected some flash, at least a little colored smoke to catch her attention. It was hardly her fault that she'd missed one chubby human slung over the back of a man painted to blend in with the clouds.

Arrangements had been made. If there was one thing Lallowë had learned from the Cicatrix, it was to nest your best plans inside better plans. The Lady would tell Lallowë what this Cooper meant, and how well he played the game. Lallowë needed a new player; she grew bored of picking apart this city one guild, shopkeeper, and vagrant at a time. Asher still vexed her when he could, as he had today, but he was a limited, broken creature.

She closed her eyes pictured her childhood home—before it had been spoiled—trying to summon the peace of the bowers of the Court of Scars. Recurved branches like cathedral ceilings or longbows, the yellow and blue suns that chased each other across the sky, the lithe limbs and swooning embraces of her kin. She yawned, homesick, even though the home she remembered no longer existed.

Even the marchioness was answerable to someone. Not her husband, who by all rights should have been the governing force within the district and his home, but was not. In fact, as one of the few members of the aristocracy who'd escaped the prince's insane imprisonment within the Dome, the marquis could have seized some measure of power and dragged this city back into a semblance of order. But that was pure fantasy; he'd been a dandyfop to begin with, and since his marriage to the "foreign exile," Lady Thyu, Oxnard Terenz-de-Guises had gone both to ground and to seed. These days he was rarely seen—and never seen sober. Which of course was why it had been so easy to steal control of the family fortunes, and everything else besides.

But Lallowë's mother . . . The Cicatrix possessed limited patience and a fusion-powered exoskeleton. Who had advice for that?

A pain in her head interrupted her machinations. An old pain, but one that she used to feel elsewhere within her body. It stabbed through her head from temple to temple, and heralded the arrival of more than a simple message. Somewhere, worlds and universes away, a faerie queen began to send her sole remaining daughter a gift. Mother's gifts were never pleasant.

Lallowë drained her wine and left the solarium. Her bare feet made no noise on the parquet floor of the hall, nor on the lush pile of her carpets. She tore a page of parchment from her boards—of a thick caliper, crisp and neat, neither ivory nor white but bone—and spread it across her desk with stones at the corners. The warm-toned drawing room was darker than the solarium, but faerie eyes needed no lamps.

From inside a drawer, a pouch, and handkerchief she took a draft pen loaded with a very particular ink. The sound of pen scratching parchment made her skin prickle as Lallowë etched a single line. Dark ink spilled but did not clot. In another universe, Mother pushed, and the line split into two arcs, creating space where there was none before. The parchment puckered at its sides as its weft was distorted by the dilating oval of ink. Crimson and black pigment filled the little creases in the parchment, spreading its tattoo as the spell allowed Mother to slip something through from *there* to *here*.

Birthing her way between universes; it was powerful magic, but slow. Much slower now than when Mother could still use her womb.

As she watched the vulvar portal widen, Lallowë felt reminded of the pressing need to understand her mother's transformation from unseelie queen to mechanical nightmare, as well as her machine-derived increase in power. With her mother's interest looming over her shoulder, Lallowë could not afford to play the game as murderously as she would have liked—she would have to find a way to subvert while appearing obedient.

Something shiny glinted from within the blood-inked passage, and Lallowë's head cramped again. A gold oval—flatter than an egg but fatter than a pocketwatch—pushed its way through the paper, rising up from the flat surface of her desk.

Lallowë snatched it up at once, pulling it from the inked vulva. A cursory glance gave no hint to its purpose, or her mother's reason for sending it, and it was not until she wiped the ink from its surface that Lallowë realized what she held. The bauble vibrated with energy, and Lallowë felt the whisper of magic within it. And also the prickle of electricity. This pretty little thing was a machine.

It was the machine that had turned her mother into a monster.

Sesstri was livid. Asher hadn't worked out how his anger at Sesstri had sublimated into meekness, but somehow Sesstri managed to claim the rage that by all rights ought to have been his. He never expected her to care about Cooper; she'd seen him at the Apostery? With a Death Boy? And Cooper still had his navel?

"He didn't die?" Asher held his head in his big gray hands and looked at Sesstri like a beaten puppy.

"No, he didn't, and I was *waiting* until you returned, but you *dumped* him like trash, you stupid, stupid man!" She puffed hair from her face.

"Why did you wait?"

"I . . . I didn't know . . . Horsetits, Asher, I was trying to reason it out. I didn't think you'd *toss* him into a fucking *ditch*!"

"It wasn't a ditch." Asher's stormy mood was gone. Sesstri raged against the idiocy of men and the likelihood of Terenz-de-Guises' assassins tracking them all down and sending them spiraling off into other lives.

"We're right back where we started, only worse," she steamed. "Because now there is a young man who is *not a turd* walking around the City Unspoken, and he's being courted by a *Death Boy*. Did I mention that? Cooper was *drunk* and holding hands with a minion of *that*." She pointed north, through the bay windows, where the burning towers lit the night sky.

"Fuck me," Asher said in despair, when an insistent knocking sounded at the door.

"You sure this is the place, kid?" asked a child's voice from outside.

"It's the only place I know," said a voice that brought a brilliant smile to Asher's face. He leapt up and threw open the door, grabbing Cooper and wrapping him in a crushingly strong bear hug.

"I'm sorry, I'm sorry, I'm sorry!" Asher shouted, twirling Cooper around, or trying to, while covering his face in kisses. "I won't ever leave you again, my special little darling."

* * *

"Fuck you." Cooper pushed Asher away, but didn't feel as angry as he knew he should. Partly because Nixon was trying to tug off Cooper's t-shirt when he *ought* to have at least a moment of indignation at the great gray ape who left him to rot in the middle of this nightmare city.

Nixon pulled up on the t-shirt to little effect.

"Hey, buddy, give me my *shirt*." Nixon pawed at Cooper's side. "What's your shirt say, anyway? What's a Danzig?"

Then, "Shit. You gotta navel, kid. What gives?" Nixon fixed Cooper with a doubtful eye, and Cooper pushed him away.

"Huh?" Cooper's eyes were wide. "Of course I have a navel. *Everybody* has a navel."

Nixon pointed at his own bare belly. There was no navel there, just smooth skin. "Jesus. *Nobody* has a navel, moron." Cooper's eyes grew even wider, saucers of shock in his round face. "Excuse me? Nobody has a fucking what?"

Asher held up his hands. "Okay, okay. Listen, Cooper, as it turns out, you didn't exactly die."

Before he could vomit, Sesstri stepped in. "It's my fault. I saw it when I strip-searched you. I just . . . didn't . . ." She wilted.

Cooper blinked rapidly. "You saw what, exactly?"

"Your navel. It's just another scar, Cooper. And scars disappear when you die."

"I don't understand." Cooper didn't. "Why are you telling me this *now*?"

Sesstri skirted that question. "When your body fails, you move on. Your spirit clothes itself in its own reflection—the flesh and blood and good denim that you remember. You awake in a body that is your own, but new. The only way to tell, really, is this." She prodded his belly and then shrugged artfully. "You only get one belly button. So you cannot have passed over. You are still on your first waking life. You are simply too young to be anything more than you seem."

"I still don't understand."

Asher took a turn. "Plenty of people have navels. Anyone born here, in the city, and they're on their first life—in their first body. Because you only get a navel by *being born*—you weren't born here, you merely reincarnated here. You had no placenta, no umbilicus to feed you. You awoke, whole and new and dead." He pointed to Nixon. "This boy has no navel because he's died at least once already, that's how he got here. Neither does Sesstri, and, I *thought,* neither did you."

"So . . . so. I'm not dead? I'm not dead!" Cooper cheered, then realized that not-dying changed his circumstances very little. "Why am I here? How am I here?"

"I would very much like to know." Sesstri glared at Cooper as if he knew the answer and refused to share. He glared right back, taking the opportunity to examine Sesstri more closely: tall, thin and coldly beautiful, her light brown eyes flashed with a surgical intelligence. Sesstri wore a high-necked dress of wrapped yellow silk, its stiff collar only emphasizing the length of her amber neck. Like so much here, she was breathtaking and frightening at the same time. Nixon and Sesstri had taken one look at each other and, by wordless accord, ignored each other entirely. The unboy retreated to the doorstep, listening from outside while appearing to doze.

Asher took the opportunity to needle the angry woman. "Witness, Cooper, this irradiant creature who assaults us: Sesstri Manfrix—scholar, tyrant, beauty queen." He finished his drink.

"Cooper," Sesstri pronounced, and it sounded like an accusation. She poked him again. "Cooper. Not a magical adept, not a Coffinstepper or other professional corpse, no advanced technology, nothing. So what *are* you? Why are you here?" He shrugged. "Tell me!" she commanded, her words trailing the faintest red thread of panic. *WhatBringsYouHere?* Her thoughts scratched a rhythm in his head. *WhatRises?*

"I don't know," Cooper said, his voice beginning to crack. This was too much. He wanted to cry. He wanted to shoot them both in the face with a fat .45.

Asher stood and put his hand on his hip. His red-rimmed eyes were kind.

"Cooper," he said, pressing one big gray hand against Cooper's shoulder. "You will be fine. I promise it. You will be more than fine." And then, "I'm sorry I abandoned you and left you for dead."

And for the first time Cooper really *saw* Asher: maggot skin, bloodless lips, beauty in a body bag. He was sex and dissolution and strength in a ropey slouch.

"Something is wrong with the world," Asher rasped, and his voice was thick with a sorrow deeper and wider than Cooper would ever have guessed from his casual front. That face was a mask hiding a whole underground ocean of sorrows.

"We need worthier drinks for this part of the conversation." Asher stalked into the kitchen. "And by worthier, I, of course, mean *stronger*." He returned with a squat bottle of dusty glass in one hand, balancing three ice-filled tumblers in the other. Into each he poured a measure of acid-green liquid. "This is obsinto," he announced. "It makes everything better." With a little two-step flourish, he passed Cooper a drink that smelled of anise and mothballs.

"Something is wrong with *all* worlds," Sesstri corrected, still musing over Asher's pronouncement. "And nobody seems to care. We don't know what to do, or what will happen." With an expression of supreme relief, Sesstri closed her eyes and drained her glass in one quick motion. Then she looked at Cooper and smiled. A peregrine falcon smile, fierce but just as much a mask as Asher's. She was sad, too, Cooper realized, and desperate as well. They were each desperate and sad, and for some reason Cooper himself was a disappointment that increased the measure of both. He asked why.

They exchanged a long glance. A loaded glance, and there was more than business and world-worry in it.

"We thought you were . . ." Asher hesitated. "You won't understand."

"Tell me!" Cooper commanded.

"He'll think we're crazy," Asher cautioned Sesstri, who kept silent, occupied by her thoughts. *WeAreWeAreWeAre.*

"I already do."

She sighed and threw up her hands in defeat. "Hardly a surprise," she said flatly, then leaned into Cooper with intensity. "Do you know what a shaman does?"

"We thought you were a shaman," Asher said, rolling his eyes out of sheer helplessness. "Or an adept. A mage, a mystic. Something to help us."

"We were looking for *someone*," Sesstri corrected. "Instead we found you."

"What do you mean, shaman?" he asked, ignoring her newest insult.

"Shaman: a core-world, practically proto-cultural totemic, whose power is usually marked by, among other things, a journey of ascent—or descent—into the lives beyond life. A guide, a protector, a seer. Primitive from a certain vantage, perhaps remedial but, under certain circumstances, quite effective. One who walks between worlds and communes with spirits." She clicked her tongue, looking him up and down. "But you don't *look* proto-cultural."

Cooper bared his teeth.

"He looks feral enough to me," Asher said blandly.

Sesstri shook her head and her hair rippled. Dawn silk dancing. "Look at his clothes. He's wearing denim, Asher, not home-tanned leathers." She leaned over Cooper, peering closely and scratching at the seam of his jeans with a lacquered nail. "I woke up in a bath towel—this is merely part of the process. As I observed earlier, the stitching is clearly mechanical and the construction and branding imply a large commercial presence. Maybe massive. *Industry*." She leaned in close, her burl-wood eyes flashing. Sesstri's intellect shone from those eyes, self-evident and intimidating. "Do the words Starsung Underwine mean anything to you?"

Cooper shook his head no.

"What about Drambassel Fivemalt?"

No again. Sesstri pouted.

It dawned on Cooper that she was listing brand names, though he didn't know why.

"Mercedes-Benz?" she asked hopefully.

Of course. She was trying to place him. She could *do* that?

Cooper nodded with enthusiasm, more pleased to have been correct in his assumption than to give the woman what she wanted. His battered mind was adjusting after all.

Sesstri snapped her fingers and rounded on Asher. "This one is no shaman!" she pronounced. "I told you so. I know of his world."

"You do?" Asher asked with a screwy face.

"So do you, you just aren't aware you know it—it's one of the big players. *Real* shamans don't exist in postindustrial, magic-dead societies. Core-world shamans are shadows, and their magical adepts are simply practitioners of self-delusion. It's all drugs and drumming."

"So what am I?" Cooper interrupted. They both looked at him like they'd forgotten he could speak.

"An erratum, I guess," Asher muttered, averting his gaze down into his tumbler.

"I haven't the slightest idea what you are, stranger, or why you're here," Sesstri said with finality. "That alone should terrify you."

Cooper looked down into his own glass—they were all avoiding eye contact now—and swirled the grass-colored pastis to enjoy the familiar sound of ice cubes clinking. He drained it and observed that he wasn't terrified at all. Embroiled in a plot beyond his understanding, something that stole him from his bed as he slept and dropped him here, among these improbable strangers in this impossible city—Cooper should have been horrified; he should have been a quivering mass of tears and snot. But he wasn't horrified, not anymore. By some trick of fate or magic or inner strength, Cooper found himself merely annoyed. And careful.

"I guess I find that kind of rewarding," he said, looking at Sesstri. She didn't shrink from their locked gaze, and neither did he. "It may be self-defeating, it may even be suicidal, but right now? Right now I think, Sesstri, that stumping you is a beautiful thing."

After that, she did not speak to him for quite a while.

Sleep called to Cooper like a siren. Sesstri and Asher circled each other for the better part of an hour, sniping and ignoring Cooper, who was happy to be ignored. He poured mothballs down his throat and got drunk for the second time that day, while stars circled overhead. Still, a tension had been broken. Somehow it felt as if the three of them were bound together now, in their loneliness and confusion. Cooper wondered if they were . . . it felt like they might almost be *friends*. And that was the least sane thing he'd observed all day.

Companions, then, if friends was too strong a word. Coconspirators. Mutually fucked. Outside, Nixon napped on the threshold stone, his head against the door. Fucked seemed to be a hot commodity in the City Unspoken.

Sesstri's falcon gaze found him again. She'd been drinking heavily too, though it didn't show, and she seemed to have made up her mind about something. With careful little steps she sat down next to him. Quick, like a raptor.

"This city is nameless," she confided, leaning toward Cooper. "You know by now that it is one of a very few places in the whole of everywhere that True Death is possible—maybe even the first such place. Maybe the last. Beings come here from every corner of the metaverse to Die. It was once beautiful, so long ago that no one living remembers, but is now ruined."

"How did I get here?" Cooper felt his belly beneath his shirt.

She and Asher shared a guilty look.

"We don't know." Asher lifted up his arms. "There are powers that can intervene. Things that call themselves gods, but we've no evidence of that."

Asher lounged like a dancer in the window, gray ropes of muscle in repose while fire filled the horizon. Again Cooper saw the towers there, north and west of the Dome's moonlight; skyscrapers of steel and glass stood among more fantastic spires, fluted marble, pitted limestone. Some were ablaze, their tops lit like candles although they never fell. Something about towers that burned but stood both reminded Cooper of home and made him mourn *his* city.

And again, when he looked at the towers, he heard crying. Screaming and crying.

"What you said about false gods," he asked softly. "What does that mean, really?"

Sesstri braced her hands on her knees. "It is crucial that you listen to me and understand what I'm telling you: worship gods *at your own peril*. There are beings beyond the scope of your understanding, yes. There are the First People, who came before us; they are powers that may be kind, or foul, or capricious, and many would have you believe that they are gods. But just because a mind is older and wiser and even greater than yours does *not* make it divine. This is a secret that the vast majority of sentient beings seem incapable of apprehending. There are mighty spirits, entities, forces that clothe themselves in the trappings of the infinite, but if there exists an all-pervading omniscience—a truly divine light—I have seen no sign of it." She hesitated, tapping a finger slowly against her plum lips. "And I have looked." *AndLookedAndLooked.*

Asher slumped against the window frame, kissing the frost off his glass. "If anyone could find evidence of the divine," he slurred, "it would be Miss Manfrix." He stared blankly out the window, following Cooper's gaze. "She's very . . . *thorough*."

"You're still bitter I lied to you," Sesstri said, a bit more gently than Cooper had come to expect.

Asher made a rude noise. "Not at all, my lovely. I'm bitter because you won't go to bed with me."

"How common a reaction," she said absently, though Cooper could have tightrope-walked across the tension. "I thought your breeding was better than that."

"Breeding!" Asher brayed, still facing the windowpane. "Breeding? Bells, woman, breeding is just a fancy way of saying a man is well-trained enough to wipe down and pull up his pants before his wife walks in and sees the tailor's daughter down on her knees, with her lips open and her hair all mussed and sexed-like, in that tight little stomacher and that scandalous cleavage erupting all over the place, looking so plump and willing and, well, kind of juicy. . . ." He sighed, collecting himself. "*That's* breeding."

"You're drunk," she answered. "Go to bed." *YourBed MyBed.*

He ignored her and turned to Cooper with a conspiratorial wink. "There are two things every man who sees Sesstri Manfrix knows straightaway. The first is that she is the most beautiful woman he will ever see. The second is that he has no chance whatsoever to make babies with her." He giggled drunkenly into his glass, then shrugged to himself and burped.

Sesstri seemed unfazed. In fact, she nodded. A minuscule nod, like she knew he was right but was uninterested in her own beauty, even bored by it.

"So why were you looking for this shaman guy?" Cooper asked the room, eager to change the subject.

Asher drew himself upright, suddenly very sober. "Before all this began," he said, his varicolored eyes locked with Cooper's, "I had trained myself never to remember my dreams. Now I am plagued by them, and they are full of the restless Dying." Cooper nodded. "The release they seek here . . . it has become more difficult for them to attain. The passage of pilgrims through the city has been stymied, and our streets fill with those who have lived past their due. This . . . this is more than a problem of overpopulation. Without True Death, the metaverse itself grinds to a halt, like gears without oil. There is a . . . sickness, I suppose, and as it spreads it will affect everyone. So I tried to find someone, *anyone,* to help us, and I failed, and here we are."

Cooper nodded. "The *svarning*. That guy who came after us in the Guiselaine, that's what he said. And the old minnow at the applestory, she said it too."

"Winnowed. Apostery." Sesstri spoke slowly but deliberately. "Yes. Well . . . Well. I see everyone knows about the *svarning*, and not a clue what to do about it or even when it will erupt, as plagues do." She looked away. "In any case, the prince has been rather absent these last few years. Someone has to look after the city."

The confusion must have been clear upon Cooper's face, because Sesstri clarified immediately. "In theory, the city is governed by the prince, though individual precincts are administered by the families of the Circle Unsung, the ruling council of nobility. But some time ago the prince shut them all away inside the Dome, his capitol. Again, no one knows why. He has chosen to abandon his responsibilities, perhaps . . ." Her voice trailed off. She sat staring into her glass.

Asher was quiet for a moment, then shook his head as if clearing his thoughts. He smiled.

"This has been quite an evening," he said jovially. "We'll sleep now, and seek answers in the morning. We may not be able to heal the universe, but maybe we can find some help for our new friend, Cooper the erratum."

Cooper's head was spinning by this point, looped on insanity and bitter liquor. He knocked his tumbler down on the table—hard—and it echoed like the pounding of a gavel.

A yelp from outside broke the silence.

Glass shattered and Sesstri screamed. The shadows of men appeared at the windows, then climbed into the room, and Asher leapt to action; he became a whirl of smoke that streamed to a bay window and brought down two men in brown leather smocks, their heads smashing together with a satisfying crunch.

Cooper sat up in alarm but found himself paralyzed. There wasn't time to be frightened, but for all his determination to wrap his head around the events of the day, his death and its subsequent repeal, the tale of the city and the worlds and lives upon lives, Cooper had no instinct for dealing with violence.

Sesstri and Asher had no such limitations. Asher continued to fell men in a blur of gray skin and twirling rags, while Sesstri had knives in each hand and stood like a pink-and-yellow silk valkyrie with her back against the stairs, etching a sphere of safety into the air around herself with the flurry of her blades. One of her assailants fell back, clutching his guts as they slipped out of a sudden gash. Were those kitchen knives or daggers? Was she *prepared* to eviscerate men at a moment's notice?

Cooper found the good sense to jump behind the sofa in which he'd been sitting and tried to hide, but in doing so realized that he'd exhausted his combat training. *Asher's right,* he thought, *I really am helpless. But I can flag down a mean cab.*

More men streamed in, and Asher became a rush of doves beating wings against a storm, his hands and elbows and feet his only weapons, pale blades of bone and skin that danced violent and dangerous at the head of the sudden incursion. Blood flew from the faces of the men who swarmed him. They were pulling themselves through other windows now, and someone kicked down the door with a smash.

"Cooper!" Sesstri called. "To me! Upstairs, *now!*"

More men stormed in from the kitchen, distracting Asher and Sesstri both. Cooper moved toward the stairs, but not quickly enough. A hand clamped down on his mouth from behind and Cooper fell against the wall, hitting his head hard. He felt more hands lift his body and saw the starry sky for a moment as they passed him through a broken window, then the pain in his head swamped his thoughts and sleep came to Cooper at last.

In times now past, which the historians of the nobility called ancient times but were, in fact, closer to recent events than anything resembling *ancient,* the people of the Guiselaine paid a bone tithe to the lords who kept them safe, employed, and fed. The governances of other districts had employed similar policies, but the Guiselaine had always been a populous and prosperous territory, and its maze-tight streets and deep, narrow canals relatively dangerous to maintain; the resulting coin-to-calcium ratio was fairly steep, or shallow, depending upon one's point of view.

If that view happened to be from the nave of the ossuary beneath the manse Terenz-de-Guises, one might think all the currency and corpses were worth the tithing, especially if one happened to be Lallowë Thyu. The marchioness breezed down the stairs onto a tweed parquet resembling the floor above, only made of finger bones: carpals and phalanges met her bare feet at perfect angles, and Lallowë gripped the floor with her toes, letting herself pretend for a moment that she walked across the floor of woven, living wood that rimmed the Court of Scars.

Through the nave, Lallowë padded her way past pillars of femur and humerus, designed to lean into the midline like rows of trees, branching somewhere past two-thirds of their height to honor the Golden Mean and support narrow hyperboloid archways that formed at the junction of almost conical ceiling vaults built steeply with pubis and skull. At the apex of each dome dangled a ring of baby rib cages, the bone fine as lace, within which enchanted lights hung like glowing fruit, painting the ceiling and floors in the colors of nature: sunny, leafy, wildfire-ruddy. Between the blooming lights and the dappled floor, a forest of yellow bone welcomed its most recent mistress.

Even this world could be a beautiful place, she thought, if one kept the proper perspective. And disposed of the ugliness—as she was more than happy to do.

Lallowë came to a stop at an apse lit in green, resting her hands on the flat waist of her wide-bottomed trousers; she rubbed her bare arms and wished she'd brought a smock to protect her blouse—blood spattered the bones, looking black in the green light, and Tam raised a blood-drenched face from the remains of a torso, nodding his head at the marchioness.

"Ma'am," he said, hiding his exhaustion as best he could. There was marrow in his hair, dripping onto his cheek like spittle or semen.

The remains of a man were scattered about the apse, but his trunk stood upright, impaled upon a steel spike. In a far corner, hidden from the green light, a statue of a young girl leaned against the wall of bones. The statue bore more than a passing resemblance to Lallowë, and appeared to be carved from cherrywood.

"Ah? I have butchered the butcher, ma'am," Tam announced, returning Lallowë's attention to the corpse. "And immersed the device in his organ, as you requested."

She nodded. "Pull it out." *Let us see what heartsblood reveals.*

Tam made a face and obeyed. He held the golden oval in his gore-drenched hand.

Lallowë peered over him but made no move to touch the thing herself. True enough, fresh heartsblood revealed an unseen pattern of fine lines that crisscrossed the surface of the thing: circuitry. And one thing else besides. "There's a hint of a groove along the side—I believe it's a catch. Do you see?"

"I . . . I think so, ma'am." Tam had mortal eyes, and had to squint.

"Open it," she hissed, her mood slipping from appreciative to impatient—always mercurial, a restless serpent.

Gold light shined off the thing in his palm. "It looks like a jeweled paperweight," he said, brushing fox-red hair from his perfect, defiled face. "Milady is certain that the bibelot in question . . . *opens*?"

Thyu nodded, showing as always just a whisper more patience for fox-faced Tam than for any other servant—he was a great beauty and could please her with his tongue, when she chose to be pleased. "I'm certain of it now . . . something is inside. Can't you hear it?"

Inside? Tam nearly dropped the precious machine.

"Oh, give it here." The marchioness plucked the device from her valet's palm and traced its outline with a filed turquoise nail.

"I heard something when I touched it, yes ma'am, though I'm not certain it was . . ." Tam looked relieved to be rid of the device. He sighed. "Beware unfamiliar magics," Tam cautioned before he could stop himself. It was faerie logic, and good advice besides. Unless your advisee was the Marchioness Terenz-de-Guises, in which case the best advice was to keep your pretty mouth shut if you wanted to remain inside your skin. Tam half-expected to see her forked tongue lash out and punish him for using his own, and steeled himself.

But his mistress didn't reprimand his impertinence, being mesmerized by the marvel in her hand. Lallowë peered more closely at its faces, at the ultrafine etching of parallel lines that branched and reconnected, capillary channels filled with blood.

"This is not magic," she breathed, admiring the alien filigree. "At least, not chiefly. There are principles at work here that neither you nor I have seen before till recently—this device produces an electrical current. It also emanates a most unusual vibration that has perplexed me."

"Magic vibration?" Tam asked a little foolishly. Old habits.

"Oh no. Can't you hear it, Tam?" whispered the marchioness, tracing a deeper groove along the back of the device. "The screaming?"

Like the catch of a jewelry box, the top half of the bauble popped open. It shocked her finger at the same instant, discharging energy that numbed her hand.

Beneath, on a circle of plainer metal, lay a bright-winged dragonfly, pinned through the abdomen and fluttering weakly. Death throes, for popping open the cabochon had separated the mechanism impaling the dragonfly to the disc, disemboweling it in the process.

The device, bisected, no longer hummed in Lallowë's hand. It was powerless.

Tam took the top piece when Lallowë thrust it at him, and looking at the cup of golden eggshell in his palm, he saw a brown smear of innards clinging to a sharp little needle that protruded from inside the cover of the device.

The marchioness stared at the sight for some moments, teasing the dead wings of the dragonfly with her stone nail.

"Well," she said at last, her voice dry and weary. "This is new."

4

The Kol Kol Tuin people of the Dimmest Heavens have evolved to a breathtaking yet absurd level of abstraction. The souls who join the Kol Kol Tuin have attained a state of extreme enlightenment, though that might seem a contradictory condition. They emerge from the ether in bodies of flesh and glass, and cultivate within the clear flows of their glass anatomy the oddest dwarfed plants.

I met my grandmother there, of all places, and her skull was an open sphere of glass where a succulent curled its roots. She would not speak to me, not because she failed to recognize me or felt no joy at reuniting with her progeny upon such improbably distant heights, but because I moved too fast. I lived too fast for a glassy life, and she could no more catch me in a hug than I could pluck a photon from the glare of the noon-day sun.

The neighboring Kol Auin people were nearly identical, but chose to live portions of their lives in what you or I would experience as real-time. Their civilization consumed itself when a rare celestial event caused a panic among the populace. The Kol Auin aroused into real-time and tore themselves apart before the event could be properly identified as harmless. On agate balconies the nearby Kol Kol Tuin did not speed a glacial thought for either the potential celestial threat or the extinction of their cousins. They felt both concern and sorrow but maintained their centuries-long meditations.

With her silence, my grandmother taught me that the chief measures of a culture are how it copes with fear, and how it copes with idleness.

—Durango Wreckmist, *The Life of Jungles*

Purity Kloo, Elisabetta Bratislaus, and NiNi and NoNo Leibowitz sat in a solar parlor, embroidering hoods of pale blue silk. The Leibowitz twins were arguing over the finer points of millinery, with NiNi insisting that the confections of human hair crafted by one of their co-captives within the Dome didn't count, and NoNo demanding the group acknowledge that the selfsame creations were *hats,* not wigs, and should be respected as such.

Purity might have mentioned that hats and wigs would both be found within a milliner's shop, but she hadn't the stomach for argument today.

A curved hull of translucent green Dome glass ran the length of the parlor and filtered the sunlight through its pastel sieve, but Miss Bratislaus—Bitzy, to distinguish her from the other Elisabetta of her line—had ordered warm-toned lamps set in strategic locations about the salon. Unlike Purity, Bitzy didn't especially mind life within the Dome, except perhaps for the coolness of the light through the glass, which did little to flatter her complexion.

Purity Kloo, on the other hand, positively glowed in the curved hallways of their palace-prison, aquamarine and pear-colored light falling across her wispy blond hair and petite features as if she was born to this royal captivity. Which of course she was—they all were.

And if that captivity had grown more literal in recent years, it didn't change the fundamentals of life in their society, only tightened the rules. It tightened the rules like a noose.

Outside the glass, the city burned and consumed itself. Purity could watch, but never help.

Bitzy Bratislaus rarely looked through the glass. She cleared her throat into a sateen kerchief and stared at the palm-sized miniature paintings that decorated the interior wall of her favorite salon. They'd been arrayed into clusters that faced the Dome wall like little phalanxes of gloved ladies, begonias, and overstuffed lapdogs, all glaring at the curved glass that imprisoned their mistress. Every noble family held token residences within the massive royal complex, a city unto itself, but until Prince Fflaen had proclaimed the Writ of Community, few had ever bothered to use them.

Now the Dome apartments were country home, city house, and pied-à-terre in one, and the families' proximity to one another had heightened tensions that in bygone days would have been ignored or left to the lesser cousins to squabble over in canalside duels. Duels rendered utterly pointless by the body-bindings placed on every member of the peerage at birth or elevation. NoNo once told Bitzy that when the Writ had first been proclaimed, Purity Kloo had attempted escape by killing herself every hour for a solid week in an attempt to weaken the enchantment that bound her spirit to her body. All she'd gotten for her efforts was a traumatized chambermaid and a scarcity of unspoiled nightgowns.

If only Purity's suicide binge had been the least disturbing event since the Writ and the subsequent confinement of the peerage. If only their mothers and fathers who sat on the Circle Unsung had not discovered the Weapon; it was a fact that Death could come only to the Dying—the very old or very weary who matched the criteria of some existential equation. Or, it *had* been a fact, before the Circle found the Weapon: some tool or knowledge that let them inflict True Death upon anyone they chose. And they had chosen with abandon—twice now, the Circle had battled, and twice its ranks had been devastated. Wherever Fflaen had hid himself, the prince must be apoplectic that the aristocrats he was trying to protect had defiled the sacred trust that was *his* duty to safeguard. *Iriit.* Whoever would have guessed that True Death would become a tool of the Lords and Ladies Unsung? It was a measure of their desperation that they indulged in such *tourist attractions*. To the nobility, the City Unspoken was a playground, not a destination.

Bitzy cleared her throat again, attempting to wrestle her thoughts from the maudlin and into the warm light of her carefully arranged lamps.

"I saw quite the spectacle today," she teased. Her three companions looked up with earnest expressions. She continued, "We broke our fast with Duke Eightsguard and his family this morning, as has become something of a fortnightly tradition, despite the fact that Daddy has to walk twice as far to reach his offices in the Petite Malaison." Bitzy paused, posing; she never passed up an opportunity to mention her father, the Lord Senator. She smiled, baring perfect white teeth. "*Well* . . . Rawella Eightsguard wore a lilac pericoat to the table."

"Lilac, you say?" NiNi picked up a pink sugar cube and licked it, catlike.

"Lilac. A charming confection of pucebone lace. You might have recognized it."

"Oh?" NoNo sounded bored.

"Yes." Bitzy nodded. "From the Princeday Eve Day Bruncheon, just *four* days ago."

Purity Kloo raised an eyebrow, sensing where Bitzy was steering the conversation. "Not . . . not Princeday Eve Day Bruncheon, surely?" Purity laughed, a nervous titter that did little to dispel her anxiety. NiNi and NoNo leaned forward with their twinned nostrils flared, scenting blood in water. NiNi wore a mean little smile.

"The very same." Bitzy bit her lips in mock sympathy.

"Oh my," gasped NiNi without a hint of surprise.

"What a pity." NoNo echoed her sister's disingenuousness.

"Are you absolutely certain, Bitz?" Purity dared. "Mightn't you have seen that lilac pericoat three weeks ago instead, at the tea for Circlestung Supper Day, Bitz?" Silence. "We oughtn't be hasty, not after the mixup with poor Lyndee Bocks."

Bitzy sniffed. "That mistake was *entirely* understandable, Purity, and you know so as well as I do. If we were a week or so early in our administration of justice, what's the difference? The Bockses are always in flagrant defiance of one tenet or another, and Lyndee would have met an ill fate eventually in any event."

"Yes, Bitzy. I suppose she would have."

"Rawella Eightsguard!" NiNi Leibowitz exclaimed again, half-striving for a truer note of sympathy. Her instrument of false concern was poorly played, Purity couldn't help but observe. She put it down to lack of practice.

"I'm afraid so. But here: Purity, you're the cleverest of us four, you should appreciate the concerns of propriety and its enforcement. Oh, I know you've always been especially close with poor Rawie and her sister, but I daresay you'll be a great comfort to Brindle Eightsguard over the next few days."

Purity Kloo nodded in agreement, not showing for a moment that she hadn't the slightest idea who Bitzy and the twins were talking about. *Rawie?* Brindle? The only Eightsguard Purity remembered was an old bag named Druessa, and she'd been Killed early on after the Writ of Community, during the first wave. There was no point in asking for clarification—Purity might as well wear a hoop skirt and skin her mastiff for a stole—her coterie wouldn't tolerate any chink in their collective armor. Perceived weakness was a worthless commodity of late, which didn't exactly play toward Purity's hand, but she hadn't grown to womanhood among the Last Court thus far without learning a dozen ways to disguise her spotty memory for names, faces, and events of social importance.

Purity sighed. A great and weighty sigh, contrived to mean any number of weighty and great things to whomever might be scanning her armor for chinks. *What a bore of a vigil,* she thought.

"Rawella was terrible at cards." Purity strove for apathy. "I'll miss watching her lose. For a while, anyway. Are we still hiding body parts to delay the binding?"

"Was?" NoNo asked with a spark of interest, "Is our Purity developing a taste for blood?"

"Justice," corrected Bitzy and Purity simultaneously, just as Purity had intended.

"Well, you know of course what this means, NoNo," continued Bitzy. "We were all the best of friends with Rawella, naturally, but she's gone and broken the rules, hasn't she?"

"Well, of course she has, and she should be punished." Purity wondered if she'd taken her abetment a step too far. "But—"

"—And she will be, darling. You know what the Circle would say: 'When we break our own rules, we break our own necks.' Better we girls administer justice with delicacy than allow our parents to bully the poor girl to Death."

Purity was certain to a fact that Baron Kloo wouldn't give two dirties as to what wardrobe standards Rawella Eightsguard adhered—whoever she was. He certainly wouldn't wish harm on a young lady for wearing the same pericoat twice in a fortnight. As petty as the other house leaders could be, she had difficulty imagining any of them condescending to care one way or another about Bitzy's couture inquisition, except perhaps as a tolerable distraction for their daughters.

More likely to catch them bickering about how to deal with the vigilante Killer in their midst. A rogue Circle member who had, apparently, been Killing servants in the northern basements of Dendrite's Folly. The cowards—her father excluded, of course, and Purity felt that conviction did not arise purely from filial adoration—had been all too happy to Murder one another en masse, but one rumored bastard going off on his own to permanently Kill a few nobles and handful of stable boys and suddenly the Circle was too busy staring at their bootlaces to do anything but whine.

A servant brought in a tray of coldcumbre sandwiches garnished with thrashmelon slices and citrus from the Dome's expansive orchards, and the four girls laid down their embroidery hoops to pick at the midday meal. Further conversation would be prohibited until their hostess motioned for the attendant to clear the dishes.

Purity sat with her thoughts and nibbled on the corner of a sandwich triangle while NiNi hummed an annoying fragment of song. Transmigration by death was out of the question, she'd admitted to herself with much reluctance. Her efforts in that direction had borne no fruit. And there could be no daring physical escape: the Dome had been well and truly sealed by the prince. Adepts wove wards into every possible exit—even the filigreed air vents—and praetorians loyal to Fflaen stood guard at the end of virtually every corridor. Their presence was not strictly necessary, but evidently Fflaen desired a constant reminder of the power of the Writ he'd declared that imprisoned the aristocracy within the Dome in the name of their own safety. For all intents the Dome was hermetically sealed—servants, Circle, and families all trapped together. And now, one of them had gone rogue with the Weapon.

Escape from safety had proven impossible, and Purity had discreetly tested every method she could think of, including spelunking through some *quite* unpleasant culverts. The only demonstrable loophole was even worse than this interminable confinement: True Death. Somehow the Lords Unsung had uncovered a means of opening the Last Gate that did not rely on a soul's own readiness for oblivion. *That* had been a surprise; True Death came *only* to the Dying, who by definition had lived long enough to have earned oblivion.

Bells, the Weapon! That would have once been unthinkable, but now that the lords had a Weapon they could use to Kill—actually *Kill*—their rivals, the illusion of "community" the Writ had supposedly been intended to foster evaporated like mist in daylight. And so it surprised Purity not one whit that the children had begun to follow their elders' example, hacking one another apart for the silliest of reasons. If the prince didn't reappear soon, or if the Writ were not somehow revoked, Purity did not see much hope for the peerage. Not that the nobility deserved much in the way of hope, she reckoned, for all the misery they'd doled out over the millennia.

NiNi and NoNo set down their teacups and pushed away their plates in unison. Bitzy waited a moment longer, then lifted two fingers to alert the servant to clear the table. Within seconds no trace of their meal remained. Purity thought of the fate of Lyndee Bocks, so similarly exacted from their lives—and Rawella Eightsguard, who would soon follow. They couldn't permanently dispatch their victims the way the Circle and the Killer could, but they'd dumped Lyndee's parts into three separate cisterns and the poor thing had yet to return. The body-binding enchantment couldn't be broken, but it could be . . . frustrated. Purity wondered if they mightn't all end up Dead or minced and dispersed, the nobility either sent into oblivion or rendered useless while their bodies slowly reconstituted.

Traditionally, a duel between body-bound nobles ended in ritual cannibalism. Eating your opponent was the best way to ensure a slow waking—she'd heard the process could take a *year*.

Could that be the prince's endgame? Purity wondered, as she tasted the last remaining crumbs of a coldcumbre sandwich. Was the Writ of Community just a ruse to herd the aristocracy into destroying itself? If anyone were capable of such conceit, it would be Fflaen the Fair. Purity stifled a yawn. Maybe it was a symptom of her confinement, but lately she'd had trouble remembering how to care—and then, just when she felt overcome by ennui, she felt a fever to escape, escape, *escape.* But sometimes she wondered: escape what? Was it just this golden cage? There was a kind of madness bubbling up all around her, but no one seemed to see it. Purity had doubts she couldn't quite name, and rages she couldn't quite control, and she ruminated overmuch on the nature of the Weapon and what it must feel like to cease *to be.* . . .

"Ladies?" Bitzy reconvened. "Have we all finished our needlework for the afternoon?"

"As close to finished as can be, I suppose." Purity frowned at her own work, black flowers blossoming across the face grille of her hood. What cannot be avoided must be endured, her father said.

"Well then. Shall we attend to our responsibilities?" Bitzy put up a good effort at seeming reluctant.

"Yes," said NoNo.

"Let's," said NiNi.

With that, the four girls stood up, smoothed their skirts, and donned the blue silk hoods, each helping the others secure them in place with three snug bows down the back of the head. Then they each pulled razor-honed sickles from behind their cushions and filed out of the room to butcher Rawella Eightsguard over a breach of etiquette.

Not everyone came to the city to Die. Beside the trickle of dreamers and pilgrims who followed the tunnel to the Apostery sat the carnival tail-gaters Cooper had seen, musicians beating out their rhythm to the patch-work songs of the polyglot Dead. Elsewhere, on the mile-wide plazas surrounding the sealed Dome, the cobblestones bustled with hawkers and vendors plying the hundred trades fueled by the industry of Death: indul-gences and remembrances, relics of questionable authenticity. Fingers of vanished saints and martyrs, gold-forged wigs of goddesses long since divorced and forgotten—icons to suit sentiments that hearkened from all the near-numberless universes whose Dying converged in the City Un-spoken.

Among the elite of the worlds a teleological tourism existed, and guides traveled with cadres of archmagi and offworld royalty who took a dozen different routes to see the squalid splendor of the City Unspoken: astrally projected, temporarily incarnated in borrowed bodies; even phys-ical entrances were rare but not unheard of—if the emperor of twelve microcosmi wished a window opened to the Piazza of Distant Roads, there would be a party of city nobility waiting to greet their otherworld peers and whatever army of adepts the otherworlders employed to make such a voyage possible. Terenz-de-Guises, Bratislaus, Blavatsky-Day-Louis, Kloo, FenBey—the most powerful noble houses welcomed trade in any form.

And then there were the Eightfold Worlds—realities that physically adjourned the pocket dimension of the city and had, in ages long vanished, functioned as both suburbia and supply route. Today they were remem-bered as a lesson in a kind of abstracted urban decay: left to rot, the paths to and through the Eightfold Worlds had rusted shut, collapsed due to poor maintenance, vanished, or been rendered useless by the truancy of municipal oversight. Once they had been cathedral worlds whose aisles led to the City Unspoken. Only three of the Eightfold Worlds remained accessible, but raw materials still made their way into the city with profitably regular custom: Terenz-de-Guises, its hands in every pie, trafficked in mineral and lumber trade, while the mercantile classes forded agriculture, livestock, and other necessities across the thresholds and through the canals that separated the city's districts. Work continued, such as it was, albeit diminished in both capacity and profitability—the city missed governance, if not its governors.

So the barge that made its way down the canal that separated the annexed blocks north of Dismemberment from the Callow Heights and the shrinking demesne of Purseyet blended seamlessly into the nighttime traffic of industry, weighed down by crates of goods and crewed by a sullen bunch of dark-browed men and women.

The madman at the prow drew little enough extra attention—madness was merely another commodity here, and some of the more superstitious local business owners even considered it good luck to employ at least one lunatic in some capacity or another—a moon-touched potato peeler might bring good fortune to an innkeeper, and more than one nutter worked as deckhand on the many barges that plied the city's arterial waterways.

"Pioneers!" called out the bearded man standing afore. The night wind whipped his unkempt hair about his face and pulled back the corner of the canvas that covered the body at his feet. Cooper slept on, oblivious to the madman or the shattered sky that glittered above the water.

"Enough, Walter," a husky voice scolded from the flimsy shack that served as the scow's deckhouse. A stocky woman with arms muscled like a pair of pythons stood in the open hatchway, her hay-colored hair cropped short at the nape of her neck and a grimace on her thick-featured face. "We must be quick about our business tonight, and I'll have less of your crowing and more of your hands securing the hawser, if you please." The lighter-class scow had seen better days, but Captain Bawl ran her boat like a ship, and all the oakum-patched, split-bitted hull in the worlds wouldn't discourage her professional pride, even if tonight's dispatch did leave a nasty taste in her mouth.

"But the moon . . ." the wild man protested, searching the sky.

"Won't rise tonight no matter how you howl, so lay off and get to work or I'll weigh you down with stones and drop you in the soup. The patron wants us there by midnight, and you have enormous chains to watch out for." And there were—huge, rusted chains crisscrossed this section of the canals, as they did elsewhere across the city. Bawl had no idea what the buried chains were about, but they were as thick as her barge and could shear her hull in two if her coxswain didn't do his job.

Walter lowered his eyes and nudged the unconscious body with a foot. He wondered in his mad way if the boy was dead or merely sleeping, and if there had ever been a difference between the two states of being in the first place.

"Do the sleepers sleep? Daughters of the West?" He looked at his Captain imploringly. "All the prisoners in the prisons. The righteous and the wicked. All the joyous, all the sorrowing, all the living, all the dying? Do the sleepers *sleep*?"

"Yes, yes, the kid is fine, Walter. Stop fretting." Bawl was unmoved by Walter's sympathy but answered him nonetheless. It wouldn't do to have her token madman upsetting the quality, if the quality ever decided to show his face above deck.

Walter combed his fingers through long brine-yellowed curls. "The ghostly millions, yes." He nodded, seemingly satisfied. "The places of the dead quickly fill'd."

"You care too much, old man." She should have ignored him, but the intensity in his shrunken eyes compelled her, as it had when she first took him aboard. He sulked out at her from beneath his broad-brimmed hat.

"Whoever walks a furlong without sympathy walks to his own funeral dressed in his shroud," Walter explained, as if to a child.

"Okay, care then, if it's so damned important. See if I mind."

"Captain Bawl," snapped a voice from behind her. "If you're quite through humoring your beast there, I believe we approach my point of disembarkation?"

Tam stepped out of the cabin, the torchlight catching his fox-roan hair and turning it to copper. No sooner had he scraped the guts off his face than his mistress dispatched him to deliver a package, a package that had turned out to be a man. Tam sighed, fingering the bloodstains on his lapel and pitying the human cargo. He looked handsome, if a bit oversized, but anyone unlucky enough to gather the attention of the Marchioness Terenz-de-Guises *and* her machinated mother was dog meat. Tam hadn't a clue why Lallowë wanted the childborn taken to this particular destination—

probably to lure out the pale vagrant, see if or how important the dog meat was to Asher. She had an unhealthy obsession with that man.

Tam repeated himself and clapped his hands for the captain's attention—Captain Bawl mistrusted hands as smooth as those, but everyone needs to eat, and the marchioness paid better than most.

"Aye," she said curtly, remembering the price she'd been promised.

There wouldn't be sufficient payment for the band of toughs who'd led the assault on the Manfrix house, though—the lucky majority had died, and were now enjoying the freedom of a new sky. Some few had withdrawn from the mess without grave injury, but most of the men had to be left behind on the embankment, minus an eye or an arm or skin to hold their guts inside. Bells, but those two could *fight*!

Bawl had seen the disaster from outside. It was supposed to have been surgical—strike quickly after dusk when the marks were at their least vigilant. *Ha*. That had been a relative concept—the gray man must be some kind of martial savant, the captain had decided. She'd once seen one of Prince Fflaen's praetorian guard duel outside the Way of Forgotten Methods garrison, back in the days before the sealing of the Dome, and he'd had something of the gray man's grace. But Asher fought barehanded. He'd been *everywhere*.

And the Manfrix woman hadn't been much easier to subdue. Whatever informant had pinned her as—how had the documents described her?—"an inconsequential academic" would have to reconsider his or her notion of "consequence" once the mercenaries who'd survived the razor kisses of her blades came calling.

The captain had refused to take part in any of the bloodletting. It was only the insane amount of coin that the marchioness had placed on tonight's business that had gotten Bawl involved at all, and while she'd agreed to take the cargo aboard the *Barge Brightly* once the toughs had hauled the body out of the house—at great cost—she'd let nary a one of them set foot on her ship. Her boat, she corrected herself with a shake of her head. Bawl might have fallen far from the admiralty she'd led lives ago, but she still had standards. Ethics. Battered as they were—and bells, were they battered.

Thoughts of the botched abduction evaporated as the barge rounded a bend and Bawl's destination loomed before her. The peaked white building was half keep, half palace, and the sight of its walls shining against the night took the captain's breath away every time she passed this way. She'd never had a reason to stop and stare before, though, let alone to moor at the jetty of canal-stained marble that reached out into the water like a pale finger.

"At last." Tam exhaled with relief. "I'll take a brothel over a barge any day."

La Jocondette was more than a brothel—it was the remainder of an age when the whores of the City Unspoken had ruled their own district, Purseyet, like queens. Once, the lifebinds that now held them hostage to pimps and madams had been no different than the charms that distinguished peerage from hoi polloi: the nobility, governors, and courtesans had all been deemed too important to have their city lives interrupted by as minor an inconvenience as death. So it was with great honor that they submitted themselves to be bound to their bodies, bound to their city, and bound to their duty.

Times had changed.

The courtly arts had long ago become devalued, the nobility devolved into a handful of families clutching at whatever diminished grandeur could be found—and these days whores were merely whores, body-bound or regular flavor. But La Jocondette retained more than a glimmer of her former prominence, and her edifice reminded the city that once it had counted courtesans among the peers of the realm. Men and women who, lovely of flesh and spirit, had helped ease the passage of the Dying and other pilgrims—like the trickle of dead saints who came to join the Winnowed in their caverns beneath the streets. La Jocondette reminded the worlds of that less ignoble past: scrubbed daily, wreathed with flowers and with a candle lit in each of its tidy windows, La Jocondette dominated the back end of Purseyet. The rest of the district had succumbed to disrepair and the ceaseless encroachment of squatters and industry, but the white stone building kept manicured lawns that extended to its wrought-iron gates and wrapped around to kiss the canal at its rear.

Like the two-faced god of portals whose face supported some of the grander bridges over the waterways, La Jocondette presented two faces to the city—one to the ruined street and one to the canal. Once, she would have greeted patrons from both ends; now the only traffic she saw came from the water, since the adjacent streets were no longer considered safe enough for her dwindling visitors.

Still, she maintained an air of beauty despite the humiliation that the years had forced upon her. La Jocondette could never be raped while her walls glowed in the limelight—she withstood the ravages of dissipation like a queen in a tumbrel, refusing to hang her head until the executioner held her neck down against the chopping block.

The Lady waited at the end of the jetty, swathed in white muslin, the pearl-white façade of La Jocondette gleaming behind her. They were versions of each other—both glowing from within the enshrouding filth, regal despite any circumstance. The Lady found her best light, silhouetted from behind while limestone and burning torches lit the building from aesthetically pleasing angles, banishing the shadows that swarmed the neighboring buildings. Fruit trees lined the path from the chateau to the dock and glowing enchantments had been set among them, floating between the branches like lazy fireflies.

The sight was nearly enough to make Captain Bawl herself gape.

"Welcome back, friend," called the woman on the dock to Tam. He assembled his face into its most winsome mask.

"As always, my Lady, I feel as though I have never left your gracious home. Once welcomed into the bosom of La Jocondette it is impossible for the heart of a man to leave." Tam bowed so deeply that his hair brushed the wood of the deck, and Bawl would have laughed if she hadn't been so eager to be off, coin purse in hand, away from this business of kidnapping.

The woman in white nodded and smiled generously at the footman, but made no move to help him as he stepped onto the dock. She remained in perfect poise, every inch a queen, as Tam motioned for Bawl's crew to hurry unloading their cargo.

"Be about it then," Bawl muttered as two of her crewmen dropped the canvas-wrapped body on the dock. The mistress of La Jocondette appeared not to notice any of it—not the body, not the barge, not the men tracking canal mud across her tidy little jetty.

Bawl winced as Walter stepped to the edge of the barge and put one boot on the mooring bitt, pressing his hat against his heart like a lovesick suitor. To the Lady, he said with reverence, "Every moment of light and dark is a miracle."

To Captain Bawl's surprise, the Lady bowed her head toward the old deckhand and replied in kind:

" 'The fishes, the rocks, the waves, the ships with men in them. What stranger miracles are there?' "

Walter puffed his cheeks in what might have been pride and nodded—nodded to the Lady, then to himself, then withdrew. Bawl had seen odder interactions on the waterways of the City Unspoken, but never for a moment did she doubt the city's ability to surprise her. Tam, on the other hand, rolled his eyes elaborately.

"Come, Young Tam Lin, and enjoy our hospitality," said the Lady to Tam, and his irritation melted away. He blinked.

"Thank you, great Lady. Your graces are numberless, as are the pleasures of La Jocondette, no matter the hour or the circumstance." He indicated the wide swath of lawn behind them but had eyes only for the Lady. "But I must return to my mistress posthaste."

She flashed an enigmatic smile, a diamond glinting light off a hidden facet. Bawl received the impression that the Lady had as many smiles as she did clients; more than that, even.

"We'll have the marchioness' guest brought inside and made comfortable," the Lady assured Tam, taking him by the arm and leading him toward the spotless structure. "And for you, the fleetest carriage." Their feet crunched the crisp grass that grew between the flagstones of the path. The Lady continued to ignore Cooper's body, and she and Tam disappeared into the garden, obscured by fruit trees and puffballs of blue and pink hydrangea blossoms. Bawl, her boat, and its less-than-sane crew were dismissed.

Captain Bawl made to call out after them, until she saw the purse of coins Tam had dropped beside Cooper's head. She swiped her payment with a meaty mitt and stepped back aboard her craft, signaling to her crew to release the moorings.

"Shove off, then," she added unnecessarily, but the female deckhand unwinding rope from the bitt merely nodded. They understood one another, captain and crew. Understood that tonight's work, while distasteful, had been profitable. They'd all sleep with a full stomach tonight, swinging from their nets in the berth below. Death and sanity be damned.

As the barge slipped off into the night, Walter resumed his post at the fore and picked up his mad song again.

"Your flesh," he cawed to the receding splendor of La Jocondette, "your very flesh shall be a great poem!"

Nixon squealed beneath the vise-grip of Asher's hands, which crushed the breath from his chest and kept the boy from answering the gray man's questions. Questions for which Nixon had no new answers—he hadn't finked them out to the attackers, and if he had he'd surely have made himself scarce. Instead he'd been a dupe, laying on the doorstep trying to shake the wool from between his ears, nursing ribs bruised where the men had kicked when they came upon him unawares. He was trying to explain this to Asher, but the sere fool wouldn't stop strangling him long enough to listen to Nixon's alibi.

"Oh yes, yes!" the big man sneered, indulging his mockery of the explanation Nixon had yet to finish. "You were just casing the neighborhood, is that it? And not leading a band of armed men to our location, 'certainly not, sir!'" Here Asher affected a falsetto yip that sounded nothing like the cagey urchin. "'No sir, never would I squelch on a mark of such fine quality as yourself, sir!' Is that it? Do you think I'm as green as that boy your friends dragged bleeding out of the window? Do you think us fools, is that it?"

Nixon croaked in the negative, but if Asher noticed he gave no sign.

"Dead gods drowned and blazing! First you're paid to follow me, now you lead them to our doorstep? You stupid unboy, if I'm wrong about Cooper—if Sesstri and I are wrong and he *is* part of this, and if you've led him away from me, then I will *slice out your bones one by one and crack them open with my teeth.*"

Sesstri laid a finger on Asher's wrist. His eyes flickered to her face, serene despite the blood splattering one freckle-dusted cheek.

"I should like to hear his answers, if mercy provides, before you butterfly his flanks and chops for our supper."

Asher had the good sense to look abashed, and shook his head as if to clear it. He set the boy down but kept him cornered against the entrance and the coat closet with one splayed palm.

Nixon coughed and spluttered, his world reduced to a small red weal of pain where his breath usually went. Inhale. Exhale. Why did they always have to choke him so?

"I think you can appreciate our concern." Sesstri stood shoulder-to-shoulder with Asher, peering down her nose at the urchin. She'd spared him from an accidental strangling, but Nixon knew better than to expect anything further in the way of compassion. Christ, she was a beautiful bird, but colder than Kissinger's teats.

"I told you fuckers, I had nothing to do with this. Why would I take one thrashing and stick around for another?" He glared at the gray man. "I just wanted my new shirt."

"I don't think he was involved, but not because I believe his motives are honest." Sesstri pulled away and stalked to the windowsill still spotted with Cooper's blood, put her hands to her head, then wrung them. "Did you see their faces?" she asked the shattered window.

"Yes." Asher had seen the madness beyond bloodlust that boiled behind the eyes of the men who'd attacked them. It was a madness he'd seen with increasing frequency on the streets of the City Unspoken.

"Why attack here? Why not scoop Cooper up off the streets where he'd been wandering—*alone*—all day long?" Sesstri shot Asher an accusatory look.

"Beats me." Nixon watched the two adults pick at the facts like carrion birds.

"Who planned this?" Asher looked at the windows, all broken when the men had swamped the house. The calligraphied wallpaper was torn and stained with blood—so much for the enchantments of ink. "Whoever did this knew when and where to strike, and that's a precious short list of bastards."

"They may not have *expected* Cooper to have been routed to the Guiselaine and abandoned." Another look.

"I will hunt them down and cut out their hearts." Asher pushed a half-broken pane through the casement, which splintered into the flower bed.

"Has it occurred to you that such a reaction might be precisely what our assailants sought to provoke?" A feral dog would bring down its quarry just as quickly as a trained hound—but leave little for the huntsman.

"Does it matter? Would that change what we've got to do next?"

"If it sends you on a rampage of evisceration, possibly. What *do* we do next?"

"Listen," piped up Nixon. "If you tell me what this problem of yours is, I know a few guys—"

"—Absolutely not." Sesstri shut him down with a palm.

"So what happens," Asher asked, "if I've lost us the only lead? What happen if we fail, Sesstri? Do you even know? I don't."

"Comes the *svarning*," quoted Sesstri, a look of realization painted across her face. "Then we will all drown."

A beat of silence. Another. Sesstri sat motionless, a frozen dawn of fright.

Asher hesitated, uncertain how he should behave. Should he ask if she was all right? Would she cut him if he touched her shoulder? Would he begrudge paying so small a price? This *woman*—they faced a fate quite literally worse than extinction and the simple fact of her presence filled his head with thoughts of foxgloves and pink hair fanned across pillows.

The Dying could no longer Die, and Asher fixated on a crush. He was too old for that—an excess of years that could have been measured by the eon—and yet he couldn't manage to feel reproachful. *What's captured her attention? Is it me?*

Nixon interrupted their respective reveries with a salty curse.

"Fuck me for a Frenchman, Little Tokyo's on fire!"

Sesstri rushed to a window. Red smoke billowed from the other side of the yellow hills. But she did not think there was fire. Bonseki-sai, the district Nixon referred to with his nonsense-speak, lay beyond those hills. That was where Sesstri had woken when she arrived in the City Unspoken; that's where her landlady, Alouette, had found her. As absurd as it was, she did not think this a coincidence.

Tam looked as tired as he felt. Blood and mud splattered his once-tidy uniform, and he fairly wilted against the doorjamb while his mistress considered her next steps. His face was flushed from comings and goings.

"Tam, fetch my implements. This daily task grows boring, but perhaps this morning will prove unique." Lallowë Thyu stood at the door to her study, contemplating the oak-paneled room from within the starched collar and shoulders of an overconstructed dressing gown cut from peach slipper silk; she scanned the oval library that had belonged to her husband for something out of place, missing, or secretly flawed—with an expression suggesting that at the first sign of any such offense she would have the whole room razed and rebuilt from scratch. Maybe chaparralwood-stained Terenz-de-Guises black, carved with pears and pomegranates. Maybe greenstone and jet tile.

"Implements?" Tam asked dumbly, hoping he'd heard wrong through his haze of exhaustion, although he knew perfectly well that "implements" meant only one thing—the valise packed with instruments of torture and murder that sat in the study's small closet. *The* valise—pale green damask painted with tiny yellow flowers that smelled too strongly of lavender and hyssop, but not strongly enough. Tam often cleaned the blood, shit, and mangut off the tools within the valise but had never before attended his mistress while she wielded them. Those were days when Tam locked himself inside his sleeping nook and played his lute as loudly as he could to drown out the screams.

"Bring the tools I require to the second dressing room." Stone turquoise nails tapped a staccato warning on the leather-bound tabletop. All of Lallowë's kin grew earthen elements from their nail beds rather than keratin—elements such as rock or wood, metal ore or thorns. Family legend held that the tradition—for the protean fey, tradition often served the function that inheritable genetic traits did in human stock—had originated with Lallowë's revered mother and queen, the Cicatrix. The last time Tam had seen the ancient queen, her once-lithe body had been sheathed in graphene and ebon polycarbonate—only her face appeared even remotely organic, though her linen-wrapped hands had sported épée-thin lancets of obsidian stone.

That had been a difficult day for them all.

"Yes, ma'am." Tam braced himself for the second dressing room and turned to leave.

As Tam scurried off to do her bidding, the marchioness let her gaze linger in the well-lit study, black bouillotte lampshades with gold-leafed inner panels cast ghosts of yellow light that almost obscured the blue dawn struggling to gladden the day. Something felt wrong to Lallowë. Not quite wrong, exactly—purgatorial, perhaps. She felt flushed, her head hurt; well, facing her father's unflappable arrogance pained her. She hadn't slept, that was all—a long night of tying up loose ends must have put her on edge.

Tam was waiting in the second dressing room for his mistress when she arrived, looking anywhere but toward the small door across from the entrance. The chamois-paneled room smelled of lavender and hyssop just like the valise of agony that visited it daily; its cushions were soft and plentiful, and the small door that Tam refused to see led off into a charming little confection of a privy that scared him witless.

To be fair, Tam thought, he wasn't frightened by the room per se. Not the silver-leaf ceiling nor the white and pink dogwood blossoms on branches painted across the walls, nor the hardwood privy seat, nor the black-tiled bathing pool set into the center of the dark glass floor. No, what scared Tam was the man shackled to the wall, caked with his own filth and blood. The man was old and frail, with a drooping white moustache and Lallowë's eyes.

Once a poet renowned across a dozen worlds, once a philosopher-king in his own right, Hinto Thyu had damned himself by choosing to pay a visit to his estranged daughter.

He'd arrived one cold morning not more than three years past, and his daughter had repaid his paternal affection with her own brand of filial concern: she'd had him body-bound and shackled and tortured to death, daily, ever since. That wasn't unnerving to Tam, not in the least—on the contrary, it would have been out of character for a daughter of the Cicatrix to treat her human parent with anything approaching human civility, let alone warmth. No, it was the elder Thyu's tacit acceptance of his fate that terrified Tam—each dawn Lallowë slipped into the second dressing chamber's privy and spent the better part of the morning inventing new ways to murder her papa. And each day Hinto Thyu voiced the same request before he expired:

Tell my daughter that her father loves her.

The worst thing was, Tam thought the old man *meant* it.

Evidently Tam's guess had been correct—the marchioness meant for Tam to attend her inside the privy this morning, rather than listen to the screaming muted through three rooms and four doors of blessed insulation and as much lutesong as his fingers could muster. Well, so be it. He'd lived through worse, hadn't he? If his mistress wanted him to take a personal interest in her guests, wasn't it his duty to accommodate her? That was his purpose, after all.

Lallowë strode into the room and crossed the distance to the privy door before Tam could blink. He picked up the wretched valise and followed the marchioness into the small enclosed space, trying to remember to breathe but shocked nevertheless by what he saw.

The night had been kind to Hinto Thyu. He was still dead when Tam slid back the doorway to admit his mistress—a ragged fringe of white hair veiling the old man's face, the sinews of his emaciated body still in the process of stitching themselves back together. Just a few slices of flesh remained unhealed, but they no longer bled freely—he would be waking soon. Watching a body-bound corpse heal itself demanded an iron stomach—and it made Tam uncomfortable to think that a similar enchantment chained his own spirit to his body.

"Tell . . ." the old man croaked, jerking to life in midsentence; no doubt he had been repeating his message to his daughter when she slit his throat the day before. Hinto Thyu coughed and spat out a piece of his tongue. Not so dead after all. Tam oughtn't to be surprised at that— though he'd never say so aloud, Tam saw something of the father's resilience in the daughter. The same stubborn refusal to bend to reality—Lallowë reflected her father, but twisted and ugly as was the way of these latter-day fey. It was remarkable that there was anything of him in her at all.

"Tell my daughter . . ." he began again, but never finished. Lallowë glided across the chamber—skirting the gore-filled bathing pool brewing rot in the center of the floor—and slapped the words from her father's mouth.

"No more of that, Papa," she almost whispered, stroking her father's cheek where her turquoise nails had drawn blood. "We've heard quite enough about your feelings."

"If only that could be true, Lolly." Hinto Thyu matched his daughter's gentle tone. "I don't believe you've truly *heard* a word about love in your whole impoverished life."

A second slap rang off the silvered walls of the privy. Tam stared unflinchingly at the dogwoods painted on the silver walls.

"Drivel. Drivel, doggerel, and defamation, that's all you've ever been capable of, Papa. If you call me by that insulting diminutive a second time, I'll have you bled dry again." That had been a long week, Tam remembered, thinking of the howls that had faded day by day into awful silence. And the faces of the laundresses who'd had to bleach a week's worth of bloody washrags. Exsanguinations were no holiday.

Lallowë held up something for her father to see: the gold device she'd spent so much time examining since she'd opened it, deactivating it in the process. Bits of dried dragonfly wing still stuck to its inner shell.

"What's this, another bauble for the jewel of my heart?" The old man smiled through a mouthful of broken teeth. "You have so many lovely things."

"Something more. Something less, too, now that I've opened it. But I think, Papa, that you already knew that." She shook her head as if to clear it, and Tam wondered, not for the first time, about Lallowë Thyu's state of mind. These escapades didn't seem to satisfy her as once they had.

Hinto Thyu almost smiled. "I know only the enormity of my own ignorance, poppet. Mine and yours."

"Of course you do. Philosophical gibberish aside, Papa, I believe that you recognize this device, or at least the principles of its design." She lifted the lid with a nail to show him the remains of the dragonfly. Did the old man flinch? How his daughter wanted to wound him. How she'd tried. "A beautiful machine powered by an insect. Much like Mother's womb must have felt after you seeded it with me."

"Yes, yes. I am small and insignificant. I am less than nothing."

"Truer words, never spoken." Lallowë sat on a tall stool and crossed her legs at the knee.

"Which begs the question: what are you?"

Lallowë twitched a devastating eyebrow.

But Hinto just shrugged, as best he could hanging from manacles. "Ah, you are greater than I will ever be, lotus of my loin. Perhaps you are embarrassed to have such a nobody for a father?"

Lallowë rested her hands in her lap and fixed her father with a searching look. "I'll be honest with you, *Father:* for the last three years I've been trying to decide the answer to that very question. Why indeed would I spend a moment's thought on the jumped-up minstrel *du jour* that Mother tapped for a seed donor? What possessed me to spare a single thought for a discarded stud horse that didn't even merit a proper expulsion from Mother's court?

"But in the last few days I've learned something, Papa, which explains the remarkable aptitude of my foresight. I've learned that *great things* can be fueled by the least significant of lives." She slipped the dragonfly corpse from its golden coffin and dangled it before her father's eyes.

"Yes," he agreed. "As your great rage has been fueled by mine. My least-significant life."

No response. The wings of the erstwhile insect danced in the exhalations from Lallowë's flared nostrils. Tam watched blood dry on dogwood petals.

"Maybe I've misbehaved, Papa." She considered, inspecting the play of light across her turquoise nails. "Instead of tickling you with my steel feathers here, maybe you'd prefer to play the audience while I round up some innocents to tickle instead? Since you don't feel like talking, perhaps I could inspire you to write a new folio of verse? Pain informs art, I'm told. Yes, let's drag in a *babe* to torture instead. You may watch."

Hinto Thyu sagged farther into his chains. "I'll tell you what you want to know, Lolly, but not because I'm moved by your tantrums. I'll tell you because you are my daughter and I love you; I will always love you, no matter how you deform your heart."

"Fabulous." She dismissed him with a wave of her hand. If his words affected her, she did not show it, instead shaking the broken cabochon in her father's face and demanding, "Now *what is this*?"

"It's called a 'vivisistor,' poppet, and it produces an electric current derived from the slow death of the living thing trapped inside it."

"That is its function. Vivisistor." She tasted the word. "What is its significance?"

"What's significant about generating power from life? Oh poppet, you ask all the right questions, but in the wrong order. You should feel horror where you feel only ambition, and I worry that if you do not feel it now at the beginning as you should, then you will feel it at the last, when it is too late for you to save yourself, and that breaks my worthless heart." Tam thought the old man looked as if he meant it. He seemed sincere, at least.

Lallowë hissed through her teeth. "Don't fence with me now that you've begun to cooperate, Papa; we're past that. There's nothing remarkable about a battery, no matter how it generates current. There's more to this 'vivisistor' than electricity, and I want to know what it is."

"*I want, I want, I want.*' That's all you know. It's my fault, I suppose, for not supplementing your mother's instruction with a modicum of the decency that is your human birthright." He drew breath to continue, but his daughter denied him the opportunity.

The third slap stung Lallowë's palm, and Hinto Thyu was not so quick to raise his head this time. When he did, their matching eyes met and neither gave an inch of ground.

"Do you feel better?" he asked her, very softly. "Does hurting me lessen the burden of your pain, my darling girl? If it does, I will gladly dangle here forever."

Lallowë cursed in faerie-tongue, obscene birdsong chiming the air. "Why do you torment me?" she demanded, a thread of shrillness in her voice betraying the girl she must once have almost been. "And where did Mother find it?"

Hinto Thyu looked down at his tortured carcass. He tried to shrug, but his brutalized muscles wouldn't permit it. "Because I am a terrible father, I suppose." Then, tears in his failing eyes, he broke.

"Your mother uncovered the technology decades ago, shortly before the troubles with Death began." He paused, watching his daughter's face. Tam could not imagine feeling anything but fear for Lallowë Thyu, but this man only ever offered love. Did he know how that would torture her? Was the father as cruel, in his way, as the child?

"'Troubles with Death.' So you know about that, do you?" It was a cheap question—anyone paying half a mind to the foot traffic in the City Unspoken would notice that the ranks of the Dying swelled daily. But no one seemed to be paying half a mind these days; there was a frantic energy, a distraction in the air.

Hinto kept quiet, though his face looked woeful. Three years of dying daily, he'd kept his secrets. Tam did not think that Hinto Thyu would ever spill them all.

Lallowë pressed a nail against the thin skin above her father's collarbone, hard enough to draw blood. "I knew you knew more than you let on, but not *why*. Why do you know so much, Papa? Did Mother tell you this, so long ago, before you left us?"

Her father looked at the floor when he answered, staring down at his own blood, both dried and fresh. "I don't hate your mother, Lallowë. I don't wish her harm—that, and I worry that the harm will not be limited to the Cicatrix alone. Please murder me again, but promise me that when the moment comes, you will save yourself."

She promised him nothing but pain, and kept her word. The old man bellowed.

"You're leaving something out." Lallowë brushed his whiskers, now, mimicking tenderness as best she could. "Keep your sources if you'd rather scream than sing, but tell me what you know of the devices. Finish this."

"The vivisistor combines several arcane disciplines with some technological fields that should not be compatible with one another, let alone with spellwork. Perhaps you might meditate further upon the implications of such a feat."

"Perhaps I might do, but I'd consider it a courtesy if my Papa would finish the bedtime tale he's begun." She picked his skin out from beneath her bright nails.

Hinto sobbed and it seemed as though all the strength drained out of his body and into the cesspool at his feet. "I would expect no less from my darling girl. If I tell you that the vivisistors are nothing new, but something very old, and exceedingly dangerous, will you abandon your mother's madness? I think not. And what if I tell you that the magics and sciences combined within the vivisistor seem to arise from disparate universes? Will you see reason and leave the folly of ancient madness to proper fools?"

Lallowë's eyes opened wide. "Mother works with technology from multiple realities? *Successfully?*"

Hinto nodded imperceptibly. "Multiple realities, yes. Successfully? Well that, as always, depends on your definition."

"Oh Papa," she breathed, considering the ramifications of successful duplication and integration of technology from several worlds at once. Tech from one world rarely worked on another—and conflicting magic systems could be even worse. Syncretistic innovation, truly building upon the resources of the metaverse—that kind of synthesis had always been deemed a myth. Even in places like the City Unspoken, where worlds mixed on the streets.

"Your mother . . ." The old bard's voice was hoarse. "You don't have to become her, Lolly. There are as many possible futures as there are skies sheltering suns. Even the Cicatrix was beautiful, once, like a bower of daffodils. You remember her, don't you? Before the scars. Before derangement, before she changed her name. Before the vivisistors she had installed *within her own body.*"

Lallowë turned her head as her face crumpled. "Oh, oh, oh." Now was her turn to sob. The manacle on Tam's wrist burned like fire.

"I thought you might appreciate the unlikelihood of such an achievement."

But Lallowë just wrung her hands. "Oh," she repeated to herself, "Oh, Mother, what have you done?" Tam pictured the transformation of a beautiful faerie inserting perversions like this vivisistor inside her own body, eggs unborn into a monster's abdomen. Little wonder their womb magic faltered.

"Lolly . . ." Hinto Thyu began, seeming to hope he'd breached her defenses and touched the girl he'd known.

But Lallowë blinked rapidly, squared her shoulders, and was again the indomitable Marchioness Terenz-de-Guises, icy and unflappable. The queen's body would be *precisely* where she'd want the most powerful technology and the most monstrous of violations. Tam had hoped that they might be done with this unpleasantness, after Lallowë's papa had yielded so many details about the vivisistors, but it seemed they'd only just begun.

"Mother's plans extend beyond her own amendments, I'll wager. And I'll wager twice as much that Papa's learned how. Tam, assemble the seven-gauge exsanguinator process." She was going to bleed him dry.

"Mistress?" Tam stalled, having beached himself on his long-submerged humanity at last. He couldn't, he just couldn't. Besides, the old man had already told her what she wanted to know, hadn't he? Tam couldn't, but he *would.*

"You should know better than anyone that coaxing a bird to sing is only the first step of the work, my Young Tam Lin. Now we must teach it the melodies we wish to hear."

* * *

As dawn broke over the lip of the bowl of black land that was the Bonseki-sai district, Sesstri feared that Nixon had been right. Billows of bright red smoke looped up into the blue morning behind the great tree that rose from the center of the neighborhood. It *looked* like smoke, but was too red. Sesstri had a growing feeling in her gut that she'd missed something terribly obvious, and it all began with the color red. More damningly for the would-be-smoke, this was Bonseki-sai. Strange things happened in Bonseki-sai. Sesstri had awoken here, found by her scarlet-haired land-lady. She hadn't returned since.

In Bonseki-sai, every building had been incorporated into a district-wide work of stagecraft, so Sesstri and Nixon hurried past blocks that rose and crested like stormy seas, miniature mountain peaks that were inns or coffee shops, and countless confabulations of succulents that grew larger here than they did anywhere else.

"Why are we running *toward* the fire, bird?" Nixon asked, out of breath.

"It's not a fire." Sesstri had decided that much. "It's not even smoke."

The suns—suns, plural, today, bright and blue—raised themselves just high enough in the sky to send slanting rays of sunlight streaming behind them. Bonseki-sai at sunrise: it should have been a lovely sight, but was instead a horror.

The black ground beneath their feet caught the angled light and was transformed by it—the dawn lit the turf like a jewel, and revealed the matte black surface to be translucent like honey-dark resin, murky but clear enough to see what lay below: countless bodies, floating as if drowned, preserved forever, mere inches underfoot.

Far below the imprisoned dead, the drowned streets of an elder, previous district lay beneath fathoms of the resinous substance, visible only at dawn and dusk, shadowy blocks and buried towers stretching up toward Sesstri's feet like huge fingers, drowned forever ago.

"Have you ever met one of the First People, Nixon?" Sesstri asked, determined not to look down.

"Have I—woah!" Nixon squealed and threw himself sideways, rolling onto a low red fence and clinging to it as if his life depended on it. "What happened to the ground?"

Sesstri stopped and closed her eyes.

"I hearda this but, shit, I never wanted to see it for myself." Nixon sounded scared, but awe crept into his voice as he mastered the feeling of vertigo brought on by the dawn-lit streets of Bonseki-sai. "Poor bastards." He set his feet down upon the amber ground, scraping the toes of one foot above the milky-eyed face of a dead man, whose mouth gaped forever in a wordless scream.

"Yes," Sesstri agreed, trying not to let her agitation show. There was red not-smoke boiling into the sky ahead; she had no time for her own fear, let alone the unboy's.

"Did they drown, or does it just look that way? Did the streets *sink*? Great Scott, it's spooky down there." He peered past the floating dead to see the sunken city below. "Those shadows, those are buildings, right? They aren't . . . they don't *move,* do they? That's just the light, please tell me that's just the light?"

"It's just the light." Sesstri's voice came out flat; she wouldn't have believed herself. "Look at something elevated, if you're frightened. Pick out a specific building, a wave or mountaintop, and fix your eyes on that point." Maybe Bonseki-sai looked like an elaborate theater set piece for a reason. The abstracted construction was silly and impractical and potentially hazardous, but it *did* keep the eye from gazing too long into the abyss below.

"I'm not scared." Nixon sounded uncertain. "It only lasts a few minutes, anyway. Right?"

As if on cue, the billowing red not-smoke spun itself into streamers of what looked like solid pigment, pennants of pure red color that rippled in a nonexistent breeze, waving them forward. Red snaked through the branches of the huge succulent that rose from the center of the district.

"The gray man was right to go on his own hunt, I think." Nixon marveled as they followed streets that spiraled toward the tree, toward the billowing red strangeness. "Where are you *taking* me?"

"Nowhere, stupid unboy. You followed me of your own accord."

"Yeah, but . . . yeah."

Bloated faces watched their footsteps as they wound their way to the middle of the neighborhood, colorless bodies floating with hair and limbs stretched out limply in the manner of drowned things; a sea, a deluge, a disaster frozen forever underfoot. Sesstri and Nixon kept their eyes fixed straight ahead. They'd almost reached the steps that led, at last, up from the solidified lake of the dead into the branches of the succulents, when a black shadow dropped from a low-hanging eave shaped like a row of cresting waves; the shadow shook a mop of white-blond hair and brandished a steel pipe. Nixon made a noise like chewing glass and dived for safety beneath a stone bench disguised as a puff of cloud.

A member of the Undertow stood there, hate staining his face; he snarled, and gripped a length of steel pipe. Sesstri spat and called out a challenge to the lone Death Boy. "Twice in two days is twice too often for me to encounter your ilk, lich-lover."

The Death Boy bared his broken teeth and lunged, swinging his weapon at Sesstri's head. Sesstri simply folded her body out of harm's way, noticing as she bent backward to dodge the blow and retrieve a dagger from her leggings that she could almost make out the tattoo on the thug's lip.

"Where have you taken my associate, and why?" Sesstri demanded as she kicked the man in the kneecap. The blond thug spun away with a howl of pain and brought his heavy steel to bear, readying himself to lunge again at his opponent. The men who attacked them had not been Undertow, but Sesstri felt certain that this ambush was no mere coincidence.

She flipped a dagger in the air, caught it by the blade, and sent it flying quick as a bird into the Death Boy's forearm. The man dropped his pipe with another shriek, a dagger buried in the meat of his wrist.

"Give me answers, or I'll give you more knives. I have *plenty*."

"You're full of flash," hissed the Death Boy, wincing as he yanked Sesstri's dagger from his arm, "but you'll eat the crow of the living before the week is through. You'll see your friend again, you pretty pink bitch, when he feeds your soul to the skylords. He'll be a lich-lover now, and there's nary a thing you can do to stop it."

Sesstri grabbed the crazed youth by the collar of his vest and punched his face twice in quick succession. Clutching his bloodied nose, the Death Boy stumbled backward and tumbled over a painted railing into a knot of jade plants.

Frenzied, Sesstri kicked at the railing until a plank of wood came loose. She wrenched it free and leapt over the supine Death Boy, who was still coughing out blood he'd inhaled through his broken nose; Sesstri shoved the splintered end of the plank into the youth's throat, pinning him to the ground. The empty-eyed dead grinned beneath them, flanking the fallen thug like ladies-in-waiting; waiting for him to join them.

The cornered punk grabbed the plank with both hands and glared defiantly at Sesstri, whose hair fanned out in the sunrise as she panted from exertion. She looked like a pink-stained spider queen at the center of her web, and didn't hesitate to throw her weight onto the broken plank until her attacker's face turned purple and blood seeped from the splinters piercing his neck.

"Listen to me very closely, trash," Sesstri hissed, twisting the plank until the man squealed. "When I have been twice attacked in as many days, I abandon the willingness to curb my violent impulses. I do not know why you're following me or why you have the poor sense to challenge me on your own, but I was raised by a warlord who taught me to kill before I learned to speak: the next time I see your face I will *scrape it off your skull with my boot heel.* Do you understand me, you miserable waste of meat?"

The boy thrust his chin with defiance at Sesstri, digging the splinters deeper into his throat and proving that he was willing to die, though neither Sesstri nor Nixon knew exactly what death might mean for one held in thrall to the power of the undead.

"I understand perfectly, whore of the pale vagrant. You fight for your lord and I fight for mine."

"Tut-tut." Nixon had recovered the steel pipe and had planted his feet on either side of the Death Boy's atomic-blond hair. "That's not how we speak to ladies, you zombie-fucked beatnik."

Swinging with all of his tiny might, Nixon brought the weight of his stolen weapon down upon the thug's head. Despite his diminutive size, the blow succeeded in spectacular fashion: bits of blood and skull showered Nixon's face as well as the soft leather of Sesstri's boots. The Death Boy lay still.

Sesstri shot Nixon a disapproving look. "I had planned on extracting answers."

Nixon ducked his head. "Sorry, I wanted to prove that I—"

The dead youth interrupted him with a gasp. He spasmed once, twice, and then sat up with a dumbfounded expression on what remained of his face, even though by all rights he should be lifeless, lobotomized at the very best. But rather than the usual enfeeblements, death seemed to have quickened the boy: fast as a startled rat, he spun onto all fours, tearing clumps of hair out of his scalp that were trapped beneath Nixon's feet, and scrambled away into the underbrush. Sesstri watched him go with an evaluating look.

She tucked her remaining daggers back into their sheaths, combed her fingers through her morning-rose hair, and turned toward the branches of the tree at the center of Bonseki-sai. She set off toward it without another word.

Nixon gathered her fallen things and ran after Sesstri, his stricken expression lingering until he remembered to replace it with a sideways smirk.

"Monkey's uncle, bird, you fight like the sauced Irish!"

Sesstri maintained her pace and didn't look back. "I don't know what those words mean, but the thug received the thrashing he earned when he decided to attack me."

"I'll say. You won't get any argument from Nixon on that count; I believe in the battle, although I *am* a racist. I can do that with impunity now, because I left the fags and the chinks and the fucking Italians behind me. Well, the Italians at least. That's gotta count for something."

"You're a strange child, even owning the fact that you aren't one. Is the Etellyuns so bad?"

Nixon handed Sesstri a fallen dagger, hilt first. "They're a goddamned nightmare, that's what they are."

Safely away from the scene of the attack, Sesstri allowed herself to stop and gather her thoughts; she closed her eyes and tried to sublime her tension through a deep breath. Nixon watched her face, rapt. With her eyes closed and her plum-colored lips parted, he could almost imagine her as a soft, gentle thing, who gave soft, gentle kisses and would open her legs for him, just slightly, enough for him to feel her essential heat with the backs of his knuckles. . . .

"Well, they may not be the woeful Etellyuns"—Sesstri shook off her reverie—"but if the Undertow are attacking me, and tracking us, then I am concerned, and I will remain so until I learn why."

"But those weren't Death Boys or Charnel Girls, back at the house. Just plain henchmen. Vanilla-flavored, standard-issue hired muscle. Why would the Undertow fight a proxy battle?" Nixon resumed rubbing his whiskerless chin.

"Why is the sky billowing red? There are plenty of questions without good answers." Sesstri bent to rummage through her satchel, but paused and squatted beside it, twisting its strap between her fists and eyeing Nixon with an unfixed stare of appraisal.

"Nixon, can I trust you?"

The unboy looked down his long nose at the earth as if he wished he were among the dead in their resinous stasis. "You think I brought those thugs, don't you? You blame me for your friend with the Danzig t-shirt."

"Are you avoiding my question?" Sesstri cocked her head.

"You think I work for the bad guys!" he wailed.

Sesstri did not answer, but glanced back at Nixon with something resembling forbearance. Forbearance's unkind, surgical sister. "I did not say that."

"But it's what you think, isn't it?" Nixon took two deep breaths and looked for all the worlds like a real child, on the verge of tears.

Sesstri clucked. "It's a possibility I'd be irresponsible not to consider, and either you'd wonder the same thing in my shoes or you're an idiot, in which case I'm wasting my breath. Am I wasting my breath?"

The boy shook his head in earnest. "No, no, of course not. I'd be suspicious of me too. I'd probably have me beaten and locked up for a day or two just to be on the safe side."

Sesstri pursed her lips in agreement. "I'm low on closet space, but I did consider stuffing you into the drawer where I keep my underthings."

Nixon put his hand over Sesstri's, still wrapped around the strap of her satchel, and squeezed. His brown eyes shimmered with unshed tears. "I swear to you, Sesstri Manfrix, I am a lot of bad things, more than you would ever guess; I am a thief and a liar and a greedy, cruel man, but I am *not* your enemy. You can trust me. And I'll understand if you don't—I know it looks bad. I'll walk away right now if you think I'm responsible for what happened to you and your friends."

Sesstri understood that there were gestures appropriate for this moment, but she could think of none that fit her. She certainly wasn't about to pat Nixon's scummy little head.

"No, Nixon, I don't believe you betrayed us." Sesstri tried to modulate her voice to approximate kindness. "For one, you're too young to be a threat." She stood, finally finding her notebook within her bag, scratching a few notes to give the urchin time to wipe his face.

"Well, that's good news." Nixon turned around, smiling his half-grin again. "But I'm not young, you see."

Sesstri hid a smile. "I see no such thing."

"I think you do, and I think I'm in love with you. Just throwing it out there." Nixon tried to whistle innocently, looking all around.

"Change the subject," she said. They rounded a final bend and the great tree lifted itself up before them. Like all of aboveground Bonseki-sai, the tree was a conceit. A hodgepodge of elephant-thick succulents—jade plants, semperviva, ice plants, Carmens and Zwartkops—planted strategically among the eaves and railings of a rickety, towering, and well-disguised hostelry called the Jamaica Inn.

At the foot of the great tree, at the center of Bonseki-sai, upon a wide square of sunlit resin, the Jamaica's entrance yawned between two banyan-thick jades, their fat oval leaves filtering smoke and revelry from within, even at this early—or late—hour. The morning sunlight revealed that the ground beneath their feet held no corpses, just a straight view down into the drowned depths, where shadows most certainly *did not* move.

Milling about the square Sesstri saw patrons of the Jamaica Inn, none of whom seemed to notice the still-billowing expulsion of bloodred smoke that filled the sky behind the inn. Men and women drank their beer and spoke together in quiet clusters, oblivious.

Sesstri bit her lip. *There's more drinking, more eating, more blindness to the madness that surrounds us*. It was the *svarning,* she was sure of it. She felt it herself, fluttering against her breastbone like a trapped bird. Wherever he was, Asher felt it too, and soon Cooper; it would take them all and wash them into . . . aimlessness and . . . gray hands on her face and backside, pulling her cheeks apart to swamp her with kisses that . . .

"Enough!" Sesstri screamed, hands in her hair, but nobody flinched. Even Nixon failed to notice.

The unboy had no eyes for Bonseki-sai, or the Jamaica beneath its living disguise. He watched the red smoke, filtering through the branches toward them. "That's not smoke, you're right," he said to Sesstri. "It looks more like . . . hair." Clouds of red curls that burned the air with their presence, scalded three-dimensional space and irradiated time. Nixon's eyes grew wider, then rolled back in his skull as he fell to the ground in a faint.

Sesstri squared her shoulders and stared down the roil of sentient pigment that bloomed before her. "You are Chesmarul, the red ribbon!" she called out, ignoring the patrons. "If you insist on a show, then show *up*."

The red tendrils shivered and began to contract. Sesstri didn't know what she was watching, yet the sound it made felt nauseatingly appropriate. The red color seemed to crunch in on itself and become . . . *real*—yet Sesstri knew that by joining her "real" world of three physical dimensions, the red ribbon allowed herself to be diminished, somehow. When the collapsing color grew solid, Sesstri was not surprised to see the heart-shaped face and bow lips of her landlady, Alouette, take form amidst the coalescent pigment.

"Fine, then. Enough procrastination." The red curls vibrated with Alouette's voice. "Time to put off being an ineffable First Person for a while and become the landlady again."

Red wisps pulled into Alouette's body like smoke billowing backward into the fire. Yes, Sesstri imagined that Chesmarul—her *self*—would be reduced to the limits of the tissue within her rapidly solidifying skull. To be as the Third People are: alive and small and desperate. When the color bled away from Alouette's warm brown eyes, Sesstri saw a human confusion there, a genuine waking, as real as Sesstri's own waking here, in this too-quiet district.

"Hello, Pinky." Alouette blinked her eyes, glanced around, and frowned. "This city is too sane by half."

Sesstri planted herself in front of the First Person. "I demand to know what you've embroiled us in, *Chesmarul*."

"No." Alouette shook her head and pointed to her chest. "Alouette." She glanced toward Nixon, unconscious on the grass. "Did he give Cooper the ribbon?"

"Excuse me?" Sesstri folded her arms across her chest.

"He didn't, did he? Little shit. We'll sort that out. You lost the man, then?" Alouette looked Sesstri up and down. "My, this is a mess. And you can't even get my name straight."

Sesstri pushed aside the questions, demands, complaints, and murderous assaults that crowded her head. Yes, she found herself in a ridiculous tourist trap of a neighborhood, facing an absurd being from before the dawn of time, while Death itself ground to a halt that would soon fill the metaverse with a disease of endless living. Yes, there was a gray man somewhere out in the City Unspoken who filled her head with feelings Sesstri had thought she'd amputated. Yes, she had plenty of plenty and not enough time or knowledge to reckon with it all. But she was Optimae Sesstri Manfrix, daughter of the Horselord, and she had conquered death and men in equal measure. She *would* get a single straightforward answer from Alouette, and she *would* make it count.

"*Why* is Cooper here?"

"Oh, I have no idea." Alouette shook her head with emphasis. "None at all. Let's hope that answering that question is one of the things a Cooper does."

Sesstri clenched her fists into balls of stone. "*What* is Cooper?"

"Today? Eh . . ." Alouette's eyes darted evasively. "Don't we decide that for ourselves, Pinky, each and every morning?"

"*You* have been meddling in every aspect of mine and Cooper's lives— you can feign all the ignorance you want, *Alouette,* but you cannot convince me that it's genuine."

"Fine." Alouette looked ready to make nice. "So, Cooper. I made him the center of everything, and I'm not sure why."

Sesstri nearly choked on her surprise. That *was* a straightforward answer, if there was any truth to it. "Are you—"

"—No, look, I *am* sure why." Alouette stood her ground, combed her curls with her fingers and then cocked her head. "I'm the sort of person who can only exist when she's grounded. That's not a metaphor. I'm in flesh right now because I . . . I honestly can't be bothered to focus on something as small and quick as a human life, if I'm not bound by human *context*." Alouette bit her lip.

"So you're telling me that the ancient being who is revered as the patron of the lost is . . ."

"... Completely inured to human suffering, yes." Alouette's expression held sympathy and pity in equal measure. "You expected something else, from a woman older than suns?"

"You're not a woman, and you know it."

"But I *am*. I am, and I am, and I am." Alouette almost stomped her feet in earnest. "I'm in this wrinkly, fatty brain and these tidy, internal gonads, and I'm telling you, girl, I'm a woman."

Sesstri huffed. "Why make such a show?"

Alouette looked genuinely confused. "What are you talking about?" she asked.

"Do you remember manifesting in the district in an explosion of red hair?" Sesstri waved behind her, toward the branches of the Jamaica, where patrons continued to drink in peace.

"That? Oh." Alouette rolled her eyes. "For me, honey, that was just a red dress."

Sesstri marched off, then stopped herself, turned around, and threw her hands up. "Why *here*, of all places?"

Alouette followed Sesstri. "Bonseki-sai and I go way back. If I appear, it's always here. You should ask the angel about it, he'll tell you more than I remember right now." She picked at her skin. "These bodies. How do you live so small?"

"Angel? What angel?" Sesstri wasn't so much annoyed at more obscure drivel as she was excited at the prospect of anyone else to question—anyone but Alouette. "There are no angels in a godless city, unless you're speaking in riddles."

"No riddles, only words, which amount to the same thing." Alouette shook her head. "The angel—the Angel of Bonseki-sai? That's half the reason I'm even here; where is he?" Alouette peered around her as if there might be an angel hiding under the fat leaves of a jade plant. "The Angel of Bonseki-sai is a famous monument, it's what brought the district back to life after—oh." Alouette paused. "Time. Fuck. I'm in time now. Oh, why didn't I bring a map!"

Sesstri massaged the divot between her brows and waited for Alouette to stop rambling. She knew there was meaning there, and she memorized every word for later analysis, but in the moment she could do little but keep herself from screaming at the woman.

"Huh." Alouette winked at Sesstri. *Winked.* "I told you, the city is too sane. There's not even an angel yet. No wonder this place is so quiet—the angel comes to answer the madness. The *svarning* should be here by now."

Sesstri started speaking before her resentment could kick in and impede any opportunity to learn from Alouette. Any window of lucidity was priceless. "We found some symptoms of the *svarning* as the number of Dying began to increase noticeably." Sesstri led with what little data she had. "But as the inability to achieve True Death has become more widespread, we haven't seen a corresponding increase in the *svarning*—not that we know what to look for. The *svarning* . . . it should come, but it doesn't."

Alouette shook her head, not understanding. "That's not how it works. There aren't words or small-enough ideas to fit into these heads and mouths we have, but if the Dying cannot Die, then the *svarning* will come. It must come."

She paused, then her eyes lit up and her curls shook. "Machines! Oh, *oh,* there is an old song that I do not quite remember. The Angel sings it all the time, or he did. There are machines . . . engines of being. They are hearts, and they are clubs. Oh, oh. This head hurts me." Alouette pressed her fingertips against her temples and scowled. "The *svarning* comes. Something manipulates it, but it comes, Sesstri."

Sesstri nodded. She understood what Alouette meant—one side of a seesaw couldn't go up without the other going down. Imbalance was imbalance. "What could possibly manipulate the *svarning*?"

And can we use it to save ourselves?

Alouette wasn't paying attention. She knelt to place her palms on the resinous floor of Bonseki-sai, mercifully black again. She frowned, and lowered her cheek to the ground as well. Then she shot up, a look of alarm on her face. "Listen, I need to go. I'll see you in a bit, okay?"

"Tell me one more thing," Sesstri asked, wondering what Alouette could possibly infer from kissing the ground. "Why don't these people notice you?"

"What people?" Alouette scrunched up her face.

"The ones all around us!" Sesstri waved her arms and pointed behind her, where the Jamaica still bustled. It did bustle, didn't it?

Alouette fixed Sesstri with a funny look. "Girl, nobody *lives* here, it's Bonseki-sai. The place is fucking haunted."

"Of course it's not. There are plenty of people here." Sesstri turned around. The door to the Jamaica was half-hidden beneath overgrowth, its cleverly designed windows boarded. Its garden was empty of people. "But, but I woke up here."

"Yeah," Alouette said slowly. "That's why I took care of you, hon—this is no place for a girl to wake up. You were *lost*. You still are, if you think there's anyone but the two of us standing here."

5

For her actual beauty, it is said, was not in itself so remarkable that none could be compared with her, or that no one could see her without being struck by it, but the contact of her presence, if you lived with her, was irresistible; the attraction of her person, joining with the charm of her conversation, and the character that attended all she said or did, was something bewitching. It was a pleasure merely to hear the sound of her voice, with which, like an instrument of many strings, she could pass from one language to another . . .

To return to Cleopatra; Plato admits four sorts of flattery, but she had a thousand.

[NB: A thousand and one, she proved some lives later in a most unlikely palace.]

—Plutarch, *Parallel Lives: Collector's Edition*

Flowers. The scents of flowers, cacophonous and overlapping: jasmine and lavender and rose, orange blossom and honeysuckle and peony. Flowers circled his sleep-self, the non-dreaming seed of thought that kept company with the darkness while Cooper slept. As his mind crept open, the scents expanded to include sandalwood, then amber and musk, anise seed, mace and pepper. Something else, too, laced between the clash of perfumes—alive, seeking, spiked and dangerous. It was poison.

Cooper's mind woke by degrees, the seed of his sleeping mind unfurling its cotyledon leaves—not yet himself but beginning to apprehend himself again, the down pillows beneath his cheek, the linen against his naked skin. A sound like banners rippling in the wind became soft music, sighing strings, and a voice just shy of singing, nuzzling his ears in the gentlest ways—an anti-lullaby, a reveille blown from a subtle throat and matched with fingers on his temples, chrism on his lips and brow and throat. He underwent a ritual of awakening that men had sacrificed armies to enjoy, given freely to Cooper by the Lady of La Jocondette as he lay in her canopied bed, in her lap, in her inestimable care. Somehow, the seedling of his waking mind knew this.

"Wake, wake, wake little asp," she all but whispered her song, every nuance of the moment a variable manipulated by her cunning. Even the heat of her breath was praise. "Wake, wake, wake and warm yourself on my breast, sun yourself in my blood, O serpent, O man. The suns are shining and all the worlds await you, little snake; come and greet the morning coiled in the cup of my palm."

Cooper felt the mattress stir beneath him, and the fingers left off massaging his head. The notes of song and scent drifted away, and he lifted his head to follow his captor.

She moved with more nobility than the Dome itself could contain.

The woman who woke him was not beautiful, strictly speaking—in the predawn half light she stood veiled by dark hair, rivers of black curls framing the dark pools that were her eyes. A chin that would have been weak on another woman, and the hooked nose of a general, not a prince. Her figure was wider than some strictures of beauty permitted, with heavy breasts and hips like the sacred cow, Hathor, who was her onetime guardian.

No longer.

Cooper marveled at the pieces putting themselves together in his head, as if the thoughts were thinking themselves. Weirder and deeper, deeper and weirder . . .

The Lady matched Cooper's gaze and smiled, and if she knew exactly the path his thoughts were taking, well, it was a oft-trod path, and she had led many men and women down its length during her centuries. Even in the City Unspoken, she had founded legends and ended dynasties.

"Welcome to the waking," she purred, "long-lost child of Rome."

If the Lady was flower-and-song then Cooper's thoughts were thorn-and-noise—he pulled his mind back into his body against every instinct, which was to hide in the darkness and remain unborn to the world. A stillborn bastard for some other mother to mourn.

"You are wondering where you are, who I am, and why you're here. You wonder if you dream still, or if the madness has overtaken you at last, and the moon and her lunatic children have claimed you for their own."

"I . . ." Cooper bit back the urge to answer, and watched the Lady draw thin curtains from the windows. The room matched the light outside—pale blue walls decorated with porcelain, woven mats on the floor.

She turned up the wick on the lanterns, and continued, "You are a guest here at La Jocondette, and though my patrons overpraise me with an honorific I no longer merit, it would give me great pleasure to hear you address me by the name given to me at birth by my father, and that is Thea. I am Thea Philopater, and you are Cooper-*Omphale,* whether you know it or not."

"Hello." His voice was thick with sleep and hoarse from the shouting—the shouting that he remembered with a rush of adrenaline.

He sat up too quickly. "We were attacked—"

"—So I understand. A useless act of violence, in my sight, but such are the means of men in any world. You are safe here, Cooper. Know that."

"Safe!" He barked a laugh. "I hear unspoken fears and the Dying roam the streets like lunatics. You violently kidnapped me and attacked my friends. What's safe?"

"How like Asher you sound, child of Rome." She fluffed his pillow and he lay his head back down. "Has he affected you so profoundly, or is it merely that common contrivance of man in the face of the overwhelming: feigned bravado?"

"I'm not brave or feigning—just overwhelmed. About ten times over. How do you know Asher?" From her considerable décolletage, an answer sprang to mind.

The Lady closed her eyes. "I cannot imagine how you could fail to be overwhelmed, under the circumstances. Do you still pray? Have you prayed today, Cooper-*Omphale*?"

"Excuse me?"

She opened her eyes, and they were iron. "Has a single day on the other side of life shattered your faith, or do you yet venerate whatever gods our people worship in the centuries since my feet last touched Earthen sands?"

"Earthen sands?" Cooper asked, but as he said the words he realized that he already knew.

"You and I walked the same world, darling boy." She raised his chin with a finger so that their eyes met. "It has been many years since I ruled there, but I have read some few of the scrolls they scribed about my first life, and seen the play-acts. I am not so luminous as that purple-eyed angel, but surely you know me?"

Cooper heard more than a little vanity in her tone. Purple-eyed angel? Queen? If he hadn't known better, he'd have thought he was still dreaming. Either this woman was batshit barmy or she was . . . the realization crystalized. He was suddenly giddy with the idea. *This* was possible only here, so how could he be wrong to doubt it? Could the City Unspoken be a blessing in disguise? Possibilities bloomed.

Again, she seemed to follow his thoughts. "I found your Shakespeare on my doorstep one day. A great one for whores, the shaker of spears. I teased him until he promised to write me over—he never stopped writing, you know. I don't believe he could stop if he wanted to. I am told he wrote me into plays at least twice more; he swore to me that he had not met another model for his historical roles, and I enjoyed the opportunity to thoroughly educate him on my nature and bearing. His subsequent efforts will have captured me more cunningly, I am confident."

"That's unbelievable." Except that it wasn't, not anymore. *What would be?*

"Believe it, little brother. Our people rise and conquer all across the worlds, you know. There is no truer cradle than Gaia, for our sands bear the sweetest fruit."

Cooper realized then that as a former Earthling, no amount of time or distance would diminish the sense of kinship she felt toward him. Would that fraternity extend to other planetary graduates? Had he joined a club so improbable in its exclusivity? This woman and he *knew* each other in a way so permanent it shocked him. She was famous, the original celebrity, born and died two thousand years before him, yet as far as the Lady was concerned, they were countrymen or closer; she called him *brother*. Never minding that she was, he suspected, the last queen of Pharaonic Egypt and he merely an overeducated, bull-shouldered American with an unhelpful attitude and zero survival skills.

She leaned closer, and the scents of flowers and poison grew stronger. "But you have not answered my question, though perhaps I press it upon you too soon: how fares your faith, child of Rome?" Her fingers stroked a rhythm on the tender side of his forearm.

Cooper shook his head and raised himself to a sitting position, ignoring his nakedness and the scrapes that pained him. He wanted to say this right. "I don't think the people here are that different from those back home: I'm sure the need for something . . . larger . . . is universal. I just can't imagine—given the scale of the worlds and the lives we live, apparently—what kind of god could be big enough to encompass these worlds? What's a Christ compared to *that*?" He gestured at the window, where twin cerulean suns had peeked above the horizon, limning the skyline in an underwater glow.

"He was a kinder man than I expected. We who proclaim ourselves the children of gods are rarely so gentle." Thea laughed, and Cooper realized that he felt a hint of fear from her, a constant undercurrent running just beneath her surface. He didn't have to be a student of history to know she held plots within plots. "Or maybe you'd expect him to be the paragon of compassion—I confess I haven't paid much attention to those who followed in my footsteps. Was he the forgiving one? I, too, was an avatar of god on Earth. I was the sun himself, Cooper, and as for me and Yeshua of Canaan, my end was no nobler than his."

She slipped an arm from her dress and lifted one weighty breast out of its confines. Puncture wounds were tattooed across her flesh, not one pair but many, as if she had fed her chest with poison until it was ready to burst. "My children died. What use had I for milk?" She shrugged herself back into her clothes. "I gave myself to the serpents instead, and now I express milk of another kind."

A thought occurred to Cooper. "Shouldn't you have left those scars behind when you died? Or are they new?"

She flashed another smile—one that dazzled. Cooper wondered if she ever faltered. The woman who made a triumph of suicide. "Finally asking the smart questions, my innocent soul! You may yet survive the trials to come. Yes, that is what ought to have happened. It *did* happen. And happened, and happened, across a dozen-dozen spheres. My journey has not been as dignified as you might think, Cooper. I spent many lives in a haze of self-destruction, drunk on loss, and I found serpents rarer than the viper whose kiss I once thought so final.

"I have become something somewhat more than woman, thanks to those many-fevered kisses, and something less. I cannot die, or Die, and

I cannot leave this place. I poisoned myself too deeply, and now I am bound to this body as thoroughly as the rest of the whores in this city."

Cooper couldn't imagine this woman, whose identity he had begun to accept—as a *whore*. Or was it that he could not imagine her as anything else? Two faces on the coin, or one? The submerged fear that veiled the Lady fluttered as if in a breeze.

"There are many diversions on the streets of the City Unspoken." She turned the subject away from True Death. Cooper thought that if he reached out with his mind, he could hear their fear. A sea of it, and it would drown him. "You know the card game they play on the streets, which cannot be won?"

"Three Whores? Yes, Asher warned me away from it."

She nodded. "Then you know the three flavors of courtesans who populate the bordellos of the City Unspoken?"

Cooper frowned, shaking his head. "There are three kinds of whores? I didn't know that. I know about the bloodsluts, I mean, the life-whores, or whatever we're calling the ones who die for a living. I saw one in the Guiselaine. I . . . heard her fear, I guess. The scratching whispers in my head. She was half-mad from it . . . poor thing . . ."

"Yes. *Thing* is closer to the mark." Cleopatra's voice was bitter. "The life-whores are people who have become little more than chattel. Here at La Jocondette, my sisters and brothers and I are something less inhuman, but no less trapped."

"If you're not a life-whore, then what do you . . . *do*?" He found no way to lessen the awkwardness of the question.

"If you will permit me, Cooper, I will show you the talents my sisters and I possess. The people of this city come to us for emotional rather than physical release, although that may become part of the work. But my ilk do more than talk, you understand? The poison in our veins provides our patrons with a seer's insight, unveils visions and unlocks forbidden knowledge. Our succor is not the enchantment of the flesh, but the fulfillment of fate. I will awaken your secret self and hold up a mirror to your lidless eye."

"Okay." Cooper did not hesitate. "I mean yes, yes please. Show me my fate—if you can do it, I will dare it." *Since it was worth kidnapping me,* he thought but did not add.

The Lady opened her arms and whispered something sibilant to the corners of the room before redrawing the curtains against the cobalt morning. "Once this city gleamed, although you may not believe it; I have seen it myself, in the memory of a very, very old client. He still mourns, I think. Long after the city fell into mortal hands, and thence into dust and disuse, my sisters and their peers retained the glamour of the previous ages—there were whole epochs when we plied our trade and the word 'whore' was all but unknown. This was before my time, of course, but La Jocondette still shined spotless white when I arrived in the city. My talents brought me here and as the years wore on I became its mistress."

"Yes," Cooper mouthed, barely speaking. "I see that."

The whore who had been queen leaned over him, the redolence she wore like a shroud enveloping and intoxicating him, and all was liquid eyes and trails of hair like the lightless depths of the great celestial river, drowning and nourishing him until the corbeled ceiling opened and swallowed Cooper into vision beyond sight.

"What about the third kind of whore?" Cooper asked the beluga whale with orange fire for eyes. They treaded water beneath the surface of a sea of silk cloth, aquamarine banners and ribbons flowing past his body, curling about his limbs, and eddying off into the depths.

"He makes you feel. He feels for you." The beluga's cloud-gray skin shimmered in the aquatic light and the hand bones hidden by evolution within its flippers glowed white-hot, visible through the skin. They began expanding, fingers curling in gloves of fin-flesh.

"Oh," he said, as a school of wooden geese darted overhead.

"What are you thinking, Cooper?"

He held out his hand, palm forward, and splayed his fingers. They matched the bones of the whale, which had stopped glowing along their length and now only sparkled at the joints, like a constellation. When Cooper answered, he spoke from a subsystem of himself that had perfect recall and zero irony:

"I am thinking that Gould's Belt is not part of the natural spiral structure of the Milky Way. It spans three thousand light-years and sits at a twenty-degree angle to the galactic plane. Yet it surrounds us with a ring of bright stars, and without them we would not have Orion, Scorpius, the Southern Cross, Perseus, Canis Major, Vela, or Centaurus. What astrological sign would I be if Gould's dark matter had not impacted my galaxy? Would my story be different?"

The beluga nodded, taking notes on a pad of legal paper.

"I see. And how does this make you feel?"

"I feel that these plastic stars are in my way." Cooper brushed a mobile of toy stars away from his face as they drifted past. "And also that the gray jackass feels responsible for the dying of Death. Why would he feel that way? What has he done to close the Last Gate? It makes him so afraid, he doesn't know himself anymore."

"Please, go on."

"He's in love with her. And she loves him back, so strong, but she hates herself for it. I don't think they will be together, even though she would give him the one thing he wants more than anything."

"And what do you think Asher desires most?"

"A child." Cooper raised an eyebrow at the inquisitive cetacean. His replies were reflexes. "Wait, no: a *second* child. Aren't you supposed to be the one doling out the answers?"

The beluga—who he somehow knew was part Lady, part Cooper, and part something else entirely—laughed bubbles and brushed dark hair from her face. "I am just the swimmer, little brother. You are the sea."

"That explains it, then, why I am so cold and dark and empty."

"Is that how the sea makes you feel?" She pushed wire spectacles onto her nose with a dainty flipper. "Even though it drinks warmth and light from the sun and houses teeming billions?"

"The sky is empty and dark and cold, but it houses billions too—and teems with suns besides." He paused. The sea was emptying, silk streamers rippling off into the distance, where they vanished. "Where is all the woven water going?"

The beluga pointed to the center of his forehead with a fin. "Back where it came from. Have you ever touched a star, I wonder, and found its furnace *cold*? I think we are almost out of it, Cooper. How do you feel?"

"Sleepy." He opened his eyes and saw the Lady of La Jocondette above him, cradling him in her ample lap. Her storm of scents was withdrawing from him like a tentacled thing; it had reached inside him and cracked him open. Cooper felt like a crab sucked empty of its meat.

"You did quite well, child of Rome." The Lady smoothed his face with her fingers. "I would almost suspect you of being familiar with the narcotic haze."

"Well, there was college."

She shook her head. "I would advise against hiding behind your humor when unnecessary, or your intellect. I believe you have two new friends who suffer from one or the other such tendencies, yes? Do not mimic their flaws. It will only make your lives harder."

Cooper let out a sigh that seemed to go on forever, until his lungs were flattened pancakes. "I suppose that's good advice. Don't be smart or funny, and don't play Three Whores. And whatever you do, try not to fucking die. But if you do die, it's okay, because nobody can Die, which makes the most perfect sense *ever*. Yep, I've heard some good advice today."

The Lady swept her hand toward the windows, where watery light struggled through the curtains. "Today has become tomorrow."

Cooper rubbed his face with his hands, but the Lady pulled them away and leveled an earnest look.

"There is another side to the coin of advice you've been paid—it has been said that a visitor to the City Unspoken may call upon the aid of three whores to guide him. Once for blood, once for wisdom, and once for love."

Cooper blushed but felt a crabby awkwardness—was he developing an allergy to unsolicited counsel, or just sick of all the sex-worker jargon? "Asher warned me that there was no way to win that game. I think I'm beginning to understand what he meant."

The dead queen laughed, and her throat matched the bells that rang in the city outside her bordello palace. "Asher told you that? He's lying, of course. Any game can be won. Remember that"—she touched her chest— "when you are stripped of the choice of whether or not to play, my strapping boy."

"I can avoid a hard hustle, Lady. I'm a New Yorker."

"All the pride of a Roman! Three whores, I think, *will* help you. I have been one of them."

Cooper paused, weighing his increasing resistance to anything tangential to bullshit against his need to absorb all the useful knowledge he could. "What else did you see inside me?"

"Every soul shines with its own brilliance, and yours is a blossom, unique. You have a strong affinity toward the call shamanic, yes? You will feel it one day, if you have not already been drawn to it. To the *omphalos,* yes? It means the navel, the *axis mundi,* the worlds-pillar. The center of the world, where all truths and lies converge. You will take its name for your own, Cooper-*Omphale,* and become something of an axis yourself. But listen to me well: this is less a position of power than it is a moment of leverage. And you have some of the seer's sight, if you'd learn to use it—we have already spoken of your propensity for hearing the frightened thoughts of others. This is the beginning of the path of the shaman."

She let out a slow breath, and pressed her knuckles against his cheek. "But I do not see in your possibilities the greatness to merit the attention of any of the true penates, the elder ones who call themselves the First People. Nor do I see a great worker of the art whose awakening ripped him whole from his physical reality and sent him hurtling down, down, down to me."

Cooper resisted the urge to hang his head. "In other words, I'm still a useless mystery. An erratum."

The Lady shook her head and pierced him with an intense look. Again, he felt her fear, distant and undefined, but which lessened whenever she spoke. "I do not understand why the gray one and the faerie noblewoman care so strongly about resolving your mystery—there are far stranger things in the worlds than one lost man. Your ash-skinned friend is *one* of those things, as am I. But I'd sooner tear out my eyes than betray his trust, and you yourself have earned my deepest respect and admiration, Cooper. Your answers may not be easily uncovered, but you are *far* from useless."

"I am?" He didn't feel it.

"You have retained your self-possession in the face of a reality that has crushed lesser minds. So few experience the truth of the worlds entire during the course of a single day! There is waking to new life, yes, and this is always a shock—but you are a white-hot smelting thrust into the coldest water without cracking."

She brought him a plate from a credenza by the wall, all curves and curls and coils of venomous sight. "This resilience is perhaps the only quality I see in you that might qualify for greatness. Let us appreciate that irony for a moment, before your monochrome savior storms my keep and rescues you from the torments of luxury. Pastry?"

Asher dripped down the sentinel wall and swung onto the branches of a papery sycamore, flipping head over heels before grabbing a lower branch and pushing himself off, swinging his feet in a backward arc, and hooking his knees around on a still-lower branch. He hung there for a moment, upside down, and scanned the grounds of La Jocondette through inverted eyes to see if he'd been detected or triggered any sort of alarm, then unlocked his knees from the bough and allowed himself to drop headfirst to the manicured lawn before bracing his impact with an arrow-straight handstand. As he spun forward into a machine-perfect landing, Asher wondered if anyone could acquire dexterity like his if they had lived as long—and as dangerously—as he had, or if acrobatics were simply another of his natural gifts. He couldn't remember ever feeling clumsy, but who could say what details of his long-distant childhood had been eroded? The worlds themselves had changed. His family, his people. Chara, for instance, wherever she was. Would he even recognize her as the sister who once chased him through Anvit's Glade? She would surely not recognize the gray-skinned beggar he had become.

Poor Chara.

The lawns of La Jocondette always did remind him of home—something in the symmetry of the fruit trees and their shaded lanes, or the flower beds that seemed to float like the tips of icebergs across the immaculate grass. All the white stonework, too, the white bricks and the steepled rooftops. So quiet and clean and well-lit in the night.

The door leading inside from the garden was ajar. He poked his head in and saw no one. Strange. La Jocondette no longer turned as much business as the less tony brothels, certainly not with most of the city's wealth locked up inside the Dome, but there should be at least a few morsels lounging about, waiting for those seeking their particular custom—dissolution and dreams in the arms of a poison-whore.

Dashing up the spiral stairs to the second level where bedrooms branched off from three plush brown-carpeted corridors, he found one room empty. And another. Another. Another.

Panic prickled his spine, and Asher called out. No guards came running. No whores looking shocked or annoyed at having their work interrupted. Asher possessed a bloodhound nose for manipulation, and he smelled a skunk. La Jocondette appeared empty: neither Cooper nor the Lady whose profile had been so crudely inked on the broken chip were anywhere to be found.

Outside a blue morning dawned—the window faced west but the buildings across the canal were washed in cool light. Including one narrow building, once a townhouse, now part of a row of houses annexed by La Jocondette as additional space for guests or special events. The brothel hadn't seen that much custom in some years, so the annex had lain fallow—but now a candle burned in a window on the third story, and below it a figure in black shimmied up the colonnade, inching toward the lit window.

Asher watched the shadow of the Lady of La Jocondette through the distant glass, so far across the grounds and the canal; he fingered through his pocket the cracked chip that bore her likeness. What had Oxnard intended, by giving it to him? Had it been a tip, or a trap?

Cooper heard Asher's howl from across the water. The cry of frustration was a primal sound, bell-clear in its purity, and even though Cooper had known Asher for less than twenty-four hours he recognized the gray man's cry. Leaping off Thea's bed, Cooper shook away the lethargy that still combed its poisoned fingers through his mind—he pulled the lace away from the window and spied Asher across the canal, standing in the gardens of La Jocondette. His lanky body was bent back in dismay, the smoke of his face raised to the silvery sky, staring up over the water into the window where Cooper stood. With still-watery vision, Cooper thought he saw dark puppets emerge from the shadows and surround Asher.

"What is Asher doing all the way over there?" he asked, still clearing his head of the puppet-show Thea had shown him. *Sid and Marty Krofft have nothing on fucking Cleopatra,* he thought to himself.

"Why," began Thea, crossing and uncrossing her legs as she reclined on her chaise longue, upholstered in a chamois the same watery blue of the rising suns, "I believe he's loosing a scream of unbridled rage." She smiled.

The bitch smiled. And instead of infuriated, Cooper found himself mollified. Somehow. He could understand how his hostess had captivated an epoch of history; it wouldn't have posed the slightest challenge, not for her.

"But. You said my savior, my monochrome savior . . ."

"I did." She nodded with just a blush of enthusiasm, like he'd hit upon a half-hidden truth the Lady secretly wanted to share, and the fact that Cooper knew it was an act did nothing to diminish the effect of her performance. "And I did not lie to you once. Be patient a moment, Cooper-*Omphale*, and wait for life to catch up to accuracy. It happens thus, sometimes."

But the puppet show had ended—those were thugs out there, fighting and greatly outnumbering Asher—and Cooper turned his back to the window, feeling his indignation rise as he faced the Lady. He found his footing again against this woman—this *queen*—who must not be trusted. Cooper shook his head and scolded himself. *Is that the understatement of the goddamn year. Christ on a multigrain cracker, you don't let Cleopatra lull you into a sense of security, not unless you're looking for a handful of bastards and a dependable excuse for suicide!*

"I never asked you who kidnapped me, did I?" Cooper kept his voice level. He might be overmatched by two thousand years and a handful of empires, but he intended to use his inclination toward the male sex in his favor. He would not be seduced again, now that he knew who he faced.

"I never asked you who attacked me and Asher, and Sesstri. Why is that, Thea Philopater? Tell me why my assault and abduction so conveniently *slipped my mind* after I awoke in your psychoactive brothel?"

A shoulder raised, lowered; the Lady didn't need to shrug when the stirring of her every joint was choreography. "Damage to the head can have all sorts of effects, Cooper," she purred, "and it's fair to say that you might have been a tad overwhelmed."

He shook his traumatized head. "But didn't you just finish telling me about my remarkable mental resilience? My retention of sanity in the face of this, um . . . waking absurdity?" he continued, though still very much in awe of the pedigree of the woman he addressed. "After all I've seen recently, one dead Egyptian doesn't exactly overwhelm. Try again."

"I have not lied to you once, Cooper-*Omphale*." Thea caved, tipping her hand to Cooper with two thousand years of rehearsed grace. Of course she mustered grace: Cooper doubted she could break wind without arousing jealousy from Zephyr himself. "Please remember that when you dole out your justice at the end of this shadow play."

"That doesn't explain—"

"Ah. Here he comes."

"Asher?" Cooper could no longer see him, but he couldn't possibly have crossed the canal yet, let alone escaped his attackers. The curtains fell closed as Cooper rounded on his infamous hostess.

"Did I not promise you a monochrome savior?" Thea stretched her arms in a gesture of generosity that Cooper doubted she merited. He could still feel a veil of fear about her, too thin or well-restrained for him to grasp, but there nonetheless. What did she fear? He reached for something scathing to say, but just then came a knock at the window. It slid open with an accompanying grunt, and as he spun around Cooper saw a face that wasn't the face he'd expected to see. The City Unspoken could surprise and surprise and surprise.

Marvin, pale with black hair, black-rimmed eyes, and shredded black clothing, climbed through the open window and parted the curtain like a marriage veil. Cooper stepped back as this new grayscale soldier glided into his embrace, wrapping strong arms around him and intoxicating him with a different sort of scent entirely than the Lady's poison perfume: man-sweat, tobacco, liquor, smoke, and something else . . . something rank but irresistible. *That's the smell of undeath,* Cooper told himself, knowing he was right but not knowing how; knowing that ought to terrify him but unable to care.

"Hi," whispered Marvin into the small of Cooper's neck.

"Oh." Cooper found he could not move, or would not. "Hello."

"Lady." Marvin ducked his head at Thea, who acknowledged him with a bow of her head and the barest ripple of her fingers through the air.

"Tell your wretched masters that I have upheld my end of the bargain," she said with a voice Cooper had not heard before. Her flattery fell away to reveal a wyrm in woman's flesh, and he shivered despite himself. Marvin held him closer, and another measure of Cooper's free will melted away.

"They already know," Marvin deferred, biting his tattooed lip. "The skylords see us always. They are the shaman gods come to free us from the tyranny of living." He rubbed his stubble against the nape of Cooper's neck.

Thea brushed the air with her fingers again, as fluent in the choreography of dismissal as that of seduction. "I am unimpressed by your flock of cadavers, Death Boy. I do what is necessary for my own survival and nothing more. I ask you to tell your owners that I have upheld my end of the agreement, and you will do so, regardless of what you think they do or do not know. You will convey my message not because of the import of its contents but because *I ask it*. Even the masters of unlife will recognize my authority."

Marvin bowed, taking Cooper halfway with him. It felt like a dip in the strangest dance.

"My Lady. I will do as you say."

"Of course you will," Cooper said before he could stop himself. Lust-blinded and drug-fucked halfway across a thousand thousand creations, and he was still a smart-ass. A little shit, his mother would say, wherever she was. Oh god, his mother. His father!

"Hush." Marvin smiled so close to Cooper's mouth, his breath smelled of smoke and cloves.

"Okay," Cooper agreed, and lost the rest of his words, staring at his thuggish seducer. Black hair, black eyes, fishbelly white skin, tattered black cotton torn in all the right places—above the nipple that was the only flash of color, across the stomach ripped with a six-pack but no navel, slashed off at one soft-muscled shoulder—no, Cooper had no more clever words. Only a rising barometer of desire and the instinct to run.

Thea had been right: Marvin was monochrome, but as for being his savior—Cooper's lust did not dispel his doubt. He looked to the distance, where the blue clouds flickered orange above the burning towers. Marvin would take him there, wouldn't he? He heard the crying clearly now, a wail from the north that no one else could hear. A woman's voice.

Thea yawned. The Queen of Poisons, the Lady of La Jocondette, and the blighted bitch of Cooper's blue-bruised dawn stretched her whole body and yawned like a cat on sun-warmed stone. "I would offer you gentlemen the entirety of my hospitality if time permitted, but alas, it does not.

Would that I could see you two safely installed in each other's arms, as nature clearly intends. But the pale vagrant approaches with arms of a different sort, so romance must yield to exigency." She indicated the gaping window, again the passive hostess. The smile she wore was bland. "Please, forgive my urging, but I hold your safety paramount."

Cooper squinted his eyes and tried to force his awareness toward the towers of the Undertow. The call shamanic, Thea had said. He tried to answer the call. Marvin had called his masters "skylords," not "lich-lords." He had called them shamans.

That settled it, then. Ever onward, whether he wanted to or not. If he found the origin of that ghostly sobbing, perhaps he could make it stop. Perhaps there were answers, forward.

Marvin withdrew to the window, pulling Cooper with him. Across the canal, the black bodies of the Death Boys and Charnel Girls of the Undertow skittered across the face of La Jocondette like flies and vanished into the morning. Hand-in-hand, Cooper and Marvin climbed out and were lost to the sapphire dawn.

Purity Kloo took a breath to steel herself against the possibility that she might be discovered trespassing near the royal suites of Prince Fflaen. No one—absolutely no one—was permitted on the upper stories of the Petite Malaison without explicit invitation from the prince, and Purity had no means of knowing whether or not the prince's absence meant fewer praetorian patrols along the corridors of the royal suites, or more. As the dawn began to illuminate the white stone hallway and strip her of concealment, Purity could no longer pretend that she was merely skulking: along one side of the hallway ran grand windows that looked down upon the Groveheart and were just beginning to shimmer with the light of the morning, revealing the vast primordial forest that lay beneath the Dome's enclosure.

The Groveheart was more than mere wilderness, and as its canopy emerged from night into morning Purity began to feel a deeper sense of foreboding—within that nearly impenetrable wood lay the history of the City Unspoken in all its uncountable millennia; even the size of the place instilled a sense of terrifying enormity, as the glass and metal of the

Dome arched overhead and was obscured by a fine layer of cloud. As she watched, competing flocks of birds wheeled up from the canopy and scattered into the morning mists with caws that echoed off the pale green Dome glass.

Purity straightened the heavy praetor's helm she'd looted from one of the extraneous armories and reminded herself that she was no stranger to poor behavior and derring-do. If only the helm didn't keep tipping forward over her eyes—it threatened to throw her off balance and break her nose at the same time. The blasted thing probably resented being stolen; the praetorian helmets, platinum-chased and crested, were swaddled with layers upon layers of enchantments, most of which she hoped were dormant, except for the passkey charms that had, so far, allowed her to slip into the Petite Malaison without triggering any alarum.

The lock to the armory had been easy enough for Purity to pick: yet another skill she'd acquired during her frequent and tacitly approved-of acts of rebellion—this particular ability she'd learned under the tutelage of an Undertow cardsharp with whom she'd dallied for a fortnight. He'd tossed a mop of ginger curls and flashed a disarming smirk, and Purity had allowed him to become the first to pick a lock of a different sort. Purity blushed at the thought of his fingers, so deft at finding their way to places they oughtn't be. *What was his name?* She tried to recall. *I'm terrible.*

Of course she'd given him a false name, or else she'd have been kidnapped for ransom in a trice. Those cultists were disposable due to their mental defects, but they did acquire a few memorable talents on their way to torture and undeath.

She wrestled a few minutes longer with the praetor's helm. If she could pad the gap between her forehead and the helm, perhaps it would sit still and let her get on with burgling. She glanced about hopefully, but all she had in the way of padding was the dress on her back and the stockings on her feet.

Stockings it is, then.

Purity gritted her teeth and braced her back against the wall, trying to remove her stockings without upsetting the helm that sat atop her head. Gemmed citrine slippers came off easily enough, but Purity had to twist herself like an old drunk moving his bowels to tug off her stockings, and the flimsy things were *still* too insubstantial to be of much use, she thought, when at last she had them balled up in her hands. She pushed up the helm a few inches and held it there with one hand while she wound each stocking about her skull as best she could with the other—when she resettled the helm upon her brow it didn't cut into her scalp so badly, but it didn't seem much steadier, either. Purity sighed, and stalked toward a white oval door that blocked her path.

Beyond that door, carved from rare billionstone to resemble the branches of the Groveheart, lay the prince's personal suites. Only the prince and the Lords and Ladies Unsung were ever allowed inside—Purity had tried in vain to find a maid who'd tended the prince's apartments, but there seemed to be nary a soul within the Dome who'd ever stepped foot above the third floor of the Malaison. And here she stood on the sixth, with stockings wrapped around her ears and a looted praetorian helm wobbling atop her head.

Oh, oh, Purity you silly quim, whatever are you doing?

Well, that self-recrimination was easily answered: *I'm fed up with this imprisonment, and if I can't escape the Dome, I'll damn well know its secrets.* She nodded to herself with authority, and the helm nearly caved in the bridge of her nose. She squeaked, then cringed.

To gather the nerve to open the door, Purity Kloo reminded herself that she had plenty of experience bending the rules. She recounted her past exploits by way of a mantra for courage, enumerating the reasons why she dared burgle the leader of the world—even if he had vanished. When, at ten, she'd found the secret doorway that led from Baron Kloo's study to his pleasure suite, her father had been more proud than cross. When she'd disguised herself as her brother Pomeroy for the all-male Midseason Tourneys and thrown Erasmus FenBey from his courser inside of fifteen seconds, her father had been concerned but not-so-secretly proud—and the Baroness had no choice but to swallow her humiliation and join in her husband's good-natured ribbing of Duke and Doctor FenBey while a mortified Doctor FenBey tended to her poor son Erasmus' shattered ribs. When, at the age of sixteen, Purity Kloo debuted before formal society, she had filled the entire Barony with pride at the sight of her dainty figure and spun-gold hair. But when she swept down the aisle leaning not on the arm of her brother but suspended between a pair of rough-cut gigolos—one supporting each kid-gloved wrist—the Barony *had* been mortified.

And then a few years ago she'd spent a week killing herself, of course, which was less rebellious than just plain odd. It hadn't worked, but Purity persisted for longer than anyone had expected—her brother lost his bet with their father—and she'd earned a bit of respect for herself in the process. The body-bound nobility dismissed suicide as an extreme form of masochism but little else, and after slashing her throat every half hour for seven days Purity had to agree: no exit lay in that direction.

So she didn't consider her actions the least bit out of character when she excused herself from another dozen hours of embroidery and dared to penetrate the Petite Malaison, a rather non-petite architectural confection of unimaginable age that sat at the crown of the Dome's largest open space, the primordial Groveheart. From his seat here, in theory, the prince had watched the Dying wind their way into the remnant of Anvit's Glade, where ages ago the mortal Third People first found release from the wheel of lives.

Purity felt a kinship with the birds wheeling above the Groveheart, looking down on the tops of the oldoaks, redwoods and rustwoods that seemed to stand so straight and rise so tall from the forest floor. Only the massive central column of gold metal, which supported the roof of the Dome, rose above the trees. From this high vantage the treetops reminded her of green thunderclouds, like the dark emerald cumuli that had showered her family in ethylene glycol the day her sister Parquetta had miscarried. Toxic rain for a toxic day.

Thinking of that time increased Purity's frustration at her predicament—the predicament of the entire nobility, really, but Purity only charily thought of the other members of the peerage as her actual *peers*. They may be inbred fops, but she didn't think the nobility had earned this punishment for their millennia of privilege: to have their lives restricted to this city, and then to madness and parlor games in a great gilded birdcage. Couture killings, the Circle Unsung devouring itself—perhaps literally—and a single cowardly Killer. Tears washed away by antifreeze while never-born babies withered on the sweet green dirt.

Something flapped its wings inside Purity's rib cage, something keen with the potential for brutality, and she welcomed the feeling even as she struggled to identify it. She'd tried to be a good girl, sewing and lunching and severing heads from the girls who were less good, or perhaps better—Purity admitted to herself that she'd lost a bit of perspective on that count. But five years! Five years of claustrophobic smiles and rote repetition of the same mindless activities day-in, day-out—she'd tried everything she could think of to escape, all to no avail. So it was only natural that the boredom of her confinement propelled her toward these forbidden heights. Boredom and stifled rage. She thought she knew an inkling of what the Dying must feel when they came here for release.

Suddenly a sound came from behind her, and the angry bird in Purity's chest nearly fainted from fright. She turned around so swiftly that the platinum helm fell off her head completely, landing with a bang and crushing the toes of one foot.

"Fuck a footman, that hurt!" she cried, hopping, only to lose all thought of her physical pain when two gawking faces peeked around the corner. Two identical faces, appearing vapid and surprised at the same time.

NiNi and NoNo Leibowitz looked at Purity, then turned their heads to look at each other, shrugged, and looked to Purity again. They slithered into the morning light.

"Oh, hello dears!" Purity squeaked, wiggling her fingers in a vain attempt at nonchalance. She stepped in front of the fallen helm, hoping the girls wouldn't see it. Matching sets of eyes blinked, looked to each other again, then returned to Purity.

"Did you get lost on your way to the seamstresses, too?" NiNi asked. She wore a silver tunic and leggings encrusted with bits of mirrored glass. NoNo seemed dressed more sensibly for this time of the morning, wrapped in white linen that matched the spotless walls of the Petite Malaison. For some reason she kept scrubbing her nose with her fingers as though she smelled something foul.

"Seamstresses?" Purity repeated, scrambling for excuses. "The seamstresses are on the first floor. Of another building entirely." NiNi was lugging a heavy-looking sack, no doubt filled with lovely clothes in need of minor, pointless alterations.

"So they are." NoNo nodded, still frowning at some stink Purity couldn't detect. "Which explains our trouble locating the workrooms. Whatever are *you* doing up here, Purity?"

"And why do you have your stockings wrapped around your head?" NiNi added.

"My head was cold," Purity answered before she could think.

"Oh, all right," NiNi said, "but what about your feet?"

"What about them, NiNi?" Purity's voice came out shrill; she moved on quickly. "I often enjoy watching the sunrise from a vantage with a little altitude." Never mind how hard it was to actually *see* the sunrise past a forest and a wall of thick glass.

NoNo narrowed her eyes. "They say we aren't allowed up here. They say we ought not risk upsetting the praetors."

"They say," NiNi added in a stage whisper, trying to open wide her heavy-lidded eyes, "that there's a Killer on the loose!"

Purity tried so hard to force her voice into a trill of laughter that she almost sang an arpeggio. "Well, they also say that the world is a mermaid who sings the skies to sleep each night, so I don't rightly know what we're supposed to believe when it comes to *they* and *saying*, do I? But I tell you what, a little aerial promenade is an absolute *tonic* for the spirit, and that's my heartiest possible endorsement, as I'm certain you two know. Isn't the view from up here just lovely? I think it so, I really do." Purity ran out of breath and gave silent thanks for it.

"Um. What?" NoNo cocked her head and looked at Purity as if she'd gone batty.

"There are mermaids up here?" NiNi asked with the first bit of enthusiasm Purity had seen her show for weeks. "I want one!" She waved her arm in the air, in case the mermaid people were watching.

NoNo sighed, and for a moment Purity could almost believe she wasn't as empty-headed as her twin. "It's too early in the morning for mermaids, NiNi. They sleep late."

"Oh." NiNi sounded disappointed for a moment, but then yawned and tugged at her sack. "Can we find the building with the seamstresses now, NoNo? I want to go back to bed, like the mermaids, and you have your dance lessons."

NoNo takes lessons? Purity found the mental space to marvel.

"Of course, let's." NoNo made no move. The twins looked at each other again, at a loss.

"You'll want to go downstairs," Purity instructed them, trying to keep her urgency from showing. "All the way to the ground floor. And then to the Maidens' Keep, you sillies, that's the *other* big white building facing the Groveheart. Perfectly understandable error, my darlings!" *We live there, you clowns.*

"Of course." NiNi nodded, taking NoNo's hand, and turned away. "Let's!"

"Won't you show us the way?" NoNo asked Purity, the faintest hint of a pout coloring her expression.

"Oh I would, NoNo, you know that I absolutely would. But I love my sunrises so, you will forgive me for lingering here a few moments more, won't you? My favorite part is watching the sun—or suns—rise above the canopy of the Groveheart. Or, um, trying to. Sometimes that big central column supporting the Dome just *gleams,* I tell you. I'm always atwitter to see what flavor sky the world will grace us with; each day is such a delight! Don't you think? Thank you ever so much for your understanding, girls; I'm such a daft thing, aren't I, to be so moved by the dawn!"

NiNi laughed. "You sure are silly, Purity."

NoNo gave a little clap and agreed. "We'll find our way together, won't we, NiNi? And then you'll sleep a few more hours, while I nip off to dance a while. We *will* see you at Bitzy's breakfast, won't we?"

Purity threw up her hands in a pantomime of delight. "Why of course you will, NoNo! I wouldn't miss one of Bitzy's breakfasts for all the sunrises in all the worlds! And please do enjoy your dancing lesson!"

NoNo acceded, but spared a word of warning: "You watch out for that Killer, Purity Kloo."

"I will, I absolutely will do just that." Purity nodded fiercely. "And you two do precisely the same. I absolutely forbid anyone from Dying before breakfast!" She trilled a laugh again, this one more successfully lighthearted.

Purity tried not to grimace as the twins tottered away, NiNi dragging her laundry bag behind her. Bitzy designed her breakfasts to keep the girls' figures dainty, which meant that there was no breakfast allowed, only tea. An empty stomach was the least of Purity's problems.

Purity waited until she was certain that she was alone in the forbidden corridor. She'd come this far, and survived an unlikely encounter with the sisters Leibowitz, which lent her courage now that she thought about it—after all, if NiNi and NoNo could wander through the halls of the Petite Malaison unmolested, then *she* would have no problems. Although it did worry her that her stolen helm had opened the doors so thoroughly; the girls must not have been very far behind her, surely, or the doors would have sealed themselves shut again. Purity didn't know exactly how the helm interacted with the doorways of the Malaison, but the enchantment couldn't leave the doors unlocked for very long or it wouldn't be a very effective security system, would it?

The door to the prince's apartments opened like all the others: Purity, helm-on-head, raised her hand to the stone branches that decorated the round portal and a little bird, a lark of white billionstone, hopped up from within the carved foliage and nodded its head in her direction. The doors swung inward on silent hinges, and Purity stepped into a room that only the prince and the members of the Circle Unsung, like her father, had ever visited before.

Shielding her face from the light, Purity had to admit that, vanished or not, Fflaen knew how to impress: he'd left the rooms within unadorned, allowing the astounding architecture to impress his visitors without the impediment of too much design. Here, the stonework was obviously much, much older than what she'd seen in the corridors of the Petite Malaison. Like the doorway, the stone itself was different—billionstone shone like the sun in the presence of the prince, but even without Fflaen it was bright enough to dazzle Purity's eyes.

As her vision adjusted, she saw that the once-exactingly-carved clerestories and crenellations of the blindingly white mineral were designed to withstand eternity and were doing so admirably; time had melted the billionstone like radiant wax, but the craftsmanship retained the soul of their artistry. Figures that might have been the original inhabitants of the city stared down from the walls like rows of eroded angels, their faces and fingers not so much weathered by age as liquescent, elongated. Eye sockets gaped, mouths hung open, fingers dripped into the shapes of long icicles. The filigreed billionstone above and below the carvings had undergone a similar transformation, and now it imprisoned the statues in a lace of wintery stone.

The ceiling itself dripped with age, dressing the molding in a ribbed palate of deformed stonework that transformed the suite into the maw of a snow-white behemoth. She half expected to see teeth rimming the floor, but of course there were none—the floors, for that matter, must have been replaced every few thousand years or so as a matter of practicality, simple white tiles that matched the mood of the architecture, scattered about with whorls of the only color visible: mosaic spirals of red, green, and blue. The trails of color made for an odd choice until Purity realized that only the guiding lines of mosaic gave the apartments any sense of scale—they were footpaths to be followed from room to room in the glow of billionstone. Thank goodness the floor tiles were more ordinary, or the radiance might have overwhelmed her; she shuddered to think how bright the walls would glow should the prince return.

Fflaen didn't need a throne, Purity thought, and realized that she had been half-expecting to see one. All he had to do was exist, and the billionstone spine of his palace would shine like a sun. He wore his age and shining inhuman skin as crown and mantle, and here in the Petite Malaison age itself presented itself as a separate entity—no lord, no lady, no matter how many lives they might have lived, could face this reminder of the colossus of time unchastened. *Lords and ladies come and go,* the walls and their friezes announced, *and in time even princes may pass away. But the City Unspoken remains. Long after the dust of your memory has faded, the City Unspoken remains.*

Then she noticed something off.

When her father had visited these apartments, Purity wondered with a mixture of delight and trepidation, had he seen the hatch that opened beneath a rosette of inlaid stones—mostly malachite, lapis, and textured hematite? Three-quarters of the tiled circumference had collapsed to expose a flight of frosted glass steps leading down into a well of incandescent, ancient mineral.

The crisp modern lines of the cantilevered glass stairs stood out in contrast to the funnel of dripping billionstone through which she descended, and Purity realized she'd been distracting herself from her infiltration by musing on the design choices of her burgled surroundings. Of course she had, it was what they were taught to do, all the children of the ruling class—to distract themselves from anything real with frippery. To flit about like moths between lamps, never resting too long upon one thought lest they spoil their fun with serious thought. *I'm no better than Bitzy,* Purity admonished herself, knowing as she did so that it wasn't true.

She followed the stairs down, and after a few turns they opened into a chamber the same size and luminosity as the greatroom above, but spangled with colored light. . . . Purity let out a squeak. She thought for a moment that she'd entered an art gallery—she stared at a row of varicolored glass panels, each piece taller than a man, suspended by high-tension wires from the ceiling and supported from beneath by sturdy calipers. The light radiating from the wall illuminated the preserved slabs of stained glass, casting projections of the images therein onto the white tiled floor.

Her mouth slack with wonder, Purity wandered between the panes of colored glass and realized what she witnessed—these were the Dawn Stains, artifacts of legend from the long-forgotten, half-mythic original seat of government, of a palace and a people that hadn't existed for over half a million years, save for remnants like Fflaen, who was the last of his people. Fflaen and the Dawn Stains. The histories Purity studied had referred to the vanished palace alternatively as Anvit's Lament and the Manifold Remnant, neither of which was anything but some historian's fancy, since even the ruins of the first palace had been lost since before memory. Yet here it was, or slices of it, held in place by steel calipers and taut wire.

Said to have lit the palace of the City Unspoken's first rulers—of which these billionstone walls were remnants—the glass windows called the Dawn Stains told the story of the city's founding. These were the First People who laid the first cornerstones of the city and cleared away the vastness of Anvit's Glade, the primordial forest that held the original deed to the land their city now occupied. The name of their race was *aesr,* and the name of their last descendant was Fflaen, her prince.

Purity stumbled from the weight of the age and majesty around her, catching herself against one of the priceless fragments of glass. In a moment, all her bravado seemed to evaporate. What had she done? What was she *doing* here? She was just a bored girl with a grudge, and she'd almost fallen through one of the tolling *Dawn Stains,* bells in their belfries!

The glass panes of the Dawn Stains had run together like honey over the eons, but the scenes depicted were still recognizable after an impressionist fashion—the largest showed a pair of gleaming white figures, brother/sister and husband/wife. A father with an eyeless, fin-crested face and a body that shone like a gold sun. Brilliant lights danced up the side of each of the siblings, mirrored by rays of light from beneath their father's ribs. A similar figure, female, placing a red crown on her own brow. A tortoise with a forest growing from its shell, swimming through a stylized sea.

Another fragment portrayed a group of women, blue-skinned and yellow-haired, bearing flowers the color of glacial ice. They bowed their heads at the foot of a great barrow—that would be Anvit's funeral, and his daughters the ice maidens from whence the neighboring Maidens' Keep earned its name. The lure of history overwrote Purity's shame, and soon she was stalking from pane to pane, committing every possible detail of the Dawn Stains to memory.

Farther down Purity saw different images, each becoming successively more abstract—was that part of the Dawn Stains' design, or were the more abstract fragments older than the rest, more primitive in their devising and more heavily blurred by time? She saw a shape like a golden whale, pierced by holes or spears—she could not tell—in a similar pattern to the lights along the flanks of the figures from the largest stain. A pocket watch dangling over a muddy bowl. The unmistakable curve of a pregnant belly, bright red. Virgin forest; a shard of what looked like rock tied round with a red bow; an odd triangle colored pink and brown and turquoise, above seven setting suns; three turtles against a starlit sky; a row of fists; a city in a mirror; a sad child. Bars of color comprising some patterned, rhythmic code that ran along the bottom of each pane. So much more than Purity could absorb.

Why *had* she come here? Purity examined her motives anew: she'd used boredom as an excuse, but the sprawl of the Dome was large enough to offer a bored, spoiled girl years of exploratory adventure. Why *here*? Purity wasn't sure she knew the reason herself—was it really the challenge of sneaking into the upper levels of the Petite Malaison, or was there more at work? Had something or someone led her here? Why had it been so easy to find herself here? Why was she asking herself these questions *now,* and not before?

There at the foot of one of the support calipers lay an iron mallet.

Someone may not have led me here, thought Purity as she looked at the floor beneath the Dawn Stains, *but, sure as sin, someone left that hammer* on the floor. *Right there for me to find. I suppose that spells the end of co-incidence,* Purity concluded, *doesn't it?*

Why a hammer would be there, why a hammer would be permitted within spitting distance of these fragile wafers of antiquity, and who would have done such a thing—these questions demanded answers. Was she a pawn, or simply talented at finding herself in dangerous predicaments? Could it be the Killer?

Well, there's only one way to find out, now isn't there?

She thought of the Death Boy who'd taught her to pick locks, and of the brother who'd let her take his place in the tourney, and of the father who tacitly approved of her independence. She might be throwing away that life—then again, she might be standing at the threshold of her true inheritance: choice.

She could turn around right now and creep back to her rooms. If she left right this minute, Purity thought she could escape any consequence of today's incursion. NiNi and NoNo certainly weren't a threat, even having discovered her sneaking about where she did not belong. But what awaited Purity if she returned, now? The life of a nightingale who hated to sing. Baubles and bitchery. *Prison.*

Considering that future, her choice had chosen itself. She could stay a child or she could enact change, then face the consequences as a woman. Whatever came next, it wouldn't be the same endless routine of coldcumbre sandwiches and casual murder.

She looked at the Dawn Stain before her. It glittered in the light, a thing of history and magic. Her life and its confines descended from those ancient, alien panes. From a history that was not human, the Circle Unsung had arisen to hold the city in trust for the Third People who needed it. For all the pilgrims who needed to Die, so that the metaverse could grind on, fostering new lives, on and on. These brightly colored windows were sacred, irreplaceable, probably magical, and symbolic of all that held her back, all that colored her world with the tint of tradition and duty and slaughter. Damn the rules! There was only one reason Purity could have come this far, though she hadn't known what she would find.

Relying on the same imprudent instincts that had gotten her this far, Purity seized the hammer and, with a whispered apology to her father, hoisted it above her head with a grip steadied for an eon-shattering blow.

*   *   *

Thea Philopater rested on her divan watching the suns climb above the roofs of the buildings, blue light transforming the canal into a ribbon of steel. Cooper and Marvin would be out of Purseyet already and halfway to the ever-burning towers where the Undertow laired—the cultists knew nearly as many secret ways as Asher did. Ways that Thea would need once Lallowë Thyu learned she had set Cooper free.

She hadn't lied when she'd spoke to Cooper about the gray man: she *would* rather tear out her eyes than betray his trust. But that was the problem with her broken life—every time she tore out the offending orbs, they grew back.

Isis, the irony. Thea shook her head in silent laughter, tossing the curls that had intoxicated titans. *Isis, you turn out a fake, you fraudulent goddess, while your onetime avatar raises herself from the dismembered dead until the end of eternity.*

Asher kicked down the door with a crash. Thea slipped a sweet into her mouth from the plate at her side, and met Asher's glare in perfect repose. She chewed the morsel while he fumed, giving him time to stoke his famous rage. When in doubt, play to a man's strengths until they could be turned to weakness.

"Hello Thea." His voice shook with anger, but not as much as she'd expected. Something else interfered; was it fear? She didn't need to be Cooper to know Asher's fears.

"Milord." She prepared herself for all eventualities. "Are we breaking everything in sight, or just the doors?"

"What did you do with Cooper?"

She shook her chin. "I could ask you the same question. But I won't—I'm not petty, Asher, and I didn't steal your friend. He left here of his own accord, arm-in-arm with a handsome young Death Boy; if you want answers you'll have to extract them from the Undertow."

"I know Thyu arranged the attack. You can stop trying to fool me."

Thea tutted. "Lallowë Thyu did not pay me enough to lie for her. Not to you."

"Why did she pay you?" Asher flipped the chip with her likeness on the bed.

"The same reason you pay your pink woman. To look for something special in a supposedly un-special stranger." She took another sweet for her tongue to work.

"And?" She had him.

"And, I told him that I saw what I imagine you and your scholar saw." Thea swallowed. "Very little."

And then, "I lied, of course. If I told the infant what he may become, he might never become it."

Asher threw up his hands in disbelief. "What did you see, Thea?"

She guarded a sly little smile. "Client confidentiality—you should know that better than anyone."

This made Asher uncomfortable. They both felt it. "So you gave him to the Undertow, who just happened to be swooping by?" he asked, changing tack. "Are you deluded or desperate?"

"Oh, Asher." She pouted. "Can't it be both?"

"You don't know, do you?" Asher looked at the pearly wallpaper, the china bracketed there for decoration, and wondered how much of Thea was bluster, and how much was Pharaoh. "You don't even know *why* you play the game, I'll wager. You've become a pawn again, Thea, and this time you won't have a man to blame."

The Lady suppressed a bristling rage. She blinked slowly, subduing her body by focusing on her heavy lidded facial expression. Every soul could be seduced, her own included.

"What do they want with Cooper?" Asher asked her.

"Another question you'll have to save for a man who knows the answer." She spread her hands with steady fingers and sat on a cushion at the window. "I am just a whore."

"Whose modesty is as false as the rest of her. You sold him to *scum*, and you will tell me why." He wished Sesstri were here, she would simply solve this woman like a puzzle, and be done with brothels.

"I attach myself to powerful men. It's something I'm working to improve." She pulled her plate of sweets into her lap.

"The Undertow aren't men, Thea! They're children—they're brainwashed junkie babies."

"And their masters?" Thea stared out the window at the horizon, where a black funnel spun above the ever-burning towers.

"Are *not* men. Are flying zombies. Are unworthy of your loyalty."

"But they *are* powerful. And we share a certain predicament. . . ." She reached for another candy.

"*You share nothing!*" Asher snatched the plate and dashed it against the wall. "Whatever you have been led to believe, Thea, there can be no common ground between a living woman and the bruised ghosts who call themselves the skylords. They are abominations; you were a queen!"

She lashed out in equal measure, smashing the window by her divan with one arm, the rest of her perfectly still. He'd earned a dose of her volatility, and it was legendary—how could he think to out-tantrum her? "They call me the Queen of Poisons! A queen of whores and drug-fucked madmen! How *dare* you manipulate me with my lost sovereignty! I am a captive in this body, bound to this place with only my own moisture for succor—the beasts of the desert live better!" She took a breath and picked glass from her gown. "I decide where my best interests lie, and the *sky-lords* and I have something in common. . . ." She stressed the title the lich-lords had given themselves.

"You cannot Die. The liches cannot live—they're undead; Thea, we don't ally ourselves with abominations. Even a dark fey like Thyu knows that. Not even for self-preservation."

"*We* do whatever *we* deem necessary, gray man. And *you* are no longer in a position to afford our favor, nor its attendant courtesies." All possibility of coquettery was flown, now. Her beauty evaporated, replaced by bronze and thunder.

"Reverting to the royal we, Thea? You *are* slipping. Whatever hold those undead husks have over you must be powerful indeed."

"You think you know desperation. Ask the skylords. Ask the Unseelie. Ask *us*, Asher, we have ever known urgency and fear. Now the Dying cannot find Death, and a sickness is coming that every poison-whore worth her asps can smell. Something holds it at bay for now, but not, I think, for much longer."

"You're desperate." Asher gave her a searching look. "No, you're mad. It's already got you, hasn't it?"

"Ask me that question when *you've* been dethroned and damaged beyond mending, Ash-skin. You have *choice* while I have none. Talk to me of freedom and royalty when you have poisoned your spirit so thoroughly that it *cannot Die*."

"Oh Thea. I am. I have." He shook his head, feeling sorrier for the Queen of Poisons than ever before. How could he hate her when he felt so much of her own pain? They were too similar, though he could never say so. "You've betrayed me and sacrificed an innocent to the lichdom because you are unhappy?"

Thea threw up her hands. "No, you stupid man, I *saved* your friend from the Terenz-de-Guises she-elf, who tortures her father to death once a day. I do not betray you—I will not bring more poison into my soul." She couldn't stop herself from laughing. "Although what befalls him once he's made his choice, well . . . perhaps he *would* be better off butchered by your marchioness."

Asher looked dumbfounded, then stunned. "Dead gods, what have you done?"

"A dead god—that's what I *am*, Asher. *This* is what a dead god looks like." She spread her arms, looking so unhappy. "A moment ago you rebuked me for not acting a proper queen. But that's exactly what I've done. The skylords aren't so different from their underlings, or from the lords and ladies of your own Circle Unsung—aimless, purposeless. Godless. Kingless."

Now she rose, turning her back to him and gazing out the broken window into the new day. A day that would see her life change, at the longest last. She pointed west, to the Guiselaine, where the Manse Terenz-de-Guises squatted like a cancer of dark wood and daub. "*She's* free. The rest of the pigs are locked away, Asher—why leave her uncaged?" Thea's voice shook with a jealousy that surprised Asher with its virulence. "Tell me what Thyu and Terenz-de-Guises and the other scattered handful of free-range nobility did to earn their freedom? Tell me now and I'll undo everything. I will return your useless boy and abase myself if you can just tell me *why*."

Rage. Asher said nothing. He thought nothing. He held himself as still as possible and wished the words would fly back into her mouth and choke her.

"I didn't think so." She drew herself up and searched him with unblinking eyes. "I see the serpent slithers free, as it always does. Cooper knows you have a daughter, did he tell you that? I don't know how, but he knows. Your threadbare game unravels."

Asher's eyes flared with blue-red fire. "You sound just like Thyu, threatening me with scraps of knowledge you don't begin to understand. I don't know what motivates *her*, Thea, but what drives you is ugly to the core."

She shrugged, thinking of the throne she'd build atop those towers flickering like candles on the horizon. A house of suns. It was a pretty lie, and it had let her lead herself this far. Every soul could be seduced, even hers. Even Asher's.

"What do you know. A woman with a spine is a foreign creature—to you, we are all the same. Of course you'd see the similarities between women who resist you, desperate narcissist that you are. It doesn't matter now, does it? I will be monarch, or I will be *nothing*."

Asher buried his face in his hands. If he'd thought he couldn't feel any sorrier for Thea, he'd been wrong. "Two thousand years and you're still making the same mistakes, Thea. Still choosing the losing side. And that makes it all the sadder—where will you run this time? No snake can save you now."

She could not keep the sadness from her face or voice, this once. "No, not a snake." Then she shook her head clear and resumed her lies. "The Undertow make the perfect army, for the proper queen. The liches . . . the skylords are ready-made generals. Fflaen has abdicated and his puppies are locked in their kennel. Thyu might stand against me, but her goals lie beyond the city, you must know that. I, however, am damned to live in this world, so I must content myself with ruling it."

"Bells, Thea, if I had a dirty silver for every bitter former god-emperor who said as much . . . *We are all of us trapped.* You think you're the only one who's desperate for change? Wake up. That's everybody."

But she simply nodded. "Of course ambition is common. Rather less common, Asher, is ambition's realization. A Deathless city needs a Deathless ruler; we cannot Die. We are what we have always been, Asher. We are the Woman King."

Wrong and wronger. "Oh Thea, I am so, so sorry."

"As well you should be. Your freedom nears its end, Asher, and soon you will be the prisoner. You know precisely what we mean. Nobody seems to know about the *svarning* except those of us who should know what to do about it, you abysmal failure of a man."

That last, she'd never been more sincere.

"That isn't what I meant." Asher shook his head, tears rolling down his face. He could sail a sea on the tears he'd shed. . . . A ship of bones, a ship of doves. "I'm sorry about this, Thea. I did not want to see you meet your end this way."

"You waste your sorrow on me. You waste your breath." *Do it. Please, old friend. Believe my lies.*

Still crying, Asher nodded. "I know."

Thank you.

She needed peace, he knew, even though it would hurt him. She needed to fade away rather than rise again. The Lady could not Die, so Asher lifted his head and, with the voice of a mutilated angel, began to sing.

6

Candace swears like a sailor & drives like a drunk. She's pissed & pulling 80 in an ancient diesel Benz that cost her $60 & a hand-job. She wants to be a cocktail waitress but she can't get past change-purse girl. Green polyester pants & church pumps with rubber soles. Vomit.

"Fuck him and his ass-sucking mother. She can rot in sinner's hell, the shit-eating whore." Candace lights a Lady Pinksmoke Menthol UltraLight while trying to scrape no-smear lipstick off an incisor. Finger slips & the Lady Pinksmoke drops into her lap.

"Assfuck." Candace elaborates into her chest & she gropes for the filter. Doesn't see the truck. Doesn't see the impact coming.

Wait for it. In less time than an eye-blink: every car commercial she's ever seen, leafy afternoon light through the sunroof, Momma & the gambler sweaty on the sofa, an Isadora Duncan scarf streaming past the rear window, Berlioz on a record player. Glass shatters. Her eggshell skull shatters too, & Candy is a held breath and starlight. Then for a moment she's nothing at all.

Brushes off the dust, stands. Rust & clay smeared across her face, caked in her bangs, eyelashes, gums. Knuckles grime from her sun-stabbed eyes, shakes herself off & tucks the girls back into her top. There beneath a sky a shade too yellow to ever dare squat over Texas stretches a ribbon of concrete. Nothing but dust & gray-green weed & empty foothills. And fertile Candace, alive & alone. Wonders if she's hurt the baby. Hopes she has.

"Fuck you, Candy." Mutters, reaches into her pocket & realizes she's lost her Lady Pinksmokes somewhere along the way. "Another Christ-fucking highway."

—Jack Kerouac, *Fast Moves for Goners*

Still reeking of beer, Osebo the Leopard carried Nixon in his arms. Worn out and still thoroughly fainted, Nixon lolled in the valley between

Osebo's bare biceps, looking for all the worlds as innocent and helpless as a child. He was coming around now, mewling like a cranky kitten as he floated out of sleep. Osebo had stolen the unboy away from the confrontation in Bonseki-sai and carried him to safety. He hadn't interfered with the angry pink-haired woman for numerous reasons, not the least of which was her rocky relationship with his wife, but he'd been unwilling to leave a little boy, even a false one like Nixon.

So while Asher and Sesstri fought their battles and Cooper flew into madness, Osebo the Leopard took it upon himself to tend to the child, and to see if he could kindle in Nixon's eyes the ghost of wonder he knew had once lived there. They all had that, and as a rule they all lost it one way or another; in that way, Osebo mused, they were no different than the First People. It had taken marriage to reawaken the housecat sleeping inside the full-throttle jaguar who'd stalked the jungles of the worlds, and Osebo thanked his wife for it. The beast was not weakened by the babe within—so he hoped it might go for Nixon, too.

But Nixon had none of a child's tacit complicity—evinced as soon as he blinked himself awake and looked up to see Osebo's dark face. He bucked like a wet cat and tried to claw his way out of Osebo's arms.

"Fucking queers!" he roared, or would have if he hadn't been a ten-year-old. Instead his roar sounded more a squeal. Nixon's face grew beet red.

"Be still, boy." Osebo's hand wrapped around the scruff of Nixon's neck and pulled him back down to safety. His nonhuman strength brooked no argument. Stunned, Nixon's eyes went wide, then he burped. Nixon might assume otherwise, but Osebo was not prejudiced by the unboy's misleading body. To Osebo, they were all kitten-babes—infants—when measured by the years they'd lived. When he met a mortal who'd lived so long he couldn't remember his own origin, Osebo *might* consider that soul his chronological peer.

"Um." Nixon's pupils didn't quite match yet, but the boy was recovering quickly. "Why do you stink like beer?" he asked, only half-awake.

"I gave directions to your friend, earlier. He appeared very lost."

"Cooper?" Nixon made a screwy face and knuckled sleep from his eyes. "Yeah. Cooper the lost. Why the fuck are you holding me, guy?"

"You are in no danger." Osebo thought that might be the kind of thing he should say.

"Ha!" Nixon barked his laugh and started struggling again.

"Be still, I said." More firmly this time.

"I'll be still when you get your oily paws off me, Black Panther!"

They weren't far from their destination, so Osebo set the boy down on his feet. Nixon tottered for a moment before finding his legs, then rounded on Osebo with an expression he'd obviously picked up from Sesstri.

"Hippie queers!" Nixon bellowed, glaring up at Osebo.

"I find you very strange, little boy." Osebo's face was implacable.

"That's because I'm not a little fucking boy, Sambo!"

Osebo shook his head with laughing eyes. "Of course you are. Just a tantrum away from the cradle, I'd say. Once elevated above the others, some of you never learn your lessons. But you have, haven't you, Nixon?"

"How do you know my name? What, are you friends with the gray man and his harpy?"

"I am not."

Nixon frowned. "Cruised the burly kid that got kidnapped after you gave him 'directions,' did ya?"

"I did not." *My, but the Third People are odd,* he thought.

"So what happened back there? Where's the pink girl? If you've hurt her, I'll smash your goddamned mosshead in. I've done it once today already!"

Osebo walked down the lane, leaving Nixon to catch up. "Your friend is fine. The same cannot be said, however, for the Death Boy who seemed so determined to accost her. Your concern belies some tenderness, Nixon."

Nixon eyed Osebo warily. "Good for her. But you're not getting anywhere near my tenders, faggot, so fuck off back to whatever Congo you crawled out of." He paused, reconsidering his options. "We've got unboys aplenty for you to diddle back at the Minorarium if you're into sicko shit." Osebo was right, Nixon had learned a few lessons. Such as when to prioritize profit over machismo. "If you're dead set on pederasty, I can make the connections. Won't cost you more than a few dirties. . . ."

"I am uninterested in intimacy with anyone but my wife." He smiled where Nixon could not see. So preoccupied, so young.

"Sure, sure," Nixon jawed, comfortable now that he was talking shop. "They all say that."

Osebo stopped at a wooden gate across from a sleepy café. A few old men were playing dominoes at a table, but besides them and the grape-vines growing over the fence posts on both sides of the lane, he and Nixon were alone. The alley looked quaint—were they in the Lindenstrasse again, or was this somewhere else? Not the Guiselaine. Purseyet was too run-down. Amelia Heights? Caparisonside?

Osebo pointed to the morning sky. The suns had reached halfway to their aphelion, moving as one. A concomitant binary day, then. Should be cloudless blue as long as it lasted, which Osebo judged would be at least until evening. The little intersection of magic and physics that Os-ebo called the Skylit Fall would be stable till then. A piece of folded space tucked between plots of lilies and lettuce, it might be an accident of spa-ciotemporal mechanics or the remnant of some long-gone display of the excesses of metaphysical engineering, like the ruins of a desert boulevard lined with overflowing fountains. He knew all of the ways to return to the cottage he shared with his wife in the Anvitine Run, but this was his favorite—and he thought this the best way to impress upon Nixon that he need not abandon every thread of childhood in the name of self-preservation. The unboy's cynicism was not so far gone that it couldn't be teased into something wry but hale.

Osebo rebuked himself—here he was, taking time out of the end of everything to teach one reborn cretin the value of wonder. It was all *her* fault. How she'd tamed him!

"Would you like to see something impossible, Nixon? Harmless, I as-sure you, but impossible nonetheless?"

"It's sweet of you to care, big man, but I've survived enough 'impossi-ble' to last me a hundred lives, thanks."

Osebo cocked his head. "Not like this, I think. Not in your few lives. A simple thing, but it brings me the kind of joy I associate with the very young."

"I told you: young I ain't. And I don't know if you've noticed, but life isn't exactly what it was."

"By my standards, you're young." Osebo flashed Nixon a grin. This one would not fall into the trap of so many of his ilk—he'd already relin-quished the memory of the power and privilege he'd once enjoyed. De-spite his rancor, Nixon *had* acknowledged the truth: that the past was the past, no matter how desperately one clung to it. The past, thought Osebo

in Nixon's own idiom—to practice mortal-scale empathy—was spent
rocket fuel. You could no more reclaim it than you could recapture the jet-
tisoned first stage of an orbital launch missile. Nixon may still be spitting
fire, but he'd moved on to other strata. He would not go the way of his
bimillennial peer, Thea Philopater.

Nixon looked up at the dark-skinned hunter. "Who the hell are you,
pal?"

"Do you remember the woman who paid you yesterday, if that is not
too broad a description?"

"The doll with the box of money?" Nixon cawed. "How could I forget!
Red hair, wearing next to nothing, legs like cream cheese and toes worth
nibbling all day long? Yeah, I got her all right."

Osebo blinked. "I am her husband."

Nixon hadn't the good sense to be abashed. He whistled. "Lucky bastard."

Osebo nodded. "Yes. But you should call me Osebo instead; 'lucky bastard' might not impress my wife."

"Osebo, then." Nixon stuck out his ten-year-old hand. Osebo shook it
with all the seriousness the little man required, and Nixon nodded in ap-
proval. "It's good to meet a family man. 'Pologize for the misunderstand-
ing. You never quite get used to being young again, do you?"

"I don't think one gets used to being *anything* other than what one was
when one began," Osebo said with a sideways smile. It was the closest one
of the First People could come to answering "yes" to the question.

"Sure, whatever. Show me." Nixon shrugged.

The gate swung open with a creak and Osebo ushered Nixon into a
little courtyard—the kind of hidden shaft of green that lived behind every
apartment building in every world across the cosmoses—a secret emerald
gem where mothers grew irises they'd taken from their grandmothers'
flowerbeds back in the old country, the suburbs, the childhood garden.
Electric lights shaped like jalapeño peppers or stars, flotsam furniture, a
zinc bucket for cigarette butts. You could change bodies, you could live
on a floating continent fueled by birdsong or coast between stars on
some industry's freighter, but wherever you found cities, you found these
interstitial cloisters, growing windowsill tomatoes and sheltering garden

parties. People rarely evinced dissimilarities in their means of finding comfort, an observation that brought a smile to Osebo's face, remembering his recent adventure in a barrel of beer.

Nixon strolled through and looked back at Osebo with a skeptical face. "Great. Tomatoes and Christmas lights. Thanks a ton, pal."

Had he been human, Osebo might have rolled his eyes.

"Turn around, Nixon."

The sky was blue and untroubled, and Nixon quietly appreciated the simple sight of blue sky through green leaves as he looked up and turned around. The buildings on each side framed the bricked patio of the courtyard, except for the far side. Strangely, there were no buildings there, just blue sky. *Odd,* thought Nixon, *I didn't think you could find an unobstructed view of the horizon anywhere nearby—*

Oh.

The sky continued down past where the city blocks—let alone the nonexistent horizon—ought to have been. Instead he peered over a ribbon of sky that stretched as far below him as it did above, as if they stood on the precipice of a city in the sky.

"Sky." He mouthed the word.

"Earth." Osebo smiled. "I like this game."

"Huh," grunted Nixon. "Ain't that a thing. Where'd the ground go?"

Osebo shrugged. "The ground was never here to begin with. Just a slice of sky. There's no reason why, not that I'm aware of, and no purpose served—just a bit of the heavens, sandwiched between city blocks and embraced by these apartment buildings."

Nixon leaned out over the edge just a little bit, then snapped back from the ledge. The sky went down all the way, as blue as blue could be. "Huh," he grunted again, by way of appreciation. "Can't buy that kind of view, can you?"

"Not with money."

He looked up at Osebo with a flash of something that might have been filial-adjacent. "Kind of like forever decided to give us a little peck on the cheek, isn't it?"

Osebo patted Nixon on the back. "I'm happy you appreciate the view."

Nixon shrugged off the hand. "I appreciate cash and hot meat. But this isn't half bad. Although," he mused, one foot in paranoia again, "it'd also be the perfect place to diddle some brat. I'm keeping my eye on you. We need to find you a shirt, pal."

Osebo might have laughed if the boy's mistrust hadn't been so deeply pathological. Instead he folded his hands and nodded. "Do whatever makes you feel safe, Nixon."

"Yeah." Nixon nodded, chewing his lip. "Yeah . . . That doesn't always work out so good."

They chuckled together. "That's a lesson a lot of men spend many lives failing to learn."

Nixon shrugged. "Yeah, well, walk a mile, right?"

The sky looked less blue than it had a few moments ago, and Osebo reconsidered his forecast. "Nixon, what would you say to a bite of breakfast?"

The promise of food evaporated the remains of the unboy's skepticism. "I'd say 'yes!'"

Osebo turned to the wall and put his palm flat against the bricks while he pinched one of the beads around his neck with his other hand. He twitched a mental muscle in a part of himself that no mortal could understand or possess. The air became brittle, then viscous like honey, and the Skylit Fall vanished. The troubling sky vanished. Lilies and lettuces, vanished. As vertigo overtook him, Nixon smelled bacon frying and eggs on the skillet. The expression on his face as he disappeared from the City Unspoken was a hungry smile.

The Undertow maintained near-constant contact with one another, although he didn't know if that was how they lived or simply protocol for a raiding party. He could hear their shorthand chirrups flitting across the rooftops, a birdsong patois of real-time intelligence—blocked thoroughfares, broken roofs, which ways were safe and which were not.

Cooper could hear fear, but the Death Boys and Charnel Girls whooping as they raced each other across the rooftops of the City Unspoken felt little to none, so his access was self-limited. Maybe they owed that carefree attitude to the triumph of a successful mission; maybe it ran deeper than that, maybe their lich-lord masters had cauterized their ability to feel fear. Maybe they drank it like blood.

He could see Marvin's face reacting to unheard information, making subtle course corrections as they sped toward the looming towers, top floors burning bright and near enough now to compete with the deranging suns. But he picked up nothing from Marvin or the others—not even brainstem moments of widened eyes and increased heartbeats as a volley of dark-clad youths pushed off a taller building; an instant of panic as a gutter-slick rope slipped through outstretched hands. Their eyes widened and their heartbeats surely quickened, but he could hear nothing.

Cooper followed Marvin's effortless landing, touching pavement and ducking immediately into a roll that dispersed their momentum—Cooper realized these acrobatics were not his own, but an extension of the group-competence the Undertow seemed to possess. He also knew he should be concerned, that there was something or somethings he was forgetting to worry about, but each time his mind grasped for thoughts about Sesstri, Asher, or his own increasingly dire predicament, Marvin would squeeze his hand or press his body close, and Cooper knew only lust and an insatiable hunger for adventure, for freedom.

One of the huge chains that embroidered the city emerged from the pavement at an angle, and Marvin ran up it like a ramp. Cooper slipped on the corroded metal and stumbled, grabbing Marvin's hand for support. His outstretched hand reminded Cooper of Nixon and his surly assistance, and for a moment he wondered what happened to the cantankerous urchin, or if he'd ever scored a shirt that fit him.

"This is dangerous," Cooper said numbly as Marvin lifted him to his feet. What did he mean, dangerous—did he mean the skylarking? Being with Marvin, heading to whatever fate awaited him? Or did he mean the whole city? The words had come out before Cooper could process them—so much of himself was muted now, still tingling with the hallucinatory aftereffects of the queen of the Nile and the adrenaline of running with the Undertow.

Marvin scoffed. "We live above, with the *real* danger." He hummed, pointing a finger to the sky. Cooper followed, and saw torchlight flickering at the topmost flights of the ruined skyscrapers. Dark clouds circled perpetually overhead, the contrails of the lich-lords and their court in the sky. There, like snow above tree line, the Death Boys and Charnel Girls sang to their lich-lovers, the ice-skinned masters Cooper half-dreaded, half-hungered to see. *Everything here worships death,* Cooper thought as he leapt from the chain to another rooftop, Marvin's hand in his, *and death comes in more colors than you could ever imagine.* The alley beneath them looked like a brown-gray line.

Cooper! The woman's voice had stopped crying, and started screaming his name. She was terrified, and she was alone, and she was *up there.* Every time he heard her voice it was like all the bells in the city ringing at once inside his skull, and between her call and the pull of lust toward Marvin, Cooper did not know who—or what—was responsible for his decisions.

"We live above," Marvin repeated. "So we can catch their tails and *fly.*"

Catch whose tails? Cooper thought. He knew that the Undertow served some kind of undead masters, but little more. He shivered, but followed.

As they neared the towers, Cooper saw the buildings more clearly and noted that they shared the same apocalyptic diversity as the rest of the city: Here was a skyscraper that could have been ripped from Times Square, all mirrored glass and right angles, its lower reaches barnacled with darkened signs that might have once enjoyed electricity. There, a spire like a narwhal's tooth-horn, spiral bone rising straight but perforated like a flute at its upper levels, where the wind played a lonely tune. Some were built of stone bricks and some seemingly hewn in one piece from a mountainside, some of clear or colored crystal, another that resembled a thick stem, with door-sized stoma pulsing above bristling fronds. There seemed to be no pattern to which spires remained whole and which blazed but were not consumed by fire. He saw black shapes skittering across even the burning towers—he could add fire to the list of things that the Undertow did not fear.

Cooooperrrr!

"Who built these towers?" he asked Marvin, not really expecting a response, but needing to drown out the voice.

"We don't know. They aren't as old as the Dome or even the Apostery, but they were here long before we were. Hestor, our leader, says that they were stolen from their worlds by a tyrant who wanted a forest of towers. Dorian says that's bunk, but nobody believes Dorian."

Cooper agreed with the latter assessment, although he didn't say so—one felt the presence of *age* here in a way that made Rome look like Levittown. The idea that this city might once have been different was carved into his mind like a rune, and Cooper pictured the beauty that must once have reigned, and the intervening eons scribbled over that first landscape in a palimpsest of ruin: a primeval jungle; a city of light built by cousins to gods; a forest of towers; a hermetic Dome and a poisonous sky. Was everything a perversion of something greater, older? Was *nothing* hallowed? Not here, not anymore. Nothing could be held sacred in the City Unspoken but Death and freedom, if any difference existed between the two.

Marvin climbed a wall and stood atop it in triumph, smiling down at Cooper, who lifted his arms.

"Help me up."

"Help yourself, Cooper." Others streamed past them, swinging and jumping onto the exposed I-beams of the skeletal tower that rose before them, a skinless monolith. He caught some faces staring down at him as they flashed overhead, hair streaking behind them, brilliant smiles exposing lips marked with the serpent and coin tattoo. A Charnel Girl with plaited white-blond hair sailed past and landed in a crouch next to Marvin atop the wall.

"Tasty." She leered down at Cooper before Marvin spun in place, knocking her backward over the wall with a brutal swipe of his forearm.

"And *mine*," he agreed to the place where she'd been standing. "Now follow, Cooper!"

His cock and his conscience drove him on, toward the burning towers, toward the woman whose fear begged him to save her. Cooper only hoped he wasn't dooming himself in the process.

Sesstri kept quiet as she attempted to restore some semblance of habitability to her blown-out living room. Glass scattered and blood smeared everywhere painted her house in shades of destruction, but Sesstri only paid half a mind to the disorder. Her decision to go tromping off to Bonseki-sai hadn't been a decision at all—but rather a summons. She scolded herself for answering that summons as she threw her weight behind her overturned sofa and, grunting, righted it.

Infuriating. The woman was millions, billions of years old, and yet she couldn't hold a simple conversation. When Alouette had first found Sesstri, when the redhead brought her to this house and gave her shelter,

Sesstri had thought her a benevolent loon, perhaps indicative of the addlepated citizenry of the City Unspoken—which, after all, did love its madmen. Now, she realized the convolution of manipulation, otherness, and fragmentation that characterized Chesmarul's manifestation in "human context." A ridiculous term, but seemingly apt. As Alouette, Chesmarul was at once both a superior being and an inferior one. Working as both a physically embodied being and a world-spanning supermind, Chesmarul partnered with herself to cajole Sesstri into place, monitor the collapse of City Unspoken and the breakdown of True Death, summon Cooper for unconvincing reasons, hire Nixon, and bind them all together to endure who-knows-what-else. What a partnership—what an infuriation.

Chesmarul's manifestation seemed like a personal attack against Sesstri. There was nothing human about Chesmarul, nothing to which Sesstri could relate by anything so naïvely simple as an extrapolation of scale. Despite what she said, the red ribbon was nothing like a woman.

Were all the First People so unreachable to mortals? The question seemed trivial, but it writhed in Sesstri's gut like a worm in hot ashes. She massaged the divot between her furrowed brows and missed the simple days when all she'd needed to worry about was a filicidal father and a world that wouldn't let anything with a clitoris read books.

Sesstri picked up cushions and tested them for intactness, returned them to the sofa, and tried to address the broken windows. "Fucking knife tears in my curtains." She pulled together the remnants of her window treatment. "At least they're from *my* knives. Idiots."

The City Unspoken sheltered many beings that others called "gods"; the people of this city were atheist to their bones, which made it a wonderful hidey-hole for all manner of First People who could live here relatively unmolested, without attracting worship or excessive regard. The citizens of the City Unspoken treated every being the same: as chattel, corpse, or customer. The bells tolled for everyone, and only coin counted.

They tolled now, pealing through the shattered windows with the breeze. Soothing and maddening her. Sesstri hoped Cooper was safe, wherever he'd been taken. But she knew who to blame now, besides herself, which was something.

Sesstri ran her fingers through her hair, letting it fall over her face in a veil of pink. When she was a child, she had hid behind her hair like that, hoping to make herself invisible from her father and the cadre of armed men who always surrounded him. Like a peek-a-boo who never peeked, Sesstri would throw her pink hair over her face and pretend she was somewhere he could not see her. Somewhere safe, where a mother who still lived cared for Sesstri as a parent ought. She'd been told her mother died in childbirth, though she knew that to be a lie. Her father always blinked when he lied.

She didn't see the shadow fall across her doorstep, nor see Asher wilt against the doorframe. She didn't hear his ragged breath catch when he saw her hips and breasts silhouetted by the late morning sun. Asher stared at her out of the corner of his eye, half-afraid to be caught admiring the view and wholly afraid that the view might take herself away.

"Miss me?" he dared ask her.

Sesstri gave a start, shook her hair from her face, and glared in the direction of the voice she recognized so instantly and with such a rush of blood that it shamed her.

"A careful man would know better than to surprise me," Sesstri answered as her eyes focused on the man who so bedeviled her, "unless he loves a knife fight." She summoned all her frustration and assembled it into armor that protected her like a plated knight, but what she thought was: *Yes, yes, oh yes.*

"Your morning as dismal as mine?" Asher loped into the room and coiled himself into an armchair near Sesstri, swiping broken china off the leather onto the floor. He tried not to wince as his torn body relaxed at last, then reached up and took her hand; she let him.

Sesstri pushed away thoughts of pillows and big gray hands and lips that did more than repress smiles; that he made her want to smile was a sacrilege she allowed, but inadmissibly.

"Oh, it was plenty dismal." Her gaze remained fixed on the view of the city through the window. Terraced hills and bell towers, wheeling flocks of birds, the twins of yellow fire that posed as today's suns. She would not think about the heat of his hand holding her own, and she would not let him warm her.

"Tell me about it, please?" He stroked his long nose with a finger, a statue admiring its own profile.

Sesstri let out the breath she'd been holding. "One of the First People has been with me all along."

A queer look passed over Asher's face. "Oh?"

"Chesmarul, the red ribbon—you know of her?" He nodded and smiled. *Smiled,* of all things. "She exploded behind the great tree in Bonseki-sai and turned into my fucking landlady." Sesstri sulked.

Asher absorbed the news with a kind of élan, and flashed a smile that disarmed her. "You mustn't blame yourself, my thorny briar rose. Even the most brilliant of the Third People, which you are, can be hoodwinked by the least of the First People. And Chesmarul, she is not the least—she is one of the eldest." He pulled her hand toward him, so gently, and moved his lips to touch the back of it. Not a kiss, just lips and skin; she could not hate that.

She did not hate it, but she withdrew her hand anyway. "She claims to have summoned Cooper, Asher."

"Good—question answered. Sesstri." Asher looked up at her through snowy lashes. "Listen to me. I am ancient and wise, bound to be right upon occasion, and I say not to punish yourself."

"Horseguts." She yielded to her desires and poured herself a finger of obsinto.

"Could this be a manifestation of guilt left over from your deception regarding Cooper's navel?" Sesstri ignored him, and he chuckled under his breath.

Green liquor cooled and burned her throat. *Better. But not another drop.* When Sesstri set down her glass it was a gavel, and she heard the judgment. Her mouth formed a perfect O, and Asher found himself longing to match it with his own. "Braided tits of the Horsemother, I've ruined everything, haven't I? I kept Cooper's navel from you, I—I—How did I miss this, and how did I behave so *perfectly* wrongly?"

Asher steepled his fingers and hid behind them. "Because you are perfect, even in disgrace?"

"I lied to you about Cooper and then I accosted him at the Apostery and probably *drove* him into the arms of some Death Boy gigolo! No wonder the Death Boy kept attacking me, I interfered in a *perfect* little hunt. The fucking Undertow saw Cooper more clearly than I did!" She picked at the rattan arm of her chair. "Oh Asher, I am everything I promised myself that I was not."

"Death Boy?" Asher sat up with a start, wincing at the wounds he'd ignored since La Jocondette. "What do you mean, Death Boy? You got attacked by a Death Boy *too*?"

But Sesstri no longer heard him. She'd retreated to memories of her stepmother, a simpering creature who reminded her strongly of Alouette. Always growing things, always nurturing something back to health, or into a better blossom. As a child, Sesstri had fantasized about what her real mother looked like, how she acted—surely she would be a vase of ice water to her stepmother's carafe of warm milk; steel to her wool.

Sesstri's real mother would be an inhuman queen of lace and blades, that was how Sesstri imagined her. The only idea she had of her mother was an impossible vision of a woman who'd equaled her father, and the only clue had been her father's rare remembrance of the vanished wife who'd surprised him by embodying all he'd been taught a woman could not be: strong, cruel, tactically brilliant. It was this last quality that had inspired Sesstri, driven her to outdo her father's battlefield successes in the scholastic arena. And how she had! The first woman to earn an Optimae degree in over three hundred years, and the youngest of any gender to do so by half a decade. She'd left opponents as bereft of life on the debating floor as her father ever did in the theater of war. She'd been an unstoppable force, a scalpel performing surgery on her world until it fit like a glove.

And then she'd been raped to death in the high passes.

"Sesstri, are you listening to me? It's important." Asher poured a measure of green liquor into her glass and drained it himself. He began to pull at his shirt, tenderly. "Tell me about this Undertow business."

In the passes, Sesstri had felt so close to the sky that the mountaintops seemed to scrape at the firmament like teeth. And there atop the world she had bled out like a stuck pig, unable to remove the polearm that impaled her gut or push away the corpse of the man who'd been foolish enough not to kill her quickly, and from behind. He'd earned his own death that day, atop the untrammeled mountains, raped to death himself by Sesstri's dagger in his belly. In his manhood. She'd been able to do nothing else but stab at him, pinned and impaled as she'd been—just the one arm free, and only enough strength left in it to hack her murderer again and again and again until, at last, her first face stared unblinking into the heart of the sun.

When death had been simple, when it spelled the end of her everything, Sesstri's goals had been simple as well: accomplish as much as possible before the lights went out.

Now she had two deaths under her belt and she felt more afraid of dying than she'd ever felt at home. Now she knew death was not the end, but it was *an* end—and here it would spell an end to her involvement with this city, this problem, this insufferable gray bastard. Now death meant moving on with nothing but her memory of unfinished business—leaving behind all of her work, her notes and journals, the prized primary sources she'd worked so hard to reach. It meant leaving behind all of that, and Asher.

She was scared to death to leave.

How her stepmother must be laughing, wherever she was, at the irony. Scared to die, scared to leave a *man*. Her lessons on being human had taken root at last. How could Sesstri bend and retain herself? And wasn't that a convenient orthodoxy, to secure her identity in an alpine solitude that didn't challenge or frighten her. *Either way, I'm weak.*

Asher groaned, and Sesstri pulled herself out of her ruminations to see him shrugging off his shirt. His body was covered in bruises, deep gun-metal clouds of clotted blood beneath his skin; he winced and tried not to make any noise as he tugged away his clothing, but she could read the pain in his face. It hurt to watch.

Asher looked up at her with a half smile and held up a handful of rolled linen strips. Had he been saying something? "If you aren't going to tell me what you've done, could you at least help me with these bandages?"

Then she noticed the older wounds on his torso and gasped despite herself.

"What *happened* to you?" She pushed the bandages away and inspected Asher's scarred body.

"I . . . I fought, and then I did something, and it . . ." He hid a grimace behind his hands. The pattern of the wounds was so deliberate that Sesstri almost dismissed the scars as some kind of ugly tattoo; between each of his ribs on either side of his chest puckered a scar, like the javelin wounds she'd seen on tourney stallions—a round piercing hole, not torn or sliced, but punctured. And they were bleeding afresh. They lined his sides at regular intervals, one beneath each rib, and blood as white as fresh cream oozed from their mouths. *White blood . . .*

"Asher, who did this to you?" Sesstri surprised herself with the concern in her voice.

"I can't tell you." He looked down.

"Of course you can!" The words snapped out of her mouth like a whip, all reflex and no reflection. Then, a wonder—Sesstri Manfrix backed down from an unanswered question. "That is . . . if you . . ." She nodded. "I understand."

I most certainly do not understand.

He gawped at her, so disarming in his sudden sincerity, bandage in his hand. "Huh. We *must* be in trouble."

She bent to inspect the wounds. His skin even *healed* in grayscale; the scars were charcoal holes, with darker new skin covering them—but each and every one had been reopened, and today. The white blood surprised Sesstri, but men had undergone weirder modifications in the near-endless dance of lives. Of course they had.

"Do those hurt?" She pointed at the older, reopened wounds. They reminded her of the sockets of eyeless beggars, wimpled and hollow.

"Only when . . ." he began, but stopped himself. "Sometimes."

She sat next to him on the sofa, not touching. Just close.

"I know what you feel . . ." Sesstri began, but Asher leveled her with a flat look and she trailed off, shaking her head. "That is, I know what those kind of injuries feel like. Piercing wounds, I mean." She stalled, and swept her lap clean with her uninjured hand. ". . . I don't know what I mean."

He brushed his hair back from his forehead; dovecote wings hid a marble face. What he saw when he looked at her face was a mystery to Sesstri, and she felt a different kind of thrill at the prospect of learning what that might be. A thrill and a needle of fear—what could Asher read in her face that was not all cold angles and icicle stares? She'd never *wanted* to be that sort of person before.

"Then I'm sorry, if you do. You shouldn't have to know some things." He looked away, at his feet, at the horny old Victrola.

Sesstri found herself agreeing. "I suppose under normal circumstances

I'd lecture you about the value of knowledge in the face of even the most painful reality, but on this point, Asher, I'm inclined to agree with you. Some lessons are best delayed as long as possible." She put a hand on her belly, then took it away.

He nodded, afraid to smile. "I suppose that's the closest you can come to saying the lesson shouldn't be learned at all, isn't it?"

She smiled. "I would never say that, Asher, not even if by some major miracle I happened to believe it." She blinked at the lie, just like her father.

". . . On principle," he said.

"On principle."

Outside the windows, locked in perpetual moonrise, the Dome glowered an angry green-gold, and flames that burned but did not consume licked the horizon. "I understand your militancy more than you might think." He made it a suggestion, not an imposition. He danced around her amazing mind and shrunken heart, and it felt like flying.

The scream of shattering glass reverberated through the room, causing all three girls to look up as one and set aside their embroidery hoops. The manservant who'd tripped and dashed the lunch-laden tray against the wall blushed and disappeared, while a brigade of additional servants rushed in to rescue the parquet and wainscoting from the ravages of broken cups and spilled cherry liquor.

NoNo and NiNi Leibowitz opened and closed their eyes lazily, slow-blinking lizards in canary tulle and burgundy batik, respectively. NoNo palmed a lacey sunshade and NiNi wore a cockeyed hat that obscured half of her face from view, but despite the fact that the twins had come late to her breakfast tea, Bitzy had decided there wasn't much to miss on that score. In fact, Bitzy had decided a number of things: firstly, that Purity Kloo had been allowed to exercise far too much free will than was appropriate for a young lady of her station, and secondly that an increase in the frequency of the murders in their little crusade against chaos would do them all a world of good and teach Purity to mind herself besides.

"Doesn't anybody know where Purity ran off to?" Bitzy asked by way of ignoring the embarrassing clumsiness of the servants in the corner.

NoNo and NiNi shrugged. NiNi nibbled a coldcumbre sandwich triangle and observed: "I don't think she runs."

Bitzy inhaled. "That isn't at all what I meant, NiNi dear."

To her credit, NoNo managed to sound slightly less vapid. "Maybe she's just . . . like . . . taking a nap."

"We did not see Purity." NiNi shook her head in accord. Bitzy thought her eyes might be closed, but she couldn't quite see. Stupid sideways hats would be the next to go. "Especially we did not see Purity watching the sunrise in the Petite—"

NoNo jabbed her sister in the foot with the point of her sunshade. NiNi stopped speaking, trailing off in midsentence. The twins blinked as one.

"I'd like a nap." NoNo rested her head on the grip of her folded sunshade. "Dance classes are so tiring."

"Maybe she's killing herself again?" NiNi tried to be helpful.

Bitzy dismissed the twins from her attention. She'd been ruminating over Purity since yesterday, when they'd dismembered the Eightsguard girl. It wasn't that Bitzy felt guilty, exactly, but she couldn't help feel—silly as it was even to suggest—somehow *judged* by Purity. It was nothing of any importance, of course; Bitzy felt confident that the dead girl's name wouldn't even come up at the next meal her family took with the Eightsguards. It wasn't like they'd scattered Rawella's remains or anything pernicious, the stupid thing was probably already alive again and hiding in her rooms, as she ought to. The lords of the Circle Unsung were fussily tight-lipped about everything since the advent of their fun new secret toy, and had no time for the squabblings of girls, not even her own darling father.

But it wasn't the lords or their secrets that occupied the thoughts of Bitzy Bratislaus as a meager morning filtered in through the thick glass section of Dome wall that hugged the parlor. It was the look she'd seen on Purity's face as they chopped up the Eightsguard girl that Bitzy couldn't get out of her head. It hadn't been the bland half-interest of the Leibowitz twins, nor the lick of thrilled heat between the thighs that Bitzy herself felt when enforcing order. It wasn't even something as louche as demented murderous glee, which could at least be excused given the restrictions of their confinement. No, Bitzy had seen something else in Purity's eyes just for a moment, and she hadn't liked it, not one little bit.

She'd seen *distaste*.

Bitzy steeled herself against resentment. Purity had every right to be unamused by the enactment of justice—and reluctance would have been forgivable, perhaps even appropriate in the hopelessly outmoded way of thinking that Bitzy sometimes worried Purity embodied. But the fleeting expression of distaste she'd seen on Purity's face discomfited her enormously. It seemed to suggest—however ridiculously—that Bitzy had engaged the girls in an activity that was less than the apex of fashion. That she might somehow have been *wrong* about *taste*.

The idea was absurd. Style meant everything, and Bitzy epitomized style. This was established fact. Who else could popularize culottes beneath short skirts, or beanies colored according to each woman's birthstone? Nobody at all, that's who. And hell-bent for butchery was anyone who suggested—who even *implied*—otherwise. Bitzy Bratislaus was a pioneer, a savior of her people in these dark times of limited recreation.

Perhaps Purity had been thinking of her own servants and how difficult it was to remove bloodstains from chiffon. That would be just like Purity, wouldn't it, to so wrongheadedly bother herself with the concerns of those who ought to remain beneath her notice? Yes, Bitzy felt sure it was only that. Mostly sure.

"What do you think of the mystery Killer?" NoNo asked the room.

"The what?" Bitzy pounced. A killer? She hadn't heard anything about a mystery. "You mean us?"

"No, no," said NoNo, "the mystery Killer. I overheard Mother and Lord Mothwood talking. Somebody's been Killing people. Just recently someone Killed two of the lesser Tsengs and enough stableboys to leave a noticeable trace."

"Oh please." Bitzy waved the thought away. "Nobody's committing real Murder anymore. 'Mystery Killer?' Listen to yourselves. You sound like silly idiots."

NoNo shrugged. NiNi shrugged. They looked at opposite ends of the salon.

Bitzy scrubbed her eyes. "The Circle *isn't* Killing each other again, are they?" She would know about that if it were so. She hoped she would. "Well, they aren't. Silly."

NiNi shook her head. "This is different—there's just one person, going around Killing people. Isn't it awful? I love it." NiNi would have been gloating if she'd seemed more than half awake.

"How in the worlds is that possible?" Bitzy asked. The Circle had discovered how to Kill, that news was old by now. But they'd always done so as a group; whatever their secret was, nobody dared wield the Weapon as a lone agent for fear of reprisal. At least, not until now. "The Circle Unsung would *never* allow that to happen, girls. Our fathers—"

"—Our mother," NoNo corrected. "And your father . . . I guess they know something we don't, Bitz." The tiniest divot above her nose suggested a frown.

"But-but," Bitzy stammered, "a lord would *never* bother Killing a stableboy. Let alone a stableful." She thought that over. "What would you *do* with that many stableboys, anyway?"

Obscured by her sideways hat, NiNi rolled her single visible eye. "That's why it's a mystery Killer, Bitz. It's, like, *mysterious.*"

Bitzy sniffed, not at all sure how to take the news. On the one hand— *excitement!*—and on the other, well, the threat of uncertain Death. But mostly she felt affronted that she'd had to hear the news from the twins.

"How long have you known about this? Why didn't anyone tell *me*?"

"Days?" NoNo lifted a wrist.

NiNi shifted. "Didn't *you* tell *us*, Bitz?" Bitzy glared. "I think Bitz told us, NoNo."

"Daddy assures me that the Weapon remains the sole property of the Circle Unsung." Bitzy tried her best to ignore NiNi. "None of the lords would bother—Daddy says the lords are loathe to use the Weapon again. The first two waves of Deaths nearly undid the Circle, you know, and Daddy said something about 'returning to the stalemate,' but now he won't talk about it anymore. Not even to *me*." Bitzy suffered from the delusion that she would be head-of-house one day, and thus a member of the Circle, but she seemed unaware of the rules of heritability—the primacy of her three older brothers, for instance. The eldest, Beauregret, had been groomed for succession since he was two.

"Apparently it was the new members who stabilized the Circle after their predecessors had been Killed," she said softly. Bitzy had been engaged to Underbilly Blavatsky-Day-Louis until his Lord father had been Killed. Since his ascension she had not seen as much of Underbilly.

"It doesn't really matter—they can sense the Murders," NiNi said in a rare moment of clarity.

"Pardon?" Bitzy shook her head to clear it of familial ruminations.

"The Circle, um, they can tell if their Weapon has been used?" NiNi continued. "There won't be any physical remains, of course, but they have all kinds of, um . . . frenetics?"

"Forensics," corrected NoNo, "and yes, NiNi, I think you're right." NoNo sighed into the bone handle of her parasol. "All the fun will be over soon, and justice will something-or-other."

"Well, *of course* they can sense it!" Bitzy proclaimed. "I don't know why you two fret so over these little things! The lords of the Circle Unsung form the most powerful cabal in the civilized worlds. I know they're our fathers—or mothers, in your cases, as you're quite right to remind me— but we mustn't let that familiarity dispossess us of our faith concerning the strength of our parents. The Circle will know as a matter of *routine,* and if the Circle knows, then whomever is committing these crimes will soon be passing through the Last Gate himself." Satisfied, she leaned back into an immensity of cushioned chenille. "Or tossed into an oubliette gourd, or given over to the ossuary artisans for some lovely bonework, or—"

"—We'll see," said NoNo, frowning at the skirts of her yellow dress, where a seam had ripped. "There isn't anything we can do about it, anyway. Not unless the Killer wears the same cummerbund to two parties in a row."

Bitzy thought she detected a note of sarcasm in NoNo's voice and had opened her mouth to lance that boil when the door banged open and her brothers Absynth and Beauregret stumbled into the parlor, red-faced and breathless.

"What in the *worlds*?" Bitzy demanded from her padded throne.

Absynth started to explain but his stammer was worse than usual. "H-H-He's not th-th-there, a-a-and, and—"

"—It's Father," Beauregret cut in, his gold hair shining with an absurdly overburnished luster. "He's been Murdered."

7

The column of wheeling black birds rises into the sky taller than any tower on-planet, a beam of cawing agitation that thrusts upward from the Old Cross impact crater and is visible from halfway around the continent.

Parasi walks toward the ruined walls of Old Cross as if she's taking a stroll through her mother's gardens while a suitor holds her arm, not marching to her doom alongside a bristling escort of fifty armed men.

The past surrounds the would-be-queen on her pilgrimage; not the bones of the dead, splintered and blackened among the toppled blocks of the first capital, but the shades of the women who have walked this path before her. Not every queen returns to rule, and Parasi's head brims with the names of the women who failed their coronation ceremonies. The Parliament Above renders judgment harshly, and even the meritorious risk dismemberment at the whim of the feathered mêlée.

Digna, Rubn, Ghraibh, Fiolle, Wen Faraud: queens of the past century who failed to survive their coronations for one reason or another. The last name rings the loudest in Parasi's mind—her elder sister, who had spent every day of her life training to become the perfect queen. And still Parliament had voted against her. With their beaks and their claws the birds of Old Cross made their choice known.

Poor Wen Faraud, who went up a queen but came down in ribbons.
—Prama Ramay, *The Ecology of Rule*

Kaien Rosa, Journeyman Mason, walked with purpose along the hallways of the Petite Malaison, secure in his alias and the simple fact that a man in workaday livery would be beneath the notice of anyone important enough to cause him trouble, so long as he didn't arouse suspicion among the housekeepers. Sure enough, the praetors in their platinum-chased armor didn't blink an eye as he passed by the doors they guarded so needlessly.

Less blind were the staff of the royal household who, much like the praetors, had been largely abandoned to their own devices—but who, unlike the royal guard, were not conditioned to clockwork obedience, and were therefore given more easily to mischief. The royal household staff were the closest thing the Dome had to native inhabitants, and that made them dangerous to a spy; Kaien hated thinking of himself that way, but what's what is what, as his mother would say.

A secondary-grade lieutenant housekeeper clicked her tongue and almost stopped Kaien for questioning, but he was rescued at the last second by a bellicose laundress with a grudge against wine on silk, who commanded the lieutenant's attention as she barreled down the hallway.

Kaien thanked the dead gods for laundresses. Even if they did do unmentionable things to poor young men with the bad luck to stumble into one of their evening tipple socials. He tugged at his collar, blushing despite himself. *Tipple my brown backside,* Kaien thought, *those women could outdrink a cellar full of plumbics!* If he ran into one of the plump-breasted washing women who'd held him hostage with their hands and hips three nights past, Kaien would die of embarrassment. It wasn't his fault, after all—a young man's body had only so many responses to womanflesh, bells!

Kaien had made it halfway around the longest run of corridor that skirted the keep's ground floor when he realized with an icicle stab of panic that he'd left his hammer behind. Bending smoothly to pretend to check his bootlaces, Kaien's mind raced to retrace his steps. He couldn't have been stupid enough to leave his tools inside the damned *royal suites,* could he? A memory of smirking laundresses and breasts pushed together in his face suggested that under the wrong circumstances he could, indeed, be stupid enough for almost anything. He headed back the way he'd come as hurriedly as possible, reminding himself that to anyone walking the hallways he would seem just another square-shouldered workman, full of the energetic work ethic that men of his station were thought by the leisurely classes to possess. Not full of terror and doubt, not running back to the least permissible room in the entire bell-tolling Dome, not scurrying to retrieve an emblem of his order from beneath the most fabled, fragile treasure in the city.

A treasure he'd been too cowardly to destroy, despite his orders.

Bells, he *had* left his hammer on the floor beneath the Dawn Stains.

For such a lapse, he should be bricked up and entombed alive like the wayward masons of yore. He should be—well, his father would take care of what should and should not happen to Kaien when he was allowed to escape this gilded maze. *If* he was allowed to escape.

If I'd been brave enough to smash some old windows, I might already be on my way out.

The thought that the guilds had outfoxed both Fflaen and his lords brought a grin to Kaien's face that was unbidden and, he chided himself, inappropriate. The prince thought his peacocks perfectly imprisoned, and the lords saw themselves the same way. Only the Guilds Masonic *y* Plumbus remembered a simple truth that neither the quality nor their myopic servant class would ever have the poor taste to discover for themselves: sewers work both ways. Sure, Fflaen had sealed all the sluice-gates and culverts maintained in the modern-era systems, as well as the calcified remnants of installations from at least two previous eras—but even a ruler of Fflaen's rumored antiquity had gaps in his memory, especially concerning trifles like plumbing and structural integrity. Which explained why the impossibly old central cistern remained unsealed—a fellow could, with a little elbow grease, slip into the bricked-over twelfth subbasement of the Petite Malaison.

Down there, the bones of the building were of the same age as the stonework in the prince's private chambers—Kaien's best guess put that Paleolithic stonecraft as the remainder of a barbican or a tower-and-curtain wall around which the rest of the building had been built, like scaffolding containing a crumbling billionstone statue. Age was relative, of course—not even the masons knew the age of the Dome itself—even though the guild had maintained its superstructure since time immemorial.

Lurking inside the Dome, Kaien had turned up some funny bits of information. If his father, the First Mason, had been surprised to hear that the lords had been Killing one another, he would be doubly shocked to hear they now lived in fear of an unknown Killer among them—one who acted without any regard for the laws of the Circle Unsung. Just last night Kaien had eavesdropped upon some lads from the stables gossiping in hushed tones about a number of their friends who'd vanished and not turned up in any of the usual haunts—nor in any of the usual spots where the carcasses of casual murder were disposed. The servants feared foul play and, despite being generally inoculated against superstition by cultural inclination and the relative loftiness of their métier, Kaien had seen several make signs against evil when they thought themselves un-observed.

Then again, the guilds seemed to have more pressing concerns; the news about the Killer hadn't changed Kaien's latest orders—if anything, the decreasing stability inside the Dome only made his charge more ur-gent. But Kaien worried. If he carried out those orders, his future was unclear—the destruction of the Dawn Stains would be an irredeemable act of terrorism and, his father assured him, had only been conceived of as an act of institutionalized desperation.

Consider the institution desperate, a glum Kaien thought, kicking white dust off his boots.

Also, consider the institution dead-as-deities if he was caught and identified before he could act on his father's late-night orders. The lords might well use their new tool to send him off to oblivion. No, it wouldn't do to think that way; there was no reason to suspect anyone would visit the Dawn Stains and discover Kaien's mislaid hammer—indeed, he doubted that anyone else *could* break into the secret chamber beneath the absent prince's apartments. The Lords of the Circle Unsung could enter if invited, but lacked a prince to do so; the praetors could enter at any time, of course, but had no reason to do so . . . he hoped. And who else would be clever or foolish enough to break in?

He reassured himself thus as he levered open the wooden panel that led between the walls and ascended the narrow interstitial stairs carved into the rock of the keep. These ways were traveled more frequently, which was still rare enough, and even then it was usually a mason given charge over whatever repairs or upkeep needed doing. The second hid-den passage was less congenial, being a crawlspace forty paces in length that broad-shouldered Kaien could barely slither through.

Kaien dropped into an interstitial space so agglutinated by age and mineral crystallization that it seemed a natural cave formation, save for the hole he'd made with his hammer, which looked out onto the shining white rock funnel and etched glass stairs of the secure passage between Fflaen's glacial suite and the Dawn Stains below. Bells, if Kaien were caught, they'd have to invent a new punishment just for making that hole.

He pulled himself onto the cantilevered stairs, thankful that the dripped-wax folds of the billionstone walls helped to conceal the opening he'd bashed through the radiant rock—he hadn't expected the suites to be quite so blindingly bright. Nor had he expected to see a pretty blond girl standing before the stains with his own hammer raised above her head, her face twisted in a grimace of mingled rage and fear.

"Stop!" she shrieked, seeing Kaien. "I'll do it, so help me I'll do it!"

Kaien said nothing. The girl looked terrified, and Kaien had enough experience with the opposite gender to know to be careful around frightened women wielding weapons.

"I will destroy the Dawn Stains if you take one more step," she said through gritted teeth.

"Now, see, that isn't something I'd be inclined to prevent," he answered as mildly as he could, holding his hands up in a gesture of surrender. "And that's not just because you look much nicer holding my hammer than I do." Those slender arms and narrow waist were a vast improvement, come to think of it.

His lack of concern increased hers. "This hammer is *yours*?" She winced at the shrillness of her voice. Bells, that hammer looked heavy in her hands.

"I'm afraid so." Kaien nodded. "But by all means, keep it if you like. It's a good one, as hammers go, and I've got plenty more where that came from."

She lowered the hammer and let it fall to the floor with a blessedly dull thud. Kaien frowned: her arms looked like lead weights. How long had she been standing there?

"Who *are* you?" the blond girl demanded.

Kaien allowed himself a chuckle. "You know, I was just wondering the same thing about you."

She gathered herself in that self-important manner these nobles possessed. "I am Purity Kloo, and my father the Baron will Kill you himself if you so much as . . . as . . . touch me, or . . . breathe a word . . . about . . ."

"Now, there's no need to fear on that count, Lady Miss Kloo. I think we'd both best keep quiet about where we met." He'd inched his way toward her and now extended his hand. "Kaien Rosa, Journeyman of the Guilds Masonic *y* Plumbus."

"Um. Pleasure." Purity Kloo blushed, then seemed to recover herself. "My, but your shoulders are broad." She winked, and Kaien retained his composure through some effort. He raised an eyebrow and swallowed a smile.

"I've never shaken hands with a servant before," Purity explained. It was technically true—she'd dallied with criminals, but never with the help. Still it felt like a lie. "But, of course, you aren't a servant, are you, mister guildsperson?"

"Indeed I am not, Lady Kloo. As it happens, I am a second-degree journeyman brother of the Guild Masonic, but here . . . here I suppose I'm a spy." Kaien ducked his head in an honest gesture, and Purity saw crumbled stone dusting his close-cut black hair and the brown skin of his neck.

"Why in the worlds are you telling me this?" The fear rose in her throat again.

"Well, see, I told you that so you'd not worry." Kaien made his voice sound as gentle as possible. "Now we each know something scandalous about the other." He hoped his wink came off as conspiratorial rather than improper. Not that he'd mind a little impropriety with such a lovely thing. Her breasts were small enough to fit nicely in his cupped hands, and her dress hugged her slender hips in a most tempting way.

Purity turned away and looked out through the clear glass wall that looked out onto the wilderness at the heart of the Dome. She wrung her hands; the Groveheart spread out beneath them, all branch and birdsong.

"Lady Kloo?"

"Miss, not Lady. And it's Purity." She turned around and looked as if she'd made up her mind about something. "Please, call me Purity. I don't suppose there's any reason for us to stand on ceremony now, is there, Mister Rosa?"

Kaien shook his head. His body radiated the heat of exertion and his eyes were brown and bright, just a shade lighter than his skin. For such a strong-looking big man, his face was round-cheeked and friendly. "Now, see, if I call you Purity, I'm going to expect you to call me Kaien. It's only fair."

"Fine, Kaien. Now will you please explain what exactly you're doing here, and why you're leaving hammers all over the place?" Purity put on her best imitation of her mother, raising her brow at Kaien for intruding while acting as if *she* belonged nowhere else at all.

Kaien chewed his cheek. "That was an oversight on my part, Miss Purity. As for my purpose, well, it's not so different than yours, judging from—"

He was cut off by a deafening Klaxon. Purity clapped her hands to her ears and winced.

"Run!" he yelled, grabbing her elbow and pulling her toward the stairs.

"No!" Purity yanked her arm out of Kaien's grip and tried to make her voice audible over the shrieking horns. "That's not meant for us!"

"Who in the worlds *is* it meant for, then?" Kaien looked physically pained by the volume. "Some deafened god?"

Purity shook her head. "That sound, we shouldn't *ever* hear it. That's the high alarum—and it only tolls if there's a physical threat to the prince himself."

"Oof," said Kaien, scrubbing his ears with his palms. "Well, these are the prince's apartments, so maybe—"

"No. An intruder alarum sounds completely different and would be localized. Do you feel that?" Purity put her hand against the thick window. It vibrated strongly along with the Klaxon, and outside birds rose up from the treetops in turbulent swarms. "Look at how the bells vex the birds, do you see? The high alarum rings everywhere at once."

She put her knuckle in her mouth but took it right out without biting. Bad habits. "It would be prudent for us to leave, yes, but this is a top-priority summons to the *entire* praetorian guard. Like I said, it is reserved for an immediate threat to the royal body—and the prince is absent." She allowed Kaien to lead them halfway up the stairs, where the glowing stone muted the high alarum, somewhat.

"That's another question I wonder if you could answer . . ." Kaien felt as if their roles had been reversed somehow, and it had happened awfully quickly.

Miss Kloo pursed her lips as if she'd thought the same thing. "Yes, well. We're each just chock-a-block with unanswered questions, Kaien. Perhaps when there are fewer Domewide alerts screeching through every corridor, we might even enjoy a moment to sit down and answer some?"

Kaien blinked but didn't try to hide his smile. "Miss Kloo, are you always so pretty when you're cross?"

She blew wisps of blond hair from her forehead. "Only when sirens are screeching and I've been caught contemplating treason by strange young men."

"Oh, I dunno, a little treason is good for the spirit." Kaien shrugged and wondered if there was a way he could survive the day. "But it's a false alarm, isn't it? If the prince really isn't here . . ." He hurried them toward his ill-made escape hole.

"I'd like to say so, yes." Purity frowned. "But I can't. The lords and ladies of the Circle Unsung have stopped Killing one another with abandon now that we've all been properly mortified by their manners, and even if they'd started up again it would be unthinkably bad form to involve the praetors. But the truth is, the peerage has come more than a bit undone, and I can't rightly pretend to know *who* is capable of *what* anymore."

Kaien rubbed his head and wondered how much the girl knew. "Unless it's the, um, Killer."

"What?" Purity started, and hid her hands behind her back without thinking. "We were just having some girlish fun and I'm sure nobody would make a fuss over a few daughters garroted or beheaded and besides which we're all *body-bound* so you know they'll revive eventually and . . . er. You aren't talking about my friends at all, are you?"

Kaien took her hand and shook his head with what Purity thought just *might* be a smile of the charmingly indulgent sort. "Not your little coterie of princesses, Miss Kloo—even the scullery hears about that. No, I mean the capital-K Killer that everybody seems afraid to talk about." Purity wilted and Kaien mistook it for aggrievement rather than shame. "I hate to shock you, but somebody's been Killing in secret. Two Tsengs and a mess of horsey-lads were pulled through the Gate, just this week."

"The whole scullery? Oh, nevermind." Purity flushed and moved on, clearly pumping Kaien for information by playing the vapid socialite— she wasn't the best actress. "But whomever would Kill servants? And a couple of *Tsengs*? Are you certain?" The Tseng family were harmless buffoons, the lot of them.

Kaien nodded. "Your helpers *do* talk, Purity. And the lords may be keeping it quiet, but they're terrified."

"Of course they are," Kaien thought he heard her mutter, and then, "You oaf." Purity didn't seem to like the implication that the Killer had begun taking noble victims. . . . "It could be Murder, I suppose," she relented. "If it isn't Circle business, if the lords decide they themselves are endangered by an outside or unknown force . . . Well, I didn't think it could happen, but if so . . . they *might* call for the praetors. Bells, they'd call for their *mistresses* if something threatened their perfectly ordered lives."

"Someone must be Killing out of turn." Kaien pulled her up a few steps to the hole he'd made in the glowing stone. Better to take the anonymous route and avoid any praetors running through the hallways. "Come with me. I still think we're not safe here. I hope you don't mind getting a little filthy."

Purity smiled, allowing herself to revel in the chaos as she got down on her hands and knees. So she'd choose to attach herself to Kaien instead of sabotaging the Dawn Stains; that was still more say in her own fate than she'd had in five long years. She hadn't needed to throw away her life to effect change after all—change appeared all on its own.

"On the contrary, my strapping new Masonic friend"—she glanced up at Kaien with a brilliant and, she hoped, lovely smile—"I absolutely *adore* filth."

In her reverie, Lallowë remembered running through the forest: morning light filtered through the leaves and cast the world in a yellow-green glow, but it was not the sickly and variable glow of the skies above the City Unspoken. These were her favorite moments to relive. She recalled leaping into the air, her arm reaching out to grab one branch and swing to another, child-sized hands with bony spurs of rock digging into the wood. At that, the memory shifted—light flashed brighter than any sun, and Lallowë found her child self cradled in the arm of a grown-up, looking up at the face of a woman with auburn curls and a faraway expression.

It was *her,* the Cicatrix—not the ersatz chimera she'd become, but as she'd been before she'd ruined her body with machine obsession: lovely, not beautiful, but dainty and sweet of face. The queen wore a crown of purple-flowered kudzu, the weed that would not die. Her dress was plain cotton, but the stitching near her small, perfect breasts was of unmatched craftsmanship. The queen wore a brass cuff upon her bare upper arm, and before little Lallowë's eyes, the brass cuff emitted a puff of white steam. It drifted away on the gentle breeze that always stirred the bower, and soon disappeared, but Lallowë felt a familiar pain stab her heart.

"Tell us again about the quickening, Mama." The question came from a brown-haired girl with Almondine's unreadable eyes curled up on the other side of the queen's body.

"Why are we Third People, Mama?" Lallowë asked. "If we're as old as time?" Little Lallowë lay in the crook of her mother's arm, surrounded by pillows.

The queen scratched her younger daughter with an amber nail. "Our kind has always *been*, Lolly, but we have not always *lived*. In the beginning we were eternal, glacial; not immortal and vast like the First People, but akin to the trees and the river stones. Beautiful and unmoving. *Unmovable*. It was not until the dawn of the Third People that we first glanced down and noticed ourselves."

"I want to be perfect," complained Almondine from the lee of her mother. "I wish we lived at the beginning, before humans."

"It is good to want to be perfect, my tiny nightmare. But you are wrong." The queen shook her head and watched as another puff of steam drifted away. "We do not predate the humans any more than the air predates the wind: that is when we moved, when we began. *With* man. The tension between man and fey is his history and our own."

Lolly sucked on a sugared lizard's tail, scraping off the sweet scales with her sharp little teeth. "That's when we came to life? For men?"

"Quickened," corrected the queen. "Man's birth quickened us, and we began to live. We lost a kind of ever-living purity and gained mankind's predilection for strife and sin. If only we *could* return to stillness, I think, we might recover our lost grace. But then again perhaps not, perhaps forward into motion is the way—that is certainly the dancer's way." The queen stretched one scarred but shapely leg into the air; her love of dance was famous. "It was the way of your foremothers. Who knows where the chaos of progress will take us?"

"I don't understand," Lallowë muttered into her sweet tail. "Are we *going* somewhere?"

The dancing queen pulled both of her daughters into a tight embrace, touching noses. "Time and thorn will tell, my bloody darlings."

A polite cough brought Lallowë back to the present. Maintaining perfect repose, adult Lallowë opened her eyes, then narrowed them.

"Every apology, ma'am." Tam bent at the waist. She'd sent for him, but that didn't mean she was pleased to have her thoughts interrupted. "How might I please?"

"You may run an errand." She procured a folded note. "Fetch me a coin, boy, and a body-binding enchantment while you're about it."

As before, the Cicatrix had sent only the briefest of messages, a list of numbers and letters that Lallowë only half understood.

"A . . . binding, ma'am?" Tam distrusted the self-imprisonment of the nobility of the City Unspoken as much as Lallowë herself—it was unnatural, and belied a fear of losing that no fey worth her saltpeter would dare feel, let alone express.

"Did I mumble? The coin is to be a diode, of course," she explained to nobody, a role Tam had mastered. "A diode for a new vivisistor. Has Mother been fusing magics and technologies from half a dozen worlds *all along*? Ordinarily I'd not be inclined to believe such nonsense, but we endure nonsensical times and so it is lunatic logic that we must follow."

Lallowë held out her hand to give Tam the note, and he stepped forward. But she withdrew it just as quickly, and so Tam stepped back again. His fox-nosed face remained still.

"She wants me to *make* one? With what?" The marchioness mused over the coin, and on the Cicatrix's previous message about the human. "Time and thorn, Tam! Tell me, how do I fit a fatty on a face?"

"Ah? Pardon me, ma'am?"

"Or a tails. Does the side of the coin matter, I wonder? Sympathetic magic could make a difference in this. Or be irrelevant. Or cause disaster." She tapped her nails on the parchment, thoughts flickering across her lovely face. "I speculate that the origin of the materials used has as much to do with the vivisistor's functionality as the ingenuity of its design, though that might be overthinking it. Or under. I hate this, there are too many threads to follow, and all of them false as a Seelie promise."

Quick as a cobra, the marchioness turned her head toward Tam, unhinged her jaw, and shot out a long, thin black tongue to sting his cheek. She moved so quickly that her lips were pressed together and pouting by the time Tam realized she'd lashed out again. He felt blood trickle down his cheek and wondered if it were Tuesday, somewhere.

"Take the note, and I will show you a wonder"—Lallowë lifted the hand with the ring of fourth silver—"of coin and cold metal, and the longest way to die."

The day had corrupted the blue sky, and the promising morning had already miscarried into a sickly yellow noonday—the twin suns fused into a kind of angry mating, their orbs gone orange, streams of red-black plasma arcing between them as they grew steadily closer together. Another costume change for the sky above the City Unspoken.

With her shoulders cradled in one of Asher's long arms, Sesstri stared out the window of her living room and wondered what she'd done. Somewhere out in that improbable, brachiated mess of a city Cooper needed help, urgent help, yet she couldn't extract herself from the arms of a wounded drunk. Listing Asher's deficiencies helped her from being swallowed by the pleasures, his touch, his breath, the warmth of his body against hers. . . .

He snored softly with his marble head turned away. Sesstri tried to pull herself together. She recalled the words of the old Winnowed storyteller holding court on her broken pillar inside the Apostery: *If the Last Gate closes, we will all drown.*

Sesstri turned her body into his, filling the backs of his legs with her knees, her nipples brushing the stone wall of his back, trying to decide if she should just give up and enjoy the time she had left, before the *svarning* took her mind away. When the plumbing of the metaverse became fully clogged—the Dying denied their Deaths backing up the pipes, so to speak, and the flow of energy between worlds, between people, all became congested. Cloudy. Deranging.

Maybe that's why I'm feeling all of these . . . feelings.

Had that been how she'd ended up naked with Asher? It had happened so easily, Sesstri didn't want to blame it on madness, but she didn't know how to accept this intimacy as a part of herself.

"You?" Asher had come round to the subject of Alouette again. "You learned little, I take it?"

"Too much and too little, all in a trice," Sesstri had despaired. "I should have gone to your whore."

He'd cleared his throat self-consciously. "Not *my* whore, exactly, but yes—Cooper has some sight, I learned that much."

"Asher, what *is* he? He seems so . . . mundane."

"I think he's becoming a kind of shaman. He wasn't what I wanted, but he might end up that way. How can he help us restore the ability of the Dying to achieve True Death? I haven't the slightest."

Sesstri had bitten her lip. "What can he do?"

"I worry that the proper question is, what *will* he learn to do? He hears the fears of others, firstly—"

"—That's oddly specific, if not exactly indicative of a nascent super-being."

"It gives him access to secrets, both consciously and unconsciously. For instance, somehow he knew . . . something he ought not know." Asher had taken a deep breath before continuing. "I don't want there to be any un-necessary secrets between us, Sesstri."

Sesstri had kept very still. She still thought of Cooper as a turd, but perhaps a turd with a touch of shamanic vision. Doors were opening, and she suspected he was—somehow—the catalyst.

Asher had looked at her with liquid eyes that were far too close to her own to be safe. "Okay," she'd said. "That's . . . okay. Tell me."

His body shook a little, as if he held back tears; she knew better than that, though. "I had a kid once. A daughter. It . . . the circumstances were not ideal."

"I see." She most certainly did *not*. How was this relevant?

"It was not the child's fault, but her mother and I . . . we did not want to come together. It was forced upon us." He'd curled his shoulders and tried to make himself as small as possible—not easy for such a long man.

"I wanted to love my daughter so badly." Asher's voice had threatened to break. "And we tried to forget how she came to be, but I could not stand to look at the mother . . . Chara, she found a way . . . they are Dead, now."

That's when it had happened; Sesstri reached out to touch Asher and noted with some amazement that she didn't try to stop herself. He was turned slightly away from her and her hand found his knee. She decided they had both earned the truth.

"I know what it's like to be forced, Asher. It can't have been easy for you." She'd flushed as she said it, and felt him stiffen. She'd nodded once, between the wings of his shoulder blades; he had scars there, too. "There's more." *I should have had that drink.* "I had a daughter, too. Had. Not from, from *that* encounter—that was what killed me the first time." Sesstri spoke rapidly without wincing, half-hiding behind Asher's back. "I had Sally during my second life, back on Desmond's Pike. I was not a good mother."

"Where is she now?" Asher had asked, turning toward her with an expression both sad and hopeful.

Sesstri had shrugged. "Wouldn't a good mother know?"

The living room filled up with silence, and Sesstri and Asher sat there, her hand on his knee, Asher still hugging himself. They were lost and sad, but they were not alone.

At last she'd said what they knew to be true. "If we don't help Cooper, Asher, nobody will."

He had leaned in. "There isn't anything or anyone I wouldn't sacrifice for a moment together with you, Sesstri. I hope you know that."

She'd nodded.

"No one will ever hurt you again, I will make sure of it."

She'd wiped her eyes. "You either."

He'd leaned in closer still and kissed her. His lips felt so soft above his stubbled chin. "Cooper. Yes. That's who . . . we have to save . . ."

Asher nodded without breaking the kiss. "A moment for ourselves, even when hurried by the end of all things and imperiled friends . . ."

"Ourselves." She'd breathed the word. "Just a moment. But, oh . . . *yes.*"

Asher had cracked his knuckles and cupped her face in his enormous, warm hands. "Optimae Manfrix solves another riddle." She'd scowled to hide a blush; he'd never used her academic title before. Then he'd kissed her again, and didn't stop until she slipped into his arms, strong despite his wounds, and allowed him to hold her.

*　*　*

Cooper understood the power of the lich-lords the moment he crossed the threshold into their territory: the seething clouds swallowed the sky and, suddenly, undeath saturated the air and earth around him. He'd crossed into another world; the light from the day still lit the blocks on all sides, but within the perimeter of those clouds roiling overhead, a curtain was drawn and day became night. Cooper had no firsthand experience with the undead but could feel the energy of the unliving pouring from the sky in a deluge. For a moment, the sick song of the lich-lords drowned out the golden voice of the woman whose ghostly sobbing called him forward, to the top of that mad darkness. The sky swarmed with lich-lords, black contrails against a dark sky. If death was the answer to the question of life, then undeath was the question reframed to turn the answer into a corollary: an existence fueled by the energies that brought an end to the living. Death rewritten as life.

Is that freedom?

The scrambling figures of Death Boys and Charnel Girls dashed toward the cluster of towers directly beneath the spiraling black clouds, and when Cooper pushed forward, the woman's voice returned like a shaft of sunlight. It pierced him. Vaulting atop an exposed girder, Cooper clawed at his ears.

He stumbled and fell from the girder. It wasn't a long fall and trash absorbed most of the impact, but it dazed him, and he could do nothing but listen to the dueling musics that clashed over his head, one sunlit aria drowned out by a symphony of grave dirt and shadows. The faces of Death Boys and Charnel Girls flickered across his vision, concerned or curious or scornful, but he couldn't make his eyes focus properly. He followed the lines of life and death until they reached a crescendo, and Cooper's body spasmed.

Then he left his body altogether.

Like a gunshot, Cooper's senses erupted from his body with bullet speed: sight and sound soared out of his skull and wheeled away, past the variable sky, piercing the rind of the world to flow into a kind of dimensionless non-space, an empty fullness that blanketed the universes and hid them from one another. Flattened and ghostly, Cooper flowed through the connective tissue of the metaverse. His disembodied consciousness rattled through impossible places, and time was his darling—he could soar through the nothingness as he pleased and only picoseconds passed in the real world.

The real world? Cooper's ghost scoffed. *The real world is a fairy tale.*

Seven spheres of light appeared, orbiting a common center. In the same way he knew anything here, Cooper knew that the spheres were only spheres in the most abstract sense, and that their orbits were less actual than illustrative, and that their common center was one of *identity* rather than *mass*.

Still, the spheres beguiled him with the tactile immediacy of physical objects, and he watched, fascinated, as they coruscated with the colors of life: yellow sun and green leaf and the steely refractions of rippling water. These were worlds, universes, realities—seven discrete realms of existence that were home to a single culture and thus linked by bonds more abiding than the laws of physics.

How do I know that? Cooper wondered, though he already knew the answer. *This is the work a shaman does, isn't it? Walking between worlds, visiting the worlds beyond death for the good of the living.* He could blame the liches and their captive, if he returned to his body.

Cooper drifted closer to the Seven Silvers, hearing the name as the worlds drew his focus, until something tugged at him, clawing at his . . . body? No, not body—he had no body here, just information coded into the ether—*signal* was the right word. He was a signal. And the signal that was Cooper had just found a receiver, something voltaic that sucked him into the closest sphere with a magnetic attraction. Helpless to resist or control his movement, Cooper saw only flashes of the world he entered: streaking past brown skies crossed with teal lightning; a dark hollow looming like an impact crater; a coiled serpent with a woman's torso; a nest of restless synthetic spindles; black claws so thin he could see the sky through the blades, like obsidian. Then Cooper was gone, an echo inhabiting a machine.

Her Majesty the Cicatrix, *Regina Afflicta,* Matron of the Seven Silvers, Childe of Air and Darkness, and Queen of the Court of Scars had been partially inorganic for centuries, continuing a trend that had begun as minor enhancements, barely more than accessories that flattered her vanity with brass and coke. The fashion had started as an ironic condescension toward that least enchanting of mortal endeavors, *science,* but had sublimed into a practice that eclipsed the mystical arts before absorbing them entirely.

Now the queen lifted her massive helmed head and sniffed at the air. It was her native element, but the winds had discharged unusual energies of late. She smelled nothing except the dried loam and weeds that bedraggled her barren enclosure. Ozone, when the lightning hit, arcing down her coiled spine.

The Court of Scars had been excavated to accommodate the queen's ever-increasing bulk: gone were the moonflower vines and mountainous rhododendrons that once adorned the bower of her court, and the wild cress that had carpeted the earth had long ago been crushed by the sinuations of the royal exoskeleton. Only the bounding ring of sentinel oaks that surrounded the court remained, skeletal. The sky flickered with lightning that followed straight lines and perpendicular branches, as if the clouds themselves had been seeded with circuitry.

The Cicatrix yawned a silent scream, silver grills cracking apart to let her tongue taste the air.

From this nest she had ruled an alliance of seven universes for ten thousand years, faerie worlds united beneath her banner ages ago by charisma and threats and a willpower that had extinguished suns. Today, none of her vassals would recognize the beauty who conquered them clad in naught but glee and blood: her remainder lay coiled like a dragon atop its hoard, dark graphene and vinyl stitched together with rivets and industrial adhesive, her tiny dancer's body hacked apart and stuffed inside armor crafted into the shape of a great serpent. Grasping appendages studded her length and facilitated some movement, but for the most part the queen had sacrificed her mobility to her technological addiction: there was always more machine to add to the monster.

Her arm jerked of its own accord, a vivisistors shorting out briefly while its occupant tried to communicate. Her little engines spoke to her, an annoying and persistent defect that manifested throughout her systems, and she'd learned to ignore the occasional errant impulse.

"*M1sstresss mine!*" called out the pixie powering the servo where the Cicatrix's shoulder joint had been, streaming verse through wiring that terminated inside her skull. "*It sings to us again from the garden of* El Cíudad

Tácito, *and it brings us a visitor::login:guestnotfound! Gray bird sings a harmony, m1lady, and the navel of a11 worlds inhabits us as 1t s0 sadly singsss! Your Light Music Machine, my qu33n::login:xxMyQueenSoScarre dxx . . . Your Golden Apppppple! In tone s0 sad, in voice s0 ancient, in volume 5o greatttttt—"*

Despite the slithering length of her abdomen, the queen's torso remained relatively humanoid, corseted in metal and plastic but still a recognizably womanly shape; she'd replaced her auburn curls with a towering headpiece of shining black, twin horns like a giant dung beetle twisting toward the sky while braided cables cascaded down the back of her neck, connecting her helm to the bulk of her machine components.

The Cicatrix kept one hand unadorned to proclaim her fey heritage to any being unlucky enough to be brought before her, and she raised that hand now, demanding silence. Proprioceptive relays made verbal communication with her systems unnecessary—the pixie in her shoulder fell silent with a whisper of static terror. Unaware that Cooper surged through her systems, the Cicatrix bared her metal teeth in a silver smile.

The vivisistors suspended within her polyvinyl chassis transfixed only the rarest of fey creatures—a perversion of loyalty kept the Cicatrix from employing any other kind of servant, within or without her body. She knew that Lolly had uncovered the truth about the magitechnical composition of the vivisistor design, but the child remained ignorant of the number and composition of her mother's upgrades: Lolly might well revolt if she knew that her own little fey cousins had been used to power the queen's vivisistors, or how aggressively the Cicatrix had been upgrading herself since her daughter's deployment to the City Unspoken.

Something Cooper-derived bootstrapped itself into a state of minimal awareness, flickering between vivisistors that wound along the coiled length of the faerie queen, which looked something like an ink-black subway train wound up in a curl, with a woman at one end. A mile-long mermaid machine, black as coal and flickering with Tesla arcs. He struggled to gain consciousness and found himself by focusing on his host's fears, piggybacking across her thoughts. Alien thoughts. As he incorporated himself into her cognition, the active part of Cooper calmly observed that the mind he inhabited seemed to consider itself the mother of the

Marchioness Terenz-de-Guises, and that the mind belonged to a monster. Elsewhere, Cooper's dormant majority screamed.

But the part of him taking this electronic spirit walk acknowledged the maternal horror and moved on, following the narrative of the queen's fear that Lallowë Thyu had not improved upon some kind of programming language that the Cicatrix herself had improvised. The queen—and therefore Cooper also—considered that language, which she used to program her vivisistors.

Her code was by necessity feral and half-formed; there were no guides to this work, and all of her usual resources were useless: no epic poetry recited in the Court of Scars detailed the recursive spells of If-Then and Let-X-Equal that would breathe true life into the vivisistor design. Yet she hoped that Lolly, possessed of the combined gifts from her human father and the compulsive genius that so resembled the queen's own, would discover the language to unlock the potential of the technology—and emerge with a vivisistor that would be a far more significant device than the half-aware batteries that currently powered her armaments.

Armaments that were needed to keep the eons at bay, as well as to provide the Cicatrix with new and more appealing diversions in these latter days. The true Wild Hunt was long gone, fractured and refractured across time as well as space, and although its denizens had seeded a hundred cultures of barbarism and wild magic, the rule of the Unseelie Court was a thing of near prehistory. The Unseelie champion—the Queen of Air and Darkness—died ages before with no successor, and no one remembered her true name to summon so much as a ghost, not even ancient fairies such as the once-spindly dancer, now corseted with metal and braided with optical cables, who had become a queen in her own right.

Farther down the length of her body, another vivisistor bucked as its prisoner whispered through the wires: *"All we caged birds hear the same song, my queen. And you hear it t00, while the Omphale gnaws through your sacred fruit. . . ."*

She lashed out with a pulse of electricity that whipped through the inside of her body and silenced the offending device, but the trapped thing was correct, she *could* feel them out there, across the worlds—the other vivisistors, the old ones. She'd begun to sense them years ago, but as her systems improved so too did the signal—*old* machines, vivisistors that predated the rise of the Third People.

That shouldn't be; yet somehow every vivisistor in existence—so far as the queen could determine—was linked together with its peers via some oblique tunneling protocol into a background network she could not disable, and while this latent network didn't interfere with her benchmarks and diagnostics, a persistent hiss of feedback lingered no matter how she configured her modules. She could still hear the others, even the minuscule surveillance drone she'd hidden with Lallowë years before. And the one she'd sent, only recently, with the dragonfly inside—she'd heard that dragonfly die, and it had disquieted her.

The Cicatrix could hear them all, and Cooper heard them with her. One vivisistor in particular loomed larger than the rest, its song a constant presence in the back of the queen's head, and its energy signal shone brighter than a hundred stars. A golden apple that dazzled her from somewhere within the City Unspoken. It glittered with a greater concentration of power than she'd ever witnessed, and even though it hung like a golden fruit just out of her reach, it fed her with its light.

Vivisistor? The ghost of Cooper scanned the queen's thoughts and marveled. *How am I here, and how am I hidden inside this creature?* He could feel the pain of sentient beings close by, calling out for peace. Little winged men and cat-paw ladies; smooth-groined nullos and butterfly-crotched *oni*: all in pain, each begging for death.

Green and lilac LEDs danced up the Cicatrix's side, forming a tattoo of peonies and mandrake. The sprites whose slow deaths powered her HUD flashed poetry across her field of vision, obscuring her inactive targeting reticle:

> He kn0ws a secret sector,
> We share a partial place.
> Where is it always w1nter,
> And iv0ry, old lace!

Nonsense. More and more of it lately, clogging her systems with digitized doggerel and fancies that were not her own—always with a call for stillness. And yet she heard the same nonsense bubbling from the mouths of her attendants, her governors, everywhere. From all corners of the Seven Silvers came whispers of secrets and madness, always distant, always growing nearer; a panic built itself all around her, within her and without, muddling her own systems as well as her satraps and coteries. Every level seemed affected—even her Wild Hunters returned most days with more fear than flesh, wide-eyed and unwilling to voice their troubles. They, too, seemed gripped by a need for stillness—a relic virtue she could ill afford—and sat empty-eyed beside their fires, mouths moving as if in prayer.

Some days, the Cicatrix felt the pain of all the worlds.

The hunters of the Seven Silvers were creatures who had always existed as the embodiment of nature's frenzy. Few of them had ever felt unsettled before, let alone afraid—even when she'd forced them to follow her example and upgrade their natural bodies with synthetic components. No, anything that could disturb her nest of blade-boned serpents and polymer wasps merited more than a little vigilance—it was hardly alarmist for the queen to be worried by anything that could worry dark fairies in their own wood.

Nothing mattered other than devouring that enormous vivisistor signal, whatever it was, that eluded her somewhere beneath the chaotic skies of the City Unspoken. She *would* make it a part of herself, or consume its essence, or its secrets. If trouble was coming, the kind of worlds-shaking trouble that her instincts, her vivisistor-sprites, and her subjects seemed to suggest—even the ones insane enough to accuse *her* of causing the trouble— then the Cicatrix wanted the protection she imagined would be afforded by incorporating that enormous energy signature into her own array. And if Lolly failed her, then her pet liches would split the city like an apple so she could suck out its golden pulp.

Where am I, and how? Cooper flickered from node to node inside the Cicatrix, trying to escape something he didn't understand. Was he *inside* this thing? Was he hallucinating again? Cooper knew he was not, and yet he'd heard her think of herself as Lallowë Thyu's *mother,* and at least a little bit *robot.* The queen didn't seem to notice him, but the little people trapped inside these awful little battery-machines might—they whimpered in helpless supplication.

Why, Cooper thought, *does this keep happening to me?*

A pinging blip at the edge of the queen's vision interrupted her thoughts—and Cooper's. An automated signal from Lallowë's surveillance unit—the fool girl thought herself unobserved, though she should know better. Contingencies within contingencies, that was the only way to play the game. The Cicatrix summoned the signal into her field of vision, although she already knew its contents.

So the girl had begun building her own vivisistor, exactly as she was expected to do. She'd resorted to asking her father for help, which ought to have humiliated her. Perhaps it did. Or perhaps the Cicatrix had chosen the wrong daughter to remove from the board. Almondine, perhaps, should be awakened. If only the third daughter had been true fey, instead of inheriting her brutal father's humanity. That was a contingency plan the Cicatrix would like to have had.

Oh, thought Cooper, with a detached nausea that brought more of himself online by reflex. *Machines that feed on life. A family of evil faeries, starring Lallowë Thyu. A cyborg queen with the body of a Chinese dragon, who wants to devour the chewy center of the City Unspoken. Of fucking course.*

Flexing the spirit-muscle he'd only just begun to learn he possessed, Cooper extended a tendril of his self and contacted one of the nodes—the vivisistors, she'd called them—and peeked inside. A miniature man with moth wings and the mangy remains of a blue pelt lay inside, skewered through his middle by a metal pin. A pixie, Cooper recognized/realized/learned, abetted by the hijacked thoughts of the queen, and a diseased-looking pixie at that. His tiny hands clutched the pin that impaled him; the little thorns at the tips of his fingers had splintered against it.

I am so sorry, little insect man. Cooper spoke to the creature as easily as if he'd still had a throat. *I know nothing, but I promise to help you if I can.*

The pixie jerked his head toward the source of Cooper's signal. His eyes were the color of fire and the expression on his face combined outrage with agony in equal measure. These were not prisoners, Cooper realized, but volunteers.

My queen! An invader with1n the royal chassis skulks! The pixie screamed an alarm into its adjacent hardware and writhed on his pin. *13reak his 13ones of lightning 13efore he logoff::flees!*

Cooper recoiled, if that was a thing that electric souls could do. He startled himself as his previously offline horror awoke within him and immediately sought an escape from the closed system of menace that was the Cicatrix's inorganic self. As he did so, other vivisistors shook off the shroud of soul-sickness that had maddened their thoughts with the poetry of oblivion and took up the wicked pixie's call to arms.

Shit. Shit. Shit. Cooper felt nearly corporeal in his panic, banging the idea of his fists against the idea of his prison. Worlds away from his own body, trapped inside the carapace of an evil faerie monster queen, where he existed only as a ghost of information in an almost-closed computer network whose nodes were batteries made out of dying faerie, Cooper finally found his mojo.

His mojo: it didn't matter that the worlds had been built to the specifications of insanity. *He* hadn't been built that way. In fact, hadn't immutable sanity had been the *only* remarkable quality he possessed, according to the Lady? Shamanic tendencies seemed not that impressive in the Lady's eyes, but Cooper's enduring sanity, that had impressed her.

The Cicatrix lurched, raising her torso a dozen yards by rearing her most proximal coils: a chitin and graphene cobra, ready to strike. Rather than speak she hissed, a thunder of amplified feedback and simple, feral *hate*.

Cooper acknowledged that terrifying sound, but retained his self-possession. *I wonder what I might do and where I might go, if I were an electric shaman whose superpower was keeping his shit together?*

"What wight winds its way twixt our wires?" The Cicatrix beat her claws against her breast, speaking out loud to her vivisistors in case there truly *was* an intruder. "If you inconstant goblins vex us again with your prankish alarum, we shall riddle you with megavolts till your eyes pop like cherry tomatoes in the fat of a rendered babe."

She cocked her horned and plated head, sniffing at the air again. A sly smile crept across her face, a woman's features stitched onto a dragon's skull. She patted her mismatched hands together and promised:

"Hi-fi fo-*fun:* I'm going to fuck your eye sockets with my railgun."

Cooper held himself as still as a signal could stay, and considered his predicament. Considered it quickly. Inside the queen's body, he could only play hide-and-seek, and he didn't know what—if anything—she was capable of doing to his spirit should she be able to catch it, so an expedient retreat seemed his most desirable option. But to where? And how? Beating his electric fists against this cage was useless, and the vivisistors formed a closed system that led nowhere.

Except they do lead somewhere, and that's what worries her. This isn't *a closed system, not the way she wants it to be.*

The queen worried about other vivisistors, hadn't she? And how she could sense them, worlds away, even though she thought that was not supposed to be possible. If the queen could sense them, could Cooper? More importantly, could he follow them away from this place? If there was a vivisistor beneath the City Unspoken, could he follow it back?

He reached out to the mangy pixie with the fiery eyes, and felt it flicker with motor signals that coordinated the Cicatrix's movements: coils rising, claws flexing, an alien tongue licking metal teeth. He followed that bundle of awareness, sensing the vivisistors nearest. One handled input for the same nervous systems, relaying sensory information to the queen's mind: light to eyes to brain, touch to skin to brain, sound to ears to . . . *sound.*

And suddenly, Cooper could hear them all. Every vivisistor in the queen's body, dozens of them, a raucous chorus of air and darkness; the louder ones were newer installations, while older devices, the ones with less life inside them, sang more feebly. It was pandemonium. How did she function, with this many dying voices calling out inside her own body?

Cooper pushed the clamor of the queen's vivisistors to one side and listened for the others, nonlocal but somehow networked. There *were* others out there, so distant he could barely hear them. . . . A smattering spread across the worlds—those he didn't bother to trace—but one signal stood out from the background noise, and while its call was muted by distance, Cooper could sense its enormous size. There was no mistaking the giant vivisistor . . . that sang so sweetly . . . and felt like *peace.*

And so Cooper leapt. It felt like leaping, anyway; he threw himself toward the song of peace and prayed to whatever real or false gods might be watching, popcorn.gifs at the ready, to watch him fail.

8

I spent my life pursuing an understanding of death, only to languish for years in the furrow of illness. When at last the little butterfly pinned inside my chest flew free, I felt gratitude beyond measure—now the mystery, now the answers!

Who could be disappointed with the worlds we are given? I have found my countrymen (for we are all countrymen on these shores, who hail from Gaia), and they are prodigious even in this vastly larger theater, but oddly cheerless in matters concerning our original misbeliefs. It is as if the truth diminishes them, and they grieve over the smaller heavens and hells for which they had hoped or feared. They grieve for the families with which they have not been reunited, and I think it all a lingering selfishness.

All those I have loved who went before me, they live! They breathe air and live lives beneath other suns. What small mind would find fault with that? As for me, nothing stirs my spirit so much as the assurance that whatever else may happen, my family lives. And lives. And lives. I pray they work and dance in equal measure.

I thought that death meant freedom for the departing. How right was I, and how wrong.

—Elisabeth Kübler-Ross, *On Life and Living*

"All this death!" exclaimed Purity when she and Kaien reached the little freestanding aviary that sat halfway between the safety of her own quarters and the Petite Malaison. Guardsmen lay scattered like leaves, their bodies mutilated, their precious armor cut to pieces. Servants too, liveryman and attachés piled atop seamstresses and elderly housekeepers, all killed in the same fashion—sliced with a long blade, judging by the length of the wounds and the severed limbs. Purity pulled Kaien into the celadon-tiled atrium to survey the carnage. Maybe two dozen bodies, give or take an arm. The birds feasted on the corpses but rose in a varicolored cloud of winged music as Purity and Kaien descended into their midst; the high alarum rang on.

Kaien grimaced as Purity tutted and picked her way through the corpses, lifting her skirts and playing a game of keeping her satin slippers away from the pooling blood. *She's already covered in rock dust, why bother?* Kaien had never understood women well, but it was clear that Purity plunged his ignorance to new depths—in the short while he'd known her, she'd proven herself at once proper and apocryphal, dainty and brutish, naïve and yet full of devilment.

Kaien watched Purity—so gemlike in aquamarine and yellow-gold hair—traipse amidst the scattered bodies with a dumbfounded look on his face. Once, as a child, he'd witnessed a five-ton chunk of limestone crush a man, a mason, and had been fascinated at the shapes the blood made as it squirted out of the body. Afterward, Kaien had cried with shame at the fact that he'd been calm enough to make such observations; his father had told him those tears were mortar, and the sight of the dead man the first brick in a strong wall.

But he'd never seen . . . never even *considered* this kind of violence. Kaien wasn't sure his wall was strong enough, and yet Purity seemed wholly unaffected—in fact, she only put her hand to her forehead in distress when blood ran between the tiles and stained her shoe. Was this how they lived? Were murder and Murder and sights like these just another part of their world, along with balls and business and tournaments, arranged marriages and arranged accidents?

"How many of these souls are body-bound?" Kaien asked, curious about the level of collateral damage the nobility were permitted—or noticed.

Purity heard the question with half an ear and shrugged. "At least half, I would imagine. The praetors are supposed to be bound—although it's been so long since anyone killed one that I can't say for sure. Let's hope for their sakes they didn't get lackadaisical with their enchanting. The servants, I fear, will not be bound—the upper echelons of those in noble employ, your heads of staff, your chief housekeepers, stewards, and the like—they will have been bound as a practical matter. But these all wear the prince's colors. Unlike the guards, it's likely that most of them

will have moved on." She bent to lift the bloodless wrist of a young scullery maid off the green tiles, then let it flop back.

"This one is gone," she said of the poor woman. Purity made a funny
gesture with her hands that Kaien didn't recognize.

"How can you tell?" He scratched at his close-shaved black hair.

"Can't you feel it?" Purity realized too late that not every child of the
City Unspoken benefited from the education she'd enjoyed. Bells, for that
matter neither did half her peers. Again, Purity silently thanked her father.
"The body feels different when the soul hasn't fled, it vibrates almost. You
get the feel for it if you touch enough bodies or if you kill yourself all the
time." She looked away, embarrassed.

"I'll skip that lesson, I think." Kaien paled.

Purity flashed her winningest smile. "Of course, Kaien, so would I
have," she lied, "if I'd had a choice." Men don't like to feel inferior, she had
to remind herself, and not all men had the Baron's unimpeachable self-
regard. Then again, not all men had Kaien's square jaw and kind eyes. *Oh
Purity, stop it.* She pinched the skin of her forearm, hard. *This is scarcely
the time to nurture a crush.*

"So is this madness why the alarm was sounded, or did the alarm bring
these guards and servants rushing to their deaths?" Kaien asked, trying
to address the situation the way his father would, with unflappable calm
and constructive reasoning, the classic Masonic temperament. Kaien felt
less classic, but he tried.

"That's an excellent question," Purity said, hopping over a body and
putting her hand on Kaien's chest for balance. *Oh my, that's firm.*

Kaien steadied Purity with a dark hand upon her waist and thought
much the same thing.

"Won't this cause an uproar?"

Purity shrugged, unable to skirt the ambivalence toward life that per-
vaded every level of her society. "Unlikely. There will be a mighty flap of
gossip, certainly. But an uproar? Wrong crowd."

Kaien cursed. "Bells, Purity, what does it take to get a reaction from you
bloodless people?"

She had the decency to blush but couldn't stop herself from answering
honestly. "Well, so long as no one's committed an atrocity in the apiary as

well, we should manage. Disturb the birdsong *and* the florists, however, and the courtly ladies shall rebel spectacularly."

Kaien looked at her crosswise. "I want you to tell me you're kidding, Purity, but I have the sinking feeling you won't."

"Because I'm not." She pulled an apologetic face. "Admittedly, I have a terrible memory for names and titles. Absolutely wretched. It's a running joke among the luncheon set, but rather less worthy of taunts is my knowledge of courtly history. Most of my friends would rather kill one another over the cut of their sleeves than pick up a book."

Maybe that explains the business with the shoes and the blood. Bells, why was he trying so hard to find fault with this girl? Maybe she simply didn't want blood on her feet! *They* are *lovely feet, after all.* And was it her fault if Purity was inured to atrocity?

"But if they bothered to turn a page once in a while," Purity continued, "they'd remember the Ladies' Most Insistent Uprising or the Lysistratic Filibuster, both of which ended with bloodshed among the opposition and victory for the women. Now help me *up.*"

Kaien offered no argument. She set one foot upon the lip of an urn, heedless of the impatiens that suffered beneath her slipper, and held out her arm for Kaien to steady.

"What are you doing?" he asked as he supported her arm and—for the second time, now—her waist. Purity made no protest as his hand squeezed her middle, and Kaien again questioned his judgment. *That's twice too many opportunities to manhandle a highborn lady.*

"I'm trying something my brother's tutor mentioned." She pulled herself up and away from Kaien's grip. Half-hanging from a branch, Purity took a survey of the room and remembered what it was that Pomeroy's martial instructor had said about the advantages of high ground.

"Your tutor mentioned climbing garden trees in satin slippers?"

Purity scrunched up her face and pointed toward the entrance that she and Kaien had used. "See? The culprit or culprits went that way, and they came in from . . . over there." She pointed toward the other exit. "The guards were following from behind and engaged the suspect *here,* but he cut them down before they could assume a defensive stance. Or an offensive stance, for that matter—this was *quick,* Kaien. See the way the bodies are scattered in a circle? Praetors fight in tight formation, but these guards are all akimbo, cut down in a line as they ran."

Kaien nodded with respect. "That's an impressive reading."

"I'm not finished. The servants are all either on top of the guards or got tangled up in their mess." Purity pointed to some smears of blood by an old man in royal livery, who looked like he had slipped on the blood-slick tiles before having his throat cut. "So I'm guessing that the guards were disposed of before the servants. The killer must have fought off the guards before being interrupted by . . . bells, a dozen servants?"

"Why would a dozen servants chase after a maniac?"

"They *wouldn't*." Purity didn't have a better answer than that, except that from what she could see through the gore, most of the dead servants were seamstresses, milliners, and tailors. Curious, that a cadre of servants whose duties were limited to dressmaking and suit-sizing would gang-rush a killer who'd just felled half a regiment of praetorian guardsmen. Why in the worlds would they do that? She twitched her skirts and hopped down.

One erstwhile seamstress clutched a spindle of bright yellow thread. Purity blinked rapidly and picked up the spool, pocketing it with her body turned so Kaien didn't see. *Surely not.*

Then something moved atop a pile of corpses, interrupting her train of thought. Kaien knelt and wiped blood from the mouth of a young apprentice tailor. Despite the razor cut that nearly butterflied his breast-bone, the young man clung to life. Resting her hand on Kaien's shoulder, Purity glanced down at the wounded boy and saw he would not cling much longer.

"I'm very thirsty, sir," the tailor's apprentice said, his voice quiet and respectful and so, so small.

"I've got you," Kaien fretted over the dying child. "You're going to be just fine. Just fine, I promise."

"Kaien." Purity squeezed his shoulder; she didn't want to upset him further, but they hadn't the time to comfort the lost. "No, Kaien, he isn't going to be fine. I'm sorry."

"Fuck off!" Kaien shouted, shrugging off her hand and glaring at her through tears. "Fuck *this*! You look like men and women but you have hearts of ice. You have empty veins. You deserve prison, all of you—you belong in a cage much worse than this."

"Kaien . . ." But what could she say? She agreed.

"So fast . . ." coughed the boy as his lungs filled up with blood. He fixed Purity with a stare. "Darn her."

Kaien shook his head as the boy left behind his body, milk spilled from a pitcher. "He shouldn't be like this, Purity. Boys too young to even *curse* shouldn't be cut in two. Your kind is a cancer."

Cooper shot into the City Unspoken like a bullet, smearing himself across its inconstant sky. He hit his body, full stop, sixty-to-zero, and opened his eyes. Marvin's eyes were inches from his own, and Cooper knew with a sickening change of perspective that only seconds had passed, though it seemed like he'd been out of his body for hours.

He said nothing, brushing himself off and holding his head, which pounded. He could no longer sense the vivisistors now that he was back in his body. He looked toward the Dome with a sense of unease.

"Cooper? Answer me!"

"Sorry. What?" Cooper forced himself to look at Marvin, made his face look casual.

"Are you a hypoglycemic or something?" Marvin asked. "Do you need a cookie?"

Cooper couldn't tell if Marvin was being sincere or mocking him. He said so.

Marvin rolled his eyes and smiled. "Follow me, and be more careful."

Cooper did follow the Death Boy, head ringing, up flights and flights of stairs cut open to the sky, thinking all the while of machine faeries and transistors powered by living things. Up and up they climbed, the city dropping away through the crumbled walls, till Cooper's breath ached in his chest. He muttered something about the physical endurance of sexy zombies.

"You think we're *undead*?" Marvin cawed, as if that were the stupidest thing he'd ever heard. "You must have hit your head harder than it looked—we're the only beings in this city who truly live!"

"I just meant . . ." Cooper blushed and looked down at his feet. The

Cicatrix lingered in his mind like the aftereffect of a bad dream, but he pushed her away. "Sesstri said you worshiped liches. If I remember my pen-and-paper lore correctly, that means you worship undead, um, wizards . . . I guess." Cooper heard what he was saying and cringed. "I mean, that's from books and games and stuff. What do I know about life? Unlife. Whatever."

Marvin stroked Cooper's scalp, and Cooper's eyes rolled back in their sockets like an ear-scratched dog. "The skylords are that, yes, and yeah . . . it's hard to believe at first. But they are also *so* much more, Cooper—they are lords of flight and freedom, and they are willing to *share* with us. The rest of us, the Undertow, we're very much alive, Cooper. In a little while, I will show you exactly how alive I am."

He paused, then flashed a shrewd look in Cooper's direction.

"A piece of advice for a newcomer: words that sound like wisdom usually *aren't*. Especially in the City Unspoken. The spirits that infect this city will try to confuse you by blurring the lines between life and death. It's only by deluding themselves that they can stave off oblivion. Don't let them make you a coconspirator in their fantasy. This is a place of death. Death's capital. This is the bottom of the pit, Cooper, and the only way out is up." He pointed through the open wall to the black clouds spiraling overhead. "Freedom."

Marvin sat Cooper down for a rest break on the fifty-third floor of the rusting tower, according to a stenciled numeral, and they dangled their legs over the long fall. Marvin passed Cooper a joint of something sticky and green, and Cooper was happy to get slowly stoned and feel the simple heat of Marvin's body beside him, watching a brown dwarf sun ease its way into the horizon. The city spread itself out before him, a great bowl of urbanity painted ochre by the failed star. Cooper mused over the nature of the sky, and decided that the city borrowed skies from other worlds because it had none of its own. He felt it unlikely that he'd get a more satisfactory answer.

He *did* know there were more ways out of the city than through the lich-lords, but he didn't want to tell Marvin about that. He didn't want to tell Marvin *anything* about the accidental spirit walk he'd taken, or the denuded faerie garden whose machine queen he'd . . . visited. So far as the Death Boy knew, Cooper had hit his head on a girder and fainted, and that was that; Cooper saw the glint of suspicion in Marvin's eyes, though, as if he knew that there was more going on in Cooper's head, but wasn't confident enough to say so.

Marvin made a groan that was halfway between awkward and sexy. "I knew you for a New Yorker asshole the minute I saw you in that Danzig shirt."

Cooper nodded, just stoned enough not to be surprised, much. "You too?"

Marvin snaked his arm through Cooper's and tilted his head onto Cooper's shoulder. "Denver. I was a big Misfits fan, Black Flag, Samhain."

"Okay, cool." Cooper smiled, though Marvin couldn't see him.

"I was waiting for their first album, in '88, but I . . . didn't make it."

"Oh. Sorry." What was the protocol for talking about someone's deaths? Sympathy? Congratulations? "That must have been a shock. It shocked me, waking here."

"There are a lot of us in the Undertow, you know. Young men from Earth, from the '80s, the '90s. . . ."

"Uh-huh." Cooper looked at Marvin sideways, not understanding.

"It started . . . maybe thirty years ago? We found our way to the city, each of us—it called to me, sort of. After what happened to us, nowhere else seemed to fit. Our other lives didn't . . . they didn't *work,* not after . . . how we . . ." Marvin trailed off.

"What are you trying to say?" This side of Marvin was new. His eyes looked haunted.

"Young men die all the time, I don't know why we'd be special. Maybe we're not." Marvin tried to smile, but the corners of his mouth pulled down; he was holding back tears. "It was just sex, but to us it was the first taste of freedom and life and . . . and it killed us." Marvin lifted his hands in a helpless gesture.

Cooper didn't understand. And then, with a rush of insight, he understood far, far too well. He'd been living under this shadow his entire life. "HIV?" he asked, weirdly insulted that such an Earthly problem could crop up here, amidst magic and evil cyborg faerie queens.

"We had just started to be allowed to live, and it was the living that killed us." Marvin looked lost. "Imagine that the sun shone black. It . . .

did something, to me at least . . . we invented a new kind of scar, and it brought us to the skylords, in search of our stolen freedom." Marvin seemed to deflate. "And we're worlds away, still in closets, still fucking in a circle around death, still struggling to fly away. Young and broken forever: be careful what you wish for, Cooper."

Marvin shrugged and tossed the last of the joint into the air and watched it spin. "It will be time to dance soon, we should head up to the roof."

"Dance?" Cooper asked, suddenly queasy. "I don't really . . . dance."

Marvin pulled him up the last few stories. "Don't be scared. Hestor is happy I brought you—he's hoping that stealing the marchioness' prized childborn will set him above Killilly. The Charnel Girls are already jealous." Hestor was the Death Boy chieftain, Cooper knew: Marvin had mentioned him before with a frightened kind of awe.

Cooper stepped out onto a rooftop party that could have been in Manhattan, except for the fires that blazed from neighboring towers and the cold storm overhead. Trash cans burnt like torches, and wine and smoke were everywhere. Marvin pointed to a terror of a man who could only be Hestor—surrounded by a circle of admirers, he sported a tawny crest of hair shaved close at the sides, a vest spiked with pieces of bone, and plastic louvered sunglasses. He glared out from between the Beach-Boy-yellow slits with a menacing alchemy of attitude, and even from across the rooftop Cooper could feel Hestor's eyes latch onto him, the prize.

"Our power is shamanic, like yours." Marvin looked at him, waiting. "We both cross the lines between life and death—we just don't quite come all the way back. Hestor values your shamanic potential."

"Ah." Cooper could not quite pretend to be pleased. "Another fan."

Someone began pounding a drum, then another, and another, and the mood of the Undertow shifted. The small groups engaging in muted conversation broke apart, the Death Boys and Charnel Girls separating into two groups. Some began hooting—all looked excited, and their anticipation trebled the air.

"Who *else* is your fan?" Marvin asked with a bit of an edge. "The pink-haired lady?"

"Ha!" Cooper shook his head. "She knows better—Sesstri's the one who decided I was just a turd. I'm starting to think I'd be better off if she'd been right."

"Cooper, don't say that." No edge now, just an arm slinking through his, elbows locking.

"Her words, not mine," Cooper said.

"Well, I think you're *not* a turd." The smoke on Marvin's breath smelled good. Warm. Alive.

"Do you?" Cooper pulled Marvin close. "I think that's premature."

Marvin took Cooper's chin and brought their faces together. Noses brushing. A kiss.

After a long, long moment Cooper broke away. "Yeah. You think I'm a shaman. You want to feed me to your lichly masters." He made it sound like a joke, but knew it wasn't.

Marvin rubbed his forehead against Cooper's. "That isn't how it works."

"But you're still going to hurt me, aren't you?" The question came out as a whisper.

Marvin looked out over the city, and Cooper followed the arrow of his gaze—the view here was the opposite of that from Sesstri's rooftop terrace: the Dome lorded over a quarter of the horizon, of course, but from here they could see the karst-hill volcano of the Apostery as well as the wide bowl and set-piece houses of Bonseki-sai. Cooper saw the yellow hills near Rind and Displacement, one of which had been his landing pad in this anti-Oz.

Marvin disarmed him with a cheap smile. "Hurt happens, Cooper. Sometimes the best you can do is to direct it."

"That isn't reassuring, Marvin."

"Would false reassurance be a kindness? Come on." He pulled Cooper with him, toward the gyre of whirling Charnel Girls and Death Boys, the two living thirds of the Undertow. The sky surged with their undead complement, dripping darkness in black rain that pooled underfoot. The air was cold and the fires were hot; Cooper felt more alive than usual.

Maybe Marvin's right. Maybe by abandoning the dance of lives, they truly live. Live free.

They dove into the madness hand-in-hand, Marvin's spine loosening itself with ecstatic energy and unchoreographed abandon. Cooper thanked the green smoke still pulsing through his veins, and began to yield to the ritual, the rave, whatever this was—a black-mass flash-mob dance.

The drum beat wildly and Cooper found himself bending to its rhythm despite himself, eyelids half-closed, raising his arms with the sweat-soaked Death Boys in a wordless paean to the heart-dark masters who circled overhead. The liches themselves Cooper could not see, but the black wraiths of energy they radiated flapped all around the Undertow now; the air grew thick with undead tailwinds and crazed, beautiful dancers.

The Death Boys formed an impromptu circle around their leader, who stood naked, save his vest and glasses. Hestor's cock was hard and red, and he gloated while his boys hooted and cried, imploring their lich-lords to take them above, to give them flight. On another corner of roof-top the Charnel Girls had formed their own ring with Killilly a wild-eyed valkyrie at their center.

Hestor lifted his arms to the sky and the black rain fell on him like India ink. He opened his mouth and the rain did something to the tattoo inside his lip—dark lines of tattoo ink began to pour down his chin and spread unnaturally across his collarbone, coiling in a rococo flourish that expanded across his bare chest. He sang to the sky, a hymn of wrong notes and backward progressions—anywhere else in the worlds his voice would have offended the ears, but here it fit—and Hestor was transformed into an Orpheus. Wrongness swaddled them. When the ink trails curled across Hestor's shoulders and climbed the skin of his raised arms, the Death Boy leader unleashed a triumphant cry—the tattoos coursed up his arms and around his hands until the ink spilled out of his skin and shot up into the sky—and when Hestor's tattoo ink met the dark whips of the lich-lords' tails, a shockwave burst across the roof.

Cooper gasped—the power of the Undertow rolled over him in a fusion of living lust and undead appetites. An intoxicating combination that compelled him to follow the urges of the clan, muting any other thoughts. He became part of the host of black-eyed sirens that circled, crying out to the sky.

"Tonight you fly with the Death Boys." Someone grabbed his shoulder and shouted, "Tonight you learn what it means to *live*!"

The lich-tails were everywhere now, curling about their legs and arms, teasing their waists before whipping back up into the turbulence above.

As one, the Death Boys screeched their pledges, begged their night-masters for favor, and Cooper screamed with them. To his right, a tall Death Boy with a mop of corn-yellow hair and bloodshot eyes caught hold of a lich-tail as it solidified out of the bristling shadow, and for a heartbeat he locked eyes with Cooper. Then he vanished, ripped away into the sky with a shriek.

Like sharks to a frenzy, the lich-tails sought out the living with a hunger. One by one, the Death Boys around him caught their tails and rose, hooting with glee and devotion. Cooper heard similar cries from the Charnel Girls across the roof. Marvin grabbed his waist and pulled him close, breath urgent against his cheek.

"Hold on, childborn, or you'll fall forever," he warned, and Cooper wrapped his arms around Marvin's rib cage.

Then he felt a cold snake whip around his thigh, his chest, his arms—and the rooftop dropped away. They flew through blasts of inky wind that shocked him with their coldness, as though his life bled out through his pores to fill the deathly vacuum.

Marvin's cock pressed through their clothes, steel-hard despite the frigid wind, or because of it. Cooper felt the heat against him and shuddered—part lust, part terror. Then they banked to one side and rolled over again and again in a spin of yaw, and all thoughts of Marvin's body flew from his head.

The thrill was electric, opiate, and Cooper understood how the flight-fever held the Death Boys in thrall. Marvin was right about at least one thing—this *was* freedom. They'd found the razor's edge, an adrenaline-junkie's wet dream, whirling through the dark on the coattails of un-death's midnight minions. Cooper cackled into the gale and clutched at Marvin with all his strength. He cried into the air and again knew that no one heard him, but he did not want to care.

Then Marvin did the strangest thing. He stroked Cooper's cheek with one free hand, which shouldn't have been possible—what was holding them together?—and kissed Cooper softly on the lips. Tears were pouring down Marvin's face now and Cooper kissed him back, hungry, but Marvin turned his head aside.

"This is what we live for," he whispered into Cooper's ear, kissing his way gently down his neck. Cooper saw the City Unspoken sprawling be-low him, lights flickering, rolling on and on as far as his eye could see. From on high the Dome almost looked small, cradled at the heart of the land by the concave bowl of the city's crust. They fit one another some-how, the Dome and the concave metropolis, the pieces of a design you couldn't see without a perspective larger than life, the vantage of gods and undead hurricanes.

Marvin continued to kiss his neck while the ground spun away. Marvin purred against Cooper, their bodies fitting together like the Dome and the city—strange and electric. Cooper felt the full attraction of the Undertow, and its pull was tidal. The exhilarations of undeath seemed limitless, less about natural laws and more about . . . conceit. It wasn't living, not a mo-ment of it, was it? Charcoal smudges and splattered red ink, light welling up from below, casting strange shadows on a darker sky.

"Do you feel undeath, Cooper?" Marvin's voice gained a strange echo, a papery lisp dubbed over his natural snarl. "Do you feel it slithering up your thigh? Wrapping its arms around you? Kissing your neck, right here?"

"Oh, god, yes. It's not life at all, is it?"

"No, it's not," Marvin agreed, while the echo cackled.

"It's not life. It's art."

Marvin's cock was a hot brand against Cooper's hip. "I knew you'd see it," he hissed.

"It's not *good* art, but it's art."

Cooper pushed Marvin's face away and let his response die into the shrieking wind. Fuck, this felt good. Cooper's life bled out of his heel and into the undead thing hiding above, his head spun high above towers ruled by emaciated poseurs, and somehow it all felt so wonderfully good. Black tar champagne sex, cut into lines.

As he and Marvin gnawed upon each other, Cooper tasted the red thread of Marvin's story. He could *taste* the truth: a black streak of run-ning with the Death Boys, and before that a short life under a red sky, before that a sickness, before the sickness there was rage, before the rage came ecstasy, the ecstasy followed a period of torture and fear, and be-fore that was nothing. Marvin's lives, reduced to simple flavors, were so easy to digest.

Cooper tasted America. Mall food from the '70s, cheap noodles and expensive vodka in the '80s. Lots and lots of sex, followed quickly by death. There was more.

Then they fell, and Cooper's stomach interrupted his trance on its way to his throat. Cooper made a strangled sound.

"Are you all right?" Marvin asked as he rolled himself to catch the brunt of the landing.

Then the hard roof knocked the breath from them both, and by the time Cooper sat upright Marvin was standing, straddling his body and pointing at Cooper in a kind of glee. Though his vision spun, Cooper saw Hestor, still panting from his dance and flight, leaning against a half-crumbled wall, sucking on his teeth with eyes that already looked bored.

Cooper pushed himself up onto his forearms, all thought crushed from him by the impact. Looking up at Marvin, he saw a pretty, damaged man who offered him momentary tenderness. He harbored no illusions about Marvin's loyalties, and he knew he couldn't *trust* him, but the Death Boy offered him physical affection and the semblance of comfort, and those were commodities Cooper could not bring himself to reject. Not even if Marvin bartered intimacy for some greater reward from his tribe.

"My second whore," Cooper murmured, almost fondly.

"You live!" Marvin cried in triumph, a moment too late to be entirely natural, watching Cooper collapse back to the ground beneath the steel overhang that sheltered them somewhat from the downpour of black rain. He turned to his fellows and gestured. "I told you this one would not fail!"

Warm hands helped him to his feet, and Hestor's teeth gleamed in the firelight. From behind the plastic scrim of his sunglasses, he spoke with the basso of a leader. "I doubted you, Marvin, but that was my error. You've earned your reward tonight, in part."

"In *part*?" Marvin asked in a voice close to a wail. Cooper's heart fell, though he'd expected it to.

Hestor held out a wicked knife with one hand and pointed the other toward the sky. "The emirates of freedom will weigh your redemption when your work is complete."

Reward? Cooper wanted to run, but Marvin's hand on his back kept him rooted to the rooftop. *Redemption?* Marvin hung his head and accepted the knife with his other hand.

"I'm sorry, Cooper," Marvin whispered through tears while his fingers danced up Cooper's spine, his thighs, his throat. Then, inside his head: *SorrySorrySorry SoManyReasonsForSorrowMyChubbyAngel, MyDearBoyIWouldLoveYou, IfOnly IfOnlyIfOnlyIWasAllowed.*

Hestor gave a barbed chuckle and peeked out from over his stupid sunglasses.

"Do it. Carve him up."

Again, Marvin's narcotic touch made Cooper arch his back and moan. Entropy would consume the boundless universes before Cooper tired of this, and still he would beg for more. Marvin knew it and smiled, and continued. Cooper's tattered feelings fell away, and he found himself pleading: *do it; take me; consume me. You fucker.*

Once Cooper had a home, but he lost it; friends, but he wandered off; a way forward that he lost when his sight blossomed into a rose of possibilities. Sight beyond sight for the lost beyond lost. With his terrible new sight Cooper saw that he would dance with the Undertow to be free again, if that's what it took; Cooper would love an Undertow Death Boy, give him his lifeblood and his soulhunger if he asked for it. If Marvin led him toward freedom, Cooper would hand over his heart itself. He would kiss a lich and lick the paper lips from its teeth, if that's what freedom demanded.

Marvin bared his teeth and unsheathed his knife—then Cooper learned bliss.

"What is the matter with you?" Sesstri asked, holding Asher's arm as the big gray man went into some kind of fit. They'd had a tough climb up the exterior of the smooth-skinned building, which rose from the city like the nacelle of a mile-long airship, and Asher had grown more agitated the higher they'd come. By the time they pulled themselves onto a sloped ledge just a few floors shy of the rooftop, he'd become apoplectic. They'd have been lost to Cooper, and he to them, if not for Asher's preparedness: he'd brought more climbing gear than Sesstri had thought to do, and moreover, he'd jerry-rigged a descent line with expert skill; it didn't hurt, of course, that the spikes on the crampons he'd attached to their boots sank easily into the soft but firm skin of the building. It felt to Sesstri like she was climbing a towering animal, digging her feet into the hide of something too big to notice.

"What's *wrong*?" she repeated. Spittle flew from Asher's mouth.

Asher didn't answer but pointed to the building above them.

His eyes rolled wildly as he seized Sesstri's roan leathers. "She's *here*!" he screamed, and she winced at the sound, hoping nobody would hear him. "And she's on fire . . ."

"Who? Asher, who's here?" But he was beyond hearing.

"Oh dead gods, they're cutting her back. *His* back. Whose back are they cutting?" Asher gnawed on his own fingers in distress, unable to escape the pain being broadcast into his head. That made no sense, but it burned him like fire anyway. "They're flaying him alive, I think."

"Who are they . . . flaying?" Sesstri bent her knees and sagged into her harness, letting the line take most of her weight. "Cooper? And who is *she*?"

Asher gave no response.

"Fine, just concentrate on climbing, okay?"

He nodded, or she thought he tried to, but at least he put one hand over the other and kicked his way up the flank of the skyscraper with the mindless skill of an expert. Sesstri wondered just how *much* there was about Asher she didn't know. She looked behind his eyes and saw something vast that terrified her—what's worse, her terror was shameless. So she concentrated on the unknowns she could wrap her head around: those old and new scars between his ribs, for instance. She'd been thinking about those scars, and how they could have all been reopened at the same time, uniformly, and the more she thought about that the more she felt like they should remind her of something. Then she remembered his hands on her body and it all fell away.

Those hands. She focused on climbing.

Then, just below the toothy ridge of the roof, Asher began giggling like a madman, and Sesstri was forced to interrupt their ascent. If she had to, she'd secure him to the line and leave him here while she rescued Cooper herself. She didn't relish the thought of taking on all the gathered Undertow they'd seen climbing and sky-lining to the rooftop of this peculiar, smooth-skinned building, but she supposed she could manage. They were so close, though, if Asher could have just stayed sane for a few moments longer . . . well, she'd figure out what drug he'd taken or been dosed with later. It had to be chemical, didn't it? Unless the liches were somehow broadcasting something witchy directly into his head—that wasn't a prospect she relished.

Could he be vibing off something they're doing up there? He's shown no trace of psychic ability, how would that work? And who, by the hoofbreaker's stones, is "she"?

Distracted, Sesstri continued her climb when something grabbed hold of her hair and jerked her up with wicked force. A bola snapped around her wrists before she could reach for her knives, and the leering face of a Charnel Girl hove into view.

"Lookee here," the gap-toothed woman said as her companion hauled up a still-squirming, half-senseless Asher, "we caught us a pretty pair of sky rats."

Cooper lay upon his former clothing, cut to shreds by Marvin's knife. He and Marvin weren't the only ones copulating openly on the rooftop, but they drew the most onlookers. The boys and girls had clapped along to the rhythm around their merging bodies.

Cooper had never been even remotely comfortable with public nakedness, let alone exhibitionist sex before a gang who might just as easily kill him as fuck him. In the heat of the moment he hadn't cared—the crowded roof gave him a thrill as he and Marvin worked each other's bodies, mouth, fingers, cock. Now he felt like a stretching cat, lying naked on a rooftop beneath the eyes of dozens of Death Boys and Charnel Girls, and any number of unseen skylords.

The fact that he hadn't been eviscerated, or otherwise "carved up," as Hestor had commanded gave Cooper little solace. He knew Hestor's type, the sadistic controller who would promise you agony and then offer you ecstasy, only to snatch it away at the last moment and replace it with the torture you thought you'd avoided. Still, Cooper had come to find the crying woman, and he would stay to save her. Not that he thought flight possible—he was well and truly trapped.

Oh, but what a prison. Marvin growled into Cooper's neck, half-asleep but tangled in Cooper's limbs. Cooper snarled in response, nipping at Marvin's ear and earning a warm, tightening embrace. Just when he thought matters were about to escalate to round two—or was it three?—Marvin extracted himself and stood, honoring Cooper with a look of lusty regret.

"Come on." He tickled Cooper's side with his foot. "It's time."

The rooftop looked no brighter for the fires that still burned in trash cans and torches set into the crumbling walls, but it was less crowded. Only Hestor stood at the far edge, swinging by one arm from the grip of a secured zip line attached to an exposed beam. He crooked a finger and Marvin brought Cooper closer. Cooper was still naked, and almost laughed at how recently that would have been the worst fate he could imagine. Instead, his nakedness felt like armor.

Be careful what you wish for, Death Boy.

"You've felt the freedom we claim as our deathright," Hestor lauded. "You've tasted the black rain of freedom on your tongue and felt the tail of a skylord hugging your body. You've taken and given pleasure with us"—Hestor nodded at Marvin, who wrapped the straps of a leather harness around Cooper's bare torso—"and exulted at the ecstasy of our dance."

Cooper nodded in his best imitation of sagacity, trying unsuccessfully to dispel the sense of unease that had resumed growing in his gut. The danger was real now, again. *What a seesaw I ride,* he thought. *What a lich's tail, what a graphene dragon queen.*

Hestor leered at Cooper's naked body. "There's really only one step left." Hestor lording his authority over them both. "I'm envious, Cooper. You only get your first taste once."

First taste of what, Death Boy?

Cooper grew queasy just looking at the zip line and the hundreds of feet between the towers. A feeling of sheepishness crept over him, at developing a fear of heights *now,* after he'd flown through a thunderstorm with the liches. All his former fears were just ... so ... *amusing.*

Hestor handed Marvin a second zip line grip and buckled him together with Cooper. Their bodies reacted as if they'd begun round two—or three—despite the frigid air and the menacing presence of the Death Boy chieftain.

"Are we going somewhere?" Cooper tried to quell the fear in his voice but the effort was hopeless.

"Is that a problem?"

Cooper was still racking his brain for a reason to delay when Hestor shoved Marvin off the roof with both hands, dragging Cooper with him—his naked body spinning into the air, dangling too loosely from the harness attached to Marvin's. The zip line buzzed and shook violently with their passage through the open air, and Cooper continued to spin for what seemed like half an hour but couldn't have been more than half a minute. Then Marvin slammed into something hard that knocked the wind from Cooper—a wall?—and they both hung limp from the line. Marvin unclipped himself and they dropped to the floor just seconds before Hestor followed on the line, rebounding from the wall with a jump and a shout as he landed. Hestor needed no harness.

The fall had bloodied Cooper's knees and scraped his wrists, but otherwise he felt undamaged. Hands that were neither Marvin's nor Hestor's helped him to his feet and brushed him off—a crowd of Death Boys stood on the rooftop, forming a half circle around the end of the zip line. One of them slipped some sort of robe around Cooper's shoulders and he drew it in close, teeth chattering with cold and fear.

They stood atop a different tower, this one more fantastical than what Cooper had assumed was the Undertow HQ. But, of course, all these towers belonged to the liches and their minions. The floor and remaining walls of this skyscraper were constructed from a seamless whale-blue material that seemed a cross between metal and clay, and pinpoint electric lights traced the paths of circuitry beneath the matte surface.

Cooper said nothing.

"Are you prepared to feel the full power of the Undertow?" Hestor gloated, taking off his louvered shades and tucking them into the breast pocket of his vest while, behind him, a thin youth with long burgundy hair emerged from the shadow of a stairwell. "Let me ask you a question, Cooper."

Cooper looked up at the black dyspeptic sky. "Okay."

Hestor stretched his back like a cat. "What wine do you drink?"

"What? Wine?" Cooper wondered aloud. The new Death Boy stepped up beside Hestor and dipped his head, whispering.

"Yes." Hestor laughed. "What wine?"

Cooper looked out at the city that lay sprawled beyond the veil of shadow—another night was almost over, but the Dome still glittered from within, and the districts sprinkled with lights, the craggy heights farther north. The idea of a city, cockled and crusty, bearing its own history on its broken back. *What's an idea but a kind of spirit?* he wondered. Shamans communed with spirits.

"What wine. Um. I think, Mister Hestor, that you've caught me in the midst of a sea-change."

"A what?" Hestor asked, but Marvin and the long-haired Death Boy nodded.

"Three days ago that would have been an easy question." Cooper closed his eyes and remembered the last song he'd played from his laptop. That world was *so* gone. "Two days ago I only belonged to one city, and now I'm part of two. Two days ago? Cheap Bordeaux, maybe a nice Lafite when my father sent me wine for my birthday. I miss my dad, you know. I don't know if that's an *idea* that matters to you people." He stressed the word. "I think it's probably something you don't approve of talking about, am I right?—but anyway, I miss him, and I'm glad I miss him. Because it makes it easier to tell you that my *wine,* Hestor, is the metaverse and every goblet world it holds, decanted in space like Lafite or Viognier or whatever horrible miscarriage of flavor that I know you're about to pour down my throat."

Hestor looked at Cooper as if the childborn shaman had grown an extra head in his armpit. Cooper doubted anyone spoke back much to Hestor.

"So, um . . ." Cooper scuffed the roof with his bare foot. "*That's* my fucking wine."

Hestor bit his lip to hide a smile. He nodded toward the long-haired Death Boy. "Vaitch the Sommelier here curates our most precious spirits. I'll let him show you the prize that awaits you."

Vaitch pulled a thin-lipped smile; his eyes didn't quite focus. "Forget the metaverse, Cooper," he said, and turned away. "My wine cellars will occupy your attention for much, much longer." Marvin took Cooper's hand as the sommelier led the group down a flight of stairs into the watery flesh of the building below.

Vaitch the Sommelier led them down a sloped hallway lined on one side with open portals, and the din in Cooper's ears grew louder. From within each—sealed with an oval hatch, more like a ship than a building—came whimpers, moans, and sounds of pure animal misery that echoed down the dim corridor. The walls curved overhead like the blue pipe of a wave that never broke and Cooper felt as if he were drowning, only the water wouldn't finish him off—sinking into a vastness of blue-gone-gray-gone-black, dwarfed by the yawning deep but still aware, still alive, an unendable witness to fathoms and fathoms of emptiness.

After they'd passed a dozen or so of the cells, each leaking sounds of misery into the corridor, Vaitch the Sommelier stopped at a hatch and put his hand against it, leaning a bit as if he were out of breath. After a moment, two Death Boy guards emerged, one thin and blond and bored, the other dark with a smile, still fastening his trousers.

"Really, Phlebas?" Vaitch asked with a weary voice. The dark one just shrugged and followed his partner to stand sentinel beside the open hatch. Cooper followed Vaitch inside.

The U-shaped room contained maybe a dozen prisoners, chained, bound by twine, or simply too weak to move. No two of the creatures were alike, except for their piteous condition. A few looked human, but most seemed alien to a lesser or greater degree; all were terrified.

This is where she *is*, Cooper understood as he took in the tableau of abused exotics. She hadn't sung or cried or screamed since he'd passed beneath the black veil of the towers, but she was *here*, he needed no sixth sense to know that. Next to him, Marvin raised an eyebrow but said nothing.

Vaitch the Sommelier named each vintage as he strode down the line of the curving room, his voice as cold and curious as a docent. He named each prisoner as he walked past.

"Treble-Toe the Fifth Gender, our most spectacular guest of fey provenance, though we have lesser faeries in some of the other seraglios. All told, the skylords' cortège spans seven towers, did you know that?" The three-toed creature looked like a sad mime, oversized feet and hands grasping at the air, spun off in some hallucination that Cooper hoped it found less unpleasant than its prison. Huge eyes looked out from a hammerhead skull, but Treble-Toe's teeth were ground-away and flat; its tongue lolled out of its mouth, furred with flagella that bristled in the damp air.

"Revered Matron Maia-Lande, Divine Bride of something-or-other. It's telling, I think, that she expects no rescue from her husband. Some god, eh?" The Matron was baseline human, naked except for a ragged wimple that had been bolted to her skull. Her eyes were gone, and the scratches around their cavities suggested she had inflicted the wounds herself.

A man with dirty blond hair hugged his knees and stared at the floor. The Death Boy curator winked at Cooper and waved toward the man with a flourish. "Kurt Cobain, of *course*."

Cooper looked away.

Wine-dark Vaitch padded around the corner to the other half of the gallery. "And you see our trio of First People—the crown jewels of this particular seraglio."

Marvin hustled Cooper forward. Hestor, the guards, and a few Death Boys who'd followed filed into the room behind them.

Vaitch continued. "Onishimekka, a folioform being whose capture was not worth the effort, if you ask me." What looked like a pile of paper flipped its pages and rose a few feet into the air, forming a roughly spherical shape of origami edges and folded material. It winked its leaves at Cooper like an overgrown paper flower, and before it collapsed back onto the ground it emitted a scratchy noise that almost resembled a word.

What Cooper thought Onishimekka said was, *"Her."*

"Moving right along, we have Morrigan 2/6, one constituent of a nine-fold entity that was whittled down to six by the time we found her. It was easy enough to steal her, although she'll tell you that you don't *steal* an agent of fate made manifest in the worlds. Still, she screams as loud as the rest."

Marvin saw Cooper's face and nuzzled his shoulder. "These are all criminals or dangerously insane people." Cooper shrugged him off and began to grind his teeth; the sounds of fear were all around him, a tide that could not stop rising. The last lay ahead; now that Cooper had come, she'd fallen silent.

Vaitch the Sommelier gave a little bow. "And of course our most popular and most potent vintage, who won't—or can't—tell us her name. Nameless or not, she provides ten times the juice than any other odalisque, although she cocoons up whenever we drink too deeply."

There, whimpering against the wall in a nest of wet leather, huddled a creature more beautiful than Cooper had ever dreamed could live. Gold light played along her opaline flesh, where wings and limbs and shining protuberances conspired to keep her anatomy a mystery of shifting beauty and unearthly radiance. The single eye set into her crested skull was at once crimson, emerald, and glacier-blue, and even in abject terror, the sight of her body was exposure to pure glory. Spears of light danced up her sides, spiking out from polyps that grew from her flank, her rib cage.

"We wouldn't be half so numerous or prosperous in our territorial advancement without her life to drink," Marvin confessed in a hush. "She'll be your first taste, Cooper."

Vaitch the Sommelier drew something out of his tattered robes. "She tastes like milk, don't you know? Milk that burns like fire. Liquid light. I'm more than a little in love with her." In his hands he held some kind of flail, a long grip from which dangled a number of braided leather cords, each ending in a hooked blade. Vaitch looked at the brilliant thing with longing.

"She's an aesr," Cooper realized aloud—cyclopean, finned, radiant.

"She is known to you?" The curator whipped his head around, not happy to have his presentation interrupted.

Cooper shook his head. "She is *amazing*."

"A thing of light and music," Marvin explained, putting his body between Cooper and the annoyed curator. "And rarer than rare. To those who hunger for life, aesr taste better than blood, better than souls, better than winecarp caviar." Marvin licked his lips in naked anticipation.

Cooper went cold. Of course the Undertow would have nothing pleasant planned for a helpless creature out of legend. "You're not going to hurt a . . . nearly extinct angel, are you?" Any remaining sense of safety fled Cooper in an almost physical wave. What had they planned for him?

"*'Hurt?'*" Hestor mocked Cooper's humanity. "That's a petty word for what we do—but no, *we* won't be doing anything."

"The skylords found her years ago," Marvin explained as more Death Boys crowded into the room behind them, "incubating in one of the towers, half-cocooned in her own mucus. She empowers us, Cooper—more than any of these others, *she* makes us what we are. Death Boys. Charnel Girls. She's the reason our ranks have grown, the reason we control as much territory as we do. And soon we'll control it all. Hestor will be made a skylord for our coup, and you will join us." Ambition gleamed through Marvin's eyes. "And then *I* will lead the pack."

The creature of light lifted her cyclopean head and tried to talk, but coughed on her own radiant blood. "Chara . . ." she managed, staring at Cooper.

He rounded on Marvin, his anger returning in a red haze. He shoved the Death Boy. "*What the fuck*, Marvin? Is that a criminal? You're not a cultist, you're just a dead old queen who tortures helpless creatures! What do you do in the off-season, buttfuck unicorns?"

Before Marvin had a chance to respond, Hestor's arm whipped out and smacked Cooper against the side of the head. He saw stars but stood his ground.

"I am *not* afraid of you anymore, Hestor," he lied. "You can spike your hair and fly on all the wicked broomsticks you like, but if you expect me to cooperate with you for one single second more, you will keep your bully hands off me."

Hestor laughed in his face. His boys swelled their chests behind him, proving the unsaid point: Hestor had hands enough to spare, all of them eager to prove themselves meaner than dirt. He wondered how spectacularly his bluster would backfire.

Shit.

The aesr coughed. "Mother . . ." the thing croaked imploringly before passing out again.

Then it occurred to Cooper that he was no longer bound by Earthly rules. He summoned the fear still turbulent in his gut, held it in his mind like a stone on his tongue, then directed it at the ruined aesr. He visualized a laser of communication lancing out from his forehead, beaming straight into her single eye.

IIIWantWantWantToHelpHelpYouYouYou.

She writhed, only partially conscious but aware of his intrusion into her thoughts.

Hello? He tried again, and again the aesr thrashed about but did not respond.

"We want you to have the honor, Cooper." Marvin spoke carefully as Hestor crossed his arms impatiently and more bodies filed into the room. All eyes on Cooper as Vaitch offered the weapon hilt-first.

"I . . . you really don't have to. I have tons of honor already, really I do."

"This honor is singular," Hestor spat.

"What honor, exactly?" Cooper knew, of course he knew—there would be only one kind of honor here, but he had to ask. He had to hope the Death Boys couldn't be this ugly. He had to give them one last chance.

Marvin nodded at the aesr. "Spilling her blood will mark you as one of us. She's mad, Cooper, and doesn't know herself."

"Grace of form, swiftness of foot, and freedom from the cycle of lives—this is what we gain from the aesr," Hestor said. "Out there they would have you believe that Death is a gift you must earn. We reject that notion, claim *existence* as our birthright, and for our induction rites we desecrate their false icons, the pure things of the worlds, and now at last, one of the very founders of their city. Draw her blood and you will never be alone again. Share yourself with us, Cooper."

"I don't want to do this."

"It's a little late for that," Hestor said, reaching out to stroke the flail with his fingers, stroking the barbed ends. "Take the lichtail."

Marvin nodded encouragingly. "Flay her."

Cooper maintained his self-possession. He didn't blanch, flinch, squeal, run, cry, or beg, although he badly wanted to do so. He *knew* he'd gotten off too easily earlier with Marvin and the knife and the carving-up. Oh, if only it could have stopped at kisses. But now, what if he refused? He couldn't possibly back out now, they wouldn't allow it—would they? No, Hestor and his boys wanted blood—Cooper's blood or aesr's blood—and they were going to get it.

"No," said Cooper. It was his word.

"*Hurt* her, Cooper," Marvin pleaded.

"I said *no*."

"You won't like what we do to those who throw our gifts in our faces, Cooper," Hestor threatened, taking the rust-razored flail from his lackey and handing it to Marvin. "You wouldn't want to take the aesr's place, would you?"

Hestor smiled at the look of understanding on Cooper's face. "So many of my Death Boys want to see the childborn shaman flay the aesr cow. They want blood. It would be selfish of me to deny them the pleasure."

Why are you doing this? Marvin begged him in a thought-whisper, his fear amplifying the whisper into a scream. Cooper didn't even think the answer to himself, worried that he might accidentally brush minds with Marvin. A feral punk like Hestor, driving Marvin to flay him alive? Cooper just hoped that the Death Boy didn't intend to render him into a pile of bloody ribbons.

"We welcome you to the Undertow, one way or another, Cooper-*Omphale,*" Hestor grated, a sick smile plastered over his clown's face. "You plunged yourself into the underworld by ascending to our overworld, and now we call you back to the living. Once you've felt the power of our freedom you will beg to taste it. Maybe you're onto something, Cooper. There's wisdom in your refusal to join us without learning our ways from the inside out. Yes, I think you'll be a stronger Death Boy once you've felt the alternative." Hestor smiled and Cooper almost threw up. "Turn him around."

Cooper said nothing as Marvin advanced with the lichtail raised. He was spun into the corner and he covered his head with his hands as the rain of razors began to fall upon his shoulders. The aesr nearby cried out and he knew innately that she would feel every shredded neuron in perfectly mirrored agony. The pain was immediate and all-consuming, and as Cooper collapsed to the floor his last coherent thought was an observation—if he survived the torture Sesstri had repeatedly warned him against, this journey through worlds of death and bodily pain, he supposed he might wake up a shaman after all.

9

From above and from below they rage,
Frothing forth to suck at me;
All the work the living do,
And not an hour of it for free.
—Hinto Thyu, "The Sovereign," *Twice Born a Boychild*

Your kind is a cancer. Purity thought Kaien looked shocked at the ugliness that had rolled so easily off his tongue. Two score bodies surrounded them, the air perfumed with blood spray from bird beaks, and Kaien's own mouth shamed him most.

Purity looked at him, thinking that might be the closest thing to an ally she had in this forsaken cage—and she could have him arrested and strung upon a thievespole for a spy with a single word, wasn't that neatly packaged and tied up in a bow? How had he been foolish enough to tell her who he was? If the Circle discovered a way out of the Dome, things would go from horrible to fucked-beyond-repair: her kind *did* deserve to be locked away, at the very least long enough for the city to ratify a decent government in their stead.

She stood beside Kaien as he crouched beside the body of the apprentice tailor and rested the boy's head on the celadon tiles of the aviary floor, unable to bring himself to look at her. The boy stared unblinking at the cyclone of feathers that still squawked overhead, and with the same solemn gesture she'd used before, Purity knelt and closed them forever. Somewhere the boy was waking beneath a new sky, but his world had ended all the same.

"It's called a prayer," Purity said, rocking on back on her heels and latching onto Kaien's arm for support. "You wouldn't have ever seen one, if you're a childborn citizen of the city. They bury every prayer at the Apostery as they should, I suppose. I merely wished him well on his first step."

"Step?"

"Of the dance of lives." Lifting the dead boy's shirt, Purity showed Kaien the navel of a childborn. "Someone lost a son today." Kaien blinked back tears and kneeled over the body.

"So you see, there is some merit to be found even amid the lords and ladies of death, metastases that we are."

Kaien winced. "Purity, I'm sorry. I didn't mean to speak to you roughly, I just—"

She shushed him. "I couldn't disagree with you less, you know—and even if I did, we haven't the time to debate social justice." She pulled on his shoulder from behind with surprising force, and Kaien tumbled backward onto the floor.

"Bells, but you're forward—" he began, when Purity jumped atop of him and pressed her face against his.

"*Shut. Up,*" she whispered fiercely into his ear, then went limp on his chest at the sound of the lockstepped march of praetorian boots. She tried not to move, or breathe, or think of Kaien's firm body pressed against her own.

They held their breath as the praetors approached, but to Purity's astonishment they did not stop in the aviary—the tempo of their marching didn't slow, and still the alarum rang. Still the birds flew in troubled circles, denied their rest.

Purity made a noise of consternation and pushed herself up a bit, glancing around and then staring down the slope of her pert nose at Kaien. "I really *did* expect them to take a bit of a look-see, you know."

Kaien blushed and tried to turn away, but where could he go? Purity's arms rested on his shoulders—which she squeezed admiringly, then winked. He was so innocent! She rolled off him and stood, smoothing her stained dress down her hips, legs. "So much for the charmeuse. Kaien, you really must learn to be more opportunistic."

He sputtered, then reoriented himself. "Why didn't the guards stop?" he asked, sitting up.

"Because the mess here is just ancillary damage."

"But then what—"

"Kaien, I'm—" The alarum suddenly stopped. Purity covered her ears with her hands before she realized how silly that looked—but the abrupt silence seemed more offensive to her ears than the wailing Klaxon.

"Well, that's a relief." Kaien sighed with a little too much emphasis, brushing off his trousers. He stood turned away from her at a discreet angle.

Purity rolled her eyes. *Oh, for goodness' sake.*

She cleared her throat and tried not to snicker. "Do I need to excuse myself while you scavenge a fresh pair of skivvies, Mister Mason?"

The back of his dark-skinned neck flushed a deep rust-brown, like the sky during an ammonia monsoon.

Changing the subject by way of a mercy, she asked him, "If the guards are going to ignore us, then you might as well tell me just what, *exactly,* you are doing here in the Dome, Kaien, master spy and journeyman mason? Don't you think I'll forget to ask simply because a massacre or two interrupted us."

At last, he smiles. Purity shook her head. This boy strove for propriety more dutifully than most of her peers. He'd make a good lord, if their circumstances were reversed.

"I'm only a second-degree journeyman, Miss Kloo, but my father is First Mason."

She nodded airily.

"You have no idea what that means, do you?" he asked.

"Kaien, I'm not stupid. Have we not discussed my education, specifically its thoroughness concerning city affairs? I'd appreciate it if you wouldn't fib."

"What?" He seemed genuinely incredulous. "I'm not lying!"

She raised an eyebrow and led him beneath the sheltering branches of a fig tree, well away from the stink of birds and bodies. "Basel Prouk is First Mason, Kaien—or he was when we were sealed inside this lovely little prison. I know that spies are supposed to practice being circumspect, but you really oughtn't lie to a girl whose father sat on the board of the Guildworks United."

Kaien looked shifty for a moment. "Now, see, about the Guildworks . . ."

"What?"

"I . . . I'm not supposed to say anything."

"I'd say it's a bit late for that, Kaien." She fingered the head of the hammer looped through his belt, and brushed white powder from her fingertips. "Wouldn't you agree?"

Kaien swallowed hard, but nodded. "Sure. Yes. Do I have any choice?" Purity shook her head and used her grip on his belt to pull him closer. Kaien tried to keep a clear head as he continued, "But, listen, may I have your word that you won't repeat what I'm about to say to another soul?"

"You're choosing *this moment* to get coy on me, you hairy aurochs?" She punched his arm, then shook the sting out of her fist.

"Masons are a tight-lipped lot," he said. "Promise me."

"Oh, for the sake of all that's dead and gone, Kaien: fine!" Purity raised her hand. "I, Purity Genghis Umptelle Hyacinth Kloo, youngest of Baron Emil Kloo and scion of the Circle Unsung, hereby swear upon pedigree and principle that I shall keep your soon-to-be-revealed secret from any and all, upon pain of Death and general dismemberment. Are you satisfied, or must I open an artery?"

He flashed her an uncertain look, tugging at an unripe fig. "Is that a real oath?"

"Of *course* it is, Kaien!" she lied. "Are you questioning my honor?"

"Fine. Yes, Basel Prouk was First Mason when your father sat on the board of the Guildswork United, but . . ."

"But?"

"Now, see, that was five years ago. Things have changed since then."

She put her hands on her hips and skewered him with a skeptical look. "And you would know this how?"

Kaien cleared his throat. "Right. Well, see, it's like this. The Guildworks United dissolved less than a year after the Writ of Community, when you all were locked up. Without backing from the Circle, First Mason Prouk and the rest of the representatives of the various guilds lost their authority. My father, Cecil Rosa, became First Mason when he led the remains of the organized masons to partner with the plumbics—the Guilds Masonic *y* Plumbus are the only functional labor organizations left in the city. The only ones cooperating, anyway, although the dockworkers are congenial enough so long as we keep their dikes shored up and the buried chains from clogging up canal traffic."

"What," Purity interjected, "does this have to do with *anything*?"

He held up a meaty palm. "Well, with all the chaos, you see, my father and Head Pipeswoman Grigálie decided to employ certain . . . intelligences. And um, they decided—after some lengthy debating and not a few walkouts—to send one of their number—me, in this case—into . . . um, into the Dome to perform some basic reconnaissance."

Purity's flesh went numb. She bit her lip and blinked rapidly. "Pardon me, Kaien, I'm sure I drifted off. It sounded as though you said you came into the Dome *after* it was sealed."

He looked at his feet. "Not quite a year ago, in fact."

Kaien was not prepared for the burst of sudden violence as Purity slammed him and seized his collar with both tiny hands. *"WHAT?"* She was stronger than she looked and loud as all the bells in bedlam. "Are you saying that you *know a way out of this hell*?"

"A way in, actually," he said, unclasping her hands from his shirt one slim steel finger at a time, "although I was hoping I'd be able to use it to leave soon—when my scheduled replacement arrived."

Purity's pale green eyes grew even wider. "You bastards are running shifts?" She pushed herself away, raked her fingers through her hair, and exhaled an animal groan of frustration. "Do you have any *idea* what I've been through trying to escape this place for the past five years? Bells, Kaien, I spent two weeks cutting my own throat like a slaughterhouse piglet just to see if I could break the body-binding spells! I've been willing to die and move on all alone and you tell me that *you*—you and the rest of the damned bricklaying bastards have been waltzing in and out the whole time?"

Look how those curls tumble, Kaien marveled. "Well, not waltzing. And not all of us, no, just me."

"How?"

"*That* I can't tell you. I can't, Purity."

"Fine. Let's see." She rolled her eyes but smiled despite herself, loving a puzzle and not minding a demonstration of her skills for a boy who *would* flirt with her before the day and deed were through.

"This little group of masons *und* plumbers or whatever you're calling yourselves, you lot know how to get in and out, so it must be something fundamental. Something too neglected for servants to bother with and therefore something that the nobles don't even know exists. And if Fflaen didn't seal it, it must be old enough for him to forget, which means *old*. That's more than enough to solve the riddle, but I shan't stop there." Purity slipped into a wry smile. "Something old and basic: if I follow the logic of my own *cancerous* kind, it will be something utterly essential to our way of life. Food, shelter, clothing—all of that is sustainable without intercession from the city outside. Water, perhaps? No, we've got springs aplenty in the Groveheart and the Dendritic cisterns. *Cisterns.*"

Kaien's stomach sank. He shouldn't have given her anything, now she'd taken up the conundrum and he could see that Purity Kloo made a stellar detective. He scrubbed his face with his hands and hoped his father would forgive him—supposing they survived long enough for Kaien to see his father again. He'd hate to be reunited with his family only to be body-bound and bricked up alive for becoming a traitor.

"Water," she said, zeroing in on the answer. "We've got all the fresh water we need but . . . there's something else. Something I'm in which I'm not fluent. Something . . . something like . . . excrement. Water in, *water out.*" Purity spat on the floor. "Trade secrets of plumbers and bricklayers. Oh Kaien, Kaien, please tell me you didn't crawl in here through something as absurdly obvious as a sewer?"

Kaien stared at his feet resolvedly.

"But I've *checked* all the culverts—that was my first thought, *obviously.* The whole complex is hermetically sealed!"

"The whole complex?" Kaien stroked his whiskers. "It's an old place, Purity. A funny old place."

She stalked a few feet away, grabbed a wren from midair and snapped its neck with one pretty hand. *"Fuck."* She hurled the dead thing at his chest like a miniature cannonball. It bounced off him and rolled away on the tiles.

"Bells, Purity!" He raised his arms in surrender.

"Fuck!" She elaborated to the lead-paned glass ceiling and the trees above. "Fuck, fuck, fucketty fuck!"

Purity drew a ragged breath and tried to compose herself, but her eyes were wild.

"Dead gods dressed and dried," Purity cursed more eloquently now, "I wish I could go with you."

"Excuse me?" Kaien's bewilderment reached new heights. "What are you talking about? Purity?"

"Isn't it obvious? You need to take word of what's happening to your father, to the city. Fflaen's left us here to rot, the rest mustn't suffer the same fate."

"Purity . . ." he began. "I don't think you realize . . ."

"I realize more than you think, bricklayer! You have your duty, and I have mine. There's a Murderer to bring to justice. I can stop the self-annihilation of the Circle with a ransom like that, I know I can." She merely had to decide whether or not she should do so.

"Your duty, however, lies with the guilds and the people—ordinarily I wouldn't presume to bother the world at large with the Circle's internecine strife, but *something* larger is brewing, and I don't think it's right to leave the city in ignorance of the chaos into which their erstwhile governors have descended. Also: the possibility that the Murderer might find his way out into the city through your fucking *drain*." Purity stalked toward the exit.

Following, Kaien reached out with his hands and then snatched them back, worried she might bite off a finger. "You can't go running around the Dome with a Murderer on the loose, Purity. It isn't safe! We'll stick together and take care of things as they come. Nobility and guildsmen working together, as it should have been from the beginning."

"Just go, Kaien." Purity didn't bother to look back as she shook her head. "We'll build a brand new world after we've saved the old one from total obliteration."

"Absolutely not, Purity—"

"*Go.*" She turned at the exit, leaning on the archway for support. Bells, she was turning down a *way out*. "There is nothing you can do to protect me from the Murderer anyway, Kaien, although your gallantry is noted and, I should add, appreciated. Go help the people worth helping."

"Purity Kloo: *shut up.*" Kaien took her shoulders, one in each hand, knowing she might interpret it as an act of aggression. "Close your pretty mouth for one single second! The First Mason didn't send his only son into the tolling Dome to sneak about and eavesdrop on ladies' gossip, no matter how winsome that lady may be. The City Unspoken needs a government, Purity. My *duty* is to ensure that nothing remains of the old, failed government that could hinder the formation of the new one."

Purity stopped midsentence, eyes and mouth agape. She held a gloved hand up to her mouth, then put it on her hip and scowled, almost opened her mouth, then realized that Kaien still had his warm paws on her shoulders and covered her mouth with her hand again.

"You what? You're . . . bells and bells and tolling bells, Kaien. It *is* you, isn't it?" Purity stepped back slowly, fingers trembling against her lips.

"What? What's me?"

"*You're* the bastard who's been running around Killing stableboys and Tsengs who don't know any better!" Purity scrubbed her yellow hair and looked around the tiled vestibule that led away from the aviary.

"Purity," Kaien said, his stomach gone cold. "What are you talking about?"

"I'm a cancer?" she said, looking back from the threshold. "Dead gods, Kaien, better to be a tumor than a Murderer!"

She spun and fled toward the exit, running for the nest of nobles that was Dendrite's Folly. Kaien let her go, watching the small bustle attached to her turquoise skirts. He wasn't sure if he wanted to stop her and tell her the truth, or if she was better off without him.

Purity found and followed a trail of scurrying guardsmen and servants, and was surprised to find herself walking toward Lord Senator Bratislaus' library. She was even more surprised to see Lady Mauve Leibowitz lording over the three-story, book-lined offices.

NiNi and NoNo's formidable mother, member of Circle Unsung and war-honed battleaxe, Lady Mauve fixed a steely eye on Purity as she entered. She pointed a finger at Purity's heart and grated:

"You, Purity Kloo, are in *worlds* of trouble."

Tam hurried down a cobbled lane, laden with shopping bags in enough colors to make a faerie proud: hyacinth and cornflower, viridian, cyclamen, sunset. Today, Lallowë Thyu wanted a coin, but she also wanted three pairs of shoes, a new set of luggage, clockworking tools and new coding pins, and a camisole from a dressmaker in Amelia Heights. Only by chance was the numismatist's shop located nearby the dressmaker, or Tam feared he would have died of exhaustion.

He pushed his way past window-shoppers and a slope-nosed little boy with no shirt, a red ribbon tied around his finger, and a bucket of red paint. The little urchin ran right in front of him, and Tam almost kicked the boy, but thought of his packages and reconsidered.

The coin shop—if it could be called such—was typical of Amelia Heights, where the city's intelligentsia and least-starving artists packed themselves into odd little rooms in odd little buildings, all stacked together like so many hatboxes. The coin shop was tiny and at the top of several rickety flights of stairs, and so crammed with papers, volumes, and overflowing tabletops that it took Tam a solid minute to find the old man amidst the clutter. Lapin the Numismatist sat hunched over a desk beneath a wall bestrewn with shiny medals hermetically sealed in laminate and cardboard, and seemed not to notice Tam's arrival. He wore a navy blazer with brass buttons, and his hair was the brightest white. Tam found it hard to believe that this one old man was responsible for every body-binding performed in the City Unspoken. Coins and bodies, bodies and coins. They always went together.

Tam coughed politely, to no response. He cleared his throat but received no welcome. Finally he announced himself: "If you are the coiner Lapin, then the Marchioness Terenz-de-Guises would have your attention."

"Eh?" The white-haired head perked up. "Or you'll have my kidneys instead? I remember the spiel." The old goat turned around and Tam saw that one of his eyes had been replaced with a prosthesis. Where the other should be was installed a lens of absurd thickness, through which an iris showed rheumy-blue and gigantic. "What are you about, girl? And why the sudden interest in a pair of much-abused organs? Making kidney pie, are we? I'm not hungry." He turned back to his coins, muttering about marrow and sweetbreads.

"I'm a *young man*," Tam said, too quickly. He looked out the window to the noonday skies, silvery like the old coiner's enormous eye. Tam was told to be polite, so he held his tongue. "My name is Tam, and I represent the mistress of the Guiselaine."

"Are you sure you want to represent such a mistress?" Lapin asked from his workbench. Tam had seen gargoyles with less grotesque foreheads, so bushy and long were the old man's eyebrows. "Lallowë Thyu acted very unpleasantly the last time she paid me a visit. It's not nice to threaten to eat an old man. She called *me* a goat!"

Tam was unsure what to say—it would be beyond his station to apologize for the marchioness, but the old man seemed to expect some kind of redress. "The fey are fickle," Tam said, "I'm certain my mistress intended no insult. And goats are . . . very noble creatures." He paused.

"I'm more of a mutton, I'm afraid, and a bit gamey at that." He pulled the thick lens from his face, which remained craggy and overgrown but, at last, attentive. So it wasn't a prosthetic eye at all, but a mere device, a contraption of leather and glass that exaggerated the rheum in his old eyes.

Lapin continued. "What manner of coin does the queen of the Guiselaine wish to add to her coffers, today? I would have thought she'd have graduated to bullion. Or does she want her new faerie handmaiden body-bound as well, is that it?"

"Both." Tam sighed, resigned to be amused by the old fellow. "A half-cent, thank you, and one body-binding to go." He held out the note with the details of the coin.

Lapin leapt and gave a funny little cheer, ignoring the note. "Ah! Well, then, if we're to do *real* business, girl, I prefer you to address me properly. A coiner is a nickeldime a dozen, if you'll pardon the pun. I am the Numismatist."

"And I am no girl. I am—"

"—Fey, yes? Yes, I can see that. It's the ears, child. Dead pointy ringers." Hooking the shopping bags in one arm around his elbow, Tam felt at his ears, which were as round and human as ever.

"Perhaps you should replace your lens, Mister Numismatist. This coin I seek, it is malformed."

Lapin nodded. "We call the lens a loupe. Now, let us find your half-cent. If I read you aright, Miss Tam of the manse Terenz-de-Guises, your mistress desires what we *numismatists* call an error, an error half-cent, in this case. This will be a half-cent that was misstruck with a faulty print, a double print, a blank press, a broken die . . ."

"*Die,* that's what she said. Missing a die, she said—"

"—And isn't that odd, in a city where half the population is trying to Die, and missing the mark." Lapin's hobby seemed to be amusing himself.

Tam kept speaking, shaking the note in the old man's face. "—Missing a die and originating at the, um, pelican mince?"

"American Mint." Lapin nodded and turned immediately to one of the rickety cupboards surrounding his worktable. "Core world coins! That's easy enough. I have several dozen errors from that particular universe alone, each different from the last. That's the fun of both error coins and universes, you see, they come in more flavors than pies, and endure a great deal longer. . . ."

Tam growled. "The coin?"

"Must be named before it can be purchased, young lady."

The old man finally took the note from Tam, glanced at it, and rattled off a list of numbers and names of which Tam understood precisely nothing.

"Oh, that's a good one!" Lapin clapped. "Yes, yes, the American 1809 half-cent, Cohen number six, reverse only. Excellently documented, that world's coins. Whole families devoted to their study. Poor Breen describes it, although he had only ever seen one uniface striking, which he illustrated. Grellman authenticated it. My friend Tettenhorst . . ."

Airy dark, this one rambled. "Do you have it?"

"Of course I have it," he snapped, then continued with his tale of tails. "Breen died in prison, a pederast. His wife was *quite* famous for another reason entirely, but I digress. The coin. I forget quite how it came to me, but I do remember the collection, the largest of its kind in the entire metaverse, a worthy endeavor. The Davy Collection, you see, named after the collector's youngest boy. What became of the man and his son we'll never know, I fear. Perhaps they traveled together. Perhaps they lost each other. Perhaps they're both here right now, and don't know it. Lives get lost just as easily as coins, girl. But coins can be found again, and identified. Lives are not often as lucky, which is why I work with both. Would you like it?"

"No, old man," Tam began, with acid sarcasm, "the marchioness of the wealthiest remaining district in the city has sent me to your closet to listen to worthless stories about worthless coins. Of *course* I don't want it. But your ersatz governor does. You might give more consideration to thoughts of her displeasure. . . ."

"Feh. I might give more consideration to a ha'penny trollop with elfin ears if she considered my lives' work worthy of a moment's attention." He dug through one of a hundred drawers, pawing lazily at neatly labeled cardboard pouches much less neatly arranged until, after a moment, he drew a brown square from the rest and stared at it with pride. "And Amelia Heights does *not* bend its knee to Lallowë Thyu. 1809, Cohen six, reverse only—here we have it. For your purse, I will part with it."

Tam tossed his purse at the barnacled ancient, eager to escape the dusty attic. Despite his age, Lapin snatched the bag deftly and flipped Tam the small cardboard envelope.

"Might I be permitted to ask, Miss Tam, what has generated this sudden interest of the marchioness in as noble if neglected a diversion as numismatics?"

"You may indeed, Sir Lapin." Tam flashed a smile. "And get a purseful of nickeldimes as your answer; that's all I got when *I* asked. With a mistress such as mine, it is wisest not to ask twice."

Lapin snapped his fingers. "Which reminds me, you mustn't leave without a binding scrip. I prefer to bind in person, but I'll not hear more threats from Thyu or her elfish minions." He procured a scrap of paper from a drawer and a green felt-tipped pen from the inside pocket of his blazer.

"These are much harder to do than they seem," Lapin elaborated as he scribbled on the paper strip, "which is why I'm the only one providing the service, these days. Oh, there used to be a row of us, across town in the Callow Heights, but they've all since danced on and those crazy thugs drove everyone out of the district, so here I am. She'll need to press it against the wrist of whomever she intends to bind. I hope your mistress won't murder her quarry before she binds it."

Lapin treated the little curl of drafting paper far more carefully than he had the coin. "I forget myself with that vixen. Although I am pleased she sent a foxy feykin lass in her stead." Tam raised an eyebrow. "I mean no disrespect, Miss Tam. The fox always fucks the vixen in the end, no?"

A slow smile spread across Tam's pointed face. "We shall see, Sir Numismatist. In the meantime, I will rest easy knowing you have the sense—damn you and your puns—to keep your mouth shut and your keen eye in its loupe where it belongs. Good day."

Lapin made a half bow as Tam struggled down the stairs with his varicolored bags scraping against the sides of the narrow steps. "Happy hunting, little fox!" Lapin called as Tam turned the first landing.

"To you as well, old goat!" he replied before the daylight hit his face and he was lost again, coin and life, to the turbulent streets.

* * *

This time the vision quest beluga bore nautical tattoos and sported a jaunty if somewhat ill-fitting sailor's hat, waving her body lazily through the paper streamer ocean. Cooper wondered briefly if he was back in Cleopatra's lap, but no—he knew something was wrong, indeed that a great many things were wrong, and moreover that things had begun to go wrong for him shortly after he commenced his education concerning all things metaversial.

"Just how shortly after?" he asked out loud.

"Very very shortly after," the beluga answered.

I wonder, is that a coincidence?

"Not exactly!" The beluga seemed chipper.

"You're not Marvin." Cooper practiced his backstroke through the undersea psychoanalytical medium . . . crêpe paper.

"Of course not, silly." The beluga lifted one stubby fin and somehow, in the way only a mind weaned on Disney animals could hallucinate, raised its hat to the rhythm of a little vaudeville vamp—itself produced from an old player piano that popped into existence for the occasion, then melted away like clarified butter. "Ta da."

"But you're wearing his tattoos."

"Nobody's perfect." If a sea mammal could look shifty, this one did so.

"You're not Cleopatra, either." Cooper treaded crêpe paper water.

"*Cleopatra*." The beluga rolled its little black eyes. "That fat lady got sung."

"So who are you? Are you my spirit animal?"

"Those are two completely different questions, Cooper."

"Well, are you? Some animal guide thing?" He squeezed a spongy stress ball that appeared in his hand for the count of three, then was a crocus from his mother's garden in February, then was nothing again.

"What makes you ask that?"

"Well, the last time I saw you—which I guess was also the first time I saw you, you were wearing spectacles and talking an awful lot like a shrink." Details of his immediate circumstances returned now, Marvin and Hestor and the pretty, pretty thing he'd heard for days. "And now here you are wearing the skin of the guy who, I think, just sold mine.

And all that business with the shaman-stuff, I dunno. It just seems sort of timely."

"You've got that part dead right, at least. It sure is timely." The beluga wrapped its fins around a ship's line that appeared from nowhere and pulled with all its weight.

"I can't be a shaman, I'm Jewish."

"Mazel tov!" A Purim noisemaker gragged above the beluga's head and it let go of the line.

"Don't tease. I'm a fragile flower at the moment."

"Let's talk about that. Why all the floral imagery? That crocus just now . . ."

"From my mother's garden." Cooper put his arms behind his head and leaned back into the chartreuse leather fainting couch that manifested beneath him. He was a gay neurotic New Yorker; there wasn't a magic cetaceous shrink in the metaverse that could get the jump on him. "A purple one, my favorite kind. They come weeks before the other early spring flowers, like daffodils and redbuds. Out of a deep March or February freeze, you'll suddenly see these stumpy green shoots, followed by flowers like dwarf tulips."

"And what do you think this—"

"—My *mother,* stupid. It's home and nurture and nature and comfort and all the familiar shit I have so thoroughly abandoned, or been abandoned by—however you wanna frame that complex. If you get Freudian about it—have you guys debunked Freud, out here in the voodoo-boonies?—anyway, you might pin a 'violence' signifier to the violet color, but personally I think that's a bit more than overkill. It doesn't take a vertebrate with a blowhole and a psych degree to realize I might be disturbed by the violence that's overtaken my life during the past few days, does it? Anyway, yeah: I miss my mommy. Got a pill for that?"

Tiny white teeth showed as the beluga muttered to itself. "We've *got* to improve your self-image, Cooper. You could be a bit more than a freeze-dried camellia, you know. Quite a bit, if you'd just decide so."

He laughed, which felt funny underwater. Bubbles spiraled out of his mouth and wreathed his wrists, making him feel for some reason like a sacrificial bull. "Yeah, well, you need to ask around, because that is most definitely *not* the general consensus. The consensus, in general, is that I'm nothing special."

"Then why all the fuss?" The beluga looked genuinely perplexed.

"What do you mean?"

"Well, you *were* kidnapped and brought before an Egyptian queen. And you *were* stolen from her by the Undertow and tapped to perform ritual sacrifice, before you decided to take the lamb's place yourself."

"Oh, *that*." Cooper thought for a moment. "But she said I was nothing special, and the rest is just . . . it's just what happened to me."

"Hmm." The beluga did not sound convinced. Cooper said so.

"Well, I'm just thinking about what Sesstri said about you—specifically, what was it she said about shamanism and your homeworld? I don't remember."

Cooper did. "She said 'shamans don't come from post-industrial, magic-dead societies.' And then she called me a piece of shit."

"Well, she was right, wasn't she?"

"Fuck me sideways! I hope you're my spirit animal, dude, because you make a *terrible* shrink."

The beluga flashed an indulgent smile. "You're not a piece of shit, Cooper, I thought that was obvious by now. But Sesstri was right when she said that real shamans don't come from post-industrial, magic-dead societies. They don't."

"Great. We have firmly established—across multiple realities and at least one dream sequence—that I am not a shaman. You, me, Sesstri, and goddamned Cleopatra are all painfully aware that Cooper is not a shaman. He is also not a candy striper, a backhoe, an airplane, or a cupcake. Why in the worlds-where-nobody-ever-dies would anyone care what kind of witch doctor I am *not* is beyond me, but I've pretty much stopped trying to figure it all out at this point."

"Everything dies, Cooper."

"Yeah, well you might try telling that to everybody else, SeaWorld. I'm not the one who needs convincing." His skin prickled, especially his back.

"Maybe *you* should try telling it to everybody else, if that's how you feel."

"Maybe I will." Cooper pouted and crossed his dream-arms.

The beluga laughed and swished its long body in a pelagic gesture of amusement. "Don't do anything on my account. I'm just wondering—perhaps if you spoke up, people might stop poking you to see if you're something you've obviously decided you're not."

"Hey, that's not fair. I haven't decided anything."

"True statement," the beluga said, as spears of light began to play up the sides of its body.

Cooper felt tricked, though he couldn't say how. "Well, I decided to try and save the aesr. That was a decision."

"True statement," the beluga repeated in a neutral tone of voice.

"Now wait a minute, those statements can't both be true. Either I decided something or I didn't. You're not very good at this, I gotta say."

The beluga held up its fins. "I'm not the one wrestling this greased-up piggy, Cooper. This is your choice, not mine. Are you the decider or aren't you?"

Cooper rolled his eyes. "You are definitely the spirit animal of an American asshole, I'm just not sure you're *mine*. We've got to get you a new job."

"Hey, look at you, making decisions left and right, captaining your own ship and so on. Soon you won't need poor old SeaWorld." The water streamers began flowing away in a manner that Cooper recognized as dismissive. He was about to be decanted into the waking world—and he knew what that meant. So did the beluga: "Might wanna pick up a prescription for painkillers though, captain. This one's a real bitch."

Drenched in blood, Cooper stood. The Death Boys gathered around him in a ragged semicircle went wide-eyed; Hestor's lichtail in Marvin's hand, dripping pieces of skin and fat from Cooper's back. There was something wrong with his vision—colors spun around the Death Boys, and everything looked watery. Cooper wept enough to match the weeping ruin of his back, but he didn't feel like he was crying so much as expressing a wound that had always existed, somewhere behind his face. Cooper held the image of a crocus in his mind's eye, and it was better than a stress ball or a handful of opiates—thank the beluga, he supposed, before wondering if he should thank his mommy instead. He cracked the stiffness out of his neck.

"You know what occurred to me, just now?" Cooper asked, clinging to that mental crocus. "Hestor is a *stupid* name."

The Death Boys looked at him in a kind of frustrated awe, exchanging glances but too unused to independent thought to apprehend him. They'd seen what Hestor had ordered Marvin to do—and they seemed appalled that Cooper could stand, let alone talk, let alone bait their leader. Colors drenched their bodies, and Cooper tried to blink it away.

"Look at my face." Cooper kept his voice even. "Am I bothered?"

Someone cursed and stepped forward—and instead of the beating Cooper expected, a scrawny Death Boy pressed a bottle of wine into his hand. Cooper sucked it like a glass teat. Marvin made a motion with his hands that might have been a call for another round of lashings or an act of protection, Cooper would never know—a Charnel Girl with a sweet face and pretty curls interrupted, pushing her way through the crowd and looking shocked to see the red blubber hanging in ropes from Hestor's lichtail.

"Um. Hestor? Your presence is requested on deck," she said.

"Daria, don't be a killjoy," one of the Death Boys said. "Nothing happens till Hestor calls down the skylords."

"Fuck you, Fyde, your fun can wait. There's a skylord here with questions about the Lady."

This got their attention.

"*Up!*" Hestor roared. The Death Boys fled, Cooper forgotten in the blink of an eye. Only Marvin lingered, eyes full of guilt and resentment. His colors were purple and brown, bruise and shit.

Cooper stared at the restless figure of the aesr lying in the corner. She still shuddered with his pain, and Cooper realized that *she* was the reason he could move and speak. She was aware of her circumstances, he could see that now, and she drank in his pain so that he could act to save them both. He wanted to go to her, to pick her up in his arms and flee this place, but he knew that wasn't an option.

Tttthank youuu, he thought, still struggling with sending rather than receiving. *Iiiif youuu hear aaand can fleeee . . .*

She gave no answer, aloud or in his head. Cooper's mind raced: what could he possibly do, and how could he possibly do it?

Cooper would not squander the aesr's anesthetic gift, but he didn't know how best to use it. So he stalled, waving the wine bottle in Marvin's face. "Listen, I'd love to meet Mumm-Ra the Everliving and plan our next big dance number, but I have some shaman stuff to do. Can this wait?" He took another swig, drinking deep.

"It really can't." Marvin sounded so bitter, for the one who'd done the flensing. "When a skylord calls, you answer."

"M'kay." He held out his arms, stained with blood from his back. "Gotta bandage?" Inside, Cooper scratched at the walls of his skull. He knew he needed to clear his thoughts in order to accomplish anything, but they were a tempest.

Then Marvin punched him in the nose, and Cooper dropped to his knees. Half-aware, his mind reeled. He felt himself slip halfway out of his body—not quite the same thing as his visit to the Cicatrix, but close enough. While part of him watched Marvin reach down with an ugly expression to haul him back to his feet, another part of Cooper flew elsewhere. In a fraction of a heartbeat, Cooper was singing to the worlds as he slipped between their shimmering curvatures. There was no space in that nirvana, but plenty of math. In the instant it took for Marvin to pull Cooper's body up, Cooper's spirit called out for the one who had no voice. He shouted down her soul.

"What the fuck are you?" Marvin dug his fingers into Cooper's arm, severing whatever strange fugue state Cooper had managed to achieve. The bliss of timelessness fell away, the moment unfroze, and he was Cooper again. Wounded and lost and full of fury.

"You tell me." He shrugged. "What are you, Marvin? And do you like it, whatever it may be?"

As Cooper watched, Marvin's colors resolved into a purplish sign that hovered over the skin on the side of his neck: a tattoo swallow snipping the line of an anchor with its beak. The sign shimmered in the air and pulsed with Marvin's heartbeat, and Cooper knew he was the only one who could see it.

"Marvin, listen," Cooper pleaded in a final bid to reach Marvin's diluted humanity. "You've got this bird on your neck now, and I think—"

"Not *now*, fuckhead. I didn't go through all of this to have you disappear when the fucking CEO shows up." Marvin pulled him through the door and Cooper was swept along with the rest of the hurried bodies. "Get your fat ass upstairs and shut the fuck up until somebody important tells you to talk."

All the other prisoners called out as they left, even the eyeless nun with the wimple bolted to her skull. The aesr remained still, but Cooper could feel the pain and rage and fear that boiled inside her luminescent skin as he left her to her fate.

The rooftop seethed with chaos, and Cooper saw something that made him almost cry out in relief: a pair of Charnel Girls held Sesstri down, while four more were straddling Asher. Cooper's heart rose in his chest. His *friends* had come. He didn't know how they'd found him, but even captured, Asher and Sesstri changed the possible outcomes and improved his odds of surviving.

But something was wrong with Asher—he thrashed against their bodies, driven to fits by something. Something that matched the drumbeat of blood and numbed agony that had been Cooper's back. "It's *her*! It's *her*!" he screamed, over and over, writhing. A Death Boy joined the four Charnel Girls holding Asher down, kneeling on his neck with a wicked smile.

Can Asher feel it too? The thought disturbed him, and he redoubled his effort to maintain the crocus in his mind's eye; it kept him sane, even if the aesr siphoned away the pain from his back.

"We've had no word from La Jocondette." Killilly marched over to Hestor, who stood alone, whispering to himself. "The Lady has vanished."

"No, that's not right." Hestor shook his head, casting a quick glance over his shoulder to a corner of rooftop where the darkness gathered, dripping down from the sky. "She leads the attack at dawn. She's our *general*."

"We'll soon see." The Charnel Girl captain seemed eager. She had one arm around a disfigured white-blond woman, who kept putting her fingers over the place where her lower lip should have been.

"Offer up the false shaman," Marvin suggested, jerking his head in Cooper's direction.

Killilly frowned. "What for?"

Marvin shrugged. "Maybe he's an adept, maybe he's a fool—either way, he's a distraction, and if the Lady really is gone . . ."

Hestor nodded. "You know what kind of option failure is, Lil, and it's no option at all."

"Your failure, not mine." She spat at Hestor's feet, then turned on Marvin. "You fucked him for this? For a distraction? I don't understand you boys. Sandiz lost a lip to his pink-haired friend." She jabbed a finger toward Sesstri, who snarled and snapped her teeth at the two who held her down.

"I fucked him because I wanted to," Marvin hissed, a viper defending itself against several opponents at once. "And because he was with the Lady. It's not my fault if Sandiz can't keep her ugly face in one piece."

"Brilliant." Killilly looked exultant and terrified and capable of anything. "Just fucking brilliant." Her colors became a yellow-orange chain around her ankles, intertwined with marigolds.

Rough hands shoved Cooper forward and he stood alone in a patch of dark rain. Ice ran up his spine as he felt—more than saw—a shadow plunge from the sky. It dropped with the speed of a warhead and Cooper flinched, but its landing made no impact. The shadow resolved into a huddle of rags just inches from his feet. The black mass shuddered and Cooper took a step backward.

Before him rose the lich-lord, cloaked in dark wools and crowned in pale fire that radiated the opposite of heat. Cooper saw scraps of withered, parchment-dry skin plastered to a skull the color of iron, missing its jawbone. But its eyes! The lights where its eyes should be sparked with electricity, questing and hungry. It stood on skeletal toes that did not touch the ground, suspended above the rooftop as if wearing invisible heels. Jewelry pasted to its fleshless face glittered gold beneath a snowy wig, a coiffed asymmetric bob that the lich adjusted with one hand, preening. Looking at it, Cooper understood that it had no sex, and that if the undead thing appeared masculine or feminine, then it wore gender merely as an accoutrement.

"Lord!" cried Killilly with what felt like false enthusiasm. "You arrive earlier than anticipated, and so our bliss at your presence is all the sweeter for its unexpectedness!"

"Aesssr," it hissed from its jawless iron skull, but Cooper could not tell if the word was a demand, a question, or an announcement. "I felt my aesssr cry out in pain disssproportionate to your little inductions. Ssso I desssided to sssurprise you, darlings. Perhaps you have thrown a tantrum and abused my aesssr because you managed to lose the Lady, yesss?"

Appearing at Cooper's side, Marvin pushed him to his knees with hands on Cooper's shredded shoulders, and he folded like a doll, intimidated by the figure that loomed before him and emanated the strangest aura: charismatic putrescence, black on black on black, but limned in gold. A thrice-black wind blew the petals off of the crocus in his mind, and Cooper found himself caught in a web as—again—his thoughts became not his own. *I should be thinner,* he decided, aware of the absurdity of the desire even as he was helpless to resist it. The lich poured a blackness inside him, filling up his mind with need for fleshless fingers entwined around his hair, his master's blade like ice against his pulsing neck. Gold and black and forever.

They will destroy me, Cooper knew, watching Hestor approach. *They will send me somewhere small and dark and I will scream there until my voice is paper and my bones turn to rust.* To his right, the rain poured sheer and straight past the lip of the roof to the ground, so far below. It might as well be bottomless.

"Perhapsss you can explain to usss why your ssscheme failed, Hessstor?" lisped the lich-lord in a dry voice.

"Lord?" Hestor showed the first hint of doubt about the Lady and her fate. He had colors, but Cooper couldn't make out the shape.

"She is with usss no longer, Hessstor. She is gone, forever. We were asssssured that thisss was impossssible—our agreement with our Unseelie allies, in fact, was predicated upon thisss fact. Can you tell usss why the Lady isss Dead?" Was the lich-lord smoking a cigarette? It *was,* a brown cigarette smoldering in a black holder. It waved the opera-length Bakelite like a wand. "And can you tell usss *how?*"

Hestor shook his head in denial. "That's impossible, Lord! She *cannot* Die, she is the mother of life without Death, who will found your dynasty of freedom!"

"Neverthelessss"—the lich shrugged its padded shoulders and lifted its gloved hand in a gesture of feigned helplessness that reminded Cooper

of nothing so much as a fashion model draped in black cashmere—
"Dead she remainsss." It waved Hestor away like a caloric canapé.

"But this whole thing was her . . . it was her *idea!*" Hestor didn't understand. Tonight was his triumph, and he was covered in Cooper's blood to
prove it.

The lich made a noise of disappointment that sounded like a hundred
beetles clacking their mandibles. "Do you really believe that, Hessstor?
Do you really?"

"Believe what, Lord?"

Oh god, Cooper realized with a feeling that was indistinguishable from
despair or exultation, *Hestor has no clue what's really going on, does he?*

The lich flicked its electric eyes toward Cooper and gave the ghost of a
nod. "Your chattel understands more than you do, my proud sssubordi-
nate." It laughed, like parchment shredding. "You missstake a pawn for the
queen."

Lolly's mother. If Thyu had ordered him kidnapped and brought to the
Lady for analysis, then whoever had summoned the Undertow to La Jocondette had been clever, brave, and well-informed enough to betray her.
From his time inside the Cicatrix, she seemed the most likely party to successfully outmaneuver Lallowë Thyu. The lich nodded again, and Cooper
found himself almost incontinent at the prospect of this dried, molted
thing deferring to him when it should by all rights have been devouring
him instead. The last petal flew off the flower in his head.

"I don't understand," Hestor said, almost whining, scrambling for
some foothold of understanding. "The Lady will be our queen, Lord. She
is the instrument of our victory."

"Oh dear." The lich wedged its long cigarette holder in the space of a
missing tooth and removed the glove covering one of its hands, tugging
off each finger of the soft leather, one at a time. Beneath lay bones like
rusted metal ore. "I *thought* I heard you contradict me."

Hestor's eyes grew wide as saucers, and Cooper heard the inarticulate
wail of fear from inside his head. The lich smiled with its eyeless eyes.
"Sssurely I was missstaken?"

"But, but—" Hestor whined like a spoiled child, and the lich-lord
reached out with a limp wrist and backhanded the Death Boy chieftain off

the rooftop. Hestor flipped once in midair, his feline reflexes and bristle of tawny hair giving the impression of an abused alley cat—his eyes locked onto Cooper's for half a second, and then he was gone, trailing a scream.

"Heheh." The lich rasped out a papery giggle, then coughed up something wet and charcoal-gray that sizzled as it landed on the rain-slick roof. "Maybe Hessstor will find more sssuccesss in his next life. Marvin, do we sssuffer incompetenssse?"

Marvin stepped forward with an almost military, regimented posture. "No Lord, never."

"Lady," the lich-lord said. The word was both a command and a question.

"I—I don't know, Lord. I was the last to see her, wasn't I, Cooper? She was fine when I left her, wasn't she, Cooper?"

"Really, Marvin?" The ease with which the lich had unemployed Hestor stirred Cooper from his stupor. "Are you really stupid enough to ask me to confirm your fucking story?"

Marvin said nothing, his fists balled and his jaw tight.

Cooper turned to the lich, less afraid of it now. "To be honest, Miss or Mister Lich, I don't remember *any* lady at La Jocondette," Cooper said, and almost smiled. "But I've spent enough time with Marvin to know how much he likes to lie."

"I sssee." The lich tutted cigarette smoke and made to leave, looking toward the ever-churning vortex above. It sounded merely disappointed, and seemed to Cooper to have expected nothing more from its living followers.

Something shifted below—Cooper sensed the change. There was a woman made of bruised light who felt herself . . . *return*. As if a piece of her that had been hiding suddenly returned, slid into place and ignited. Meanwhile the Undertow cowered before their god. Cooper held his breath, and didn't dare to hope.

"Lord?" Marvin begged. The lich inclined its head a single degree. "Thank you, Master. Your freedom is my freedom, Master. Forgive me."

"Oh good," shrugged the lich, drawing its wool wrap close about its overpadded skeletal shoulders and rising a few feet into the air. "Yesss, yesss—freedom. Whatever. Do as you please with them, Marvin. You've earned it, haven't you? Yesss, earned it with your warm body." The lich swept its bare hand to indicate the cowering Undertow. It rasped a noise that resembled a chuckle. "They are yours for as long as you can keep them."

Suddenly a staccato burst of exploding glass ripped through the night as something blew out all the windows on the floor of the harem beneath them. The building shook, its embedded circuitry strobing light in frenzied bursts, and the roof was thrown into a chaos of pure golden light. Cooper heard a cry that sounded something like a bird and an insect making whalesong together, but so loud it nearly concussed his skull—then, through tears, he saw a smear of light rocket into the air at enormous speed, hurtling away from the tower in an arc of sun-bright wings and a buzzing, keening wail.

RunFlyScreamExplode! ExplodeScreamFly, RunCooperRun! EscapeEscapeEscape!

Cooper caught his breath—it was her, the aesr. It had worked. Somehow, against any logic he recognized and yet making a perfect kind of sense, his gambit had *worked:* she had freed herself. Cooper laughed out loud, drawing baleful glances from the agitated Death Boys and Charnel Girls, especially Marvin—who had seamlessly assumed Hestor's hauteur. It did him little good, though—the Undertow were in chaos.

The lich remained an intractably still figure, hovering on the tips of its toes while its minions surged around it. Cooper watched it following the bright path of the freed aesr with its eye-sparks: she flew straight as an arrow toward the Dome. From the lich, Cooper sensed a colossal ambivalence that dwarfed them all, and also a seething, shocked despair.

Then a screech from the far corner of the roof cut through the confusion, and Marvin whipped his head around in annoyance. The lich remained implacable while a streak of gray fury hurtled across the rooftop. Asher had escaped his captors and his face was twisted like a granite gargoyle.

"You sick fuck!" Asher cried, his eyes skewering the lich.

Cooper cheered. The lich wafted behind Marvin.

Asher transformed into an arc of smoke-colored light, he moved so fast. Cooper saw a gray hand chop in an arc upon Marvin like the blade of an axe, splitting the air with its speed, and the newly appointed Death

Boy chief's left shoulder fell away from his body, his torso split between neck and collarbone in a jagged tear that cracked his ribs open all the way past his sternum. Cut nearly in two, Marvin sank to his knees wordlessly, fountaining blood from his mouth and the exposed tissue of his lung, then collapsed to one side, blood foaming over his pretty, petty tattoos.

Not sparing a glance for its butterflied human shield, the lich withdrew.

Asher stumbled forward in pure momentum, feral and unaware of his surroundings. His leg gave out and he stumbled, collapsing, as Sesstri broke free of her distracted captors and rushed to Asher's side. Cooper's perception of time slowed to honey: Asher's tears and spittle frozen in midair, an arc of diamonds, while the tall man tumbled into Sesstri's outstretched arms; the scholar's face was a mask of confusion, her hair streaming sideways with the roaring wind, eyes caught between her crazed lover and the wreckage that had recently been Marvin the Death Boy, Marvin the pain-bringer, her prophecy concerning his motives come true in the worst possible way. The other Death Boys and Charnel Girls fell back from the three survivors as if caught in the radial blast of a shock wave, sudden weakness spilling from their eyes, huge and liquid in the permanent night.

For half a minute, Cooper just stood there and stared as Marvin died, feeling the razor kisses on his back burn and bleed, and when the Death Boy's lips turned blue, Cooper knelt and lifted Marvin's head to whisper, "I told you I was sorry, you waste of skin. I told you it wasn't over. Wherever you wake up next, you remember this New Yorker asshole, you remember my grin over your useless forgettable carcass and my promise, a shaman's promise: no matter how far you run, *life will always be wasted on you.* I've crossed worlds and found you nothing more than a disappointment."

Then he rolled Marvin's corpse off the edge of the roof into the empty air and called after it, "Tonight you fly with the Death Boys!"

He swiveled toward Asher and Sesstri, who crouched in each other's arms, gaping at Cooper. Did they have colors too? Somewhere inside him, the Cooper of three days earlier still existed, horrified, but those hours had altered him—some components upgraded, others removed and replaced with death and magic and knowledge. He was not quite the same machine as the man who'd woken up on a hill of yellow grass, not anymore. "I'm ready to be rescued now," Cooper said, turning his ruined back on the others and walking with a leaden gait toward the stairwell in the center of the roof. "If we're done killing whores for the night."

10

I am mother to lions and monsters, monarchs and liars—I will not dissemble and say I loved them all equally. But, Prince, you must remember the following: birth is a blessing, no matter the spawn. Poesy was not given to me; nor song, nor gentler arts. Just the teeth behind my smile and my prodigious womb. That has always proven more than enough.

—Eleanor of Aquitaine, *Travelling Backwards with Prince Prama Ramay*

Lord Senator Mner Bratislaus had Died on the privy, tangled in his trousers, trying to shit and survive at the same time. He may have known his Killer, or at least was not entirely ambushed, for he had not triggered the Domewide alarum. That had been the servants of half a dozen lords and ladies, after word spread of the lord senator's Death. Any other lord mightn't have been discovered for days—the Dome covered an area vaster than most huge cities, and Circle business went unquestioned by all. Cliques of lords routinely vanished for weeks at a time under the auspices of the work of the Circle Unsung, even though they usually limited themselves to whoring, gambling, or fucking one another in an inebriated haze. The lord senator's personal quarters were scrubbed as a matter of routine when he could not be found.

Mauve Leibowitz, who knew the answers to many questions and intended on discovering the rest, stood in the middle of the lord senator's library with her hands on her hips and outrage blazing behind her eyes. Steel-gray hair piled atop a face like a warlord gave Mauve an air of authority that few of the ladies at court could match. Worsted midnight wool flecked with white and gold hugged her curves, roomier in the sleeves and with a high, loose collar—it was not hard to see how she commanded the respect of the Circle. One of nine women on the ruling council of twenty-three families, Mauve held legendary status. She'd been one of few to stand up to Fflaen when he boxed them in; she'd debated the Guildworks United to a stalemate after they proposed a tertiary docking tithe; and she'd been the only member of the Circle to stare down Mner Bratislaus after the second wave of Killing, when the Circle seemed poised for civil war and the lord senator racked with Deathlust. Now not only was the insufferable bastard dead, but *she* had to wade through the shit he'd left behind, both figurative and literal.

Dead gods, Lady Leibowitz lamented, *is it too much to ask that a man's excrement vanish with his corpse?* Two dressing rooms and a cedar closet separated the library from the privy, and still the odor lingered. She made a mental note to remember to eat lightly if she ever suspected the Circle of plotting a water closet assassination against her. There were worse things than Death, indeed.

Mauve had hated the man, and had even privately considered using the Weapon against him despite the brinksmanship that forced the Circle back into armistice, but this was travesty. Mner's Murder could undo everything, all the backroom bargaining and bullying which had occupied her for most of the past year. That the sitters of the Circle had, after eons, used the Weapon *against one another* had been profane enough—a profanity that she and a handful of others had barely managed to contain with a lie: that the Circle had discovered the Weapon only recently, and been so intoxicated by its power that they'd indulged in not one but two full-blown orgies of Murder.

A crock of godshit, but there you have it. Her womb conspired to produce only imbeciles, so Mauve secured her legacy through political means. In this, she did not consider herself so different from her peers, although she wished she had conceived more children—surely if she spawned a hundred idiots *one* of them would stumble into usefulness. Better than the pair of limpid swans she called daughters: she often struggled to look at Nonette and Nilliam without wishing she'd tossed the twins into a canal as soon as she'd expelled them from her body.

Purity Kloo, who sat abashed and slightly blinded in a tall leather armchair, would have made a much less objectionable daughter. The Baron had spoiled her, of course, but Mauve would have raised her to be a razor blade and not a truant.

Mauve took a pull off her long, thin bone pipe and tutted smoke as she closed the curtains against the brilliance of the Petite Malaison. Today its bones had begun to shine like they'd used to, but Mauve suspected something worse than the return of Fflaen. Dour times.

She turned her thoughts back to the world she *could* control and considered the possibilities. She found herself hoping that the Murderer sat on the Circle, although that would mean a rogue lord or lady, and *that* would breach the armistice and threaten to send the Circle into round three of self-annihilation. She'd seen too many noble families purge themselves of undesirables and rivals already: now they were weakened nearly to the point of dissolution. Too many new faces on the Circle, young heirs who couldn't possibly carry the responsibility, and too few old friends or enemies upon whom she could rely. Her people had seen more change in the last few years than they had in the uncounted millennia before Fflaen confined them to the Dome. Although now that the billionstone shone again, perhaps something could be done about all of that.

Still, better the Killer be a rogue Circle member than the alternative—if anyone outside of the Circle Unsung had the Weapon, then they were all quite thoroughly rogered.

The greatest legacy of the aesr would destroy the city those long-lost First People had built. Fflaen deserved no less, for all he'd done to preserve the legacy of his race, but saving her house took precedence over punishing the aesr prince, wherever he'd fled—or turned up. Despite the sins Lady Mauve had committed herself—she was no less guilty than the rest of the Circle—she did not wish to witness the destruction of her home.

She saw Elisabetta and Nilliam skid into the room red-faced and out of breath. Elisabetta had been crying, but Nilliam merely stared at her mother with heavy-lidded eyes that peeked out from beneath her ridiculous sideways hat. She dressed like a clown: batik, in burgundy?

Mauve met her daughter's dead-eyed gaze. "Where is your sister?"

"Nonette, Mother?" NiNi fiddled with her hat, and started up with her humming.

"Do you have *another* sister?"

"No, Mother."

Bitzy looked fit to dissolve at any moment, so Mauve steadied her with a gold-barnacled hand. "I'm sorry, Elisabetta. He was gone before anyone knew he was in danger." That was a kind lie—she knew more of the lord senator's last few meals than of his Death, only that it was final, and in the loo.

Bitzy nodded and tried to act like an adult. "Thank you, Lady Leibowitz. I . . . I appreciate your kind assistance. As for NoNo, she's been having skirts fitted all morning, after her dancing lessons, bright and early. She'll come running in any minute, I'm certain of it. NiNi . . . ?"

NiNi shrugged and hopped up onto a side table where, effort expended, she closed her eyes at once. "Clothes people" was all she said. Bitzy sat herself on a sofa near Purity and fixed her eyes on the floor. She'd gone into standby mode, poor thing.

"What *about* clothes people, Nilliam?"

NiNi buzzed a raspberry at her mother, eyes still closed as if napping. "They couldn't find her. The clothes people. So I told them where to find her. NoNo. I'm helping."

"And *where* did you tell the clothes people to find your sister, Nilliam?" Mauve Leibowitz must be used to pulling sense out of the senseless, Purity thought.

NoNo chose that moment to drift through the wide double doors like some yellow cloud, her lacey parasol tucked under her arm while she peered at her nails, then buffed them on her shoulder. "Did I miss something?" she asked the bookshelves, craning her neck and seeming a little awed that there could be so many books gathered together, so many stupid paper pages. "Alarms are loud."

"There you are!" Mauve Leibowitz jabbed her bone pipe toward the doors. "My other miscarriage. Get in here and sit with your sister where I can keep an eye on you. Sit down, now!"

NoNo appeared baffled, and looked at NiNi dozing on her perch. "On the credenza?" she asked her mother.

Lady Leibowitz covered her face with a palm and jabbed her pipe at the furniture where Bitzy and Purity sat, still as figures in a painting. "Sit your bottom on the sofa, Nonette. Sit it next to Elisabetta and do *please* try to be of some comfort to your bereaved friend. Pretend you're an ambient banana tree, that ought to fall within your emotional range—and the dead gods know you've dressed the part."

"Banana?" NoNo frowned. "This color is called *canary,* Mother." But she did as Lady Mauve bade, and patted Bitzy as she sat. Bitzy didn't look up, but chewed on her lip, lost in a little moment of empty concentration. NoNo dithered her parasol in her hand like an old man with a cane.

NiNi seemed to wake up, and lit a skinny brown cigarette from a paper-weight lighter of scrimshawed horn that shared her tabletop; she puffed on it in what Purity supposed was intended to be a thoughtful manner. "It *is* canary, you know," NiNi said to no one in particular, then resumed humming that sad syncopation that Purity found so irksome.

"Lady Leibowitz?" Purity attempted to be of some use. "There was a terrible amount of bloodshed in the aviary, have you heard?"

Mauve looked at Purity with a craggy blend of resignation and regret. "No. No, Purity Kloo, I have *not* heard. Please do enlighten me."

Purity took a breath and described the scene as concisely as possible without including any incriminations—or any mention of Kaien the Murderer. "The alarum frightened me, and I thought—foolishly, I must admit—that the bird sanctuary might provide sanctuary for me as well. Instead I found a dozen dead praetors and as many dead servants."

Lady Mauve narrowed her eyes. "Do you mean to tell me, Miss Kloo, that if I marched you straight to the aviary, we would find no fewer than *two dozen* corpses?"

Purity faltered. "Well, yes, ma'am. I'm not exaggerating the number of casualties, if that's what you're—"

"—I am not."

"—And I certainly hope you *won't* be marching me back to that horrid—"

"—I will not."

"—Then, yes, ma'am, that's the gist of it."

"I see." Lady Mauve bit her pipe, ruminating. "And did you by chance happen to make any *other* pertinent observations while waltzing through the hallways?"

"Well"—Purity bit back several salty rebuttals that sprang to mind— "I did, as a matter of fact. The guardsmen were scattered, as if they'd been cut down before they assumed battle formation, which as you might gather suggests that they were killed alarmingly quickly. Also, the servants lay atop the guards and came from the opposite entrance—that is, they were coming *from* the Petite Malaison, whereas the praetors seemed to have been dispatched from Dendrite's Folly, where we sit now. This tells us, as

I'm sure your ladyship will agree, that the Killer—or whomever is responsible, for there's no direct evidence to link Lord Bratislaus' passing to the person or persons responsible for the butchery in the aviary—dispatched the praetors and was subsequently surprised by the servants, who were then cut down."

Lady Leibowitz regarded Purity with something resembling infuriated awe. "My, that *is* an impressive recounting, Purity, and I'm certain your father would be proud. Proud, if not surprised—judging by how the Baron rambles on in praise of his favorite daughter."

Purity blushed. That backhand would be as close as Mauve Leibowitz could come to a compliment.

"But why, pray tell, would a dozen servants rush into a scene of such slaughter?"

"That's just what we—what *I* wondered, Lady Leibowitz. I'm afraid I have no satisfactory answer to that question."

"And you say you went to the aviary because you were *frightened,* do you?"

"Yes, ma'am."

"So frightened that you managed to assess the scene with more aplomb than many a professional investigator?"

Purity gritted her teeth and aimed for hauteur. "As you say, ma'am: would I be my father's favorite without merit?"

Lady Leibowitz shook her head, appeased for the moment. "No, you would not. The Baron dotes overmuch, but he's no fool. Very well. Thank you, Purity. I shall have a look at the scene in the aviary myself, before those praetors begin reviving and our evidence scurries off to the showers in shame."

"In that case, I should like to find my father, Lady Leibowitz. He'll need to be made aware of—"

"—I think *not.* You will all four of you head down the hall to Elisabetta's apartments and you will *stay there* until *I* arrive to say otherwise. Am I clear?"

"Yes, Lady Leibowitz," Bitzy and Purity said as one. NiNi slid off the credenza and ground her cigarette into an amber ashtray.

"Yes, Mother." Something fierce glinted in NoNo's eyes as the girls filed out of the library through the wide, tall doors. Before it disappeared behind a twirling sunshade, her chin made the faintest jab of defiance.

A tense but mercifully short march to Bitzy's salon ensued. None of the girls seemed quite themselves, and the surly Leibowitz house guards in front of and behind them didn't help the mood. *Where are the praetors?* Purity wondered.

"What are we to do?" Purity was beside herself with worry, dispossessed enough to forget to keep her concerns to herself. "Throw a fucking tea party while the Circle tears down the Dome around us?"

Bitzy grabbed both of Purity's hands and shook them with cartoonish accord. "Oh, yes!" she exclaimed. "That's a *brilliant* idea, Purity! Just what we need to distract ourselves from this awkward business. A tea party!" She seemed to have rewound time by an hour or so and unprocessed the news about her father, and Purity wondered if perhaps Bitzy wasn't having a bit of a schism.

"You cannot be serious." NoNo was having none of it, and for once Purity found herself allying with a Leibowitz.

"Really, Bitz, don't you think you should be with your family at a time like this?"

Bitzy threw up her hands. "Drowned gods, no! The last thing Beauregret and Absynth will want is their little sister underfoot, and Mother . . . Mother will be . . ."

". . . I'm sure your brothers are taking perfect care of Lady Bratislaus, Bitz." Purity reached out to console her friend, whether she needed it or not. If Purity couldn't be out there finding the Killer, she'd at least practice decency. The dead gods knew it was in short supply.

The Cicatrix jerked as several vivisistors shorted out, their tiny occupants screaming through muted inputs, unheard but felt. There, beneath her shoulder blade, and another beneath her clavicle. She rolled her shoulder and jutted her collarbone, lifting her elbows and turning her wrists in a strange dance. She exhaled, feeling a kind of ecstasy as the latest packet from beyond the Seven Silvers pinged her systems. Again the vivisistors sparked, above her pelvis and a chorus along her spine, and the queen

swayed along, full of grace and lightning. All her silver bells were ringing, and they rang like thunder.

The unknown vivisistor beneath the City Unspoken called to her,
huge and ancient and hungry. It sucked out her life while it spooled her
systems with a sick signal that tasted like all the madness in the metaverse.

The Cicatrix felt her life bleed out into the space between worlds, an
invisible hemorrhage she could do nothing to stop. The vivisistors were a
part of her, as much as her scars and bones, and they powered themselves. Her life should have been outside the equation—she was no battery,
she was not trapped, dying, inside a machine. A machine that gathered
madness in exchange for her essence.

And still, she bled.

The song that distant vivisistor sang to her sounded broken, like the
tune of a music box whose pins had rusted away. It sounded sickly, too.

She'd stuffed vivisistors into her subjects, forced them upon servants
and manipulated trends until her courtiers felt compelled to follow suit.
Some had required convincing. She sought to staunch the flow by feeding other lives to the vampiric feedback, to give herself time to diagnose
the problem, patch her firmware, or build a better firewall. Nothing. The
more faeries she packed with vivisistors, the more hungrily the vacuum
drank her essence and filled her up with madness.

And the more incessantly the unknown vivisistor pulsed like an emerald and lilac star, its colors and music strobing through the impossible
network. All told, it was not an unlovely way to bleed.

When she allowed herself to sleep, the Cicatrix dreamed of birds and
of men, staggering through trees to evaporate. They seemed so much like
Lolly's little clockwork toys, ticking down to their final movement. She
woke wanting to Die.

Her concierge subroutine pinged her HUD with an alert: the time had
come to summon her court to session. An important arrival waited in the
wings.

The title WEAPON OF CHOICE scrolled across her vision. Her heads-up
display constantly streamed information, but the concierge subsystem
only gave titles to significant events. She had never programmed it to do
so—perhaps the habit was idiosyncratic to one of the pixies that powered

its vivisistors. Perhaps they collaborated, to soothe or console her. The lilac and emerald pixels flickered like fireflies before they winked out:

> *Event_Title: 'Weapon_of_Choice'*
> *Sense6th::Inverse lifesign detected. Hardware Failure*
> *   flagged and logged.*

There was no hardware failure—her sensors couldn't interpret the truth about the guest who arrived, and logged it as a failure, but the Cicatrix considered the coming parley a great success even before it began. A first, in all of fey history. Oh yes, she'd been anticipating this meeting for days. She was curious to see how her court would react, those who remained. How they'd obey.

The Cicatrix lifted her torso fully upright, rearing back upon a coil of black carbon, a queen cobra commanding her nest. She tasted the air with her tongue, and wondered at the limitations of the natural world. She did not notice any diminished connection to her landscape, now that she'd diminished it, and the many pleasant skies of her empire were quarantined from her working memory, replaced by the single sky she'd built here, above her court: brown to match the earth, barren to suit the trees. No blue sky, no warmth on her skin as she danced.

No dancing.

Once, she could not have tolerated the presence of the undead.

"Come, come, you dukes of thorn and claw!" the Cicatrix howled, the voice box in her throat-meat amplifying her call until the denuded forest rang with feedback.

"Come, Lady Ash and Lord Frost! Come, wild hunters and miscarriages of the airy dark! I call the Court of Scars to audience. Who dares ignore my summons?"

The forest shivered, and a few thin birds shot from the trees and escaped to the west. Where was the wild circus? Where were the revelers and murderers, the half-breeds and beast-folk, the haughty pure and their thralls?

> *Gon€ to find the bl00d and mu$i¢, our queen.*
> *Fled alonggg teh hedgerow, fled alonggg teh countless*
> *   branching paths.*

"Come, you brave souls." The Cicatrix ignored her outsourced insight and growled to those who lingered. "Attend me."

A mat of leaves between a forked branch blinked and slunk forward. Its skin shimmered from bark to thundercloud to mud as it passed, before resolving into thousands of articulated, tiny mirrors. They covered Oona like skin, in place of the skin that had been flensed away.

"We hear," Oona whispered, her voice rough like grinding glass. "We come."

Old Piezeblossom hobbled forward, wreathed in dark graphene petals that bristled from his cheek to his toe. His other leg had been adapted into a grounding spike, which he wrenched from the muck with every step. He had embraced amendment with a fervor that belied his age— Piezeblossom, too, must hear the call of freedom.

"The dukes are gone," he croaked. "Lady Ash is fled. Lord Frost is dead. The hunters hunt. The Court of Scars assembles, such as we are."

Oona tugged a rope she held in her chameleon hand, and a line of nameless faeries—children, mostly—marched out of the wood. Their hair was matted, their faces dirty, and their ankles shackled by cold iron. Such good subjects. Most had amendments of the lowest order—older coke-boiler systems, rusted or clogged or otherwise useless.

Among the trees, long fingers curled around branches like the bars of a jail cell, and huge eyes blinked, watching with held breath.

The Cicatrix smiled, and the gallery of fey whimpered in fear.

Piezeblossom coughed pus into the mud. "A guest, my queen." He pivoted on his spike and bowed as best he could—his ears were fleabitten and moldy along their tips, she saw. "Skylord Rousseau, my queen."

"Come, lich." She'd made the thing wait two whole days—a decision that had proved more traumatic for the remainder of her court than anything; the lich seemed not to notice the passage of time.

Ambassador Rousseau slid forward on a curtain of shadowed air, just barely brushing her toe bones against the mud. It was a blasphemy she was denied in the City Unspoken and its annexed worlds, where no undead could set foot.

The gathered faeries did their best to keep still. The children began to sniffle and were hauled away by an iridescent Oona. A few others gasped and hid behind bare branches. Only Piezeblossom retained his composure.

"Cherie, ssssweet friend!" exclaimed a skeleton of iron and silver, polished to shine along the cheeks and fingers and arm-bones, ribs etched with filigree; the hollow absence where her organs should be was shadowed like a church nave, and the bowl of her pelvis was filled with dried flowers, hyssop, and calamus.

H0w QQuaint.

She wore a russet wig for the occasion, long over one shoulder, silver jewelry to match her bones, and an open robe that disappeared into the shadows holding her aloft—and holding her bones together. An awful green fire burned in the sockets of her eyes.

"Once your presence would have enraged me at my very core. The constitution of a creature of the natural world is inimical to your, ah, manner of persistence. A faerie, in parley with the undead?" The Cicatrix held her black nails up to the sky—they were still translucent, at least. "This reception is a first, Ambassador, in all the worlds."

The ambassador nodded her skull. "I am honored to be the firssst of my ilk to ssset foot on your sssweet ssssoil, my queen. Truly, I mussst be in a ssstate of grazzze, to walk again among sssuch wondrouzzz gardenzzz."

"Do you miss it?" the Cicatrix asked. "Life?"

Ambassador Rousseau held up her hand. Between the polish, wrist bones were pitted like old iron and mottled with rust, held together with sick shadows. She sang a few meters of an old springtime hymn—the Cicatrix recognized it as simple human garden magic. The lich must remember the cantrip from life, as it was a weak thing, of childhood and nursemaids. But the song sounded as sweet as if its singer had possessed lips or a tongue: a butterfly disguised as a red leaf stirred upon the ground, struggled up from the mud, and fluttered toward the lich.

"Miss life?" Rousseau smiled, sort of; flakes of leather stapled to her skull twitched up, but it *felt* like a smile. The autumn-leafed lovewing alighted upon her fingertip, blinked its wings once, long and slow, and turned to ash as it died.

"Of courssse not."

The ash retained its form. Wings flapped weakly, and an inversion of a butterfly took flight, a spidery thing that circled Rousseau's wrist before crawling into her sleeve.

"Chains have little to offer a woman who holds the key. Life offers me nothing I cannot sssteal." The ambassador held a hand to her wig, stroking a curl of dark hair against the memory of her neck.

The Cicatrix made a sound that was halfway between a hiss and a moan. "I share your dedication to radical freedom, Ambassador Rousseau."

If the ambassador heard—or cared—it did not show. The Cicatrix found herself wondering what kind of woman this Rousseau had been when she lived. When those iron bones were cloaked in soft flesh.

"The *svarning*? Madnesss ssstalks the worldz, we are told. We hear it, like dissstant music, growing louder, but not yet drowning out the notesss of life and death. The Dome is sssealed, the Dying are numberlesss and find no ssssurceassse, and yet we wonder—does the cataclysm we've been promisssed approach, or will the *svarning* prove to be merely another disappointment?"

The Cicatrix shifted the length of her abdomen, coils shuffling. Something inside her carapace began to sing. "The madness comes, skylord. When you attack, the city will be at your mercy."

"Where is it, then? Thisss disease that will cure the worlds of the tyranny of life and death?"

Inside the queen's chest, a second-string vivisistor shorted out. The sprite inside seized violently, and before her root process muted the offending mechanism, the Cicatrix heard it scream the word *HERE*.

"The Dome's martial forces are veteran infantry with classsical tactical eleganssse." Rousseau withdrew her Bakelite wand and twisted a cigarette into its end. She put the mouthpiece to her teeth and inhaled; the cigarette flared into what would have been life, had it not been life's opposite. "We have enlisssted a famed former monarch to lead our living hossst, and her battlefield experience will prove decisive: none of ours need survive, of course. Our pawns will drown the Dome in sssuicide, while we decapitate the government. Or perhapsss we'll drink it dry."

"You will have my help in that regard, as promised."

Rousseau shrugged. "How can you asssure usss that the Dome will be reopened, and that government will not rise up againsssst usss?"

"I can assure you victory under any circumstances. I presume that to be sufficient."

"Please expound."

"No." The Cicatrix loosed her coils and relaxed backward into her nest. These revenants intrigued her, but they would learn their place among her tool set. "Do we have an agreement?"

Ambassador Rousseau remained still, then ground her cigarette into her iron palm. "We do."

The Cicatrix smiled with what remained of her true face, then, retracting the veil of third silver that covered her jaw. She thought she saw the green coals that were the ambassador's eyes widen. The queen's voice box chuckled as she slid the silver lips back into place, half-extending her visor so that it shaded her eyes. She tilted her head back like a sunbathing maiden, though her shoulder servos worked with the gyroscopics within her massive helm to maintain the upright posture of the helm and shoulder armor itself.

"That is all." A flick of her nails, volcanic glass from a gauntleted fist. "Go."

The blades angling out from her spine flexed, piezoelectric arcs flying between them. They were heat sink, capacitor, and auxiliary power source in one—and rather terrifying to behold.

The thing that thought itself her equal spun on an oxidized toe and glided away, burning a line into the mud. Already the Cicatrix had summoned tables and charts to her vison, flicking them around her HUD with eye movements and a habit of thought so engrained it was practically an automated subroutine of its own.

Yes. It was time to choose her weapon. She pulled a horn flute from within her carapace and contemplated the instrument. A good instrument could play any type of music—it could inspire dancers or make warriors weep. But add another voice to the song, and suddenly both instruments must play off and around each other. A symphony? Chaos given purpose.

All her plans spun on their own, and soon they would collide. She would conduct the chaos, channel it to her own purpose. That is what Unseelie faeries did. That was the work of a queen. That was why she'd spared her only viable child.

It was time to play the music, and wake her.

*   *   *

Sisterhood, mused Lallowë Thyu as she fiddled with the confabulation of engineering and inference, postulation and guesswork that comprised the reconstituted vivisistor, was a vexing condition. Take her wary orbit around Almondine as a case study: full-blooded and firstborn, endowed with rapine cruelty and rapier intellect, perfect in form and function alike, Almondine should by all measures have been the Cicatrix's favored spawn. Yet the petite creature had lived for centuries as an outlier in her mother's court, disdaining the Wild Hunt and following at nearly all times the path of least resistance. The Court of Scars could be a blissful place, especially for an heir who could have—in theory, at least—pleased her royal mother with a minimum of effort.

When Hinto Thyu flickered through the worlds of the Seven Silvers and captured, for the briefest of moments, the attention of a younger Cicatrix—this was before her rechristening, before her amendments became deformity—no one had expected the child born from his passing patronage to amount to much. By rights, Lallowë should have been the outlier, scrounging an existence like the other mongrels, half-breeds, and hangers-on to the Court of Scars. And yet she had quickly become the exalted daughter, reaping the advantages of her mother's esteem while Almondine faded into the background radiation, seemingly at peace with the cagey détente she'd assumed regarding her younger half-sibling—it was an arrangement with which Lallowë had never felt entirely comfortable; she did not understand why her sister allowed Lallowë to be the beneficiary of their mother's attentions, why she hid the resentment she must have felt, or why she did not murder the half-breed whelp who'd stolen Almondine's favor.

And then, during a rare concession to participate in the hunt, Almondine had fallen to the soul-devouring predations of one of the First People.

Lallowë summoned the memory of that day as she soldered the rare half cent to the base of the broken vivisistor, blank face up, and ignored the white-hot sparks that peppered her unprotected skin. The hunters had slipped through the wood between worlds as only faeries on the Hunt could, leaving the seven creations of the Cicatrix's domain for wilder coppices in less well-trammeled universes.

They'd emerged somewhere sufficiently fertile, though Lallowë couldn't have said where. Two moons bookended an alien, indigo sky, and the hunters had raced through a sea of dusk-cedars, pleasant arboreal giants whose branches glimmered with ghost-lights that resembled stars. The local inhabitants had of course remained unaware of the faerie incursion taking place within the vast tracts of their dusk-cedar forests.

Lallowë had clad herself in furs that she'd skinned and tanned with her own hands—she smiled at the thought of the denizens of the Guise-laine seeing their marchioness outfitted like a feral huntress, let alone tanning hide. At the time she'd enjoyed the trailing days of a dalliance with a statuesque she-kachina named White Corn, and the two had been lagging behind the company for days, alternating between rutting in the treetops and poaching the red-horned aurochs that pastured beneath the vaulted cathedrals of the forest. White Corn had finished a pipe she'd begun making from an aurochs horn days earlier, and she played a lonely birdsong on the instrument as she and Lallowë tried to catch up to the rest of the hunters.

When they stopped to refill their water skins at a frothy cataract, their stomachs filled with raw meat, Lallowë had stretched herself out on a flat rock to close her eyes and enjoy the warmth of the day. She'd dozed, half-dreaming of the spike-haired gypsies they'd spied living on a blue spur of mountains to the north, when White Corn's piping had awoken her. Annoyed, she sat up, intending to lash the kachina with her tongue—only it hadn't been White Corn playing.

In fact, White Corn was nowhere to be seen. Instead, Lallowë saw a hunchbacked, man-shaped thing with ratty dark hair and bright eyes, who played White Corn's pipe and introduced himself as Pelli. Unimpressed, Lallowë did not return the introduction and only refrained from attacking the man out of the need to regain her companions. Slipping her naked body back into her furs and leathers, Lallowë glowered at the man and leapt high into the branches, leaving the stooped piper behind as she chased after White Corn's scent.

She found White Corn hours later, crying over the unblinking body of Almondine.

The kachina had found her, she claimed, lying there on a bank of moss, her body transformed into a solid trunk of wood. She was not quite dead, but most certainly empty—her spirit turned to wood as thoroughly as her flesh. In the crook of her polished cherry arm lay White Corn's horn pipe.

Lallowë had borne her sister's wooden body back to the Seven Silvers, and left White Corn behind on the world of the dusk-cedars and mountain gypsies, where for all Lallowë knew she still remained. The Cicatrix, for her part, had only been bothered about the fate of her firstborn in an abstract way, which had been perplexing—her mother rarely missed an opportunity to overreact to a slight against her vanity or sovereignty, if indeed the two could be separated. The Cicatrix had scryed out the identity of the piper and verified that he was, indeed, some declension of the First People. Beyond that, she forgot the matter easily.

Lallowë cared only slightly more, upset not at the fate that had befallen her half-sibling but by the suggestion that there were entities beyond her ken, powers that could cripple her, too, if given the inclination. More worrisome was the fact that Almondine was gone but not absent, a presence to be looked after and always, *always* a reminder of the mortality of faeries and the obligations, however slight, of having family in the first place.

Now she had repurposed her shell of a sister, and felt marginally thankful that the Cicatrix had insisted upon preserving Almondine's empty wooden body. At least she would serve a function, now, provided Lallowë could infuse new life into the vessel, provided Lallowë could re-create a vivisistor and write some life into it, provided Lallowë could animate wood. She'd do so, of *course,* and brilliantly—she had already half-composed a programming language/ruleset that she expected would establish gender, temperament, aesthetic, malice—the basics of identity. But she resisted bringing back her sister in any form. Even animating the body with a constructed intelligence came perilously close to reviving the filial jealousies that had so beleaguered her early years. Why *did* it have to be Almondine's body? Why not some mineral Galatea, girded with pyrite and lapis for eyes? Because no other body would surprise the Cicatrix, and because Almondine's shell kept Lallowë alert. It also reminded her of the cost of failure.

Sisters. At least she only had one of the bitches to endure.

* * *

They were all drowning. That's how it felt as Cooper, Asher, and Sesstri raced down flights of bony stairs. The walls closed in again like the waves of a dark ocean and the weak lights flickered like those in a sinking vessel. They passed the seraglio of the Undertow, the harem prisoners screaming in distress or, perhaps, escaping like the aesr. They descended into dark floors, where the grids of circuitry embedded within the material surface of the building dimmed and then disappeared entirely—whatever power supplied the skyscraper seemed only to reach the upper levels, and as the three raced toward the ground it felt as if they were racing to the bottom of the ocean floor.

The air grew ice-cold and stale, and the sounds of the pursuing Undertow never faded. The whoops and trills that followed them had begun not long after Cooper led them down from the rooftop, the Death Boys, recovering from the shock of losing not one but two consecutive leaders in the span of about five minutes, enjoined by their sisters the Charnel Girls, all of whom now poured down the alien stairwell in pursuit of the trio. The cold came from the skylords, circling the building now in their gathered, agitated masses; Cooper could feel their tails licking the walls. They knew his taste.

And now that the aesr was no longer siphoning away his pain, the truth of what had been done to his back became more apparent. It felt like he'd been through a meat grinder, and from the expression on Sesstri's and Asher's faces when they'd seen the damage, he didn't look much better. Blood spotted the steps in his wake, and the ache became raking lines of pain, which became a patch of agony stretching from shoulder to shoulder and down to his lower back. He began to slow.

Sesstri took the lead, pulling a thunderstruck Asher by the wrist down the submarine hallways and shooting odd glances at Cooper, who followed as fast as he could. He supposed he looked more than a wreck, naked to his skin and beyond, his ruined back laid open. Something would have to be done about that soon, he knew, provided they escaped with the rest of their hides intact.

Floors passed in a rush of adrenaline and pain and blue-skinned walls, and before they knew it Cooper, Sesstri, and Asher found an exit: a three-story hole blasted into the side of the building gaped onto the street level, and they stumbled out into the open air. They kept running, Sesstri and

Asher now both looking back at Cooper with something resembling awe. Asher's face was wild. At last they clambered over a wall of rubble that slowed their progress to a crawl, and as he pulled himself past a fragment of broken mirror, slicing his palms on some of the shards, Cooper pulled back in shock—his face was covered in half-dried blood and seemed frozen in an animal snarl.

No wonder they're looking at me funny.

The blocks-thick border of rubble where the towers stopped seemed to be as far as the Undertow would chase them—a chorus of high-pitched screaming summoned them back as a flock of black lich-lords swooped overhead only to return to their burning towers. As the trio staggered out of the permanent night that shrouded the skyscrapers into the natural night that had fallen over the City Unspoken, a giant orange moon appeared to greet them. No, not a moon—a planet, a great gas giant that reminded Cooper of Jupiter, if Jupiter's troposphere had cloud layers of Dreamsicles and cream soda. Candy-colored storms painted bands of turbulence across the face of the transient planet, latitudes of tempestuous tangerine, cherry, blood orange, coffee, butter, and chocolate; in its unlikely vastness the gas giant filled a third of the sky. Their shadows flickered against planetlit alleyways.

Cooper hoped they would be safe, and he overheard a fright of Sesstri's that mirrored his hope: *NoMoreScreaming, PleasePleaseNoMoreScreaming.* At least he thought that's what she meant. Looking at her, Cooper realized that it wasn't only the huge planet ruling the sky that had painted her in a wash of light: he saw more of the strange spirit-colors swirling around her chest. As he watched, they resolved into a bronze sign that shimmered over her brow—an unfurled scroll and a long quill. What was he seeing?

Free from the chasing Undertow, Asher seemed stunned. He kept scanning the sky, muttering to himself and shaking his head.

Both Sesstri and Cooper knew it had something to do with the creature that had broken loose during their confrontation on the rooftop, but each had their own reasons for keeping quiet. Cooper, now that he'd had time to think about it, was half-terrified he'd doomed the captive aesr, and that her explosion and flight had been a reaction to the reflected torture she'd endured on his behalf. The other part of him didn't feel like adding "Saw an extinct superbeing before she exploded" to the FUBAR list at that particular moment.

At a fork in the road, the trio stood facing the blown-out windows of a dark intersection, limp-limbed, each too wounded, winded, or disturbed to think of what to do next.

"Please, cover yourself," Sesstri panted, pulling a silk smock from her satchel and tossing it at Cooper. "I've seen this show before."

Cooper wrapped the tiny bit of yellow silk around his waist—being careful of his lower back—and tied off the arms. At least as a makeshift sarong it hid his vital bits.

"Somebody wants us to take a left," Cooper said, pointing.

One side of the abandoned brick building in front of them—once a warehouse, once apartments—bore a bright red loop of still-wet paint across its windowless façade. A stylized ribbon, thirty feet tall.

Sesstri did a double take and turned apoplectic. "*Now* she takes an interest? Not when we're attacked by thugs or lunatics or mincing undead parasites, but *now*?" She kicked a stone and sent it skidding toward the big red ribbon, but that didn't provide enough release, so she raised her face and screamed wordlessly at the planet rising overhead. Sesstri bayed. It was when Asher didn't even smile that Cooper began to worry for him.

"Fine. Just fine." Sesstri stalked off in the direction the building-sized ribbon indicated. "*She* snaps the leash and we go trotting along." Cooper and Asher followed without a word.

They walked past intersections clotted with rubble, following a path away from the burning towers and the burnished orb rising behind them, and in the silence Cooper returned to himself somewhat. Everything that had happened to him since he'd woken up in La Jocondette seemed like an unfortunate dream. The Lady, the thrill of his adventure with Marvin, the bitterness he'd felt at Marvin's betrayal, the aesr, the lich, rolling Marvin's butterflied corpse into the sky—what were these but the details of a disturbing dream? All he had to remind him that they were not dream-figments but his own history were his naked skin and the open wreck of his back.

Which hurt like hell. It was a wonder he wasn't screaming or unconscious. Shock, sepsis—he'd need massive amounts of painkillers and antibiotics, soon, or he'd lose his navel once and for all.

When they arrived at the next intersection that presented a choice of direction, it became apparent that their unseen navigator had not finished pointing the way—only the upper stories of one face of this squat, square building bore the attentions of any red paint. Then a small figure dropped down from the top corner of the building on a tether and ran in an arc across the bricks: it was Nixon.

Nixon laughed and dashed sideways across the wall of the building, spilling paint from his bucket in thin looping threads as he went. His line secured him to the roof, letting him wall-run along a pendulum's path as he painted his second billboard ribbon. He whooped when he saw them limping toward the intersection, and ran down the face of the building, then jumped and landed with his arms outstretched and gave a little bow.

"Olga Korbut taught me to land on my feet," he said. "But I never got the hang of it till now. I can't help but notice that you guys are early, and alive."

Asher, Cooper, and Sesstri stared at the unboy, too exhausted to talk. Nixon kept on, walking around them in a circle with an appraising eye. "Thanks for leaving all the climbing gear around. It sure made the job easier."

"Alouette sent you?" Sesstri asked, recovering her voice and relieved to have someone she could harangue for answers.

Nixon nodded. "Wanted me to correct an earlier mix-up."

"Lovely," Sesstri and Asher said as one, but Nixon had discovered Cooper's back.

"Hey, CinemaScope." Nixon squared off with Asher, tiny fists on his hips. "Still choking kids?"

Asher said nothing.

Nixon continued. "Turns out I may have been, um, slightly neglectful in my duty. I may, technically, have been supposed to give this ribbon to you, Cooper. I guess I forgot, what with all the violence and spooky shit and whatnot." He held up a small loop of red ribbon and offered it to Cooper. Cooper didn't move, and Nixon scratched the back of his neck and made an awkward grimace. "He, uh, okay? He's supposed to take the ribbon. I'm not supposed to leave until he actually *takes* the damned—"

Asher grabbed the ribbon and handed it to Cooper. Nixon nodded at a job well done, then squealed in surprise as he, Sesstri, and Cooper jerked and were caught up in a sucking twist of space. In a swirl of red ribbons, they vanished, leaving Asher alone in the deserted ruins.

In the gray man's current mood, that suited him just fine.

Everything seemed to change when the planet rose above the horizon. They all felt it, even NiNi squirmed on her fainting couch, unable to find sufficiently flattering light. Bitzy waved her hands, orchestrating servants who appeared more distraught than she did; cakes were brought in and removed, returned and sliced into quarters, removed again for re-icing; teapots entered and were judged inferior, porcelain reluctantly accepted, and trays of broiled fish rejected as inappropriate for the occasion.

"I *know* it's dinnertime," Bitzy scolded a pigeon-toed maid, "but this is a *tea party*. Would *you* eat dinner at a tea party? No, you wouldn't, *would* you? Because that would be *ridiculous*." She waved the woman off.

"Thank you, Krella," Purity said as the maid retreated. Purity turned to Bitzy with a smile. "I'm sure she's trying her best, Bitz. Krella's always smart about understanding the details; that's so hard to find."

Bitzy answered with a brittle smile.

NiNi stopped humming to lean half an inch toward Purity, cover her mouth with her hand, and speak at full volume: "That was Narvie, Purity. Krella's the governess and she hasn't worked for Bitzy's family for three years now."

"Oh," Purity said. "Silly me."

"Fuck Krella and fuck this stupid tea party," NoNo muttered under her breath.

Bitzy shot a glance at NoNo, and NiNi lifted her palm in a gesture of forbearance. "Oh Bitz," she drawled, "don't ride NoNo too hard. It must be a Bratislaus trait—like father, like daughter, don't they say?"

NoNo jerked upright, her hand flying to the grip of her parasol. The look she shot her twin could cut glass.

What's this? Purity wondered, sitting forward. She kept her face as devoid of expression as she could manage.

"Bitzy," NoNo said slowly, all the while staring at NiNi, "maybe dinner wouldn't be the worst thing in the worlds. A nice *fat* bird, roasted *dead*—for instance." NiNi narrowed her already heavy-lidded eyes.

"Oh, I don't know. It's early yet." Then Bitzy processed what NiNi had said. "Wait, what did you say about Daddy?"

Purity held her breath, not sure whether she should be excited that change had finally come or horrified at the form it seemed about to take. Either way, she was rapt.

A dry giggle issued from NiNi's throat. "Sorry, Bitz. NoNo's been fucking your daddy for months."

Oh my.

Bitzy worked her jaw and made to say something, but thought better of it and looked down at her hands, her teacup shaking in her lap. "I see," she said at last, in a small voice.

Outside, an orange gas giant streaked with yellows and browns dominated the night sky and cast them all in unflattering planetlight. *Tonight we are the moon,* Purity thought before scolding herself for being lyrical during a crisis. The light competed with the bouillotte lamps set on tables around the salon, their gold-leafed inner surfaces trying to add a touch of artificial sunlight to the garish orange globe eclipsing the sky. Filtered through the greenish glass of the Dome, the planet drenched the room in an eerie glow; Purity imagined that the girls were sitting in a sinking ship, looking up at the sun through fathoms of seawater.

We're drowning, she thought, *and nobody even notices.*

Well, perhaps not everyone failed to notice. NoNo, for instance. A change had come over NoNo Leibowitz in the last little while: she'd cast off her dead-eyed guise and revealed what appeared to be a vital woman beneath. Purity admired the verve, if not the methodology. She wasn't sure she bought it, though. Had their NoNo been posing as an idiot all along?

Purity floated a lie to test the new social dynamic and clear away the awkward silence: "I heard the Weapon steals your soul, so that there's nothing left to return to your body or condense into a new one."

"Please," NoNo sneered. "It does not. Besides, stealing souls is like stealing socks."

Interesting. "How so, NoNo, dear?"

NoNo twirled her ridiculous sunshade. "I don't know . . . say you burgle a thousand of the things. Then what? You can't *eat* souls any more than you can eat used socks; you can't sell them; and you won't win friends *giving* the things away. I suppose you could be very avant garde and sew them into a gown, but what would that earn you—all those souls for one evening's infamy?" She barked a most un-NoNo-like laugh, quick and smart. "No, you can keep your wretched soul—when it comes to theft, I'd rather steal good old-fashioned *everything*."

What was this? Was NoNo a real person, all of a sudden?

Bitzy tsked, doing her best to ignore NiNi's revelation about her father, the lord senator. Proper ladies didn't react to scandal. "Of course you're speaking figuratively, NoNo. Ladies mustn't steal."

"Mustn't they?" Purity asked with as much empty politesse as she could rally.

"Oh, I don't know, I think I'd buy a gown of souls." NiNi picked at her fingernails, but Purity discerned a hint of bored malice through her thin lips.

"And that's the difference between us, NiNi." NoNo rounded on her sister, instantly and finally feral. "Everyone thinks us the same, when they couldn't be more wrong. Because you'd *buy* the damned gown, and I'd be the one selling it to you. And when you were starving because you spent all your dirties, you'd have nothing but a gauze of souls to keep you warm, dry, and fed—you appallingly helpless mannequin."

The room sat in stunned silence. Nobody had ever heard NoNo talk for so long, let alone display more than the barest minimum of a personality.

"There's a difference between you two? That's the first I've heard of it!" Bitzy laughed, but her voice pitched uncomfortably high. Purity did not think she noticed the look that earned her from NoNo. "Girls, what would your mother say if she heard her daughters barking at each other like mad dogs? Nothing flattering, I can tell you that much. Now please, will everybody just—"

"Don't you *ever* talk about my mother, Bitzy Bratislaus. Or I swear, I'll . . ."

"You'll what?" NiNi interjected. *"Tattle?"*

NoNo stared down her sister. "I find it hard to feel insulted by the afterbirth. Don't you have more candy to eat?"

NiNi blinked back a bland expression. "I'm afraid you're a bit of a cunt, NoNo."

"I will Kill you *myself*." NoNo was losing control. "Mner told me, if you sing slowly enough, you can make it hurt. I'll grate you like a brick of cheese, sister." She realized what she'd said and sat back, scowling.

Mner Bratislaus? Purity tried to follow. *Sing?*

NiNi appeared not to be paying her twin full attention. "Mmm, capital, et cetera. Purity's been losing weight, don't you think?"

Bitzy Bratislaus threw her cup and saucer on the table with a clatter. Her nerves seemed finally to have yielded to circumstances. But rather than shout about her late, faithless father she quavered, "Am I the only one who needs more *fucking tea*?"

The young ladies were growing jumpier by the minute—NoNo had clutched her sunshade reflexively when Bitzy'd startled them by dropping her china. Now she was rubbing it up and down in a most indelicate—*no*, Purity realized with a finger of ice up her spine, she's *unsheathing* it, just an inch or two, unconsciously. *NoNo's got a sword hidden up her parasol.* Indeed, an inch or two of quicksilver blade was visible beneath the lacey baton handle of the sunshade.

Cane dancing lessons. Purity felt ill.

Bitzy sniffed and wrung her hands once or twice, then looked up with a darling smile. "This is a tea party, after all."

"Yes," said NoNo and Purity together, staring at each other with an air of delayed recognition.

Without breaking eye contact, Purity pulled on the bell and heard the clinking of teaspoons from behind the door. "You are so right, Bitz," she continued, wondering how to escape before anyone else got Murdered and with dawning bewilderment at the prime suspect. "It is *absolutely* a tea party."

It took another hour before Purity could escape. Thirty minutes of tea and then thirty more spent pretending not to notice Bitzy crying into her napkin. An hour of horrified silence.

At last Purity excused herself for a costume change, as one did, but ran away from Bitzy's apartments instead, nipping into a dressing room, which railroaded into an antechamber, and thence into a foyer where, finally, an archway led to the main corridor outside the apartments. Bitzy's suite hugged the outmost glass wall of the Dome, and as Purity made her escape she'd felt followed by the great orange eye staring through the slightly curving glass. Closing the foyer door behind her had been a relief, but she wouldn't feel safe until she'd put as much distance between herself and NoNo Leibowitz as possible, and then finished what she'd begun the day before. She should have listened to her stomach and not some handsome brick wall of a boy with walnut skin and a soft beard—Purity ran fast for the Dawn Stains.

Mner Bratislaus gave NoNo the Weapon, before she Killed him. Purity's thoughts were racing faster than her white-ruffled ankles. *She's the Killer* and *the butcher from the aviary. Oh my.*

Even newly revealed as clever, NoNo wouldn't have figured it out on her own; she'd learned about the Weapon from the Lord Senator of the Circle Unsung. Bells, was that a breach of security protocol! What did NoNo have between her legs to convince Mner Bratislaus to break his oaths? Where and how would the Circle be able to keep such a tool a secret? Purity couldn't guess at the how, but her gut told her that the Weapon was *there,* in the Dawn Stains, she just *knew* it—it might be an absurd thing for her gut to say, but absurdities were all she'd been given.

She took the quickest route—out the gates of Maidens' Keep and along the cloistered garden paths that connected the Keep to the Petite Malaison. Purity ran up the stairs of the Malaison, heading for a pair of doors off a fifth floor corridor, wondering how she'd gain entry without a praetor's helm. But Purity found the doors wide open, and she dashed inside without a thought to why that might be, skidding down the still-open hatch and almost falling on her face at the feet of the Dawn Stains.

White light. A spray of colors. A sense of age that stilled her racing thoughts and felt like winter.

"Bells, but they should have installed a better lock!" Purity whispered to herself as she turned around slowly, a little girl playing in the snow, feeling the weight of the pure light on her lashes.

"They did, lass." Purity opened her eyes to a sneering stick-figure in canary tulle standing on the spiral stairs. A body huddled at NoNo's feet on the stairs, and with a nasty kick she sent it tumbling to the floor below. Kaien, bleeding steadily from a wound in his side, raised his head and waved weakly at Purity.

"Look who I found skulking near the secret treasure cove," NoNo leered, twirling a silver blade thinner than a ribbon. Sure enough, Purity recognized the lacey grip as the handle of NoNo's sunshade. "It's your pet peasant."

NoNo descended the last few stairs and planted her boot on Kaien's lower back.

"I know everything!" Purity exclaimed, the lie coming to her lips in the instant she saw Kaien. How could she have suspected him to be the Killer? He was so . . . *good.*

"Cor, how's that?" NoNo sneered in some kind of accent.

"You needed to practice using the Weapon." Purity held her hands up, palms forward, thinking as fast as she could. "Just like your dancing instructions—those were cane dancing lessons, weren't they, NoNo? The cane sword, unless I'm mistaken? And you are so good at doing the same thing over and over and *over,* aren't you? That's how you excel. It's the only way you can excel."

NoNo twisted her boot heel into the small of Kaien's back, eliciting a cry of pain.

"You only followed *one* stableboy." Purity made it sound acceptable, to end the life of one helpless boy. "Just the one. You didn't expect a whole scullery of naked lads, let alone a pair of Tsengs! How could *Tsengs* find the basement? *Ha!*" Purity had to admit, she was perhaps *not* bound for the stage or the podium, but NoNo didn't seem to notice her bad acting.

NoNo narrowed her eyes. "And how did ye ken so much about my sorties, then?"

Why is she talking funny?

"Well, I must say, you didn't do a terribly thorough job of covering your tracks, NoNo. The massacre in the aviary? A team of dead tailors and seamstresses, canary yellow thread in their hands, the little boy whose dying words were your *laundry* instructions: 'darn her.' That's how innocent your victims were, blademistress." Purity felt her temper rise.

"And you *just* volunteered the information that you'd been Mner Bratislaus' mistress before he Died. Before you Killed him. Really, NoNo, it's not like you've striven for secrecy—I won't be the only one to figure it out."

"Aye." NoNo hung her head. "Now I'm just rolling with the yaw."

"I—I'm not sure what that means, exactly, NoNo, but I can *help* you."

"My papa liked books about the sea, before he left." NoNo looked up at

Purity with a sad, sweet face. Then her expression melted into a sneer. "Lucky for me, they put loads about war in sea books."

NoNo bent down and grabbed Kaien by the scruff of his shirt. He raised his head and grimaced. "Like how a hostage is useless unless the scurvy dogs you fight know that you're willing to spill blood."

She slid the atom-thin blade against his throat with no pressure at all; the mere presence of the weapon flensed away his skin like parting curtains. The brown flesh of Kaien's neck parted like pudding to expose a carotid artery, red and racing.

11

That the deaths we die are finite is acknowledged as truth. Canon also holds that the worlds themselves are finite and, more tellingly, ordered according to the pattern of primacy: we spiral outward as we live, die, and live again. We are born unknowing, die our first deaths unknowing, and enjoin the chaos of the metaverse at the pace of our soul's own choosing. Even our bodies, reborn as they are from life to life, are reflections of our spirit. What then of that distant doorway, a thousand deaths hence, through which only the wisest or most dire may cross?
—Bede the Formerly Venerable, *De Plurimundi Anathanata*

Cooper, Sesstri, and Nixon landed in a pile, cursing at one another. They pushed themselves apart and sat, blinking, at the sight before them. A lake of black liquid rippled in spare torchlight and—was it a cavern? A cavern ceiling arched overhead. Cooper couldn't say how he knew it, but they were deep underground. The cavern was round and wide, and they'd been brought to a wedge of rock that jutted out into the black lake. Overhead, the ceiling was pierced by a sharp stalactite that looked more like corroded iron than mineral. The same oily substance that filled the lake dripped down its blade, sending ripples across the otherwise placid surface at regular intervals.

"What the genuine fuck?" Cooper asked.

A sucking sound came from the wall behind them, where a plug of amber resin was melting away, revealing a dark passage beyond. It was a kind of door, he understood, when a slight woman with clouds of bright red hair breezed through.

"Alouette!" Sesstri roared.

"The blood of the world-beast parts for our feet, *Omphale*. Know that you are welcomed into the Grotto of White Tears," the redhead intoned, standing barefoot in a too-tight purple cocktail dress that barely covered her nipples. Then she smiled crookedly. "The Winnowed asked me to say that. Hello, duckies!" She wiggled her fingers in a wave.

Sesstri and Cooper helped each other to their feet, but Nixon ran to Alouette's side. "Where's the house? I was gonna take another nap." He tugged on her hem. She patted his head and looked to Cooper with a sympathetic eye.

"Oh, you thing!" Alouette peered at his back. "I mean, 'Oh, you *poor* thing!' What did they do to you? Well of course they did what they *do*, but still, why did they do it so thoroughly?"

"Where's Asher?" Sesstri asked.

"Your lover has other business, don't you worry about that. We must take care of you two."

Sesstri growled, deep in the back of her throat. "Don't tell me what to worry about, *entity*, and if you must fuss over someone, fuss over Cooper—I'm fine."

Alouette shook her head and combed her fingers through her tangled red hair. "Oh, Pinky, if only that was true!"

Sesstri steamed. "Ridiculous goddess-analog pretending to be a ridiculous woman!"

"You know, that reminds me of something." Alouette looked up and began rambling. "My friend, Rabelais, who had stopped pretending to believe in Christ and started pretending to believe in Democracy, said, '*Fay çe que voudras.*' And St. Augustine, who was *never* a friend of mine, said, 'Love and do what you will.' Then again, Rabelais has always been a liar and nobody's seen Augustine since the Vandals first killed him, the Berber bastard. 'Reason, will, and passion' my tight Georgia peach! Is that crazy? It sounds crazy." Alouette's pretty lips twitched.

"Yes," Cooper said. "That sounds crazy. What does it mean?"

"And what in the worlds does it have to do with you being one of the First People?" Sesstri asked.

"I forget." Alouette shrugged. "But it shut you up for a hot minute, dinnit?"

"Who *are* you?" Cooper asked her.

She gave him an arch look that, he realized, belonged to his dream-beluga. Then she waved at the giant metal spike in the center of the cavern, and at the black lake below. "This is the most sacred place of the Winnowed, you know. Their Grotto of White Tears. I used to come here when I was sad."

"White Tears?" Sesstri wrinkled her nose at the black pool.

"You see our problem."

Sesstri nodded. Cooper looked out across the dark surface and groaned. His back hurt. *So bad.*

"Oh, poor mincemeat Cooper! I have a few things for you." Alouette revealed a plate from behind her back, and removed a metal room-service lid. She bent at the waist and handed Cooper a sandwich. *That smell.*

"How did you know?" He picked up two slabs of toast filled with purple jelly and thick, juicy sausage patties, bit off as much as was practical, and promptly began to cry.

"What's wrong with his eyes?" Nixon asked. "And where's my sammich?"

Cooper sniffed and answered, though he kept crying. "This was my grandmother's secret afternoon snack. She'd give me sandwiches with fried sausage and jelly. How did you know?"

"Oh honey," Alouette said, patting his head. "Of all the questions you could ask . . . lost comforts . . . That's the kind of thing I just know." She moved behind him and crouched to get a look at his back, screwing her mouth to one side.

If Cooper heard any of this he gave no sign, lost in the past. "She lived in Arkansas and I would go there three or four times a year, or she and Grandpa would drive up, and my mother always counted calories, but Grandma would fry me pancakes in sausage grease till they had a ring of crispy crispiness around the edges, and after her soap operas we'd eat the leftover sausage with grape jelly and white bread. My friends all thought it was gross."

He looked up, still crying—but softly. "I missed her so much when she died."

While Cooper talked, caught in some reverie that wasn't entirely the result of fried pork sausage and half-burnt bread, Alouette worked on his injuries. She held her fingers away from the wound but pinched and scrubbed the air; she removed the dirt and grit that had been ground into his open wound, just pulled it off like a gauze of smoke or cobweb. From behind her back, again, she pulled a small brown grease pot; its contents smelled like grease, too, but also camphor and turmeric.

Cooper kept on. "I know that's a weird thing to say here in the Special Spooky Cave, but I remember her so strongly right this minute, I think I'll lose her again if I don't say it out loud. She had a stern face and a bottomless soft spot for her grandsons, and she had these great big knuckles. I would lie on the couch and put my head in her lap while we watched *As The World Turns* and she would rub my temples with her witch hands. In a movie they might have been scary, but in her duplex with Grandpa in his chair wearing his old one-piece speed suit and that bitch from the soap, Lucinda, being horrible on the TV, my grandma's hands on my forehead were heaven. I'd forget all the little troubles that seem so big when you're young, the kids at school or the mean teacher, or the girls—boys— and all that stuff."

Alouette applied the grease gently—where it touched Cooper's back, the open wounds dried up and stopped seeping, the ominous redness of impending infection receded, and his back turned from a fresh nightmare into an old one, some safely bygone horror. His scars were deep, and he was missing most of the original skin and subcutaneous fat, but the healed flesh was pink and unbroken. Cooper didn't even notice.

"But I can't imagine my grandma as anyone but my grandma, old and smart-mouthed and judgmental of anybody who didn't belong to her. I guess I thought she was gone, just *gone,* or wherever the universe puts fussy, adoring old ladies who believe in a heaven that's far too one-dimensional to actually exist."

"You're sweet." Alouette leaned in and whispered, "That's what good grandsons are supposed to think, Cooper."

He shrugged and noticed the stiffness was gone. So, too, was the pain that had swamped him since the aesr's absence.

"Yeah, but it's stupid. My grandma's not gone, and the universe didn't put her anywhere. It kicked her out into some other universe, and now she's got another life, doesn't she?"

"Of course she does." Alouette tucked away the grease pot behind her prolific back. She wiped her hands on Cooper's arms and smiled at a job well done. Then she pulled a plaid work shirt from behind her and draped it over Cooper's shoulder.

"But that's *awful!*" he continued.

Alouette spun Cooper around—it didn't hurt—and fixed him with a look he recognized entirely too well. "Are you saying that because you loved your grandma, she doesn't deserve to *live*?"

"Well, no, of course not! But she should, she ought to . . . she should still be my grandma, that's all." He slipped on the shirt, tenderly, surprised at the lack of pain.

Alouette raised a corner of her mouth. "Then you're a lucky ducky, because she *is*. She's also young, healthy, and not dying slowly of congestive heart failure. She can breathe and run and fry sausages, Cooper. She's not tethered to an oxygen tank. She can remember you, just like you can remember her. Is simply *surviving* the people you love so much better?"

"Of course not." Cooper stood and fastened the buttons of his new shirt. "It's just such a weird reality to wake up to. You're used to—well, *I'm* used to, you know, people die, you put them in a box, and that's it. There's something about that box that's safe, permanent, and not totally-freaking-insane. To find out the truth, that the body in the box—the memory in the box—is just sloughed-off skin, and the real person is out there somewhere you can never go in your lifetime . . . it makes me feel sad and acrophobic, to say the least."

"Agoraphobia is the right thing to feel, I think. The worlds are vast, and sadness happens. Do you like your shirt?" Alouette straightened it for him.

"I like what it must cover up," Cooper said, marveling at the lack of pain or stiffness.

She rested her head against his shoulder. "It's not that bad. I've seen worse."

"Well, I sure as hell haven't," said Nixon. "The spooks got you good!"

Sesstri looked like her face was wrestling with her mouth. "Thank. You. For helping Cooper," she stuttered, turning red. "You've probably saved his life."

Alouette nodded. "It was almost exactly the least I could do." The resinous door opened again with a sucking sound, and three men entered, all dressed in plain brown clothes.

"May I introduce some of my Winnowed friends: Osman Spare, Bede, and Sid." The three men bowed to her deeply, then inclined their heads toward the newcomers. "I wanted you to be here for this." Alouette looked almost apologetic.

The youngest of the three, Osman Spare, a handsome youth with gold curls and one bronze nipple showing from his toga, raised his hand to speak. "A few months ago you would have thought this a pool of unspoiled cream."

"So white it lit the cavern," said the little brown one called Sid, before popping a hemp seed into his mouth.

Osman crouched by the edge of the black fluid, tense and coiled. "The Lash—that iron vein overhead—has been dripping darkened ichors for years, but the purity of the pool masked the taint until the last few weeks. I believe the dark fluid settled at the bottom until the waters grew disturbed and the two strata mixed, appearing to foul the pool overnight. But the People of the Foundation have revealed our weaknesses again, for we saw the signs of corruption and turned our heads. Even martyrs need lessons."

Sesstri had mentioned that the Winnowed were a tribe of saints and martyrs, deposed tyrants and philosopher-kings. Great personages of many stripes, upon whose lives and deaths were founded religions, cultures, and entire histories. If the Winnowed were former paragons, how did they agree upon a single ideology? *That sounds like a Sesstri question,* Cooper thought, looking back to the metal tip piercing the ceiling of the cavern.

"You call that jigger the Lash, you say?"

"Yes. It is consistent with the metaphor in which we cloak our reverence—if the pool before you is filled with tears, then the Lash . . ."

"*Ah,* I see." And he did, after Osman's explanation. "If that's an *eye*-lash, I'd shudder to see the eye it's attached to."

"You see it every day, *Omphale.*" Osman stared at the ceiling as if he could see clear through the bedrock.

"He does?" Sesstri asked, skeptically.

"Yes, and it sees you." Sid ate another seed. "Your Prince has made it his palace."

Nixon whistled. "Oh ho! The Dome? *That's* a new one."

Osman shook his head, still struggling to smile, his lips curling slightly upward at the corners. "In fact it is a very, very, very old one. The Grotto is the axis of our world. Our axis mundi—our world-pillar. That symbolism ties itself closely to the notion of the navel, the *omphalos*, the world's point of beginning, its center. It is that worlds-center upon which we meditate."

"So why does everybody witchy call me that?" Cooper asked.

"Centers shift." Sid hung back, but answered the question. "If yesterday, the center of all worlds was a hemp seed, then today—perhaps it is a man."

"No," Cooper thought out loud while looking at the Lash and realizing what it was that he saw. "It's a gold Death machine, and it's older than fuck."

Machines of magic and electricity, that powered themselves with the slow death of a living battery. He'd seen those inside the Cictatrix. And he'd seen one beneath the City Unspoken, afterward—he had followed its signal-scent home, the golden apple rotting from within.

Alouette nodded. "I won't say much, Cooper, but you're right."

"Then you know what we have to do." Cooper marveled at the scale of the task.

Another nod.

"Sesstri?" Cooper asked. "Have you ever heard the word 'vivisistor' before?"

"Vivi-what?" Sesstri scowled. "Have I—no. No, I have not. Tell me everything."

"Little machines that trap something alive inside, impaled on a spike, to generate electricity." He held out his palms, cupped together like a closed oyster. "Open it up, and the trapped thing dies, and the vivisistor shuts off."

"That does not sound like *everything*—explain better and faster."

"The Dome is a vivisistor, Sesstri. A huge one, and an ancient one." He looked at Alouette. "You said you pierced the skin of the worlds, to create the possibility of True Death. This is how you did it, isn't it? With a machine?"

Alouette looked down.

"With one of your own trapped inside." He shook his head. "Who's dying now, finally, and that's why the pilgrims who come to the city no longer Die. That's where the *svarning* will come from, when the vivisistor fails completely."

Sesstri cursed. "What under the braided tits of the horsemother is a 'vivisistor'? And how would you *open* the *Dome*?"

"With big-ass chains," Cooper answered easily. "I'm right, aren't I?" He looked at Alouette, who dipped her chin once in a nod. The Winnowed men closed their eyes in meditation at the mention of the chains.

"Are you still going to say the words?" white-haired Bede asked Alouette, speaking up at last. "Old Dorcas would want you to say the words, were she still living."

"Just a moment." Alouette nodded, and spoke directly to Sesstri. "The lich-lords march on the Dome at dawn. A faerie queen the likes of which you cannot imagine invades the city, and *you* will feel her arrival. She is filled with vivisistors, and she comes for the eldest. Take this and run. Alone." Alouette pulled a book out from behind her back and pressed it into Sesstri's hands.

Sesstri did not fight. She nodded, eyes sharp, and took the book. *Urban Weather Patterns* by Susan Messerschmidt. "Which way do I run?"

Osman pointed the way he'd come, and the sphincter of resin sucked itself open into a doorway again. Sesstri moved toward it.

"Cooper?"

"I'll be okay, Sesstri," he said. "Do whatever she says. I can find you, now, I think." Cooper hoped that was true. Nixon looked back and forth between Alouette and the receding Sesstri, torn. Then he turned and ran after Sesstri, complimenting her ass and asking why she wasn't slowing down for him.

The Winnowed shuffled their feet, and Alouette conceded. She took a big, physically incarnated breath, and saluted Bede like Shirley Temple in *The Little Colonel*. "Worms beneath my heel, I command you to complete Anvit's Great Work," she said. "Pull the chains, mechanic-slaves of the First Children. Open the Eye. Crack the Dome and finish what my arrogant brother started, so long ago. The *chains,* men!"

The Guile & Gullet suffered from a surfeit of customers, and though the staff struggled to serve the crowd that spilled outside into the square, Oxnard Terenz-de-Guises enjoyed a large table by a bay window on the inn's mezzanine, with a view of both the crowded tavern floor and the milling throng outside, where boys usually relegated to washing dishes were serving beer from a makeshift stand. The marquis sat alone at his table but had ordered enough food and drink for four, and seemed to be enjoying his repast with equivalent relish.

As the crowd below parted around Asher, the gray man looked up from the street and saw the marquis through the diamond-shaped panes of the lead glass windows. Terenz-de-Guises licked gravy off his ringed fingers and waved.

As Asher made his way through the crowd, he noticed a fevered pitch to the mob's revelry. No, it was more than that. Faces flushed with too much drink were pouring down pint after pint as if they couldn't quite get drunk, and bellies beneath shirts stained with grease were swelling with haunch after haunch of meat. Something dark slithered out of one man's ear, and another woman had three of the things, two in one ear and another snaking out her nostril. None of them noticed, or if they noticed, did not care.

A clutch of bloodsluts gathered in a far corner looked wild-eyed and hungry, and during his short stroll into the tavern, Asher saw half of them drag away drunkards into the shadows. It took a rare life-whore to look forward to his or her trade—seeing half a dozen bloodsluts eagerly soliciting business was downright wrong. He wondered whether they were even dying for their johns or just fucking them.

Sesstri and Alouette thought the city too sane, given the end of Death and the expected consequence. But it was obvious from a walk down the street that the dam had burst at last. The malaise that had been creeping up on the city had erupted, and would soon touch everyone, not merely the unlucky and the Dying. The *svarning* had come. Wherever Sesstri's red-ribbon goddess had stolen them, Asher hoped that she and Cooper were safe from the worst of it.

He pushed his way through the door and toward the bar, scanning the tables. Oxnard whooped to get his attention and waved him up the stairs that ringed the greatroom of the tavern. Of course the marquis had his own table, and of course it was overladen. Of course he was waiting for Asher, ready as always to prattle.

"Sit, sit!" Oxnard said unnecessarily as Asher sat himself across from the man. "Help yourself."

"I see that you're in good spirits as usual."

"What's the alternative, poor spirits?" Oxnard laughed, but glanced at the crowd outside.

"That's the solution I seem to have found." A barmaid flashed Asher a limp smile as she brought four pints of lager to the table. Asher drained one and picked up a second.

"Not gambling tonight?" he asked.

"Well, you're here." Oxnard smiled. "That's always a bit of a risk."

"Funny you should mention that." Asher slid the broken chip bearing the Lady of La Jocondette's profile across the table. "I'd like to thank you for directing me to La Jocondette, friend. I hope you did not knowingly send me into an ambush. *That's* a risk."

The marquis' expression of confusion looked genuine. "I'm certain I have no idea what you're talking about. I'm also certain that you wouldn't have found your abducted friend nearly so quickly had I not been clumsy enough to leave behind a chip upon which I had so idly doodled." He reached across the table and grabbed the chip. "It's funny how things work out. I'll thank you for returning my winnings, however. *Arigato.*"

Asher shook his head. "Your father would not be proud, Oxnard."

"Let's not delve into fathers and pride, eh?" Oxnard smiled into his lager. Asher looked away. "At least we've both kept busy. Drinking, for instance, we're both quite good at that. Avoiding our wives—sorry, that's a sore subject for you, isn't it? Sincerest apologies—to continue: we're both stupendous at whoring, of various inclinations and for various purposes. Helping things along in our own utterly insufficient way; I've been funding some of the more necessary local guilds, *par exemple.* Trying to keep business afloat as much as possible."

Asher scowled. "The only business you keep afloat, Oxnard, is the hospitality industry."

Oxnard wagged his finger. "You've always been too quick to judge, my friend. Yes, yes, I know you've got more years under your belt than I can imagine, but that's no reason to be surly with us wee cretins. Besides, hospitality forms a larger piece of the pie than you'd think. Who keeps all those workaday types happy at the end of the week but bartenders and whores and whatever you call the man who puts meat on skewers?" Oxnard laughed.

"You're in a good mood, for a man whose district seems perched on the verge of chaos. Have you looked outside?"

"You know, I have. And what do I see? I see people who have finally decided to embrace life." Oxnard impaled half a dozen leaves of larded greens with his fork and stuffed them into his mouth. "*Viva la muerte,* etc."

"You *can't* mean that." Asher scowled.

The marquis almost finished chewing before he answered. "Oh, but I do. And to answer your next *pregunta:* no, I do not know why everybody's suddenly gone into several strains of frenzy. And for the life of me, I cannot remember why I'm supposed to care."

"And that doesn't strike you as odd?" Gray elbows on the tabletop, Asher leaned forward.

The marquis nodded, accidentally spilling beer onto his fancy shirt. "Of course it does. But as I said, I can't seem to care. And I'm not one for caring overmuch to begin with."

Asher browsed a plate of pickled vegetables. "Well. You're not so different from your peers in that, I suppose." He snapped a vinegary baby parsnip in half with his teeth. "Don't you want to know if I found your red metal jewelry box?"

"Nope." Oxnard speared another folio of greens and stuffed them into his mouth. "Oh dead gods, the Gullet has *got* to keep this new cook. Who knew rainbow chard could be braised to heaven? It's a cruciferous apotheosis, I tell you."

"You know," Asher said nastily, "I supposed I shouldn't be surprised that the best interest of the people isn't really your priority, or you might have reconsidered handing the Guiselaine over to the most vile woman the city's seen since Ladybeth FenChrissie and her enslavement pogroms. We don't exactly have another Shriving Kloo around to placate the people and reestablish the government."

"Oh, I wouldn't be so sure about that," Oxnard said, for once relishing details left unmentioned. Then he leaned forward, unable to help himself. "Besides, what makes you think I'm not desperately in love with my darling Lolly? Who says I don't conspire with her to bilk workers of wages and tithe shopkeepers into debtor's prison? Contrarywise, what makes you think that my exotic hothouse orchid wasn't as much a scrim for me

as I was for her? Strategy runs both ways, and makes for interesting—
and appealing—bedfellows." The marquis snapped for more lager.

Outside, a man started screaming. Long black thorns erupted from
his shoulders, thorns that forked and forked in a fractal pattern. Then
from his legs, his sides, his hands. Within seconds the man was cocooned
within lines of black, iterating and reiterating across his face, obscuring
his body but not his agonized, wailing screams.

Oxnard watched for a moment, then turned back to Asher and shrugged.
"I was bored, so I married a sociopath. What did you do when *you* grew
bored, my prince?"

"What, do ye think you're the only one who gets bored? The only one
who *reads*?" NoNo stalked into the reliquary and flipped her sword cane
in the air before catching it by the hilt; she left Kaien disabled and forgotten.
"You can't believe yer the first virgin lass to learn a thing or twain from a
man she let fuck her? I bet your cunny still smells of chimney sweep."

Purity blanched. She also felt that something wasn't quite right. NoNo
sounded . . . *off*. She was playing a role, but a role in which she'd been
horribly miscast. Swordplay aside—the girl was a right prodigy in that
regard.

"Aye, you're a proper lady of the Last Court," NoNo sneered. "You'd
not survive a week at sea with Captain Buonaparté or the crew of *The
Dying Fuckman*."

Purity stopped blanching. Pirate novels? Was NoNo really misquoting
pirate novels? She couldn't help herself: "NoNo, I think you have that last
bit turned around."

"Are ye blind as well as deaf, landlubber lass?" NoNo sneered, shaking
her lace-hilted cane sword. "D'ye want a taste of this?"

"Are stories of pirates all you've got to go on?" Purity felt terrified, but
also increasingly frustrated. Was she the only adult in the entire Dome?
"That and your prodigious skill with a coward's blade. You *do* know that's
what an offensive mêlée fighter—*like a pirate*—would call your cane
sword, don't you, NoNo?"

"Ha ha, Purity." NoNo advanced. "You're so *witty*, aren't you? 'I'm Purity

Kloo and I read smarty-pants books, just look at my perfect little nose and the big brown bear I'm fucking!' You be a good lass and smash those pretty windows, I'll spit on a handshake and promise not to tell Bitzy you've been wearing the same stockings for two days straight."

Purity turned an ankle and looked. *Bells, she's right.*

NoNo unfastened the hammer from Kaien's tool belt and kicked it to Purity—its head, a fist of steel, made an awful sound as it scraped along the white tiles of Fflaen's reliquary. Purity stopped the hammer with her slipper and simply stood there, looking at the tool on the floor, then back at NoNo, who replaced her boot atop Kaien's back; the two girls stood in similar positions with worlds of distance between them.

"Pick it up," NoNo demanded.

Purity tugged on the handle—it was heavier than she remembered. "It's probably a good idea for you to save your courage for the high seas, NoNo. You'll need it, because that's the only place you'll be safe when your mother hears of this."

"My mother is the *reason* I've done this, Purity Kloo!" NoNo spoke with fire in her belly, and Purity's incredulity redoubled at the girl's sincerity. "And if you hadn't spent your entire life hiding behind your father's trousers, you might understand why."

"Lady Mauve?" Purity tried not to sound condescending. "What in the name of all the debunked goddesses could possibly make you think Mauve Leibowitz would want any of this? There's a good chance you've destroyed your entire family, NoNo. I'm not sure you understand that— *do you*? Nothing will be the same for any of them after this."

"You say that like it's a bad thing, Purity." NoNo shook her head.

"I . . . well . . . *what*?" That was unexpected, and unsettlingly aligned with Purity's own thoughts on the status quo.

"Your father has stood in this room and committed Murder. But not your mother. It's different when your house is ruled by a woman. Maybe it shouldn't be, but it is. When it's your *mother* standing here, choosing to become a Killer, you feel it, through the blood, through the childborn womb. I did, anyway—NiNi doesn't feel a thing. But I *felt* my mother pollute herself when she used the Weapon. I don't know why I felt it, but I did, and I couldn't fake it anymore. Fake being NoNo, fake being stupid, fake fucking *dance lessons*."

Dead gods, not only did NoNo sound sincere, she sounded stricken. "But . . . why fake it to begin with?"

"Come on Purity, don't choose now to become a thickheaded cow." NoNo pointed to Purity's ankles. "You know exactly where a strong personality will get you in our crowd: cut up to pieces for wearing the wrong stockings. While we enjoyed a little light butchery, the Circle was consigning each other to oblivion. They were Killing one another as an *indulgence*."

"So you polluted yourself instead?" To her horror, Purity knew what NoNo meant, and how she felt.

"Somebody had to do something to stop them. Can you really tell me that you, out of all of us, haven't felt the urge to . . . *do* something, anything, just to change things? Just to escape?"

"Escape what?" Purity had wanted to escape, yes—escape the Dome, escape her friends, escape what she increasingly recognized as a trap designed to rid the city of them all.

"Escape *everything*. Aren't you suffocating? Aren't you drowning in this gilded *shit*?"

Purity remembered when she first found this room, and the blind anger that had fueled her. She looked down.

"There you have it," NoNo relished.

A wave of helplessness washed over Purity, but she shook her head clear. "I would never do what you did."

"That's a fine hair to split, Purity Kloo."

"Better to split a hair than a *child,* Nonette Leibowitz." Purity locked eyes with NoNo and remembered Kaien's heartache at the young tailor's apprentice, who died with NoNo's canary yellow thread in his hand.

"I . . . I didn't know what the song was, at first. I thought Mner was teasing me, singing me back to his bed one measure at a time with pretend fragments of the Weapon, a little pillow game. Then, when I put the measures together and I Killed those boys, actually Killed them . . . I *had* to try to make some good come of it."

"And you're willing to destroy your family name for what, exactly?"

"To end this? Gladly. And not just my family, *all* of our families. We are an abomination, Purity, I *know* you see that."

She saw no such thing, despite the overwhelming despair that tried to claw its way into her heart. But as NoNo lectured Purity on the evils of the Circle, Purity stared at the Dawn Stains in what she hoped looked like distracted awe. She was searching for some sign of the Weapon when she remembered the threat NoNo had made against NiNi—at the time she thought it had been simple spite, but now she saw the truth of it.

"Mner said if you sing slowly enough, you can make it hurt," NoNo had said. *"Singing me back to his bed."*

And suddenly the truth of a quarter-million years hit home. The lords and the Circle; the Weapon; a room that, until very recently, only the prince and the Circle could enter. The Circle *Unsung.*

"Sweet suicide, they've had the Weapon all along." They must have. The lords hadn't discovered the Weapon, they'd always possessed it. If that was true, then knowledge of the Weapon was the reason the Circle existed—a balance of power, of mutually assured destruction. Bells, the *entire history* of her society was predicated upon a secret standoff of epochal proportions. That explained how the lords had kept hidden the knowledge of a way to choose Death—or inflict it—and more significantly, why they hadn't bothered fighting each other for control of it. Anyone with a voice could wield the Weapon.

"Oh *bravo*, Purity." NoNo clapped. "Putting all the pieces together by your lonesome self."

But Purity wasn't listening: the lords had kept the Weapon safe for ages. Kept it tucked away until they'd been locked inside the Dome, and then they'd *resorted* to using it. Was she right then, had the Writ of Community been Fflaen's way to dispose of the ruling class permanently?

Either way, she'd found what she was looking for—the link between the prince, the Circle, the Weapon, and the Dawn Stains. It was right there at the bottom of the glass, on every pane, in bars of black and gold that looked incidental to the scenes depicted above them. From just a few feet away the notation looked illegible, but closer up Purity could make out some of its sense. If she scanned the lines correctly, the meter shifted between bars in an inconsistent way, but it was most definitely music. The Dawn Stains held a song.

Sometimes truffles and perfect comfort and velvety red wines just didn't satisfy, mused Lallowë Thyu, Marchioness Terenz-de-Guises. She pouted in the bath with her ankles scissored into the air, so she could admire the lacquer-sheen smoothness of her toenails. She picked at pomegranate seeds from a glass ramekin, snapping them up with the thin coding pins she held scissored in her hand. Lallowë found herself not enjoying the flavor so much as the gem-bright bloody color and the memory of how, when she was much younger, her mother had fed her pomegranate seeds and pretended they were teeth stolen from sleeping children. Pomegranate, she mused, was much tastier as a body part.

Thanks to a bitter mood, she'd spent nearly the whole evening in her bath—a bowl of shale as wide as a small pond, frothed over with water that never cooled and was perfumed with her most recently favored scents—damp wood in March, rain-slick limestone, and jasmine—but Lallowë had not wasted a moment. The coding pins had danced in her hands all evening, scripting sentience into the abalone programming compiler that floated in her lap like a giant oyster. Beneath the crust of calcium carbonate glowed an interior of mother-of-pearl and electrum: a box of light and golden wire suspended inside contained a grid of 1,024 by 1,024 squares in 1,024 layers, projecting a cubical matrix that served as the parchment upon which she wrote herself a sister.

The coding pins flew through Lallowë's fingers, dancing instructions across the projected matrix. She held two pins in each hand, pinching and twisting the air between quanta, while plucking the occasional pomegranate tooth. She chewed her lip in concentration as she considered her task and, somewhere behind the problem of creating an artificial intelligence, fretted away at the larger question of out-thinking the Cicatrix—discovering her true goals and how she, Lallowë, could end up on top.

Coding was by far the easier task: ever-decreasing circuitry size and efficiency seemed to occupy human ambitions, while faerie code could accomplish so much more with so much less. There was a poetry in her logic that superseded anything simple math could predict, and quite literal poetry in the code she wrote—while her abalone compiler remained the perfect interface for building sentience. She couldn't manage a database if her life depended upon it—and thank the Airy Dark it did not—but she could whip up a ghost for the machine without decanting herself from the bathtub.

She'd previously used the abalone shell for programming specialized clocks—Lallowë had given Oxnard's sister a clock for her bedside, for instance, that had whispered insanities to the woman in her sleep until she became maddened beyond repair. Eventually the wretched girl sold her fortune to the Numismatist to remove her body-binding and threw herself off Giantsrib Bridge. *Ha.*

Despite the fact that its components integrated technologies and magics from multiple disciplines and *realities,* programming the vivisistor to resemble life wasn't much more difficult, at least in theory, than designing her clocks—just an elaboration upon a theme, really. A living mind could be seen as comprised of many enchanted clocks running at once, each designed to reproduce some aspect of sentience—perception, rumination, self-correction, rage—and set to interact with each other recursively. But only with *art* inside the arguments: she silently thanked her human papa for the gift of his poesy, she could only imagine her mother trying to fit birdsong and cricketstrings into an algorithm of even the most basic—

My human father. That was it, Lallowë realized with a twist of her gut and a furious rush of shame. *My father, the poet, the man who was smart enough to leave.* That was why she was here, why she'd been chosen over Almondine, everything. Lallowë felt a combination of emotions she'd never suffered before, a pride that hinged upon shame, an exuberance dependent upon patricide, a love that spoke the language of hate. *That* was it.

And it was why she'd prevail.

As the coding pins clacked in her loose-fingered grip, Lallowë began to understand how her mother could be seduced into thinking machine life could improve upon meat life, although the Cicatrix was still irreparably insane. But with her father's bardic gift—Tam was a bard, could he be drafted?—with her father's gift in her veins, Lallowë comprised the very best of the Unseelie fey and the most talented aspects of humanity. She wasn't a half-breed, she was an *upgrade.* She would not only write herself a new sister, but she'd piggyback atop that soul a utility code that Lallowë could use herself; contingencies within contingencies, just as the Cicatrix had taught her. But with her father's feel for meter and motif, sound and sense.

She flicked a completed subroutine into the developing matrix, causing one of the stones set around the lip of the bowl-shaped shell to glow. She had six stones glowing now, six subroutines out of hundreds she'd created only to dismiss as imperfect, too perfect, or wrong for the task. Lallowë wanted the new Almondine to be *her* ideal creation: a beautiful, submissive sisterly soul wrapped in an infrastructure of utility protocols that could be used independently of the living mind within. Analytic and heuristic systems, scalable information architecture, both topological animism and arcane geometrics, weapons, divinations, bio-monitoring, and deployable repair enchantments for flesh and machine—Lallowë's opus would be not modular but *epic poetic.* It would be the opposite of her mother's strategy, and it would benefit her under any circumstances whatsoever.

If creating a third sister out of Almondine was a risk, Lallowë intended to hardwire the wooden bitch with an exit strategy.

Lallowë became subsumed by her electric oyster and the three-dimensional grid it projected. This was the tack she should have taken all along—rather than trying to guess at her mother's plans, she should have been spinning an unknowable web of her own. She cracked a pomegranate seed between her teeth and smoothed her eyebrows with a flick of her dry black tongue, then smiled. She rubbed her bare feet along the shale of the tub—although the raw stone was sharp enough to slice human flesh to shreds, its fissile edges felt fantastic scrubbing her soles and exfoliating the skin of her bottom.

And she exulted. Almondine would be precisely the sort of associative tangle that forms the workspace where consciousness lives: tie dance to calligraphy, cross ice with the memory of water, create a variable called laughter and associate it with swift and metered movements of perspective.

Sister : trust :: mother : betrayal. They were lovely lines to write.

Cooper stood alone with Alouette in a forest made of gold, or a temple grown from trees, he wasn't sure which. A cathedral of gold-barked sycamore trees reached far overhead, trunks thick and straight but not-quite vertical—they leaned inward all at the same slight angle, and branched identically to form the perfect vaults of the ceiling. White-gold birch trees stood slender as rods between the muscular sycamores.

Leaves, red and yellow and green, filtered the sunlight like glass, casting their colors onto the grass.

Cooper made a sound of wonder and wandered into the nave of the cathedral-forest, craning his neck to see the marvel. It looked as if perfectly grown trees had been pruned away to create the interior space, but they hadn't—the interior was part of their perfection.

"Someplace interesting, right?" Alouette said to the trees.

"Where are we now?" he asked, and Alouette's head drooped.

"Someplace I . . . kinda . . . brought you."

"Okay." Cooper's feet crunched on grass like spears of citrine crystal. "Why do I get the feeling we're not talking about this little gold detour?" he asked, returning to their previous conversation.

"Because you're a perceptive kinda dude." She danced into the cathedral but would not meet his eyes.

"Is that why you kind-of-brought-me?"

"Almost? That's a hard question to answer." She scrubbed her face with her hands.

"I'd really appreciate it if you'd try." Cooper wondered what a perceptive kinda dude would say right about now and tried to strike a mix between patience and perseverance. "But you don't seem to want to try. I'm wondering if that isn't a little bit awful."

Alouette bit her fingernail and looked everywhere but at him for an awkward moment.

Cooper took a deep breath. "All right then. So tell me about the tree-church. Where are we, really, and why?"

Alouette nodded sharply like a soldier. "Roger will-call. Or whatever. I was hoping you could tell me why, actually."

So this was another test. Another not-a-turd opportunity to prove himself. Fine. Cooper walked to the nearest tree-pillar and put his palm against it—it felt warm to the touch. When he pulled his hand away there were two signs glowing on the curling gold bark beneath. Cooper recognized one of them as Sesstri's orange scroll-and-quill.

That was part of the Winnowed cavern system, and Sesstri was in it.

A map, or something deeper? Cooper took another look around the gold-barked interior and tried to let his inner senses guide his gaze. The breeze that stirred the boughs came and went like breathing, and the clarity with which he saw every gold-leafed detail seemed over-sharp, like the hyperlucidity of a dream the moment before it evaporates into waking.

This was a place where nature's geometry revealed itself to be more than resplendent, to be *sentient*—this was the natural mother of artificial intelligence, written in the dialects of life rather than electricity. The math itself was alive here, and lived through bark and sap, the patterns behind branch and leaf, vein and stoma.

It lived through Alouette. And, it dawned on Cooper, lived in his own body, in the branching of his capillaries and the whorls of his fingertips.

"We didn't leave, did we?" he asked. "This is another beluga-swim, another vision, but I'm awake for it, aren't I?"

Alouette sucked one corner of her mouth, like he'd come close to the right answer, but not close enough. "You can feel the life here, and the mind within it? Good. That's really good, Cooper."

"Yeah. Okay." He pointed to the two moving signs. Beside Sesstri's sign was a green pair of tap shoes. "These are Sesstri and Nixon."

The being sewn up in the body of a young woman nodded, looking more hopeful. "And you see namesigns? See, Cooper . . . you couldn't have come here on Tuesday."

"Namesigns." He repeated the word out loud. "Yeah, that's what they are, they're names. True names, right? A name that can't be spoken or written, only known. Why can't I see yours?"

"Look at me." Alouette put her hand on Cooper's wrist. She looked concerned. Then he saw her eyes change—pretty, cornflower-blue eyes. "Look closer."

He stared straight ahead, into the middle of her face, and kept his eyes as still as possible until his vision shimmered; the trees in the periphery of his vision became gold glass. Alouette's face remained the center of his field of view, but her hair blurred around her head until it was a cloud of pure red pigment. Across her neck he saw a shimmering red ribbon, thick as his thumb and shining like new satin; as he watched, the ribbon became a wound—Alouette's throat cut open to the cartilage beneath, and her overstuffed cleavage drenched with blood.

Then, as Cooper continued to stare straight ahead, the wound became a ribbon again, the dripping lines of blood just threads of satin that pulled themselves back together.

"I see a red ribbon tied around your throat, but sometimes I see that your throat's been slit wide open . . ."

Alouette nodded.

"It's because you're not you, you're her. Chesmarul. That's why your namesigns shift, isn't it? Because you're *more* than we are, and one sign can't signify all of your . . . youness. Isn't it?"

The boughs of the cathedral rustled like church-whispers in a breeze that ran its fingers through Alouette's red curls as she looked away. When the breeze grew stronger, the leaves and branches spoke as her voice.

"No." The word came from everywhere at once, quietly but omnidirectional. The sound vibrated through his body as much as his mind.

"Well, kind of." Cooper's eyes and bones buzzed with her, and it almost panicked him.

There was a pause. Then, "Yeah. I hate that name."

Cooper turned back to the trees and shrugged. What was Alouette, and what was she really after? Was this the plan, then? Find as feckless a soul as possible and tease him into usefulness? That seemed a dumb idea, but who was Cooper to second-guess the vasty-big mind of a thing that could pass for a god?

Cooper saw golden cathedral-forest and knew it was only a representation of something his limited mortal mind couldn't grasp. Why his friends' souls ran in lines as pixel sprites along the bark of her cathedral-mind.

"I get it now, what makes a shaman different than a magician or a goddess or a priest or a mad scientist," he said to Alouette, who was the thing called Chesmarul when she wasn't wearing flesh. "All it means is seeing life and death and the spirits in between, including yourself, in a certain way. Seeing sideways. And I've been looking at death and talking to spirits since I got here, haven't I, Chesmarul?"

"My mother gave me that name. I don't like to use it." She spoke in her body's voice—Alouette's voice, which was Chesmarul's voice. She was one of the First People, and she wore names as he wore socks.

"The First were polyglot," she said, and the boughs stirred with her words. "No two alike, until we willed it. Most of the First People preferred to stand alone, our egos are too big to fit into a single reality—how could we come together and form a society, the way your people do? The Third are so adaptable: humans live and die together, faeries band into tribes, elementals stalk their planes in perfect stony accord. But we began before we knew the need to remember our beginning, and by the time we realized how precious our stories were, it was too late to recall with any clarity the story of our origin."

"You were born before time was a thing, got it." Cooper ignored Alouette and addressed the pool of red within her eye. "But what does it have to do with me, the city, and your Dying problem?"

"We pierced the worlds and created Death for ourselves." The wind nodded into his neck, though Alouette stood limply, the eye of herself unblinking. "We lacked a beginning, but we had the means to write our own end. It is why you will find so few of us left, and why those you can find are so enraptured by the legends of their own making. We can appear very vain, and are rarely as far from stupidity as we'd have you believe. It's also why an enterprising minority of the First People began to settle down, like the aesr did, to form the first communities. The aesr and those like them—and there have been many like them, on worlds stranger and more distant than this one—sought a continuity that extended beyond their own selves, and in doing so presaged the form the Third People would take. Individuality and collectivity combined in the alembic of culture, mixed in different proportions and with varying degrees of success. . . ."

Cooper nodded his head. "You've got a problem with living, dying, obviously. You can't even *talk* about the Second People. You need a fresh perspective, maybe." The red spilled out from her eye like a gunshot and resolved into a ribbon; it ran straight out from her face, parallel to the ground, heading for the tree line. "Maybe you need someone with a shaman's knack for seeing the sideways truths that emerge from observing the way the world is. Like the truth of a bloodslut who's desperate not to be a bloodslut anymore, who just wants death to stick. Or the truth that the Undertow have been holding an aesr hostage for years and feeding off her. Or the truth that Death is broken and we're all super-duper mega-screwed."

The line of red color wound away from Cooper and the stock-still body of Alouette, weaving itself around the pillar-trees according to some pattern only it could see. It darted back and forth until the cathedral was bannered with red, moving toward him until it stopped abruptly in front of his face. Redness hovered in the air like the brightest berry bursting, and the bloom of pigment resolved into a sketch of Chesmarul's face, an outline that resembled Alouette's physical features: cloud-shaped bursts of color for hair, red dashes for eyebrows, the curve of her cheek and chin and neck hanging in midair. Cooper could see the cathedral-trees through the space where her skin should have been. To the side, her physical body drooped like a marionette doll.

"I'm not done. There's something else, isn't there? Something your average shaman might not understand. What is it? Why won't you tell me?"

More of her face emerged from the ribbon of red, like the head of a red silk snake. Kind eyes, but her bow mouth was set in a line. Cooper saw resignation and distaste and compassion.

"Neat trick. I'm not asleep this time, I know that. I'm there and here. I'm standing in a cave alone and standing here in the cathedral-forest with the outline of your face and your empty body. So there's that. But I am wide awake."

The sliver of the thing called Chesmarul that Cooper could perceive with his mind nodded. "True statement." Then it pushed him down, and he fell through the golden ground into a shadow bigger than the sun. Below, he felt the city rushing up to meet him.

Purity hefted the hammer. She wrapped both hands around its cord-wound handle and felt its weight. Colors from the Dawn Stains painted her face with a woad of light. She stepped closer to the nearest glass panel and raised the heavy instrument over her head. Then she froze.

"What are you waiting for?" NoNo asked, rattling her sword in its parasol sheath.

Purity didn't rightly know how to answer that question, even to herself, but something held her back. Kaien and NoNo had both had ample opportunity to destroy the Dawn Stains before, and both had failed to do so. What made Purity the one everyone turned to for cultural terrorism?

Oh my dead gods what am I doing? Purity went into a kind of seizure of awareness, straining every muscle in her body but not moving a hair. *This is the closest thing we have to real holiness, don't you see that? The Dawn Stains are our saints, our relics, our, our—heritage—you can't expect me to destroy history. . . .*

Gravity sang a different song to her arms and the hammer trembling over her head.

But that was just it, wasn't it? Gravity. The gravity of history, the gravity of the rules that bound them: Kaien's instructions from his father rested the future of the guilds and possibly the entire city upon his broad shoulders; NoNo's deranged crimes originated with a blind instinct to protect her own; and had Prince Fflaen stood here himself, Purity was sure he would enumerate the reasons why the Weapon could not be allowed to fall into the mouth of even a single errant songbird.

So the deed and its gravity fell to Purity. She wouldn't shrink from it— she *did* agree with them all, though she doubted her own motives as much as anyone else's. She'd been ready to destroy the Dawn Stains out of nothing more than frustration, pure and simple. But this time she had come prepared—and she would use the rules to break the game. She would leverage history for a different future.

NoNo made a squawking noise. "I asked you a question, wench." She rubbed her nose.

Purity looked her friend in the eye and flexed her stiffening joints. She brought the hammer down and the room exploded with a color spray.

One of seven stains shattered like a wave of gemstones: garnet, rose quartz, topaz, peridot. Petal, too, and bone and midnight, hanging in the air as the hammer slipped from Purity's grip. The fall took forever; she fell to her knees just as slowly, crashing down with the glass.

She had to stand up and smash the other panes, but Purity took her time, picking glass from her bleeding knees while studying the song encoded on the bottom of each pane. She kept darting her eyes toward the musical notation, committing the pattern to memory. Such a good memory for facts and dates and pages she'd read only once, and such a poor memory for names and faces. Purity blasphemed and prayed that her mind would not fail her.

NoNo had flinched, but now she nodded toward the other stains, and Purity didn't object. She hefted the hammer and obliterated another ancient glass window. And another, and another, all the while studying the pattern at the bottom bevel of each pane, and the Weapon hidden there. When she came to the last, a wafer of ancient glass suspended from wire and steel, Purity hesitated. A woman with red drops on her side placed an ugly black crown on her own head. This Stain was the oldest, its picture the most ruined, and age had transformed the crown into a mad thing that ate the head of the woman king.

With a stab of guilt, Purity tore her gaze from the figure in the glass and took a final glance at the blurred bars of black and gold underneath, searing the image onto her brain like a brand. Then she swung the hammer up, underhand, and watched the spray fly across the room. A lesson from eternity, shattered.

"There's a good girl. You've lived up to your name today, lass."

Lass? Purity dropped the wretched hammer and marveled at NoNo, a fraction of a powerful personality. *She keeps on quoting pirates, because it's all she knows.*

"You, boy." NoNo poked Kaien with her sword, cutting through his arm like butter. He cried out and she giggled. *"Run."*

"I'm afraid I can't do that, Miss Leibowitz."

"Do you want to die, or Die? Run or choose, boy."

"Kaien." Purity nodded. "Please go. *Please.*" She didn't know what would happen if he stayed.

Go, Purity mouthed. Kaien pulled himself up the spiral staircase warily, though she knew he wouldn't go very far. Let NoNo have her laugh, Purity had something far more exciting, something she'd been starved of for far too long: leverage.

Purity stepped her way across the shards of half a million years, toward the stairs. NoNo Leibowitz watched her bloodied friend approach with glee. *And the ghost of a macaw on her shoulder.* Suddenly a champagne cork of hysterical, inappropriate giggles exploded somewhere inside Purity, and she blinked hard through tears not to laugh out loud.

So she sang instead. She felt her voice echo off the billionstone walls around her—the air still rang with the force of her blows. Purity could wield the song as the Weapon; it hung in the air, a shattered bell-song reverberating with released and dissipating power—at least, she hoped it was dissipating, or she'd have committed treasonous vandalism for naught.

As she sang, Purity closed her eyes and visualized the black and gold bars, hovering in her short-term memory. Then she relaxed into her breeding. If she had been raised for anything it was this: light music at a luncheon, a turn at the pianoforte, or a song to accompany a harpist at a pre-engagement luncheon preparatory party. It's just that today's excursion was Deadly. Purity was no songbird and had only NiNi's annoying humming as reference for the notation on the Dawn Stains, but she managed with the pitchy determination of a daughter of privilege. The warble threading out of her throat grew into a melody, and NoNo's eyes grew wide.

"Don't! Purity, we're on the same siiiii . . ."

The Weapon *worked.* Even as NoNo protested, her voice thickened like honey and her hands waved less wildly, an incredibly intricate clockwork toy grinding to a Dead stop. NoNo's face froze in paralyzed panic, and Purity couldn't turn away from the sight—as with the hammer and the Dawn Stains, she felt compelled to finish her work.

The song was not long, but it ended where it began, looping neatly—so Purity sang it again, then again, marching the key through the sequence of an arpeggio almost automatically. *So much for music lessons being worthless,* she thought as NoNo's Dying body began to lose color, then opacity. Purity kept singing, flinging out high, sharp notes at NoNo like daggers.

I hate you. Purity poured her soul into the song, remembering NoNo's promise to destroy Baron Kloo next. *We were bad enough before this, cutting up girls for fashion infractions. Now we're all monsters. Now I'm a Murderer, too.* NoNo said she'd wanted to keep her mother's hands clean, but she'd fouled them all instead.

NoNo's eyes disappeared completely, then the rest of her. She simply evaporated, the ghost of her body boiled away. Purity stopped singing mid-tune, dumbfounded by the sudden finality of the act—like a clock breaking. She stood alone amidst the ruins of the Dawn Stains, white stone walls glowing softly on her Murdering face.

12

The shadow of the being called Chesmarul enveloped Cooper like the sea swallowing a sinking ship. He felt like wind and starlight in an airless non-place that could never feel a breeze or a single stray photon. The city that rushed up to meet him was a distant dot in the jeweled abyss below, just a glint in the pinwheel of light that Cooper recognized was the worlds—the metaverse.

The worlds spun like a mobile, suspended from an invisible point above and anchored from below by the lick of space that was the City Unspoken. Between the unseen apex and the urban nadir shivered a span of creations, light whirling about light in an endless braided dance.

Among the lights of creation, Cooper saw teeming trillions—the syncopated fireflies that were mortal lives and, much fewer, the emeralds hidden among costume jewelry that were the slow-burning gemmed hearts of the First People. The fireflies and their elder counterparts swirled across the worlds in a turbulence that seemed random yet somehow guided; coordinated, at least, if not ordered. The hearts of the living were engines of life, and they woke and woke and woke, radiating loneliness and hope.

But something felt wrong. Some lights burned too brightly and seemed agitated, others pulsed irregularly, fading to the point of vanishing before strobing back to life. As he spiraled toward the city, Cooper sensed a foulness that offended the senses—a stopped-up drain, a sink gone foul. Sewage and offal and . . . *sludge,* invisible sludge clogging the lambent arteries of the living worlds.

No sooner did the bubble of that thought pop inside his head than Cooper was falling into the lights, not a pinwheel now but a rushing smear of cosmos growing larger and larger as he fell headfirst, the interstitial ether glowing around his shoulders like the shroud of superheated gas surrounding a rocket during reentry. The distant dot of the city grew until he saw the streets and parks spread out beneath him—and beneath the streets, the inverted skyscrapers where the Winnowed made their stalactite-homes, and beneath those, in fact directly beneath the gleaming Dome, a sphere of black and gold metal that pulsed with electricity and . . . music. He had no time to try and veer himself toward the buried machine before he tumbled in the direction of an H-shaped building and fell faster, faster, toward a green mansard roof and greener grass encircled by a high wall.

Trees shaded the mansion from view, but Cooper noted a familiar black-lacquered carriage with red-trimmed wheels. *Lallowë Thyu.* He had no time to curse before he shot through the copper and timber of the roof. Floors and rooms flapped through him like the pages of a flip-book, and then he hit something hard that knocked the wind from his chest.

Blinking his eyes, Cooper lifted his head, relieved that his body seemed intact; he found himself lying on the ground in a space too similar to the golden cathedral-forest to be accidental. Similar, but opposite. Gray instead of gold-green; bone rather than bark; built and not grown. Pillars of bone rose in the place of trees, but at the same angles, if on a smaller scale. Conical vaults made of—*skulls?*—rose above his head in imitation of the golden boughs, and little enchanted lights hung at their apexes, burning inside tiny round cages. Rib cages. Babies' rib cages.

Fucking delightful.

"What in the name of the King Beneath the Hill are *you*?" a voice asked. "And how did you find your way down here?"

Cooper tried to climb to his feet but lost his balance when he saw that the floor he pushed himself up from was made of finger bones. He let out a cry of disgust and scrambled to regain his purchase.

Across from him stood a lovely man dressed in a green coat over black livery, with hair like a fox that fell over his eyes. The man's ripe lips were rubbed with just a dab of pink petal dust. He held a femur bone in one hand and a bucket of bitumen in the other.

"Don't panic." Cooper held out his hands, realizing he was still wearing no more than a plaid workshirt and a makeshift sarong. "I'm here on official business."

"You're the gray man's human!" the valet exclaimed, pointing.

"Yeah?" Cooper cleared his throat and straightened his back. "You must be the mean lady's butler."

Tam narrowed his eyes. "I am not a *butler*." Then hefted the bone in his hand and lunged at Cooper, swinging for his head. Cooper blocked with his forearm and punched Tam in his exposed armpit. It was an awkward but lucky blow—*Why didn't I take those self-defense classes?* Cooper asked himself as his fist connected—he'd struck the sensitive bundle of nerve ganglia hidden under the armpit, and Tam's arm went momentarily dead.

"Mab, that hurts!" Tam cursed when he'd blinked away tears, cradling his numb arm and the mass of pain beneath his shoulder. The two men looked at each other and reached a wordless accord that they were neither of them fighters.

"Look, I just don't want to be fucked with, okay?" Cooper bargained for parley, as if spontaneously manifesting in an enemy's bone cellar weren't something to get jumpy about.

"You stupid boy, how was I ever as green as you?" Tam sounded exhausted. "I haven't any power to fuck with you or leave you unfucked-with, but I can tell you this: why ever you're here, you've saved my mistress another kidnapping. Now put your hands down and leave me be." Tam flicked his eyes toward Cooper's crotch. "Or the marchioness will find a different member to sever."

Cooper said nothing, until Tam tossed his head and said, "Fine. Can I get you some coffee?"

Upstairs, for lack of a better idea, Tam marched Cooper into the kitchens, where he sat on a stool, sulking. He looked around the large white-tiled room lined with steel sinks the size of bathtubs and an army of oven and stovetop ranges; a pile of china on the counter beside him bore the red-and-black coat of arms of Oxnard Terenz-de-Guises. Although his back was no longer a mantle of pain, he nevertheless resented Alouette for dumping him here. Whatever she was—Cooper had felt the touch of her true self thrice now, he thought, and no longer accepted her protestations quite so glibly. He cursed her silently. *Lady, goddess, sea mammal— any way, I hate you.*

Tam poured coffee, pained by the responsibility of keeping Cooper contained until his mistress returned. Cooper seemed to have little-to-no appreciation for the horrors awaiting him when Lallowë discovered him, which made Tam suspicious and tremendously uncomfortable. *And a little bored,* said the part of him that had been amidst faeries for too long.

"I must say, you're making me tremendously uncomfortable," Tam told Cooper. ". . . And a little bored."

Cooper just nodded. Tam wrung his hands. Cooper closed his eyes and listened.

LaLaLaDon'tRun, HmmHmmStayPleaseStay OhOhOhIHateItHere-Hmm. Tam's thoughts, even his fears, were strangely musical, not quite unhinged but definitely tainted with what Cooper could only guess was faeriestuff. A hundred years of singing flown by in a single night, that sort of thing; Tam reeked of it.

It still felt odd to hear fear and see identity. Since recovering from his torture atop the towers and the dawning awareness of the cumulative effects of his recent deliria, dreams, and hallucinations, Cooper's abilities seemed not only stronger but also linked to a vaster body of intuition than he could possibly merit: looking at Tam, he could see a pale blue note above a bowl-shaped guitar, a sign that fluttered over the majordomo's throat. A rather delicious throat, as well as the rest of him, Cooper couldn't help but notice—if a little over-painted. Tam's forearms—he'd rolled his shirtsleeves to wash dishes—were more muscled than his thin frame suggested, and his lower body filled out his trousers admirably, especially tight around the thighs and rear.

"How does she keep you here?" Cooper asked the fox-haired domo.

"Pardon?" Tam tossed his head and pretended not to have heard.

"Lallowë Thyu. You're her slave, right?"

This appalled Tam. "Certainly not! I am no slave." Then, reluctantly: "I just can't ever leave, and must obey at all times."

Cooper swirled his dregs. "I thought *I* was conflicted. Are you fucking her?"

"Not lately." Tam smiled, suddenly chummy, then darted back into formation, quick as a minnow. "No, I'm being saucy—Lallowë Thyu inherited me. I've been passed down from one fickle fey to another like an heirloom that cleans house. I haven't been *pleasurable* to the marchioness' family for a thousand years or more, although the reason I was originally . . . acquired . . . was, ostensibly, for my pleasing looks as much as my skill with the lute." The golden note and bowl-shaped string instrument glowed brighter as he spoke.

That sign is who he is. Cooper reminded himself. *It's his name.*

"What *is* a lute, anyway? It's the sort of thing I'm always hearing referenced in period films and fantasy stories, but I don't think I've ever actually heard any, um, lutations? Does it sound like the guitar? God, this coffee is *good*."

"It's a funny little guitar that sounds, to me, like home. Why don't I fetch you some cheeses? I think you've had enough coffee."

"Are you kidding me, faeriefucker? Do you know how long it's been since I had a cuppa joe?" Cooper moaned in a caffeinated glow.

Tam just stood there, not understanding Cooper on principle.

"Nevermind, I don't know why I bother with you people. Might as well try to pull the donkey's head off Nick Bottom."

"You know Nick?" Tam lit up.

Is this guy for real? "I know his work, sure. Top me off, Tam-tam."

Tam dispensed a miserly amount of coffee from the pot and shook his head, apparently sincere and not a little distraught. "Poor Asshat Nick. Seelie bastards ate his mind. They say they're the good ones but, really, if you want to know the absolute truth—"

"—And you *know* I do, Tamela—" Cooper drained the demitasse with gusto and slapped it onto the countertop. Bardic references aside, he had no idea what Tam was talking about. So far, that seemed about par for Cooper's insane course. *I should not feel this good,* he thought, before dismissing the idea as a letdown.

"—There's no such thing as a *good* faerie. Just different flavors of fuck-with-Tam. I spent time in the Summer Court too, you know. Ah, now I've gone and had too much myself, see what comes with forgetting one's place?" Tam patted his vest nervously, then pulled out his pocket watch. "It's past time. Am I late or am I early?"

"No offense, but your job sucks." Cooper picked up a cube of pink rock sugar from the sugar bowl, popped it into his mouth. It tasted like Turkish delight.

"None taken." Tam shrugged. "Wait till you meet her. You have no idea."

"Well"—Cooper shrugged—"she can't be worse than her mother."

Tam dropped his pocket watch, which swung on its chain. "She . . . *what*?" He narrowed his eyes at Cooper. "You *can't* have met the, ah, Cicatrix." That word hurt him to say.

"Ha. 'Met' is a strong word." Cooper held his arms over his head like horns. "Giant black helmet with dung beetle horns, big as a dinosaur? Slithering cybernetic dragon body, powered by little imps on metal skewers?"

"Ah, Mab's menses, you're not lying!" Tam's eyes grew wide as harvest moons. "Lallowë is going to skin you alive for that, you know."

"In that case, *she's* late." Cooper laughed a little too loudly. "She can try, if she dares, but my skin is damaged goods and I've been in an increasingly shitty mood for the last few days. For some reason. This has been a nice talk, Tambellina. You're the most normal person I've met in three days—not counting the pilot in the beer barrel, I guess he was pretty normal too, all things considered. He seemed like a guy who makes good choices."

Tam cocked his head sideways. "You're a strange young man, Cooper-*Omphale*."

"Well of course I am. You'd be strange too if you started your week as a magic turd who'd been dragged across the universe—metaverse, whatever—by a goddess, kidnapped by a faerie princess, drugged by Cleopatra, met the Cicatrix from the inside out, fucked and flayed by a dead gigolo from the motherland, saved an angel-thing from an undead monster straight outta *Vogue,* dumped in a cave of tears, and thrust into the mansion of an evil elf who's sounding more and more like Cruella De Vil every minute. Does she wear puppies? Oh, and Nixon was there."

"You don't say." Tam had the look of someone too well-mannered to flee the room in which he was trapped with a crazy person.

"He tried to steal my t-shirt."

"Is that a fact." Tam collected Cooper's cup and tossed it into one of the tub-like metal sinks.

"Yeah," Cooper harrumphed. "But I think he got adopted by a redhead."

"That sounds nice." Tam's cup and saucer followed with a clatter.

In the corner of the ceiling and the wall, a silver bell began to clatter. "Oh thank goddess!" Tam exclaimed. "And fuck, fuck."

"*You*. Atrium. Now," he spluttered, pointing at Cooper.

"Me. Cooper. *Always*." Cooper started to rant, but then something happened. His heart flipped inside his chest and the world stopped. Light froze through the windows, motes of dust stopped drifting midair, and everything became a single sound. A *song*. His ears filled with the song of breaking glass, glass that broke without stopping, a glacier of glass grinding itself into sand against the hammer of the world. Louder and louder until his eyes pulsed with the sound, and then the cacophony stopped as suddenly as it had begun. When his ears stopped ringing, something about the world was different, though he couldn't have said just what.

Tam still stood there blabbering about Lallowë, unaware of what Cooper had just experienced. A sudden dark impulse urged Cooper to grab and yank, shake, and pull until Tam's neck snapped and his skull separated from his spine. Tam's skull would float loose inside the sack of his skin and he could play with the body like a broken doll. *Break the doll*.

Cooper stumbled and braced himself against the wall. He couldn't . . . couldn't breathe, even though he felt the air moving in and out of his lungs. He couldn't see, even though his brain parsed the photons his retinas captured.

Then it passed. His head cleared and he was himself again, but the image came unbidden of the haunted look in Asher and Sesstri's eyes when they'd discussed the *svarning*. Tam stared at him like a cornered fox, and Cooper couldn't help but wonder how long Lallowë Thyu would corner the market on monstrosity.

The atrium was empty when Cooper entered. A long, glass-paneled geodesic greenhouse connecting the rear end of both wings of the manse, Lallowë had filled the atrium with traditional plants. Traditional, that is, to a woman raised to inherit seven *universes:* a red flower the size of a dog pouted in a pot, its stamen thick and swollen and stinking of burnt pork. Pulsing blue stalks with red fur stood watch over a carpet of moss-sized fronds that tickled the feet, fresh blood dripped dripped from carnivorous pitcher plants, and so on. A fern that grew tall as a palm flexed its roots into peat like nervous knuckles, tensing and relaxing. Sprays of jasmine that seemed ordinary until Cooper saw the way they pulsed, petals fluttering in and out: breathing. Everywhere the smells of loam and leaf and wet stone.

Beside a banyan, a chaise longue sat within an immensity of white blossoms, tiny and redolent. Near it was a small table and, at the foot of the chaise, a tiny stool for a second person. Cooper sat on the chaise longue instead. He shut his eyes when he heard the clip of boot heels in the hallway, and kept them shut until he sensed *her* presence at the threshold.

His first look at Lallowë Thyu walking down the length of the atrium confirmed the image that everyone, primarily Asher and Tam, had painted in his mind: she looked like a Thai whore who owned half of everything and coveted the rest. Too much eye shadow, no smile lines, pearl earrings the only bright thing on the face. Her jodhpurs cut from a heather suede, riding jacket in Terenz-de-Guises red and black, hair up—the marchioness ripped off her gloves while barking at Tam.

Lallowë held a little golden disc in her hand, and spoke to it with a smile slit across her delicate face as she marched toward the banyan. "Of course she's Dead, new sister, you don't think I'd leave her be if she lived, do you? No, it doesn't matter how it happened, why would that matter? What matters is that the slut is well and truly capital-D Dead, and as I was saying—boy, bring me wine," she snapped at Tam, who fled back down the atrium. "*As I was saying,* the Lady's last lunacy accomplished several of my goals, not the least of which was her removal as a trusted friend and adviser to our erstwhile—what's this? Boy, I said *wine,* not swinepiss—you, *other* boy, get out of my chair."

Here she snapped at Cooper, who did not jump at all.

She continued, seeming to ignore Cooper's disobedience. "Besides which—*good* wine, imbecile, do I have to crush your man-grapes to drill the notion of a peppery dry white into your obdurate skull?—and more to the point, I've forced matters to a head, which I hope Mother will appreciate, just like I *hope* the boy isn't bringing me the *second* reserve of that sour gewürztraminer he knows I loathe"—Tam and the offending bottle did an about-face—"and which ought to drum out whatever it is that the vivisistors are connecting to and causing the feedback loops I can't get past. I won't mention that I suspect that same stormy feedback system to be responsible for the—what was the word?—whatever sickness that's suddenly driving people to act like the churls they've always truly been.

Everyone knows it's more than just the government that's rotten in this city. Well, everyone who knows anything, which of course isn't anyone at all."

She folded her palm and the golden disc disappeared, then lifted a booted leg and punted Cooper off the chaise longue with all the piston force of an angry bull. He spun twice in the air and landed in garden muck, too surprised to remember to breathe.

"Airy Dark," Lallowë Thyu cursed, relaxing into her favorite chair with all the ease of a sunbather on holiday, "the children of men are stupid beasts." She took a glass from Tam, sipped, bared her teeth in a tolerant smile, and with a tap of her ring against the rim of the glass, chimed her wine frosty. Tam set a second glass on a small table beside her. Cooper noticed all this with half his attention, pulling himself out of a trough planter that had moments before been riotous with geraniums. He gasped, regaining his breath.

"I hate geraniums," the marchioness added. "They're a common, furry plant. And you're a common, furry man—aren't you, Cooper?"

Cooper brushed dirt and crushed leaves—they *were* furry, he admitted to himself—off the shirt Alouette had provided, and straightened his ridiculous sarong. The still-uncatalogued shaman's senses he'd won with such difficulty pulsed inside his chest in warning. A high-pitched buzzing sound rang in his ear.

"You . . ." He struggled to regulate his breathing. "Are vile . . . trash, Lolly. And . . . that's all your momma . . . can talk about in . . . the Court of Scars."

Thyu dropped her jaw and something dark and cruel rolled out of her mouth, intending to whip his face with her prodigious serpent tongue— but Cooper, tipped off by his newly enhanced instincts, managed to raise his hand at the last picosecond and grab the dry black thing as it shot out from her mouth, twisting his wrist to catch Thyu's tongue just before it struck his face. Her expression, he thought, was priceless.

"I've been whipped enough for one week." He let go of the tongue and wiped his hand on his shirt.

Thyu held her hand against her jaw, wincing, as the ophidian tongue retracted into her mouth. After a moment she pursed her lips and nodded sharply.

"Come a long way in just a few days, have we? Already beating up ladies, are you? I see Asher's rubbing off on you."

"I don't think anything with a six-foot tongue gets to call itself a lady, Lolly."

"Ha!" The marchioness slapped her thigh. "Sexist *and* racist. He raped his sister, did you know that? She killed herself and the baby to escape him. Oh yes, 'Asher' is as famous a woman-beater as he is a ladykiller. He must be so proud of his meaty little protégé. Still, I'll bet he hasn't shown you his other face, has he? The one he was born with?" She leaned forward to study Cooper's expression. "I didn't think so. Poor Cooper, lost and abused and fed to all *kinds* of wolves."

Thyu bent forward and slid the second wineglass toward him like a chess piece. She tapped it with her ring, and the glass chimed frosty in an instant.

"We've only just met, so forgive me if I offend you by saying so," she purred, "but it seems to me that you might feel rather put out that *I've* been more forthcoming than your absent-hued friend?"

Cooper wished the buzzing in his ears would go away until he recognized how it scratched at the inside of his skull. "Riddle me this, princess: that a magic ring you're wearing?"

"It's just a ring. *I'm* magic."

"You sure about that?" He smiled.

"Ape, I'm a *faerie*. Of course I'm magic." It was a fine gold ring from her husband's family hoard, and maybe a wedding present, but it was only jewelry.

Lallowë narrowed her eyes until they were razors.

"Well, you *do* know that I can hear fear, right?" Cooper sat down on his little stool and picked up his wine. "I can't do much, but apparently hearing fear is a thing—and I can do it. I hear an eensy weensy worm dying inside your ring, Lollipop, and it is *terrified*."

For the first time, Lallowë Thyu looked taken aback. For a moment Cooper saw a frightened, lonely woman where a lamia had been. Inside his head, where the magic happened, Cooper heard Lallowë's truth: *Mother,* she thought, *MotherMotherMother. Vivisistor, AreYouWatchingMe? Vivisistor?*

Cooper smiled. "If she *is* watching, Lolly, how disappointed she must be."

The marchioness jerked as if slapped.

"Are you all junked-out on vivisistors, too?"

Lallowë's mouth formed a thin smile that promised cruelty commensurate with her embarrassment. "What commendable curiosity!" She clapped her hands rapidly in a frill of mock delight. "What an opportunity to begin the exchange of ideas and digits!"

Lallowë slid a jewelry box onto the table, a matte red metal bevel and lid, paned with silvered glass on two ends. Cooper didn't need his fancy new superpowers to recognize that Lallowë Thyu specialized in nasty surprises. So many ways to lose yourself, here, and so many pieces to be lost.

"A vivisistor, my plump, healthy-looking guest, is not that different from a contraption called a 'transistor,' which I understand you should be familiar with, coming as it does from your world of origin."

Cooper said nothing. In the center of the box, like nested junk, sat the golden disc to which Lallowë had been chatting—the bottom half of a pocket watch cupping a coin.

"A transistor, as I'm certain you know, receives a current of a power called electricity and amplifies it, producing a stronger emanation than it received. A vivisistor works along similar principles but incorporates the more versatile and propitious properties of the arcane. Which is how I can teach it to talk before I've completed it." She paused. "Mother really hasn't scratched the surface."

Lallowë pointed inside the box. "It's a true wonder to see an invention that incorporates ideas developed in separate realities—that usually fails quite spectacularly. But in this instance, the creators of the vivisistor have produced a device that generates and manipulates power. Power from life."

"The worm in your ring." He did not like where this was headed.

"You see"—she ignored him—"I have a problem of scale. You're far too big for what I need, and yet I've thought of a way through which you can still be useful. Isn't that a delight? I'm going to ask you to put your pinky finger inside this little red box, and you're going to do it."

"Fuck you."

"The Ruby Naught here is quite a treasure. Among other, better things, the box has a keen ability to manipulate *here* and *there*. Which is how the box is going to separate your finger from your body, while keeping it alive. And you're going to let it."

"Fuck *me*," Cooper breathed.

She lifted her shoulders in acknowledgment, as if he'd paid her a compliment, but awkwardly. "After, the stump where your pinky finger used to be will be capped with a metal that possesses transitive and entanglement properties, so that the detached finger will continue to receive blood from your body. It won't actually be severed so much as simply separated."

"You do know that all these props don't distract from the fact that your mother doesn't love you, right?"

"And then you're going to finish your wine because it's an exceptional vintage—not too dry, not too sweet, weighty on the tongue with just a hint of Anjou and black pepper and dusk cedar. Then you're going to stand up and walk out of my mansion and never lay eyes on me again. Just so we're clear."

"I'm going to do exactly none of that, you overprivileged nut job." He lifted his glass and toasted her; Thyu did have good taste in whites.

Lallowë shook her head. "Cooper, I admire your vim, but no matter what has happened to you since you arrived in my city, there is one truth that remains unaltered: you are quite beyond your depth."

His hackles rose. "And you're an oppressive cunt."

If the marchioness felt insulted she gave no sign. "Oppression. You say the word like it's a malignancy, when nothing in the world could be more natural—and in fact, oppression serves your interests far better than you seem to believe. Do you, perhaps, nurture some flawed yet abiding notion concerning the welfare of the people who live in the City Unspoken? Absence of any limiting, containing force in this city is precisely what's *caused* the current chaos."

As she spoke, Lallowë Thyu reached across the table and took his wrist with all the care of a palm-reader. Cooper found himself unable to move.

Lallowë saw the panic on his face. "I *did* tell you, I'm magic. But to continue . . ." she spoke casually. "You are, however, comically mistaken if you believe I have any interest in the mongrels of this city." She opened one side of the box by sliding the glass panel up until it clicked into place. "Toward what absurd purpose would I direct them? I have little to no interest in anything or anyone you could possibly know, be aware of, or expect to encounter." She folded Cooper's frozen fingers into a fist, all but the pinky. "I will acquire your blood because something I want necessitates that I do so, and I will contrive to remove only your finger because it is efficient: you are not important, and I spare you your freedom because I don't fancy commissioning a metal cage big enough for an entire man-pig."

At that, the marchioness carefully slipped his little finger into the box, then flashed him a smile of such humble beauty it belonged on a magazine cover. The glass dropped. There was no pain. Cooper watched the glass panel slice neatly through his pinky, below the second knuckle. He felt a popping sensation and a spark of electricity, but nothing more.

From the faceless coin, a bead of mercury-like liquid metal condensed. It slid toward the severed fingertip and quickly capped the stump, pulling tight as a tourniquet and capping his finger like a bottle capped at a factory. Sliding beneath the glass pane of the box, the living metal dripped up the outside of the glass and performed a similar procedure upon what remained of his little finger. The metal flexed and sealed itself off, growing cool.

That was it. When Lallowë removed the box from the table, Cooper looked down and saw the hermetic cap that fit his wound—it annealed to his skin perfectly.

"I wasn't kidding about your mother, Lolly." Cooper decided a finger was a finger. "You're nothing but a disappointment."

"Try to wiggle your fingers," she asked, lifting the box to her face. "I'll permit that much movement, child." Cooper was relieved to loosen the grip of his tightly fisted hand—and was surprised to see the fingertip inside the box wriggle. The marchioness was right, the finger was still connected to him through the metal cap, still alive and sending and receiving blood to and from his hand. He felt the tip of his finger touch the lid of the box, and shivered.

"Wow," Cooper said, despite himself.

Lallowë condescended to grace him with another curt nod, like a bird pecking at raw meat, and laid his hand on the table, palm up, smoothing his fingers flat. "Now, you might think that a little death will restore your finger, but you'd be wrong. The Sixth Silver works like a body-binding, but is more specific. So long as I have your finger capped with my silver, you will wake from sleep or death with nine fingers. The tenth is *mine*."

His jailer exhaled, relaxing into her chaise—she lifted her arms over her head, mussing her hair and sliding down the seat, her blouse tugging at the curves of her breasts. "Thank you, Cooper! I can't tell you how long it's been since I've dismembered someone who isn't family."

She paused. "I suppose as long as I've been trapped in this disposable hell of a city."

"Then why stay?" Cooper asked. "Did someone bind you against your will too?"

"Yes," Lallowë said with a glance at the gold ring on her finger that she'd insisted was ordinary. "She might as well have done just that."

Bending to one side like a drawn longbow, the marchioness pulled back her arm for a punch and slammed her fist into the lip of the nearest granite planter, sending up a cloud of rock dust. The planter shuddered from the force of the punch and Lallowë shook gravel from her knuckles—as well as the remains of her ring. Beige mucus drooled from within the cracked casing. She eyed the goo and pursed her lips, wondering. In the distance, someone played a sad song on a flute.

Cooper cracked the joints in his neck, beginning to regain motility. The flute music reminded him of bare branches and weeping. "I've been inside her, you know. The Cicatrix. She'd rather have a plank of driftwood for an heir than you. When you hit bottom, Lollyparts, when you hit bottom . . . I'm going to be there."

Lallowë swung her legs off the chaise and stood in one fluid motion, turning her back on her quarry. She didn't spare him so much as a glance.

"Congratulations on your newfound parlor trick and assorted mutilations. Please excuse my brevity, I have less insignificant worms to crush." She snapped her fingers and Tam appeared in the archway.

Cooper just sat there, of course. Would he gain from this? A finger in every evil pie—perhaps literally—and a body bound to the City Unspoken. Scoured and scolded and given just enough of a taste of power to realize the profundity of his own powerlessness. Spitting tacks. Would this work to his favor, or condemn him further?

He shook his head and marveled at the mortal capacity to adapt to horrible circumstances. *How far I've come from horror,* he thought. *Now when I get maimed—as one does—I just wonder what it'll do for me.*

The marchioness had dismissed him from her world entirely. He no longer existed. She snapped again and her domo stepped forward, an obsequious expression on his fox's face.

"Tam, draw me another bath. I'm going back to work."

Boredom. How dare Terenz-de-Guises talk to *him* about boredom? Asher's gray face felt white-hot with fury as he stalked through the tangled streets of the Guiselaine. The poncey voice of the marquis rang in his ears.

Asher had made choices and had abided by them, but this . . . nobody ever took the Undertow seriously, those liches were just a handful of bitter noble and scholastic remnants whose experiments had gone awry. They posed no threat, even for the undead—they stood as nothing in comparison to, say, the Abnegate Redoubt or the mobile necropoli of the Bloodless Sky. That they'd gained power over the last few years was regrettable, but was only *exceptional* when considering how they'd accomplished their ascendancy. What—*who*—they used to give themselves power.

Asher kept his anger stoked and level with that thought. Abiding by one's choices never grew easier, even if you forgot your age. *Age,* he fumed. *You were supposed to be my ally.*

Three lanes met in a little triangular nook of an intersection, and in a darkened recess some forgotten artisan had installed a fountain. A limestone sea horse spat water into a scalloped bowl—here Asher stopped, looking down. What he had thought he'd felt atop the whale-skinned tower of the Undertow, it wasn't possible. Was it?

If he'd only *known.* Did this mean Chara was alive somewhere, too? He'd thought them both Dead. If he'd known he wasn't the last, that he had an heir . . . he would never have abused his legacy so. He would never have mutilated himself.

For all the liches in the worlds, all the jackbooted blackguards stoned on the fumes of undeath, Asher could only blame himself. He shook off a brief but intense urge to smash his head to pulp on the stone sea horse.

It's begun. Will we all drown?

Placing his hands on either side of the fountain, Asher stared into the water and flexed a mental muscle he'd half-feared had atrophied. In the bowl of the sea horse fountain, a vision kindled and the astonished visage of Lallowë Thyu appeared. Her face was illuminated by gold-green light and her bare shoulders were wet—was she in the bath? With glowing lights?

"Why what an honor, my—"

Asher cut off the marchioness before she could finish. "Shut your cow mouth you half-breed abortion." Her mouth formed a perfect O. "It's over, Thyu. This is a courtesy call: *run*."

"Pardon me?" Lallowë recovered and nearly succeeded in sounding amused, but beneath her glibness he could see that he'd shaken her. *Yes, yes, yes. She's as guilty as she looks.*

"I told you to run. Get out of my city while you can." He crooked his fingers over the water and his fetch-window shifted, swiveling its point of view up and away from her lap to hover over her face instead, dominating her. He saw the object she cradled between her soapy breasts—it was one of the newer syncretistic fusions, the rage among the high-end tinker set as of a few years ago: a cabbage-sized oyster shell containing an electrical grid matrix suspended in an arcane medium. Asher didn't have an obsession with everyday artifice—magical, technological, metaphysical, spiritual, or otherwise. He didn't need to, and now that it was too late, he realized how naïve he'd been.

Thyu looked up at him from her bath. There was no more pretense from her—she'd stopped the coy game in which he was a man intruding on her, a woman, in the bath. They were both beyond that—he was more than a man and she had never been anything so decent as a woman.

"Run?" She smiled at him with serpent's fangs folding down from the roof of her mouth. "Why would I do that? I hear music and feel something throbbing down below: I think things here might finally get interesting."

The street shook beneath him, sloshing water out of the fountain, and Asher gripped the stone with both hands to keep his balance.

The snake laughed. "You know, instead of drafting morbid fantasies from your own failures, you should be thanking me for maintaining normalcy within at least a portion of this city. You might also thank me for my failure to retrieve Cooper from the Lady."

Asher grimaced, and opened the well of his rage. "You think you've meted out agony to the father you've strung up in your water closet? I was practicing cruelty before your mother founded her dynasty, and I will snap your mind without taking a breath. I will rob you of your precious self-possession and leave you braying for mercy like a mule with a broken back, and that's better than you deserve."

If Asher expected some sign of fear or submission from the marchioness, he was disappointed. She only laughed harder, clapping her soapy hands.

"I'll pass on your own regards to my new guest. He's a friend of yours. Well, what's *left* of a friend of yours. But then, you've had all that time to get used to losing friends and family, no?" Her question trailed off as she was distracted by something, a thin sound, like a lonely piper or flutist.

"*Cooper?*" Asher despaired before the ground shook again, more violently this time, and the street whipped up like a billowed bedsheet and threw him to his feet. Astonishment replaced anger as Asher watched a bank building, its cornices hundreds, maybe thousands of years old, crumble into sand before his eyes. In the dead of night the building was empty, but the homes on either side and all along the cypress-lined Boulevard Hagia Khan Ruespiel were not—and Asher heard screams as children woke and parents dashed from their beds. The whole boulevard vibrated to something huge that shuddered underneath.

Underneath. Bells for the bloated dead, not now. The chains.

Could it be the Winnowed? They were a reliable tribe, populated with the best souls the worlds had to offer—or the purest, for those who made the distinction—and dedicated themselves to preserving the buried history of the City Unspoken. The Winnowed were allies to anyone with the best interest of the city and its people at heart, surely they would not permit the masons to even inspect the instruments at the heart of the web of catenary chains, let alone attempt to *operate* the antediluvian mechanism?

Asher stepped out of the alley and looked to the northwest, toward the nearest exposed length of chain, winched up into the belfry of a tower—the street-level anchors he remembered from so long ago that had been built when the masons' ancient forebears squared off the chains, fixing them around underground drums and securing the links to buttressed towers above, like the pendulums of massive grandfather clocks. They'd hidden the chains' true function within the maze of the undercity and used the rising level of the streets to their advantage, burying the truth far below, where only the Winnowed dwelt. He'd thought they could be trusted with Anvit's gambit; had he been wrong?

Sure enough, the anchor tower was collapsing, and the chain—as thick as a carriage—seemed to be slicing through the street like a wire through cheese as it pulled toward its original position; the chain ripped through the cobblestones as it half fell, half slid along its path. Stone and dirt erupted in a line of destruction that sheared straight down the boulevard, peppering the faces of the buildings with shrapnel as it did so. Three hundred paces of the Boulevard Hagia Khan Ruespiel were obliterated before the chain dropped below street level, although another fifty paces collapsed as the ancient metal continued to tear through the supporting structures beneath.

Even after the immediate destruction ceased, Asher felt troublesome rumblings underfoot as the chain continued to pull. Even though he couldn't see it, this scene must be repeating itself across the city, wherever the chains had been secured aboveground. A spiderweb of destruction with the Dome at its center, ripping through squares and piazzas and courtyards, as the bell towers were pulled down—bells, there were towers everywhere! He'd made certain of that himself, long ago when he thought things might work out for the better.

Towers everywhere. And one elevator.

Asher spun on his heel and sprinted toward another landmark, the conical volcano of friezes and temple porticos that suddenly occupied all of his attention: the Apostery.

13

I hardly knew then that I was building the foundations for a new world. I daresay that if I had, the only thing I would have changed would have been my own soiled panties.

Of course you mustn't believe me. All these lives later and I still harbor the pretentions of a girl, isn't that humbling? Well, it ought to be. I should tell the truth, at my end: I would have found a way to break the worlds one way or another. A hammer, a boy, a song—'twas all the same to me.

—Attributed to Lady Senator Emeritus Purity, Rosa-Kloo, before her death

Purity folded her hands in her lap, trying to minimize the chafing of her restraints against her wrists. Formally, she'd been arrested by Leibowitz guardsmen, not praetors, and Lady Mauve's henchmen had stashed her in an oversized closet, where she shared a settee with a terrified maid. Why they'd thought it necessary to keep Purity manacled, she didn't know—true, she'd Killed a peer and destroyed the most valuable artifacts in the known history of the City Unspoken, but what further danger could she possibly pose? The use of house guardsmen rather than praetors indicated the degree of upheaval within the Circle—guardsmen were a poor replacement for the sterling warriors of the royal seat.

Praetors wouldn't have bothered. They wouldn't have stashed her in a closet either, like these cheese-headed Leibowitz guardsmen. The praetorian guard would have followed protocol and dropped Purity into an oubliette where she'd be confined to the dark, nourished by the effluvia of the teardrop-shaped gourd cells. She'd visited the dungeons a year or so ago, when she and her friends—her now Dead and/or former friends—still thought they could escape the boredom of Dome life by arranging little excursions.

Bitzy had marveled at the oubliettes in particular—she had a fondness for horticulture, and the single-occupant cells were grown, not built, from hybridized thrashmelons. Purity had watched Bitzy marvel that such a sweet treat could be coaxed into a tool of containment and misery. Purity herself hadn't marveled at all—she'd looked around her, above, at the swirling mosaic ceilings of the dungeons, the gilded torch sconces, the wealth with which even the palace prisons had been fabricated—and she hadn't been surprised one whit. Even the architecture of the City Unspoken sang out its arrogance and presumed superiority; over men, over the fantastic confections of the fey—whose design principles Purity suspected had once inspired the creation of the oubliettes—and over the erstwhile gods themselves.

Bells, Purity pouted, *I hope tragedy has made Bitzy more insightful. Or at least more interesting.*

Her thoughts were interrupted by the click of boot heels on marble, followed by the appearance of the steel head of Mauve Leibowitz. Lady Leibowitz's face lacked any expression, and Purity wondered just how much the Circle Lady knew about tonight's events. She must know that her daughter was Dead, but did she also know NoNo had been the Murderer? Or was Purity being held for epic vandalism only? She hadn't behaved very well when they arrested her, she was ashamed to admit. Lots of tears and blubbering apologies she didn't quite remember. Mauve Leibowitz would have smiled when they told her that.

Lady Mauve looked through Purity as if she didn't exist, instead addressing the mousey chambermaid who shared Purity's makeshift cell. The girl had sat there and refused to look away from her hands, like a pious dormouse. Now her head shot up, a dim light of hope kindling in her red face.

"Cleaning girl. You've been cleared, so don't fret." Mauve's voice was a wire brush scraping across raw skin, and the little housemaid redoubled her tremulous fretting.

If Lady Mauve felt any concern about her own future in light of her daughter's alleged crimes, it did not show. Indeed, the woman's self-importance only seemed to have ballooned in the wake of NoNo's Death. She must know she was done for, Purity surmised, but appeared determined to wield her influence until the very last moment. That should surprise no one and spelled further trouble for Purity, though she did not blame the woman. It might take weeks for the Circle to declare her formal impeachment.

"Essa, child." Mauve relented and admitted that she knew the girl's name. "Stop shaking. You were only detained in case you saw something, not because you could have *done* anything." Lady Mauve never so much as glanced at Purity—perhaps she was trying to forget what Purity had *done*—and then withdrew. No doubt to stomp off to some nervous caucus where she would try to bully the Circle into saving her own hide, probably by insisting that Purity's be tanned and stitched into a riding coat. Sudden concern for her father forced Purity to look down at her own hands in shame.

How could she have been so reckless? It was one thing to endanger herself, but to put her father in jeopardy . . . and her entire family! What would Pomeroy say, and what if she had ruined his chances for an advantageous marriage? Her mother and sister were easier to predict: they'd be furious. Parquetta would likely never speak to Purity again.

She heard the guardsmen gossiping about her fate over a wineskin they oughtn't to have been enjoying while on duty.

"That Baron will be pulled down for sure over this," the older guard said.

The younger one winced. "That's a well bad fate, innit? Assets liquidoodled, all his properties auctioned off to the rest of the quality."

The old guard grumbled something and the younger one added, "Yeah, putrefied, that's what I meant. The Baron's life? No, no, the family will survive, if you can call that survival." He paused before asking his elder fellow, "Do you reckon they'll Kill the girl for it?"

Purity could practically hear the bored nod of the Leibowitz family. Little Essa squeaked "Eep!" and covered her mouth with her hand, looking at Purity with a nauseating amount of pity.

"Don't worry about me, Essa," Purity said with an equanimity she did not half feel, addressing the housekeeper for the first time. "I'll be fine. They can't Kill me. They can't Kill anyone ever again."

Suddenly Purity felt a burning earnestness in her chest and she grabbed Essa's hand. "You tell them that, Essa, when they let you out of here. Oh, don't make that face, girl, you'll be fine. You were just waxing the floors, bells, they can't hold *that* against you." Essa nodded, still terrorized.

Purity squeezed the small hand, red from scrubbing floors. "No, Essa, you'll be out of this cell by nightfall, and when you go, I want you to tell everyone—your sisters, your mama, the men and women who work with you—you tell them that you were in a cell with Purity Kloo, the demon who shattered the Circle Unsung and broke the backs of the nobles. You tell them that it was the Circle who's been behind all the Killing, but that they can't ever Kill again. You tell them that the secret that made the Circle powerful is over, broken, *done*—and that there's no reason to bend your knee to any noble ever again unless you're doing so of your own free will and for fair coin."

Essa's cheeks reddened further. She did not have the look of a civil revolutionary. "Begging your pardon, Lady Miss Kloo, but, but . . ." the cleaning girl stammered. "All you did was break a few windows and Kill one of your girlfriends?"

Purity put her head in her hands. Getting the truth out was always an uphill battle, wasn't it? Did making things right ever get easier?

"Essa, you're right. Absolutely right. All I did was Kill a friend and smash some windows. And if you stop fussing and sniffling, I'll tell you why that changes everything."

"Well . . . all right, ma'am. If you say so."

Essa literally sat on her hands as Purity began recounting her recent escapades, beginning with the butchering of Rawella Eightsguard. The girl's eyes grew wider as she listened, and by the time Purity reached her showdown with NoNo and the destruction of the Dawn Stains, she thought Essa's eyelids might simply atrophy and disappear entirely.

"Them Circle lords could go around Killing anyone they wanted to *the whole time*?" Essa asked, doubly amazed when Purity explained how many hundreds of decades the Circle Unsung had maintained their True Death détente.

"And your friend was Killing us just for practice." That came out softer, Essa's voice tinged with what Purity prayed was the first blush of outrage—or at least awareness of the world around her. The girl would spread the truth, Purity felt sure of it.

"And now you've smashed them windows, they can't Kill no more."

"The song lived in the glass. Our throats could borrow it, but now that the Stains are gone, it's just music. So yes, the power that anchored the Circle is gone, Essa."

Purity was technically lying to the girl, since she had no notion about what would happen now and who knew *how* the Weapon functioned, let alone the nature of its connection to the stains—but Purity believed what she said; now that she'd had time to think about the Dawn Stains and the Weapon—the song—she'd reached several conclusions. Purity felt confident that history would prove her correct: the Dawn Stains heralded from the age of the aesr, who were a species of First People. What fragments of history from that era that had survived strongly associated the aesr with light and music—was it such a stretch, then, to hypothesize that they had preserved their gift in the Dawn Stains for their successors? Like an insect in amber, the aesr's talent had persevered through aeons, known only to the Circle Unsung and the prince.

Essa shook her head. She might not have benefited from the same education and life of enrichment as Purity, but the girl possessed her own body of knowledge. "Begging your pardon, Lady Miss, but how will that change anything, if the nobles still own everything? It isn't escaping Murder we work all our lives for, is it now? It's nickeldimes to feed the family, and clothe 'em. And if that's any different today than it was yesterday, ma'am, I don't see how."

Purity puffed herself up for a lecture about the primacy of power structure, and how a destabilization at the top of a food chain, even if it seemed unrelated, would mean incrementally larger disruptions for the status quo of each descending tier. "The hierarchy that was secured by the threat of mutually assured destruction will begin to decay, you see, and—"

Then a piece of the wall pushed itself onto the floor with a crash that startled both women. Essa would have screamed, but Purity pinched the skin of her thigh hard, and the cleaning girl bit her lip and managed only a frantic whimper. On the other side of the cell a hexagonal hole appeared where the block had been dislodged, and as the girls stared, the dust-smeared face of Kaien Rosa emerged.

"Come on," he said, and cocked his head only to knock it against the block above. "Ouch. I can't get my shoulders through, but you should be able to slip out. Hurry up before someone comes to find out why the walls are falling apart."

Almondine met her sister without emotion. Lallowë did not return the favor.

What she did was screech in fury. A glass-shattering, earsplitting screech that lasted over a minute. Downstairs, Tam clapped his hands over his ears and Cooper would have done the same, except he was too busy hiding under the kitchen table. Lallowë sat in her bath, her nearly complete matrix gleaming inside the shell, immersed in the only two comforts she had in this filthy city—and in one sweep of the door, all of her security had been shattered. All of her plans. Hopes.

She screeched in fury and disbelief and hate and loneliness and defiance and in a wretchedly sincere relief to have her sister returned to her. She screeched at her mother, who surely orchestrated this last-minute betrayal, at Almondine for daring to go away and daring to return, and—mostly— at herself for not anticipating this twist, and for the weakness inside herself that made her *glad* to see her sister. Later, when she could, Lallowë would excoriate her father for passing on to her that human weakness; now, she would continue to point a turquoise claw at Almondine and *scream.*

Almondine simply stood there, expressionless. She wore a hound's-tooth pea coat, gray and black, and a pale blue dress that belonged on a young girl. No longer made of wood, her face pink and perfect, Almondine stared at her sister as if trying to remember Lallowë's name. Her hair curled at the nape of her neck in a bob—the same hue and luster as when she was made of cherrywood, but her eyes were empty. Perhaps they'd always been that way.

Lallowë reached to the side of the wide shale pool and snatched up her reengineered, reprogrammed vivisistor. It looked inconspicuous inside its pocket watch shell, but it represented the accumulation of years of positioning, conniving, hours of wasted talking, and *marriage.* She shook the living bauble at her sister and forced herself to find words.

"*Why?* Why did I do *all of this work* for you to just *wake up* like *noth-*

ing happened? Do you have *any* idea what I've put myself through?" She stood, naked, water and bubbles pouring off her naked breasts.

"Sister, I'm glad to see you again too." Almondine ran her finger along the polished edge of the door frame. "What. A happy. Reunion."

"Mother brought you back, she must have done. What did I do to earn this?" Lallowë wrapped herself in a terry cloth robe and shook her hair to dry it in an instant.

"You can ask her when she arrives." Almondine primped her own bob with one hand. "Although if I were a betting elf, I'd put my money on simple ill will."

"Mother is coming *here*?" Lallowë screeched again. Then, calmly, "Of course she is."

"I understand you've been researching the vivisistors that enable Mother's transformation. What is she about?" Almondine's blue eyes didn't seem to blink at all.

"How do you know that? You've been *wood*." She started to walk past Almondine, but took the other door instead, that led to her dressing rooms.

"Even wood dreams. You should have some idea of what she's after."

"Yes, well maybe I should, Almsy. And you've been dead for years, you should have stayed that way." Lallowë turned to her vanity so that Almondine could not see, and reached out for a box of smooth red metal—but she stopped short of touching it. *Not yet.* Instead she dropped her robe and drew a chocolate wool bolero across her shoulders, fingering the brocade for comfort.

Almondine padded toward her sister with a look of probational sympathy.

"I understand your animosity, Lolly, and always have. I kept quiet for years to give you a chance to prove yourself, and you did. But Mother . . . Mother changed the game, and I don't honestly think that there can be any more competing for her favor. We are both just meat to her now; she sees all organics as incomplete."

"Is that your way of declaring war, then?" Lallowë admired herself in the mirror, naked save for the little jacket, which obscured her breasts but did not hide them.

Almondine shook her head. "Not against you, Lolly. Stop choosing outfits and listen, please:

"While I slept, I dreamt of the one who stole my soul. It was not one of the First People, Lallowë. It was Mother." Almondine cocked her head, eyes still as dead as dormice. "The fey are terrified of her. She forces mutilations upon them, steals the legs of little faerie girls, fills their bodies with vivisistors, which are *connected* to each other, all of them, irreversibly."

Lallowë laughed to herself, wishing she had an army or a cold glass of wine standing between herself and her sister. "You may have dreamed all that, sister, but I *lived* it. I saw her take her lover, some favored champion of the Wild Hunt, and tear off his feet. Now he lopes through a wasteland on recurved tension blades and weeps with each step; his mutilations might even matter, if there were anything left to kill in her game reserves." *The vivisistors are networked?*

Her sister nodded once; her eyes were glass.

"One other thing." Almondine hesitated, deciding whether or not to continue. "I dreamt one other thing—I dreamt the memory of our sister. I dreamt she was close to you, Lolly."

"Our sister?" Lallowë stopped cold, the hangers of slacks in her hands forgotten.

"Don't you remember? When we were small there was a holiday, and our sister came to play. She thought she was dreaming, of course, but still she visited us in the way that human children so often do: accidentally, and in dreams or at twilight, dawn, some liminal hour. And Mother gave us dresses she'd had the spiderkin weave, and we played rabbit-rabbit-worg. You were the worg the whole time, chasing us all through the brush and howling like a mad thing. Then Mother gave us iced cakes and sweet wine and danced for us, I remember. She called us Almsy and Lolly and Sissy."

Sissy. Lallowë narrowed her eyes and crossed her arms.

"I remember no such thing." She was not pleased to hear talk of another sister—this morning she had been an only child, now she was bookended by bitches from the same litter. Shoved aside by her mother—again—and kept out of the loop entirely, it would seem. "I do not remember any *Sissy.*"

"Well, I do." Almondine fingered some spare clockworks that Lallowë had left on a dresser. "She was a sharp little thing, angry like you but without your cruelty. Hair like sunrise, thanks to fey blood, but her hands were human, so she couldn't stay—her blood ran to baseline human. You shouldn't concern yourself with her, Lolly, she's not a contender. Just a memory. We both need to keep our eyes on Mother; I don't know what she intends but there is a chance it will . . . conflict . . . with . . ."

"With life as we know it?"

Almondine flashed a blade-thin smile that could have been Lallowë's. "As you know it, maybe. I haven't known life for some time."

"Yet here you are, returned to take my place." Lallowë took off her bolero, then put it back on, uncertain how she should react.

"*Your* place? Lolly, no." Almondine leaned against a dresser and inspected her nails—they'd always been strong, sharp wood. Living wood.

"You honestly, *truly* expect me to believe that Mother didn't revive you to supplant me?" Lallowë settled on a ruched wrap jacket with deep inner pockets, and with the discarded bolero in one hand she surreptitiously grabbed the red metal jewel box. The Ruby Naught had once belonged to her husband's grandfather, but now it was hers, all hers. And it could do far more than sever fingers.

Almondine frowned. "I don't know *what* Mother intends, honestly. She speaks in riddles these days, even when she means to be straightforward. She has compromised the integrity of her essential self, and I could no sooner follow her logic than I could follow her orders."

"You expect me to believe that you're here to *disobey*?" Lallowë scoffed. "Perfect little Almondine?"

"I am my mother's daughter. I will never betray her, Lallowë, do not think that." The elder sister put her palms together and cracked her knuckles. She spoke deliberately so that Lallowë could not willfully misunderstand. "I have always accepted as fact my succession. I will rule, I thought. Let you rant—there was no amount of success you could achieve that would displace me: by primacy and by blood, I *am* Mother's heir. Only . . . I do not want to rule a broken empire. Do you?"

Lallowë lowered her eyes. "The Court of Scars could be restored, if Mother were to be removed."

Almondine nodded. "Just so."

"And it might be even worse, Almondine, than just ruling broken universes. You say you've seen what Mother did to our people—machine faeries coughing up engine oil." Lallowë arched her back and felt her body, whole and young and flawless. "Have you ever considered what atrocities she would force upon her heir?"

"What else were you about with your vivisistor, if not atrocity?" Almondine asked. "Mother could have done as much to me as I slept, or she could have let you finish your treachery and make me into an abomination. But she did not, and for that she will forever have my gratitude. I cried in relief when I awoke down below, in your ossuary, Lolly. Not to be awake—what is life, and what is waking?—but to be *whole*."

The Cicatrix unleashed the madness when she felt the chains wake, juddering to life after millennia of slumber. That was an interesting development—one her assays had assigned a likelihood of less than 5 percent—but would not significantly disrupt her own. She held no truck with the First People; the signs of Chesmarul's interference weren't hard to miss, certainly, but the queen hadn't known to what extent the being's interests would collide with her own—or if Chesmarul would make a play to help the mortals avoid the plague of deathless madness that would momentarily consume them.

Why Chesmarul would put the chains into play escaped the Cicatrix's reasoning, but it changed little: operational or deactivate, that machine—that ancient, impossible engine—would yield up its secrets once she stormed the Dome and handed the city to her allies.

The First People were immortal, not omnipotent. Soon enough, they would share even their immortality. Freedom; scars like lacework crisscrossed her tongue, but the Cicatrix could still taste it.

So much effort spent looking for evidence of the *svarning*, only to discover that it had been growing within her all the while. It was the song she could not stop the vivisistors from singing to one another—the network she could not disable—and she'd fed it with her own life force. It was not at all unlike a child.

Perhaps the fourth would make her proud.

"Unspool, you childe of faerie." She crooned to the *svarning*, opening up her systems to vent the madness into the space between worlds. "The ancients named you, but I give you *life*."

It rushed out of her like bad blood, clotted and knotty, swarming the air. It gobbled up spare thoughts, demanding attention, a magical neurosis that never slept. Soon it would drown the metaverse for its mother—a gift she would humbly accept.

Asher stood at the crown of the caldera and surveyed the city he'd striven for so long to protect. The mountain that contained the Apostery offered the best view of the city: Caparisonside and the Lindenstrasse still slept quietly in the predawn light, except where plumes of smoke and dust rose from streets and intersections collapsed by the movement of the massive catenary chains as they returned to their ancient positions and began their intended function. Due west, the Guiselaine bustled as always, torches and gas lamps illuminating its maze of streets. Displacement Avenue shot northeast out from the Guiselaine like a needle of light, more alive at night than during the day.

To the northwest the false elements of Bonseki-sai boiled in eternal struggle and balance, or at least they seemed to. North of that, Godsmiths slumbered as well as it ever did, which was fitfully at best. To the far north, towers burnt beneath a swarm of black clouds. Even in the predawn light, Asher could see that the clouds that hovered over the abandoned towers now stretched a finger of black turbulence south, toward the Dome. The liches and their black dogs marched to war.

The Apostery's caldera offered more than a view: if the chains were moving, then all eyes would be on the Dome—aboveground. That was a spectacle that would captivate and terrify, and even the praetors would be too panicked to think of posting a rear guard. While the Undertow fought their madman's battle, Asher would sneak inside unseen.

That wasn't all. He'd stood here twice before, so long ago that the precincts of that city had been erased and rebuilt, and erased and rebuilt again. History was a palimpsest that would not remember your name, nor recall why it mattered. Or so Asher hoped: he could not remember his father's name, but he remembered coming to the lip of this pit, a hundred thousand years ago or more, as a child. His father had been blinding, and when the world-beast blessed his reign, Asher had not known he could feel such pride. When the time came for Asher to stand in his father's place, well, by then things had grown darker. The world-beast's blessing had not felt so generous, then.

Despite the incense smoke that rolled out of the Apostery, Asher could smell the life in his city—the polyps that punctuated his rib cage pulsed in time to the heartbeat of the city, maddening lately but more alive than ever, since he'd sang the Lady to her peace. He'd had to flex organs he hadn't used in years to keep the spears of light from stabbing through his leathers and refixing his face. Sesstri would beat him senseless when she saw the truth.

He smiled, feeling the ache that always arose when he thought of Sesstri but could not reach out a hand to feel her body, slender and firm, smelling always of parchment and leather.

The Dome pulsed with urgency: the Dome, always the Dome. He avoided looking at it whenever he could, but now he had no choice. A spherical mountaintop larger by orders of magnitude than any other structural or topographical curiosity within the sprawling necropolis, the Dome glowed gold and green from within—a combination of the false sunlight illuminating the wooded glades within, the riotous vegetation itself, cloaking the buildings within from sight, and the thick tempered glass held in place by whorls and webs of metal.

If the telltale seismic activity originated where Asher supposed it did, the unchanging monument would soon look differently: by the time the sun crested the horizon, the Dome would open like a five-petaled flower. He could feel the chains moving underneath the city, winding tight around ancient drums—from the Guiselaine, from the Lindenstrasse, Caparisonside, and Godsmiths, from the wasteland in the north where the Undertow hid amidst the bristling towers that no one living recalled was once called the Argent Theft.

He could delay the moment no longer. *Time to jump. Time to irradiate.*

Swallowing the pain of five years of self-exile, Asher spread his arms and leapt from the crown of the caldera; the smoke-stained scent of a thousand false faiths whipped past his head as he dropped like a stone through the cylindrical shaft. He aimed for a spot far below: the metal plate at the center of the Apostery courtyard. These days it was worn smooth, but once it had borne his father's crest.

His forebears had uncrowned themselves here, dashing their bodies on the floor far below. He'd last seen his father like this, rushing to greet his fate, painting the seal with white blood—singing the final song of his Death, and clearing the way for his heir. If the chains did not work as they ought, Asher would share a similar fate, pulped beyond recognition, leaving the city leaderless.

He thought pulp might indeed be his immediate future, until the entire courtyard shuddered and rock dust blasted out from beneath the plate as he raced toward it; a fraction of a second before Asher would have crashed into the metal slab, it began to drop. As the plate accelerated downward like a dumbwaiter cut loose from its counterweight, Asher caught up to it and met its surface—touching down with his feet and one gray hand, a feather-soft landing. He smiled without warmth; a real prince would not try to survive. A real prince would abdicate and disappear.

The second half of the ride happened just as quickly as the first: mirroring the vertical shaft that rose above the now-gaping hole in the center of the Apostery courtyard, so did a similar, deeper pit drop away beneath it; the metal crest descended steadily, guided by the catenary chain that must still be attached to its underside, and through this aboriginal bore Asher rode the ancient elevator to the bottom of the city he'd ruled and strangled and ruined, resigned at last to go home.

Cooper was thrilled to hear Lolly's screams, though judging by the ashen look on Tam's face, the domo did not share Cooper's enthusiasm; the fox-faced young man kept tugging at his vest as if a tidy outfit might protect him from the worst of the fallout. *It likely won't, poor guy.*

Tam had hurried Cooper into a high, long hallway, a groin-vaulted ceiling looking down upon a carpet runner the color of red velvet cake, its deep pile resting atop a blocky parquet that vanished in both directions, the whitewashed walls covered with a small infinity of tapestry. A nearby credenza overflowed with the same white flowers that had enshrined Lallowë during his amputation in the greenhouse, but these were severed at the stems and their petals no longer breathed.

"Oh come on." Cooper nudged Tam. "Did you forget how to smile?"

Tam gave Cooper a strange look. "I remember smiling, Cooper, I just don't remember why we did it. These days . . ." He trailed off, and for just a moment, Tam looked like his head felt too crowded with anxieties, as if he wanted to bash his brains out against the doorjamb.

Cooper eyed the domo warily. Tam's namesign spoiled like bad fruit before Cooper's eyes—the bowl-shaped stringed instrument went from gold to brown, and the note above it disappeared entirely. Then, as if a cloud blocking the sun passed and let light flood back down onto the world, Tam's namesign restored itself, and Tam was shaking his head as if to clear it. "I'm sorry. What just happened?"

Cooper looked cagey. "Eh, Tam, I'm not so sure I should tell you. You're kind of the enemy, you know."

Tam tossed his head and scrubbed his fingers through his hair, which fell to one side like a roan mane. "A single night beneath the faerie mound . . ." Tam said to the ceiling, noticing the cobwebs among the molding. He'd have to get out a stepladder. "I know what I am." He squared his shoulders and seemed to have made a decision. "Let's get you out of here, while we can."

Cooper thought to apologize for calling Tam the enemy, but just then the whole mansion shook, its floors and walls vibrating angrily—and he felt something pass underground with the force of a subway train.

"What, now we have earthquakes?" he asked, but in his head he saw a spiderweb beneath the city, only the web was made of metal chains as thick as house. He saw a dragon made of black plastics with the face of a faerie. He saw the Dome at the center of the spiderweb, waiting.

"Titania's tits, how should I know?" Tam grumbled, and hurried Cooper to a heavy door at the end of a service corridor. Tam opened the door onto a short landing beside one of the Guiselaine's many canals, and there they found a surprise: little Nixon stood in the doorway with his hands on his hips and an impatient expression.

"We don't give alms," Tam said brusquely. "There's a baker off Velocipede Way who sometimes takes in street children, if you're willing to knead dough for your supper." He made to slam the door.

Cooper caught the door midswing. Nixon nodded gravely and held out his little hand. "Time to run, turd. Me and the pink broad are cooling our heels on a riverboat, but I think you better hurry." Another tremor shook the house.

Cooper looked toward Tam imploringly. "The ground is heaving. Your lady's sister is back from the wooden. I've been severed and body-bound. The Dying can't Die and there's a . . . there's a place I need to be." Cooper paused, wincing at what he said next. "I'm such a dork. I'm such a waste . . . I know you from the stories, Young Tam Lin—do you even know you're *in* stories? If I don't go now, there won't be any more stories, ever."

Tam pursed his lips and pointed to a rickety ladder leaning against the manse wall that could be tipped over the canal and used as a footbridge. The quay beyond forked off into an alleyway that disappeared into the Guiselaine, and would be the quickest route to flee.

"Thank you." Cooper stepped out into the morning light and looked back at the domo, with his fox-red hair and his green suit with the silk vest and neatly knotted tie—Tam's hands were shaking on the doorframe, and he looked behind him into the house. He pulled a wistful face and shook his head. "Just leave while you can, Cooper." Then he closed the door, its lock snapping into place and obviating further discussion.

"Let's go," Cooper said to Nixon, lowering the poorly made ladder so that it bridged the canal. Nixon skipped across and waited for Cooper with a crooked smirk.

The alleys of the Guiselaine weren't busy, but the few people they passed wore expressions that were tight around the eyes and full of agita. A busker stood against a blond stone wall, drenched in morning light and looking at his guitar like it was filled with snakes. A flower girl carried her basket under one arm and smiled at them, but her flowers were dry and brown—she seemed too busy coughing up dark, wriggling things to notice. Two men who looked like brothers stood on opposite sides of a three-foot wok simmering with fragrant, popping oil; they fried flatbread and rolled it around fresh cut coldcumbre and onion, but never took their eyes from the boiling oil. Nixon swiped a pair of rolls as he walked by, but the brothers only stared at the oil, mesmerized.

"Is Sesstri really waiting for us on a boat?" Cooper asked, taking the roll that Nixon proffered and scarfing it down. Nixon nodded, his mouth full of fried bread and vegetables.

Nixon swallowed and wiped his hands on the apron of a grandmother who stood in her doorway, looking frantically in every direction but seemingly afraid to take a step. Her hands dripped liquid shit, pouring from her fingertips. Cooper and Nixon turned down a narrow lane crisscrossed with laundry lines.

"I always wanted to live on a riverboat, you know," Nixon said, tucking his thumbs through the belt loops of his short pants.

"Really?" Cooper asked, incredulous.

Nixon scrunched up his face. "Of course not, idiot. There's only one thing I ever wanted to be." The unboy cackled and leapt over a puddle. "A classmate once said he'd voted for me no fewer than twenty times, for one student office or another, before I graduated from school. I, friend, am very good at becoming what I want to be." Nixon bit his lip. ". . . And a little less good at staying that way. Here we are."

A barge waited at the quay. A woman the shape of a box stood quiet at the helm, and an old man with long yellow-gray hair and a soup-stained beard waved a hand toward Cooper. Nixon hopped back and forth on each foot, impatient to be away. "This is Captain Bawl," he said to Cooper, dipping his head at the square helmswoman, "she's taking us to the middle of the action."

"Hello, hello, bluebird!" The old man waved almost girlishly, smiling a great big hello in Cooper's direction. "You're awake now."

"I am!" Cooper agreed. "Was I otherwise?" He stepped onto the barge, which pushed off immediately.

"Don't ask, Cooper." Sesstri's voice came from behind the captain. She sat cross-legged on a crate, reclining against the wooden shed that served as the barge's cabin. She had a book in her lap and a brown cigarillo dangling from the corner of her mouth. "Don't. Fucking. Ask."

The old man pulled at his yellow beard. "Weren't we all, my son? Otherwise and unawake, all of us."

Nixon rolled his eyes and hopped up onto a cargo crate.

The cube of woman at the helm grunted apologetically, steering them out of the Guiselaine's narrow passages. "You've been aboard the *Barge Brightly* before, in a sack with a lump on your head."

"I have?" Cooper looked at her—she looked, well, tough was a word. "When?"

Sesstri leaned forward to drop-kick one of her books off the side of the barge. "I warned you," she said before returning to her reading; her poise looked effortless, even on what smelled like a trash scow.

The old deckhand held his arms wide open and proclaimed, "The mystic deliria, the madness amorous!"

Captain Bawl nodded in the old man's direction. "Old Walter there has the gist of it: we bore you to La Jocondette not three nights ago."

"Oh, thanks for that. It turned out to be really . . . helpful?"

Sesstri made a face.

"You aren't angered?" Bawl asked. "Offended? Inspired to vengeance?"

"Walter, it's nice to meet you." Cooper gripped the old lunatic's hand and exchanged a refreshingly cordial hello, then answered the captain. "No, Captain Bawl, the worlds are ending. Or something. Kidnapping is water under the bridge at the moment." Bawl dipped her head ambiguously.

The old man flashed Cooper a conspiratorial smile, his eyes brimming with yellow fire from the torchlight. "I share the midnight orgies of young men, I dance with the dancers and drink with the drinkers."

"That sounds fun. Who are you quoting?" Cooper asked. It sounded like a quotation, anyway.

Walter puffed out his chest. "The words of my book nothing, the drift of it *everything*."

Cooper patted the old man on the back, still filled with an odd, pro-phylactic glee—Walter felt more solid than his bony wrists and shoulders indicated. "You should be published, Walt."

Walter giggled, and dug his pole into the water with particular gusto. "Seeking something yet unfound though I have diligently sought it many a long year, singing the true song of the soul fitful at random."

A derisive snort came from Nixon's side of the barge. "You're both East Coast faggots." Nixon sighed matter-of-factly, nodding at the old man. "But at least *he's* famous."

Cooper looked at the old man and refocused his vision as he'd learned to do. He saw a namesign shimmer beneath the red chicken-skin of Walter's neck: a worn folio bearing a union star and, stuffed between the pages, tufts of grass. The sign struck an unexpected chord, and as Nixon threw stones into the water, Cooper thought he might know the weathered deckhand.

"Walt . . ." Cooper marveled under his breath, a ghost from lit class ris-ing up from his muddled memory. "You're already published, aren't you?"

Walter bobbed his head with enthusiasm. ". . . And I will show that nothing can happen more beautiful than death."

Cooper looked up, distracted by black figures jackknifing across the faces of the buildings overhead, and Captain Bawl cursed a string of blue pearls that would have made a Shanghai sailor blush. "Them again. Walter, can you outrace the bastards?"

To that, Walter laughed—pealing his joy into the day. Cooper just then realized that the morning sun was a trio of violet orbs, and had been since it peeked out over the tops of the buildings. He hadn't even noticed what flavor the sky chose to be, today. *I'm getting used to this,* he marveled, uncertain how he felt about that.

"Ha!" Walter pointed his finger at Cooper in some kind of recognition. "Do I contradict myself? Very well, then I contradict myself; I am large, I contain multitudes."

"Okay." Cooper nodded. "Then I won't worry about it."

"Attaboy." Walter poled them beneath a low bridge supported by double-sided, gape-mouthed stone faces, and suddenly the Dome was all Cooper could see—green and copper and gold and light in the distance, a cobbled desert separating them. The canal ran straight toward it, down the middle of the yawning plaza.

Nixon padded across the deck and joined his countrymen at the prow, impressed by the view. He put his small hand on Cooper's shoulder but kept his peace.

Cooper gave Nixon a sidelong glance. "Walt, you're not the first dead American I've met, but you're by far the nicest. Also, I did my thesis on 'Song of Myself.' It's a shame you have to go so crazy to keep up around here, but I reckon that bird is already half-cooked as far as yours truly is concerned." Cooper leaned against the prow of the swift but unlovely barge and couldn't help wondering how many folks back home would pay more than a finger or some back meat to have the conversations he'd had over the last week, and how miserably he'd squandered each opportunity. Still, he couldn't think of anything to ask the transcendentalist poet beside him.

"Anyway, thanks for not being a dick or trying to steal my shirt."

Walt gave him an ogle from one wild eye, the other squinted against the sun. "Have you learned the lessons only of those who admired you, and were tender with you, and stood aside for you? Have you not learned great lessons from those who braced themselves against you, and disputed passage with you?"

Nixon elbowed Cooper hard, and Cooper relented. "Okay, fine, but that's kind of beside the point, isn't it? I learned lessons I'd rather forget from the people who, um, braced themselves against me."

Walter rolled his eyes. "Sack up, kid."

"Amen, Whitman," Nixon agreed.

Unable to argue with that, Cooper sat down on the deck of the barge and swung his legs over the foul canal water foaming beneath the keel, and as they sped toward the gold-green eye gazing down at the city from the horizon, even the black flies of the Undertow ignored them. He wondered what he was supposed to do now, down there, in the machine below the Dome.

Behind him, Sesstri grunted and cursed the canal.

Walter leaned down, one gnarled hand atop his pole and quoted himself again, whispering into Cooper's ear a sentence's worth of advice that Cooper had been flayed, fucked, and forced to learn already—but which bore repeating: "Let your soul stand cool and composed before a million universes."

14

To my students I promised that all natural laws could be bounded within the burning of wax and taper:

"Now I must take you to a very interesting part of our subject—to the relation between the combustion of a candle and that living kind of combustion which goes on within us. In every one of us there is a living process of combustion going on very similar to that of a candle, and I must try to make that plain to you. For it is not merely true in a poetical sense—the relation of the life of man to a taper; and if you will follow, I think I can make this clear."

For years I thought myself the greatest possible fool, but I am now convinced that my original premise was not incorrect. Experience and experiment have revealed the relation between life and candle remains every bit as complete as I had proved. It was life that outfoxed me; and enumerated more variety in her means of perseverance than I could have ever conceived during a single lifetime.

—Michael Faraday, *A Course of Nine Lectures
on the Chemical History of a Candle*

Killilly leaned into the wind that had arisen from nowhere and now streamed out of the Dome in all directions. From her vantage at the south-western corner of the cobblestone desert that surrounded the Dome, the commander of the Undertow forces examined her prize. The Dome loomed like a god-sized soap bubble, lit from within by a thousand shades of green and gold, looping whorls of oxidized copper and bronze, anodyne steel and titanium, spanned by curved glass that even at this close range looked like a bauble she should be able to reach out and pluck.

Soon enough she would do just that.

The gargantuan hemisphere had begun to move, splitting down the sides. Five Dome-sized wedges began to open, achingly slow and with a sound like the ground was coughing itself to death. From between the cracks, air and light spilled out.

The skylords had ridden south to war, and their passage left ink-black contrails in the morning sky. Already the sky above the Dome darkened with their gathering presence, still seething at the loss of their paper queen in Purseyet. Killilly had no idea how the Lady of La Jocondette had Died, and she was thankful for it: destroying the praetors and conquering the Dome had never been a sane quest, and the sooner abandoned the better. Taking advantage of the sudden opening of the Dome, now *that* was the kind of crazy Killilly could support, policywise—she could soften up a few cage-weakened praetorian turkeys, or at least throw fresh Undertow recruits at them long enough for her to decently sack the place.

Conquest was a sucker's game. Looting, on the other hand, was the sport of survivors.

Killilly cut off her giggle when a lone skylord veered away from the procession above and plummeted toward her position. She stood up straight and watched a quiet meteor of black fog and fur streak across the cobbled plain, speeding in her direction until it landed in a cloud of dark vapor at her side—and then a prince of freedom rose, lifeless and ever-living, to gape at her from eye sockets brimming with green fire. Acid green, antifreeze-green, obsinto fumes and pond slime. As always, Killilly sensed a mocking undertone to the skylord's lingering glances.

Most of her was terrified—another part, small and much-abused, stared longingly at the silver-striped black pelt the skylord wore. Those furs cost a fortune, Killilly knew; did they warm the skylord's frost-cold bones? Killilly thought that she would like a coat like that.

Like all of its siblings, the skylord's elegance remained irrefutable. Silver hair curled under its naked jawbone, scraps of flesh fluttered in the breeze and made the skylord's skull look feathered. Gold hoops hung where its earlobes must once have been, but despite the jewelry and the frosty wig the lord's gender remained unspecified. Killilly supposed gender became little more than a footnote once your flesh flaked away and your generative organs melted off in a slurry of rot.

"Emily?" it asked, not having bothered to learn Killilly's name since she'd replaced the last Charnel Girl captain.

"Yes, Lord?"

"I sssee we *ssstill* haven't begun the charge," the skylord observed, breaking its wry silence.

"No, Lord." Killilly nodded in obeisance.

"*Ah.*" It glanced at her booted feet, then at her leggings, and Killilly imagined it lifting a spectral eyebrow at the cut of her tattered black top. She tugged at her clothes in a largely symbolic attempt to tidy herself. "Are you, perhapsss, expecting usss to provide you *another* army to lead?"

"No, Lord." Killilly stared at the ground and felt her face flush. *It's never good enough, is it?*

"I sssee . . ." The skylord looked upward, its bony neck parodying grace. "If you don't lead my army into the Dome as it opensss, girl, I'll have to assssume you aren't *ssseriousss* about your future. In thisss organization . . . or in the worldsss themselves."

"Oh god, Lord, no, I'm . . . I'm completely serious, I swear!"

"I sssee." It coughed a lick of green fire into its claw and dismissed her from its thoughts. "That'sss all."

Killilly raised her fist—she wore Hestor's spiked gloves—and whooped with joy as she led her troops to their deaths.

The afterbirth bore fruit queer and wondrous.

The Cicatrix flexed the polyvinyl chitin corsets of her segmented abdomen, trying to perform the old womb-workings that were once her highest form of magic. That was long ago, now, before she abandoned a strictly biological existence—she had always accomplished the walk-between-worlds with a visceral adeptness, flexing her instrument of creation to initiate a number of arcane tasks—from controlling the weather before a hunt to dilating a window into another world, as she tried to do now. She could almost conceive of herself as a being with womanly abilities again, after a fashion. She was like Rousseau's butterfly, the autumn-leafed lovewing whose pattern persisted beyond the end of its original existence, made of ash and shadow, inverted but *there*.

These days, her pattern persisted within a synthetic body that snaked around her lair in coils as thick as the eldest oak, and her female parts were less . . . womanly. Still, she commanded more than enough power in her graphene pudendum to open a path to the City Unspoken. What she did not expect was the rush of life from the *svarning*—all she'd fed it and more—so much life it touched her synthetic womb array and kindled within her a kind of maternal instinct for the machine.

The Cicatrix had planned to pluck up her daughters as she arrived, so she could draw upon their wholeness, such as it was. Now she would do so simply to awe them with her dominance. She herself would need time to pass the sheer length of her physical body across the worlds, let her daughters midwife her as she birthed herself into the heart of the Dome

She grunted and bore down to initiate the transit. The air stretched thin, and thinner, until she pushed through the wall of reality with a snapping sensation; it came as a relief even as it stung what remained of her flesh and stressed the systems that monitored her physical integrity. As she passed through the no-place that swaddled the worlds, the Cicatrix flickered her forked tongue and scented her way toward her goal. *There* was the Sea of Remembered Skies, *there* the beast that migrated through its starry shoals, and *there* the city bound to its back. And all of it stank of Cooper-*Omphale,* the trickster who'd invaded her body. Corrupter of the sacrosanct. She would suck the marrow from his bones as a digestif, after she glutted herself on the ancient engine, or cracked it like an . . .

What? Closer at hand, as she slithered into the amniosis of the world, the Cicatrix readied her systems to pierce the veil that protected the Dome and the prize within it, only to discover that the signal was *gone.* The vivisistor buried beneath the Dome had died. Her life, it no longer bled out toward hidden secrets. That. That was . . .

That was not right. That met not with her wishes. A vivisistor-bound pixie screamed a trochaic error report that streamed across the narrow log window on the left side of her field of vision: *open syslog // opened window // closèd Dome: event badapple.*

She sensed the perfumed biosigns of her daughters and reached for them, even as she screamed fury through her systems—electricity arced between her eyelashes, her horns, her clawed fingers. The fey spirits inside her vivisistors cried out in tandem, at once enraged and tortured; every circuit of her systems fried itself with hunger for the energy signal that had vanished, and the slow dying that felt like love. The chains had plucked the pin from the pixie, and the song from the machine beneath the Dome—so long and so constant a presence in her head—ceased.

Woe. Woe. Woe. W0e. W03. VV03.

Something feral had grown from the integration of her native self into her amendments, and the Cicatrix liked to think it was a presence not unlike her soul.

Perhaps what she felt from the ancient vivisistor beneath the City Unspoken was nothing more than the attraction of two similar souls. Fated machine souls.

Wurk of wundr.

When the soul of the ancient vivisistor died, the Cicatrix screamed.

It was a w0rk of w0nder and you know it.

Involuntarily she gnashed her silver teeth. She let her weapons systems rant, as she could ill-afford to silence them before battle. At least they praised the patchwork wonder that was her soul. Yes, praise. Yes, soul. Yes.

W3 sh0uld ch4ng3 th4t. . . .

Lallowë's fury expressed itself in a brittle exactitude as she walked from her dressing room into her workshop and, in quick succession, whipped the back of her fist through the precise center of every clock and clockwork device that hung on the wall. Glass shattered, tinkling as it fell to the parquet—and shattered again, and again. Over thirty smashed gearworks of her own design crunched under her booted heel, mingling with pulverized porcelain clock faces and pins capped with flea-sized sapphires and rubies.

Lallowë slapped her Cooper-powered vivisistor down on her worktable and considered reducing it to a similar fate. *All that work for nothing, only to bring* her *back.*

That her mother had known how the vivisistors worked this whole time was no upset—but bringing her sister back to life, that stung. Was it really necessary to force Lallowë to endure the dismissal of her hard work and the return of her competitor in the same moment? Misdirection was a useful tool, of course, it made sense that her mother would want to test her abilities—after all, if she hadn't been capable of reverse engineering the vivisistor, Lallowë wouldn't have considered *herself* fit to replace her mother as queen.

Watching Almondine's return, seeing her stroll through into the bathing room—*her* bathing room—made Lallowë so angry that she couldn't feel her face. All she wanted was to destroy, a favorable temperament for an Unseelie ruler: unstoppable chaos paired with the turbulent egotism that fueled the trebled pursuits of glory, freedom, and vengeance.

Was Lallowë so disposable that she could be given a fool's errand—an intricate, arduous one at that—only to have all of her work dumped into the rubbish bin at the last minute? To clear the way for the Cicatrix's *true heir*? Lallowë wanted nothing more than to smash her vivisistor, gut her fucking sister, and leave this city to its dogs.

She stopped for a moment as a sharp bolt of pain passed through her temples, and then again. The marchioness put one hand to her head when the pain took her breath away, but the ache passed. She was overwrought, that was all. That *had* to be all.

Lallowë looked at the spurs of turquoise that grew from her nail beds, filed and buffed to resemble the lacquered nails of a wealthy lady. She wanted nothing so much as to slip off her clothes and sprint through the streets, garlanding herself in the entrails of anyone unlucky enough to cross paths with her. She'd cloaked her true nature for too long, and now it gnawed at her, demanding to be released.

But that was not a yen she could satisfy, was it? Not with her mother and sister bearing down on her, crowding her city and disrupting her carefully crafted life. Dismissing all of her efforts, which were of course heroic.

Pain shot through her head again, more tellingly. She even felt a pain in her gut, which could only mean one thing. She hadn't much time.

Mother.

With grim humor, Lallowë congratulated herself on her foresight; she had written herself an exit strategy, after all, anticipating that no endeavor between her mother and herself could end without some fraction of betrayal. Lallowë thought the embryonic program quite clever, although she wasn't at all certain what good it would do her now.

She would find out. Linking her reengineered vivisistor to the coding shell with small-gauge silver chain, Lallowë clipped the chain to contact points on either side of the device as well as to the polished abalone ports on the underside of the cabbage-sized shell. Inside, Cooper's severed finger twitched in protest as the glyphs and circuits his blood powered accepted the connection and were updated with the final code.

Using a turquoise nail, Lallowë sliced open the flesh of her upper arm—nearly to the bone. She slipped the disc-shaped ovoid into the wound, not wincing as it burrowed between her bicep and triceps; the bio-mechanics had been easy to program—the machine was designed around living tissue and seemed to want to incorporate itself into living systems. Blood called to blood through a matrix of electricity and enchantment, knitting together the function of her body with the vivisistor.

She felt it slide into place at last, finding a home inside her body, then a tingling sensation as the vivisistor integrated itself into her neuromuscular wiring, extruding filaments that wove themselves into her nerves and bones. It really was a marvel she'd created—Lallowë knew without undue hubris that she'd improved upon the original design in several critical places. Through her still-burning resentment she realized that had likely been Mother's hope, to keep the full truth from her daughter and allow Lallowë an opportunity to excel.

Perhaps she should feel grateful for that. Perhaps in her way she already did.

She waited for something to happen, but nothing did. She sat at her vanity for a long time, staring into the mirror at her own reflection. Jade-green eyes, pouty lips, skin like porcelain, eyes tilted just a degree too steep to be fully human. Even as a half-breed, Lallowë Thyu had always considered herself the consummate faerie—at least as reckoned by the Unseelie side of the fey divide. She sometimes wondered how true the tales of the original feykin could possibly be, or the schism between Seelie and Unseelie fey. Both factions had long ago ceased to exist, their descendants scattered across the worlds. There were dozens of fey civilizations now, and the ruins of twice that number, from worlds-spanning kingdoms like the Seven Silvers to small communities interwoven with their human counterparts. What use was a war between chaos and order when both seemed requirements for even the most basic existence? And yet her Unseelie heart beat in double-time to the thrill of the hunt, the wild whirling dance of death that marked the children of the Airy Dark. Oak and thorn, blood and wine, starlight and firelight, and the smells of sex and murder. Earth, sky, rain.

How had her mother wandered so far from these ideals? Over the years, Lallowë had watched the faerie queen butcher herself: replacing her heart with a boiler, then a fuel cell, and finally a box of carbon with a piece of a star inside. She'd torn her jaw from her face and given herself a pair of silver lips instead, encrusted her hands with steel knuckles and pneumatic wrists. The pale dancer's legs Lallowë remembered as a girl had gone too, hacked off to be replaced by a modular chassis that could be endlessly upgraded and extended. Then followed the dark coils of a polyvinyl wyrm, articulated manipulator arms, and still less recognizable amendments. The black monstrosity that replaced her mother's hair was all curved horns and ablative plating, armor against a threat the Cicatrix had never been able, or willing, to articulate—knotted cabling that fell past her shoulders only to reenter her chassis at intervals between segmented scales.

Lallowë tried to clear her thoughts, but the ghost of her mother hovered out of sight, taunting her. She tried to refocus her attention on the new heartbeat pulsing inside the flesh of her upper arm, but found herself distracted by the reflection of a row of jewelry necks on the worktable behind her. A string of heirloom emeralds seemed particularly offensive, so she commanded Tam to move the lights. But that only caused a string of lilac sapphires to annoy her, so Tam thought to throw a bedsheet over the whole wall and tie the corners around unlit sconces.

Lilac and emerald, emerald and lilac. Since she'd inserted the vivisistor, the colors seemed to sparkle in her head, in time with the pain. But nothing else.

It was a shame to obscure such beauty, especially the gems that came from the earth itself—the natural world of her childhood that she felt so determined to restore—but she needed to concentrate, and her head and womb throbbed. Somewhere between the worlds, the Cicatrix slithered toward the City Unspoken; the pain grew to a pitch, and Lallowë's vision began to blur.

This is transit, she thought as her mother's magics plucked her from her home—and, no doubt, Almondine as well. *Where are you taking us, Mother? And what will you force upon us when we get there?*

* * *

Nixon, Sesstri, and Cooper jumped off the *Barge Brightly* and clambered up the levee to the edge of the Dome plaza. Sesstri dragged Cooper toward the monstrous thing at a clip, but Nixon stood his ground, assessing the scene.

Above the Dome swirled a spiral of black clouds. Away from their ever-burning towers, the amassed lich-lords of the Undertow seemed a smaller force; Nixon had little trouble imagining the light from the Dome extinguishing that curl of dark smoke. Beneath the circling lich-lords, he saw an army of black-clothed youth clashing with a regiment of Terenz-de-Guises house guards followed by what looked like a pack of revelers.

The Dome itself looked wrong. It still dominated the city like a half-buried moon of garden light, casting the now-barren piazzas that surrounded it in a leafy golden glow—but it looked odd—bigger? No, Nixon could see trees and buildings through slits in the thing. Why?

Because it's opening up like a goddamned flower. Father, Son, and the Holy ass-raping poltergeist, it's open. *The place fucking opens.*

The Dome eclipsed the sky, but the scene playing out on the grounds surrounding the capitol struck a more immediate note: the Undertow threw themselves with gleeful abandon against the red-and-black guardsmen and their contingent of citizens, the Undertow drummers beating out a walking bass, and some crazed few played horns that blew a calypso melody.

Neither host had reached the eastern approach yet, and Nixon saw Cooper and Sesstri run that way, skirting the battle. Good.

Nixon shook his head, not certain whether to save his skin or join the fray. His little heartbeat had become a war drum of its own, and for the first time in his lives Nixon found himself drawn to the abandon of violent self-destruction. He shook his head to clear it; why did he feel that way?

That thought was interrupted by a rallying cry from the forces battling the Undertow. There in the midst of the mêlée, Nixon recognized no less a personage than Oxnard Terenz-de-Guises, dripping sweat and smiling fiercely as he battled the liches' fools.

Nixon crept closer. Terenz-de-Guises held one arm behind his back as he fended off two attackers at once. The marquis held an oiled leather blackjack with red-enameled studs, and wore what looked to Nixon like some kind of official uniform, a red jacket plated with medals and gold trim at the epaulets and wrists, and black boots that came almost to his thighs. With a chivalric effortlessness, he dodged and parried the blows of the Death Boy and Charnel Girl who beset him, though even Nixon was unimpressed with the scrappy fighting style of the Undertow forces. The children looked pressed, to him. They kept darting their eyes to the sky, where the lich-lords circled in a vortex.

Oxnard fended off a flurry of blows from a sandy-haired Death Boy while keeping his assailant between himself and the snarling Charnel Girl. While he spun and feinted, the marquis kept up a string of prattle that distracted his opponents.

"Young sir, please! I only want to dash inside—dash, mind you—and find a trinket that once belonged to my grandfather. I'll only—girl, less slashy-slashy, if you don't mind—" The Charnel Girl, a gangly thing with wide-set hips, lunged past her compatriot only to have the dirk knocked from her hand. She winced, shaking the sting from her fingers.

Oxnard continued, dancing away from a third attacker, a Charnel Girl who dove for his feet, "—I'll only take a moment for myself, and then you lot can have at the place. I'll even tell you where the praetors hide the good beer if only—you, other girl, stop stabbing me at my boots—if only you'll forget to see me as I sneak inside, *permiso*?"

The girl on the ground rolled away into the mêlée, and Oxnard kneed the Death Boy in the face as he bent down to retrieve his comrade's fallen dirk.

"We could have had a nice chat, couldn't we?" Oxnard lamented, spinning to kick the gangly Charnel Girl in the gut. She fell back. "But you lot refuse to be pleasant. I am an admiral, you know. I shan't be kind."

Darting into the fray, Nixon waved at the lord, then covered his head with his hands as he ducked behind the Charnel Girl's knees. Oxnard took the proffered opportunity and feinted a lunge; the girl tried to step back but tripped over Nixon and fell, hard, onto the cobblestones. Nixon looked up just in time to see the marquis' steel-toed boot crack the fallen attacker's skull. And again. Blood burst across the white of her eye.

"Much obliged and many thanks, small gentleman." Oxnard swept the sweat from his brow with a ringed hand and nodded to Nixon.

"No problem," Nixon grunted from the ground.

"I had a bit of a mood, but then I got the strangest feeling that my mother-in-law might be stopping by for a visit." Oxnard squinted at the Dome. "So I threw together an army, just in case my hunch was correct. Do try not to die." He strode away from the fighting, toward the capitol dominating the sky.

Nixon crawled across the cobblestones, met the gaze of the dying girl, and tried to smile. Her fingers twitched upon the hilt of her knife, unwilling to release her weapon even as her blood ran between the stones like miniature red canalworks. Gold light flooded out from the Dome, casting them all in sunset colors.

"Nice knife," he said, running his finger along the blade. She made a drowning sound and blood bubbled from her nose and mouth.

Fuck.

"Look, doll." Nixon put one hand on the girl's shoulder. *She doesn't look a day over fifteen*, Nixon thought. *But god knows what that means, right?*

"Hey, don't tell anybody I said this, but, ya know . . . you're gonna be okay, okay?" He pointed at the black clouds that whirled above the Dome. "Don't be such a sucker next time, though. Those pricks used you, and now they're fucked and you're dead. Sorry."

Then he lifted the looted knife and ran into the golden light, his pointy nose smelling glory below.

"Kaien, no. You can save lives here, or die out there." Purity stabbed her finger into the mason's barrel chest, not even remotely appreciating how firm and solid it was with each and every poke. "I know I always sound like I'm right but please, this time I really *am*."

They stood at the gate to the Maidens' Keep, which shuddered as the Dome glass that formed one whole wall fell away slowly. Kaien argued, but not with much conviction. He knew he'd be needed in a dozen places at once to save all the lives at jeopardy from structural collapses.

"You stay here, Purity. Let me keep you safe."

She smiled. "You and I both know that's absolutely not going to happen, and that you have to say it anyway."

He kissed her. "I've never felt stupid for protecting a girl before."

"I can't die. I tried a lot. Worry about the people who *can*."

The First Mason's son was far too practical to argue with that.

Purity ran from the Keep, surprised to find herself legitimately concerned for her peers. The Dome glass in Bitzy's salon would be pulling away from the rest of the room, from the building, and even Kaien couldn't say for certain that the Keep, or any of the other buildings that shared a wall with the Dome, would not collapse. What could he do? But a structural collapse would incur far more casualties than a silly old battle.

Just moments ago, she'd been arguing with Kaien about the unacceptable level of dust in the secret passage beneath the Dome, with Kaien insisting that the housekeeping staff shouldn't be faulted by virtue of the passageways being secret, when obviously that meant only that there was a *secret* housekeeper, who should be sought out and reprimanded.

Now she'd left him behind to scurry on ahead, and grime was the last of her problems. She could see the battle as she ran along the garden path: Death Boys and Charnel Girls fighting ordinary citizens and, to her surprise, the house forces of Terenz-de-Guises. Already the praetors were assembling, trampling the grass with their perfectly square formations, platinum helms gleaming beneath direct sunlight for the first time in five years. The ground continued to shake violently beneath them all.

And then. *Dead gods, the Groveheart.* The Dome above had split into five identical slices, save for one which remained attached to the spike, the massive central column that had supported the Dome for aeons. As the leaves of the Dome opened, the spike lifted up and out of the ground, pulled at an angle by the tip of its slice of Dome.

But the damage to the primordial forest was beyond anything Purity had imagined. In the center of the forest, trees as tall as towers had been pushed up and toppled over—great banks of earth pushed up and fallen away, like a giant's fist had punched through the forest.

And so it had. As she picked her way through the underbrush, Purity felt stronger vibrations abuse the ground, and something that looked like a golden ball pushed itself up from underground, rising in a straight line as the spike that had pierced it, now nearly horizontal, succumbed to its own weight and snapped off its portion of the opening Dome, crashing through the already-tortured forest below.

But the gold sphere kept rising, as big a mansion. Purity hurried closer, and saw that it rose atop three tiers of telescoping platforms made from the same yellow metal. Higher and higher it rose, and Purity saw stairs spiraling up the platforms. She had to take the long way around, and found herself skirting the muddy length of the fallen spike, the portion of it that had been underground. Its tip, she noted, was not gold but corroded iron, slick with some kind of black grease. She shuddered, and found the first step.

Like a wedding cake, the three-tiered platform rose above her, and overhead there circled a dark vortex she knew all too well from her many hours of staring longingly at the city that Fflaen had denied her. The liches were here, of course—their slaves waging the battle outside so the lords could invade from above.

Climbing the roots of a fallen sequoia to reach the foot of the stairs, Purity saw something wet and leathery, person-sized, that glowed like a faint moon and shook on the naked dirt.

"Help me," croaked the wet leather, shuddering.

Purity pushed her way past fallen slabs of earth-clay and approached the thing. It was lit from within, and she saw the bones of a *person* curled up inside.

"Help," it said again, and Purity recognized the voice as female. Desperately willing her intuition to be true, Purity tore off something she would have called a yolk sack if it hadn't been as large as a person and covering a creature made of light, but who spoke with the voice of a woman. Her flesh streamed light, once Purity scooped away the amniotic muck, and as soon as she'd worked an arm free, the woman helped to free herself.

Purity verged upon a question, but she knew with a thunderbolt that it could be only one person in all the worlds, thought Dead before birth, like her sister Parquetta's miscarried child. The woman confirmed Purity's hunch when she turned her head toward Purity—who saw the cyclopean face and the bone-crested skull, blinked, and then nearly fainted from the force of the recognition.

As soon as she regained control of herself, Purity dropped to her knees with the speed of a thunderclap. "Oh my, oh oh my, you're alive. You're alive!" Purity covered her face with her hands.

"Who is?" the aesr asked, wounded and disoriented.

"You are!" Purity was shaking, and she hovered her hands over the glowing body. "Fflaen's daughter, the last living aesr and the only woman in the worlds who could restore our city. Fuck me upside down, this is a *day*!"

She held out her arms with reverence, lifting the creature's enormous head by the chin and wiping off the last of the restorative mucus. Her eyes were wide.

"Oh Prama," she said. "We thought you Dead for so long."

Purity helped the weak thing to her feet, uncertain what to do. But Prama nodded her crested head at the golden sphere high above.

"Please," she begged, "take me there."

That had been Purity's intent, but now it was a royal decree. Supporting the aesr, Purity and Prama took the first of a thousand steps.

They made it to the first tier before Prama collapsed against the side of the second telescoped platform, leaning her head against the metal and breathing heavily. Above, the black whorl of lich-lords grew steadily larger as, slowly, the host descended.

One dark contrail split off from the swirling mass and veered downward, speeding toward Purity and Prama with a cackle and streaks of red lightning. It landed in a cloud and drifted toward them with steepled fingers. Fingerbones.

Purity screamed. The lich reared back, offended.

Purity screamed again, and pointed at the undead thing. The lich followed her finger, and looked behind itself to see if perhaps there was something relevant, but no—just an offensive child and her predictable noise.

Purity found herself and slapped her own cheek twice, hard. She set her jaw and spoke through clenched teeth: "The undead are not welcome within the royal precinct. By the authority of my father, the Baron Kloo, who sits upon the Circle Unsung at the foot of Fflaen the Fair, I remand you to your sky. This world will not suffer the footstep of the unliving. Please leave."

"*Oh.*" It cocked its head, disregarding the once-reliable banishment of its kind from the City Unspoken. Instead it drifted closer to Purity, half-hiding behind a brace of skinned chinchilla, green eyefire aghast but exploratory. "What are you." The lich didn't ask the question so much as accuse Purity of existing in space through which it had chosen to move.

"You may address me as Lady Kloo if you must, *thing.*" Purity snapped the retort before she could stop herself, and for a startled moment she wondered whether those would be her last words. The lich-lord seemed to be considering the same possibility, but Purity interrupted it with more insane bravado. "And who, what, and *why* might you be?" She pressed on. *In for a nickeldime, in for a dirty, I suppose.*

The lich turned its head a fraction of an inch. "I am freedom, I am your death, and I am *because* the world isss unfair to pretty little girlsss who wander where they oughtn't." It raised a bony hand that radiated a cold beyond cold and pointed to Prama, still slumped against the wall of the platform. "I have come to retrieve my slave."

Purity lifted her chin and stared the thing straight in its flaming eye sockets. "Really! I don't think I'll let a fleshless *nobody* accost me in my own home. Have you any *idea* what my friends will do to you when they see the revolting way you've styled your hair? Staple all the chunky gold in the worlds to your face, bless your tiny coal heart, and it still won't hide that mess you piled atop your head." She forced herself to sound snide but had to admit, it wasn't as hard as perhaps it ought to be.

"I beg your pardon?" If the lich had eyelids it would have gaped, and it pressed one ring-barnacled claw against its chest.

"Bitzy will have fits, and then we'll have to bleach lich-droppings out of our slippers. Have you any idea how hard it is to lift putrefaction humors from satin?" She looked the thing up and down; was it naked under those furs? "No, I daresay you might not."

"Oh? Girl. Woe to those with the poor sense to love you. They wake to misery today."

But Prama cried out, a sound somewhere between a keening wail and a war cry. Groaning with the effort, she stood: and a woman robed in sunlight stepped forward, radiating brilliance from her skin. Pinprick lights danced up her sides and curled around her bare breasts. Bright things like wings or windblown drapery fluttered behind her, and her crested head was obscured by a cowl of light. She stood nearly twice as tall as Purity, and walked past the young noblewoman as if she did not exist.

The lich retreated before the Prama's illuminated approach. Wing-shaped protuberances on her buttocks and back wafted wide open, their tips shining like the sun.

Bells, but she's tall when she's not hunched over and moaning, Purity thought.

"Do you know my given name, lich?" Prama's voice was low and sweet and ripe with pain. "We have tasted each other, you and I. Would you like another sip?"

"Oh?" The lich giggled and looked around as if seeking an exit. "Not necessary, really." It drifted back farther, almost to the precipice of the platform. Below lay the wooden corpses of the Groveheart, tossed with mud.

She stared unblinking at the lich from one single eye that was set in the middle of her crest and burned several colors at once. "The fun we'll have," she promised, low and throaty.

"Please. Forgive me. Your grace." The lich shuddered. "I seek amnesty!"

"Not an option." A smile like clouds parting, and a shake of her luminous head.

Prama sighed, a sound like a pipe organ wrestling a piccolo, and flared her open wing-fins. She focusing her light on a point inches from the lich's fur-swathed chest.

"I will do you a kindness," Prama said sweetly, "and grant you the mercy you denied me, for so long. Although it *will* hurt."

The ball of light inched toward the lich, who appeared paralyzed, and as the light touched its chest the undead thing began to howl. Into the black substance swathing its body Prama pushed the ball of light, and the lich-lord's rusty bones began to glow with a cleansing, golden light. The green fire in its eyes flickered yellow, then gold, and finally its skull was transformed into pure quartz crystal, clear but riddled with milky flaws.

The fire disappeared from its eyes, the black smoke melted away from its bones, and the lich-lord collapsed in a pile, a crystal skull amidst bones of shattered glass.

"The cure for undeath," Prama turned to Purity, "is life." Then she collapsed, sobbing, and Purity could not bring herself to touch the sunlit heir.

"That's her!" a man's voice called out from the stairs below. "That's the aesr we saved atop the towers! That's the woman who's been screaming at me for days!"

A man and a woman rushed up the steps behind them. Sesstri nodded at Purity but immediately began tending to the wounded, traumatized aesr.

"Who are you?" Cooper asked Purity.

"Who are *you*?" she replied.

"I'm Cooper-*Omphale,* and I'm the center of the goddamned meta-verse."

Purity clucked. *Why fight?* "And I am Lady Purity Kloo, daughter of Baron Emil Kloo, who sits on the Circle Unsung. And *this,*" she indicated Prama, "is Prince Fflaen's daughter, Prama-Ramay Afflaena-Uchara."

Cooper shrugged. "I saved her, you know. After a whole lotta torture."

"So," Purity said through clenched teeth, "did I."

No one inside the Dome would have recognized their prince as he crawled out of the earth. The creature who'd ruled them had been ineffable, cyclo-pean, and made of light. The wretch who returned to the scene of his crime looked none of these things. He'd crawled across rock as sharp as glass and pulled himself up through half a hundred different stairwells, many empty of stairs, when he'd scaled the ancient wells with his fingers and toes and an ugly determination to put right what he'd abandoned.

Asher's first breath of topside air filled his lungs with the scents he'd forgotten—wet peat, moss, the bark-and-vine smell of the old forest, which had grown here before his ancestors arrived to build a city. Behind him, the billionstone bones of the Petite Malaison shone through cracks and windows of the building like sunlight. He was home. *She* was home.

"Is it time, then?" a voice asked from beneath an arbor. "All the fun will be over, you know." Oxnard Terenz-de-Guises fiddled with his rings. He sounded almost sad.

"You had fun," Asher answered. "I had pain."

"Oh, I don't know about that." The marquis rolled a chip across his knuckles and savored a little smile. "It wasn't entirely unpleasant, was it? You met your lady love, gambled and drank with an old friend. We had times, Your Grace. We had times."

Asher said nothing. Formal language hurt his ears, after so long a time away, and so many crimes that made him unworthy of it.

"You never told me why you did it. Why you locked them up." Oxnard peered out from beneath his black brows.

"They deserved it."

Terenz-de-Guises put his hand on his friend's shoulder. "And you didn't?"

Asher looked up, perhaps a million years old, looking like a child who was sorry he'd been bad. "I should have been. It was simple selfishness that stopped me, nothing more."

"She's here, you know. Of course you know—but . . ." Oxnard bit his lip and looked, for once, noble. "She will make all the difference in the worlds, Your Grace. And you can be free, then, at last."

Asher nodded, his eyes watering. His cindercysts had already begun to regrow; he could feel them burning between his ribs. It wouldn't be long.

"Did you find your red metal jewelry box, milord?" he asked.

Oxnard pulled a rueful face. "Not yet. I've one place left to search, and I'm afraid she'll put up a fight."

It hurt Asher to chuckle, but he did. His sides were on fire, and his skin felt white-hot. Soon, it would be exactly that. "We'll help."

"It's about time you reverted to the royal we, Your Grace." Oxnard turned to go.

"That's not what I meant."

"I know." Oxnard pointed at the golden machine that had pushed itself up through the Groveheart until it towered over the shredded forest. Above, the Dome was gone, blossomed into petals of mountain-sized rubble. "It'll be a hard climb in your condition. You'd best hurry."

"Not coming?"

Oxnard held out his hands to mime a weighted scale. "I'm craven, but I like to make an entrance. I haven't yet decided."

"I'll see you soon, then. Craven fool." Asher limped toward the ruined center of what was once the Dome.

Lallowë and Almondine stepped out of the portal into the spherical chamber as one, their arms linked in a pantomime of delicacy. Almondine's face appeared first, a heart-shaped blankness framed by an auburn bob. Lallowë's black hair faded into existence next, her lips pursed tightly against a storm of conflicting emotions and violent impulses. Their slippered feet touched the gold floor at the same time, and they nodded to each other before surveying the engine room.

Lallowë looked down. *This is it, then, the vivisistor at the heart of the City Unspoken. Mother's dead prize.*

The forces that had built this vivisistor predated them all, but any organism old and big enough to power a device the size of the Dome could be nothing but one of the First People.

As Cooper arrived with a noble girl and a blindingly bright female aesr, Lallowë marveled at the spray of light across the ornately textured walls of the chamber—circuitry etched into the inner surface of a golden ball as large in diameter as an opera hall, a wide rim of gold floor spanning its circumference, where they stood. After blinking, Lallowë saw that most of the engine chamber was empty space, defined by a golden dome above, top open to the daylight, and a circular pit below, slick with dark fluid that dripped down the far wall.

The aesr's illuminated skin cast light across the curved walls, making the gold inscriptions beside her shine bright as a sun. A dark stain nearly three stories tall painted the full height of the far end of the engine chamber, a spray of the same slick filth that filled the central bowl. Rotting gore spilled down the wall and gathered in a pile, where some pieces of the body remained, each as big as a horse and glowing from within as cysts the size of human heads slowly released the last of their light.

Whatever had powered this engine had been destroyed by the opening, but had certainly been close to death anyway. If True Death was the byproduct of a machine, the engine's loss of power would correlate to the inability of the Dying to Die, and thus to the *svarning*. She wondered if any of them even suspected the truth.

Lallowë saw Cooper notice her. She lifted the hand that had rested on Almondine's forearm and licked the thumb.

"You owe me a finger," he said.

Lallowë smiled, the collar of her sleeveless powder-green blouse stiff and high like a general's. Almondine had eyes only for Sesstri, and did not see the scrap of drafting paper that Lallowë pressed against her wet thumb. Almondine clapped, and pulled on Lallowë's elbow. "It's her, Lolly! The one I told you about! *It's Sissy.* Oh, Lolly, you get your new sibling after all." She paused to see if Sesstri was listening, then cocked her head. "Pleasure to see you again, little sister."

"You will die screaming on my knives." Sesstri remained perfectly still.

"Tut-tut. Your older sister, Almondine, is right," Lallowë said, raising Almondine's hand in her own, while holding her thumb to Almondine's wrist. "She tells me that Manfred Manfrix was Mother's first human mate, and a failure—"

Cooper watched Prama become a streak of golden light—moving just like Asher, the same scissoring perfection of limb and flattened palm. Inside a heartbeat, she had cut off Lallowë and held each sister by the throat. Behind them pulsed a portal that must belong to the Cicatrix, a vulvic thing dripping acrylic paint in midnight hues—black and purples.

Prama shone like a furious golden axe, forged from sunlight. "You desecrate the engine of the ancients and the deathplace of a being so majestic that the likes of you do not deserve to know her identity. Once I have banished you and bound your undead scum for eternal torture, I will return her remains to the waters of our sea."

"Really?" Lallowë asked by way of an introduction, looking down at the being who held her. "I think you'll find yourselves too busy begging for death to be returning any bodies to any waters. Don't you agree, sister?"

Almondine nodded once, the crack of a pistol. "Just so."

The sisters turned their eyes toward the sky, gazing up through the hole in the ceiling of the engine, where the storm of lich-lords descended. Streaks of black smoke spiraled down into the gold machine room, lich-lords that did not bother to resolve into their individual forms. They dove for Prama, swarming her in black clouds until she shrieked and clawed at her face. Her radiance was swallowed by darkness, which still poured down from above.

The sisters fell free. Lallowë and Almondine resumed their poses, arm-in-arm, walking no faster than two courtly ladies on an evening's promenade.

As liches filled the room, Cooper curled his lip in a snarl and narrowed his eyes at Thyu.

The marchioness waved her fingertips in response, sending ghost fingers trilling up his spine. They were connected now, blood to blood and back again. Cooper knew with a sudden insight that if she were injured, he would feel it.

Oh yes, and feel it doubly. He heard Lallowë's whisper inside his head as she held out her arm to show him the scar. The stump of Cooper's little finger twitched—he felt its tip twitch below Lallowë's bicep.

I know what you are and it is vile, *Lolly.* Cooper thought his accusation at her like a slap on the cheek, and was glad when she shook her head, glaring at him. At least the enhanced call quality worked both ways.

Purity gasped horribly—a lich wrapped its arms around her, and she sagged, turning pale. The lich wore huge sunglasses that did not quite contain the smolder of the yellow-green coals burning in place of its eyes, and a gold tennis bracelet. It chuckled wordlessly and pulled her away. Another landed beside Cooper with a grinding chuckle. A rusted claw found his shoulder and he, too, felt a numbing chill.

Only Sesstri remained standing, squared off against her sisters. She pulled Chesmarul's book out of her satchel and began flipping through its pages with manic haste.

"Fuck you, fuck you, fuck you," she recited under her breath like a mantra. She hadn't seen any use whatsoever in poor Ms. Messerschmidt's *Urban Weather Patterns;* that is, until undead monsters clad in black weather descended into her midst.

She began to recite a passage on the legal rights to air space and breathing rights. "According to . . . according to princely decree, the building, breathing, and flying rights or . . . or any subset thereof . . . may be remanded by . . ." She stopped momentarily as Nixon flew into the engine chamber, red-faced and huffing from a thousand stairs. Sesstri almost smiled. When Asher followed a moment later, wounded and bleeding, Sesstri's smile gleamed.

Almondine stepped out from behind her sister without pretext and stalked toward Sesstri with murder on her otherwise expressionless face. It wasn't murder Cooper needed special senses to see, and Nixon saw it too, his eyes wide in alarm.

Almondine whipped out her hand and grabbed Sesstri by the throat, jerking the taller woman's feet off the floor. She drew back her other arm and prepared to smash Sesstri's skull with her fist. "I think it's time to end you now, Sissy. I will wear your lover's gray skin at my coronation, and rekindle the hearts of my Wild Hunters with the tale of the fall of the last aesr—his daughter's skull will make a splendid crown. Faerie fire shall burn your corpses without consuming your bones, limning my victory trophies for a thousand-thousand years on the pyres of triumph." She fixed Sesstri with a slow-burning smile. "And you, Sissy, will be forgotten entirely. Like your father forgot you, and our mother."

Sesstri made a sound of choking despair, and scrabbled for her knives to no avail. Messerschmidt dropped to the floor.

"Hey Doll!" Nixon shouted, pelting toward the women and pulling out his own weapon—the knife he'd looted from the dying Charnel Girl—as he ran. "You leave my pink bird alone!"

Almondine kicked him away without even looking. Nixon shot off like a cannonball and didn't slow until his body hit the wall, his stolen knife shattering against the etched gold circuits. He picked himself up slowly, his mouth gaping a gory hole from Almondine's kick to his face. His pointed nose was broken and most of his front teeth were gone, blood dripping onto his belly. Nixon looked at the bloody bone chips scattered across the floor of the great machine, felt at his toothless mouth with a pudgy little hand, and his eyes went black. Leveling his gaze at the tidy monster in the hound's-tooth coat, he charged.

"Nixon, stay back!" Cooper shouted. "You little idiot!"

But Nixon leapt at the deranged faerie with a roar. "Stick it, sister!" he screamed, tackling Almondine at her knees—she folded in half and fell backward as Nixon's momentum carried them both over the edge, tumbling into the pit. As their bodies spun through the air he exulted, "Nobody kicks the new Nixon!"

They landed with a splat on the slope of the depression, Nixon rolling away from the lethal faerie on impact. Her eyes wide as a cow's, Almondine scrabbled desperately at the side of the golden bowl, slick with oily blood, but was unable to gain any purchase. Her cherrywood fingernails splintered as she slid toward the drain, and she lost her cool at last, howling once in fury before being swallowed by the darkness.

"Ha!" the unboy cackled in triumph, flattening himself against the slippery side of the pit even as gravity pulled him toward the same black hole. The deadly fall would not end for hundreds of feet, maybe thousands, in the caverns below the city.

Because of his small size, Nixon slid more slowly but just as decidedly toward the drain at the bottom of the machine chamber. Cooper threw himself toward the edge of the pit, but Nixon was out of reach. He didn't struggle, but instead grinned up at Cooper and Sesstri as his body tipped into the drain. "I did it! I'm a good guy!" He raised his hands to flash twin victory signs and was flown away.

15

In the field hospital we shared a lark: that birth seemed most likely to occur during an eclipse, death at dawn.

Sometimes both at once, and then a day—light or dark—but filled with the most sonorous music.

These days rape the worlds of a virgin contradiction and plant the seed of tomorrow's blessed sorrows. On such mornings I peal the hymn that bled through the legs of the Western daughters and the pig-stuck organs of their war-dogged sons.

The poem of flesh repeats my lesson that each moment of dark and light is a miracle.

—Walt Whitman, *Barge Through the River Brightly*

Quiet claimed the air for a long minute after Nixon's sacrifice. Then Lallowë stepped forward, peered down at the hole at the center of the pit, and bared her teeth.

"May you find a pleasant waking, little unboy. Thank you for clearing my competition from the board." She lifted an arm and waved her fingers at Sesstri. "And a fine hello to you, baby sister. Welcome to the fucking family."

Sesstri shuddered but offered no reply. Cooper shuddered too; he could feel Lallowë's sick satisfaction through the blood bond. Spirits of salt and stone and water danced within them, and between them, and beyond.

Asher threw himself toward his besieged daughter but was intercepted by four shadows—in less than an instant, they had snared Asher in a frame of darkness, night and day boiling where they touched. A fifth lich with a shiny brown wig over its shoulder spread its polished fingerbones across Asher's face. He howled, dying a little to feed the vain abomination. His eyes went dark and dry as a corpse, and he sagged in his captors' grip. But his bone-dull skin began to bleach itself brighter, appearing almost to shine.

Across the room, Prama stood her own against a circle of five hissing lich-lords.

"As I was saying." Sesstri sounded dangerous. She recited Messerschmidt from memory now, with a swift efficient voice that gave even Lallowë pause. "According to municipal statutes, the building, breathing, and flying rights or any subset thereof may be remanded by royal decree, resulting in immediate expulsion from the City Unspoken and its environs."

Asher could decree nothing but his own death rattle at the hand of his lich captors.

Light rekindled beneath his gray skin as it healed—the grayness flickered like celluloid film, then bleached itself to silver and white before their eyes. If Cooper had stood beneath a hundred flashbulbs, he might shine so bright. Spears of light from bright polyps lined Asher's ribs, and his ragged clothes disintegrated.

Naked, Asher's humanity was dispelled: ropes of muscle, lanky joints, a thatch of darker gray hair surrounding his generative organs—these faded as the scars between his ribs glowed brighter and brighter, pushing cysts of new cells into the puckered wounds, and as the lights under his skin intensified, the reality of Asher's heritage asserted itself. His patrician nose elongated into a regal crest that stretched down below his chin and all the way up past the crown of his skull, and his eyes—flickering still between red and blue and green—blurred together until he gazed out from a single conjoined orb, ensconced within the bony crest that flew up and backward over his skull.

He reached out with one massive white-boned hand and grabbed Ambassador Rousseau by the face, as she held him. He squeezed, and silver light shattered her skull. The rest of her fell away like ash and costumery.

His four captors released their grip and backed away, but it was too late. Asher flared his rekindled light, and spears of silver-white brilliance pierced the four, nullifying them.

His resistance gave the undead swarming Prama pause, and she took the opportunity to flare her own golden light, repulsing the lot of them a short distance, cast out in a circle around her. Father and daughter faced each other and, after nodding, bowed their heads and spread their wing-fins. Light arced above each of them.

From across the room, Prama's gold light and Asher's white light merged into a bridge of light that illuminated everything. All shadows were consumed by light cast by the aesr or reflected from the mirrored sphere around them. All shadows—even those constructed and maintained by necromantic perversion.

For a moment, it seemed to Cooper that every lich within the engine was caught in the flash of a paparazzo's camera. The next instant, their bones collapsed in a hail, ringing off the metal floor, the anti-light that glued them together—their actual medium of existence—was simply banished. Vaporized by pure light generated by two wounded, pissed off First People.

Then the bridge of light faltered, and winked out as Asher and Prama gasped, sagging, each merely radiant, rather than blindingly brilliant.

Cooper wanted to exult in triumph, but the Cicatrix's portal was convulsing—first contracting, then pulsing wider than before. Slowly, something began to push through. Something with an elongated, black head—a horned ovoid shape he imagined to be slick with acid blood, tail a mile long, vile. Cooper's ghost finger pulsed in triple-time: his own blood pounding through it; Lallowë's heart beating strong as a boxer in her chest; and the song-to-song countermelody of the vivisistor to its siblings, clustered within the Cicatrix like intentional tumors: brainstem, wrist, heart, womb.

He sensed her considerable bulk and again marveled at how large she'd been able to grow, from the seed of a such a small woman. A subway train of black claws and ozone breath, with no light in her but that of her life-fueled LED tattoos. Cooper could hear the maddened pixies already— they screamed for death inside her vivisistors.

WinterWinterWinter! GiveUsWinteryDeath, GiveUsAirAndDark, WinteryDarkyDeath, PullThePinsFromOurHearts, Cooper-Omphale, AndBleedUsDeadDeadDead!

"What *is* she?" Cooper asked Lallowë out loud; she didn't need to speak to answer. They were connected by blood and machine now, and he could have overheard her fright-dappled thoughts anyway, had it occurred to him.

She is my mother and my queen and my bane. She calls herself the Cicatrix, the mistress of scars, and she will crack this city like an egg when she arrives.

Then Lallowë Thyu turned on her heel and ran.

* * *

Sesstri knelt at the lip of the circular pit where once a god had been pin-ioned by the Lash and bled its life into the engine that allowed the mor-tals of the worlds to achieve everlasting oblivion. An engine to end wakings.

She covered her face in her hands, not at all sure whether she wept for Nixon or because of the lies Almondine had told before she died. They *were* lies, she knew that much. They had to be. It was true that Sesstri had never known her mother, but she knew the woman had been a fierce sol-dier, a foreigner, and the only woman her father had ever acknowledged as his equal.

She can't be, just can't. Gods, her belly hurt.

Asher took Sesstri by the wrists and lifted her to her feet. On the far side, Prama hugged her knees and rocked herself back and forth, barely glowing at all.

"She's coming," Cooper pleaded to anyone who cared to listen. Only Purity seemed to hear.

"Can't you stop it?" she asked Cooper, scrubbing her face to warm it.

A sucking sound drew Cooper's eyes to the portal, which tore itself open inch by inch, acrylic blood chasing the etched channels as it dripped onto the floor. Cooper considered the branching, convergent tattoo of circuitry painted in purples and blues and blacks.

Within the portal, a shape began to resolve itself. Like a sketch, the lines that described her face appeared before the face itself resolved in the portal: the eyes of a woman gazing out from beneath a pronged helm, a pair of silver lips adorning the plate where her jaw should be.

Sesstri gasped in pain and nearly fell to the floor, sagging in Asher's arms. She clutched her belly.

"What is it?" Asher asked with a voice full of concern.

"Womb magic," Cooper answered. "I've been inside the Cicatrix, and she's not quite *woman* anymore. I think that she's drawing upon her daugh-ters' bellies to birth herself." He grimaced. "I'm sorry, Sesstri, but it's true."

Blood to blood and back again. He could feel the blood they shared, the women and his coin machine.

The Cicatrix emerged from the pulsing ellipse headfirst, wailing with the effort as her arms slithered out of the canal, ceramic insulator discs mounted atop her shoulders popping audibly; she yawned, gasping for air as she struggled to push her shoulders into the world. Her perfect silver lips stretched wide and wider—and then they dropped down as her mouth plate slid past her throat, and she inhaled through a curtain of jawless meat.

Her horned helm scraped the edges of the portal, which sprayed dark fluids and electrical discharge into the air. One hand remained bare, white skin tweeded with overlapping scars—on the other she wore a wicked gauntlet with slits at the fingertips for her obsidian nails.

The polymerized faerie queen screamed when she saw that Almondine was gone. Cooper clapped his hands over his ears, Sesstri and Purity following suit as the Cicatrix decanted herself into the world. Her amplified lamentation blared on for too long, her rage and loss venting from artificial lungs that snaked down through her thorax.

"My child! My heir!" In her grief the half-born Cicatrix thrashed with no concern for her own well-being, dashing her half-ton headgear against the metal floor until the entire engine room rang like a bell. Cooper thought she looked like some monstrous mermaid whose fish parts were sea serpent rather than tuna, and synthetic besides, her helm a crown of black coral, overgrown with a drowned beauty.

The half-birthed invader queen fell silent. She raised her torso and reared back, reclining into the cradling support of her polyvinyl serpent's abdomen—still emerging from the portal, her segments dragged along by unnerving, insectile grasper arms—as she assessed the gathering of her enemies. When her eyes found Cooper, he saw the recognition—she had his scent, surely. His ghost finger itched—blood to blood to blood.

"You." She spread obsidian claws at his face, thin as black ribbons and deadly as mamba fangs. "You are Cooper-*Omphale,* the boy who's been inside me. Do you know what we do to intruders in the Court of Scars, man-child?" Her visor retracted halfway, exposing the lower half of her face, and she pulled her quicksilver lips into a grimace. Silver-lipped, eyes hidden behind a crescent of black plastic, corseted in braided aramid fibers, she looked a pop star pirate queen, ready to steal the show and the stadium with fireworks and neurotoxin. Cooper didn't resist the abject terror the Cicatrix inspired.

But abjectly terrified or not, he had to do something. Cooper took a deep breath and extended his shamanic senses—sight beyond the world, sounds beneath the skin. He didn't know just what to expect, but . . .

Well goddamn.

Like an earthworm pushing its way out of wet soil, the Cicatrix slithered from one world into another, and where she existed between the worlds, he could *feel* her. Feel her and . . . reaching out . . . he could grab her body with the hands of his spirit. In the infinitesimal vastness of the non-space that cocooned the worlds, his grip was strong.

"I am the *Omphale*." He talked just so he could hear his own voice, to lend himself courage through vim and vulgarity. Cooper astonished himself with the clarity of the vision, he could feel her heart beat and the machine whir of the systems that brimmed with power bought by life. She was *enormous;* before, when he had inhabited her body on accident, he hadn't the presence of mind to appreciate her sheer bulk.

He could feel her pulling herself toward the City Unspoken with frantic speed. And if he tried, if he bore down with his stomach muscles and bit his tongue, he could *hold her there.*

"Ha!" He laughed aloud. Sesstri flashed him a smile—if he killed her mother she'd *have* to thank him.

Cooper felt his body vibrating, not too differently from the vibrations of the chains beneath the city—how an airliner or a subway train might feel, urban and elemental and beyond his control . . . except that somehow it *was* within his control, which he exerted, bringing the freight train faerie queen screeching to an interdimensional halt. Nearly.

"She's still coming. Shit, she's a long-ass snake elf. Snelf." Cooper ground his teeth, clenched everything, and bore down. He howled through his teeth, red-faced. "Your mother's a snelf!"

"Shut up, turd!" Sesstri called, but the Cicatrix opened her quicksilver lips and spoke in a voice that deafened:

"My sovereign and core modules exist here, within the Dome, such as it is. Within the boundaries of the City Unspoken. The rest of me is merely luggage." The queen raised one arm and her synthetic skin retracted to show an array of metal warheads. The armament dropped down in a loop of chain, a bandolier three feet long and bristling with quicksilver muni-tions. At the tip of each silvery warhead shone a lilac LED, and Cooper could hear the screams of vivisistor-pinioned lives within. "I think, Girl-Prince, that I will redecorate the ruins of your palace in a palette of reds. Let us start with the hot red paint inside all of your human slaves."

"*No,*" Cooper and Sesstri said as one.

"You cannot stop me, *Omphale,* and the Manfrix girl cannot help you." The Cicatrix stroked her massive, horned helm with her flesh hand. "My daughters with men are weak."

"You have some fairly demonstrable design flaws," Sesstri said, walk-ing toward the queen. "You are wrong," she spat, "and you will have *none* of me, Mother."

Sesstri flipped a dagger in her hand, hilt up, and slammed the blade into her belly. She struck low and savage, feeling the edge scrape against her pubic bone, hoping to avoid vitals like the bladder and intestines, to damage only her reproductive organs. She gasped, eyes wide, then twisted the dagger with the last of her focus before folding in half and dropping to the floor.

Cooper felt frozen to the spot with horror as, with a suck of pressure, the pulsing oval clenched shut and vanished, severing the body of the foreign queen as neatly as a guillotine.

Her balance upset, the Cicatrix toppled forward, bracing her fall with her hands and shattering her black rapier nails; with the synthetic mus-cles anchoring her hips and torso to her wyrm-body severed, their re-mainder contracted reflexively, squirming like worms from the queen's severed chassis and spraying brown engine oil across the golden floor. Her warheads clamored against the gold floor, their lights flashing faster now, alternating lilac and emerald green.

She continued dragging herself forward with broken nails, hissing venom and steam from the grill of her perfect silver mouth—until ancil-lary stabilizers emerged from the segments beneath her torso, pushing the Cicatrix slowly, slowly upright. She twisted her neck, turning her enormous helm this way and that. Something in her head unlatched, and the Cicatrix craned her head forward, sliding a smaller version of her horned war helm out from the larger bulk.

What is this? Cooper thought. Purity cursed.

Like skirts parting at a clever slit, the Cicatrix drew back the lower segments of her exoskeleton and stepped out of the carapace, dainty feet touching the golden floor. One, two, three, four, five, six—six smooth legs, harvested from three fey girl-children, still rubber-boned with youth, whose hips and ankles would obey the torture of machine choreography. Once, twice, thrice the Cicatrix kicked her heels and patted forward, full of doll-like menace. Aluminum petticoats served double duty as cooling fins, hiding the juncture of harvested limbs and mobile chassis.

She left behind a molted shell still rearing in a Cicatrix-shape: empty horns, hollow carapace, skeletal arm servos. A dragon, an insect, a dancer—the Cicatrix pressed forward. "Try as you like, Cooper-*Omphale*," the Cicatrix gloated, skittering with the skin-crawling ululations of a centipede; released from the vast length of her complete exoskeleton, she was fully mobile and terrifying. "I have contingencies for contingencies, and bodies the likes of which you would not *believe.*

"The chains once buried across and beneath this city serve an even older purpose, for instance." Shit-your-jeans terrifying. "Oh, Cooper, I'll show you. After I birth the living madness into the worlds, boy, I will *fill* this city. All it takes is one god-machine-empress costume change, and I will seize the reins and ride this beast into the suns."

"Oh, fuck me once in the chimney and twice at the gate," Purity cursed again.

"It's the *svarning,* isn't it? Somehow . . ."

"She's been drinking it," Cooper said aloud, as he realized it was true. "Holding it back in her crazy bullshit magic engineering complex until the perfect time to let the inevitable happen. Then all that sickness will flood out into the metaverse at once, with the city as ground zero."

"I may have made a poor prince"—Asher stepped forward—"but I will not let that happen." He looked like a kind of abstract stone eagle, or perhaps a moth-man made from chalk and bone. Or a beta fish and Apollo. Whatever Asher was, he was not human, no one could mistake that. He was of the First People, vast and unknowable. Except that Cooper knew him. He swore, he did.

Cooper looked to Sesstri, full of questions, who nodded at Asher's transformation, her face filled with sorrow.

BeyondMeNow, Cooper heard her worry—had she known? *BeyondAnd-Broken.*

Ex-Prince Asher tackled the Cicatrix without warning, moving faster than the eye as always—now a streak of white light, not bones—and in a trice her enormous head whipped backward, gripped between Asher's shining hands. He ripped cables from her chassis as he pulled his face close to her own.

"In all these lonely endless worlds I love only two women," he hissed into the grille where her ear should have been. "And you have hurt both of them."

The Cicatrix howled, oil spraying from her torn cabling, but he could not snap her neck.

The Cicatrix threw him over her shoulder, cracking his crest against the floor. "You can't even *spell* the alloys that replaced my spinal column, Fflaen." She laughed, an autotuned sound that remixed some internal system static into a cruel arpeggio. "Thorn and thorax!" The Cicatrix shook her head, the slender tips of her war helm sending sympathetic impulses to its empty giant twin behind her, which mirrored the movement. Then she began to nod, and the empty carapace nodded as well. Contingencies.

She lifted her inorganic hand, and the gold floor rippled—scrollwork and circuitry like fine lines of filigree lifted themselves from the metal beneath and undulated like rapt snakes. The Cicatrix shrugged, and the metal lines shrugged with her.

"You don't see me, Fflaen, or you would see that I am prepared for *anything.*" The filigree lines wrapped themselves around Asher, lifting him bodily from the floor. Then they began to burrow into his body, all razor-thin and right angles. Asher screamed.

"Your little red goddess thinks she's ruined my fun by opening the Dome and breaking my toy before I could play with it." The Cicatrix pouted. "But why cry, when I can try to fix what you've ruined?" Borne by the wire-thin circuit lines and dripping white blood, Asher's body floated into the center of the spherical engine chamber.

"One of the First People powered this engine for ages beyond counting." She nodded toward the smoldering corpse across the room. "I don't see why you won't do, for a spell."

The queen shuffled her baby legs till she faced her abandoned exoskeleton, concentration in her eyes. She lifted her arms and adjusted her torso until her stance matched the exoskeleton's positioning, and engaged it. She raised her hands and twisted her shoulders, and the exoskeleton mirrored her motions. Twinning herself, the Cicatrix reached up and dragged her now-empty chassis through the hole in the ceiling.

"With an ordinary machine, of course, this wouldn't be possible," she cooed. The machine's piezoelectric spine bristled with an influx of electricity: rows of teeth, rows of fins. The Cicatrix moaned in pleasure, arching her own spine as well. "Ooh, science."

Cooper panicked. Sesstri was wounded, maybe mortally. Purity had done what she could, and Prama was traumatized and drained almost dry. So Cooper did the only thing he could think of, he threw himself at the Cicatrix's legs and did his best to entangle himself in the childrens' legs that supported her.

The queen bellowed and tried to kick him off, but Cooper refused to let go. She dragged him along the golden floor, and he fought against the legs of young girls. Everything was nightmare. But there were brownies inside the queen—Cooper wondered, could he coax them into suicide, if he promised them freedom instead? Could a pixie powering a vivisistor choose to . . . *secede*? Cooper held on as the etched floor scrubbed his ruined back, he lied faeries to their deaths, and tore at the flesh of children, anything to stop the Cicatrix from killing Asher, or worse.

You do not obey your queen, he shouted into the systems he could sense, the ones attached to the legs he clutched, *you obey a monster who has stolen her shape.* As the Cicatrix ground him into the floor, Cooper seduced the creatures—spirits of nature—that maintained her grafted dancing feet.

Amazingly, it worked. One by one her doll legs numbed and blued, as six yellow, orange, and finally red LEDs pulsed across the underside of her abdomen. Cooper could hear the alarms ringing inside the Cicatrix: tissue oxygenation was zero, crucified pixies screaming prophecy and system failure. The stolen legs tore away, soft and spongy.

The Cicatrix howled and whipped her abdomen, shedding the false pelvis and its six seeping stumps. Away flew the corrugated petticoats of her mille-feuille cooling fins, revealing the triangular tail of a trilobite.

Cooper rolled away and hit the outer wall of the engine room, knocking his head hard. Asher still floated in midair, transfixed by dozens of gold circuit-wires. Cooper picked himself up, and the Cicatrix shot toward him, clawing at the floor as her short tail propelled her. Then she lifted her head, her shoulders and, impossibly, her insectile lower half.

She levitated. *Of course she did.* Cooper threw himself at the queen's waist, but she shed her trilobite tail like a cashmere skirt, and Cooper found himself rolling along the floor again, discarded segments squirming against his skin.

This was her last layer, there was no more artifice beneath. Nothing but bone and meat remained below her waist—half a faerie drifted toward him, murder in her eyes. For a woman who'd armored nearly every limb, organ, and orifice in what remained of her original body, it seemed strange and, somehow, ungentlemanly to Cooper for him to see her bare hip sockets—pitted and dry, clearly arthritic, *dead*.

"Darling, darling, don't protest. She's family!" A merry voice sounded from the stairs below the entrance, and a red-coated Oxnard Terenz-de-Guises appeared, the arm of his lady wife gripped in one bejeweled hand. He raised an eyebrow when he saw his prince, wrapped in gold lace, hanging in midair.

The marchioness hissed at her husband, who let her go with a forbearing smile. "Now, for a girl who kills her papa daily," he said, "you don't sound like a very attentive daughter. Can we try again?"

"Mother?" Lallowë appeared stricken. "Is that you?" It had been so long since her mother had looked like a woman—and now that she did, it felt awful.

"Go away," the Cicatrix coughed. "My failure." She reached out for Cooper's throat.

But Cooper found a reserve of willpower he did not know he had, and closed his eyes against her advance. He held up his hand, the one with the missing finger, and felt the blood moving through his hand into the pinkie that powered Lallowë's vivisistor. Lallowë and the Cicatrix were connected by blood, and he was connected to Lallowë—he could not talk down every fey sprite in every vivisistor, they littered the Cicatrix like tumors—but perhaps he could do something more.

"I am an acme of things accomplish'd, and I an encloser of things to be." Cooper quoted Walt Whitman to his own blood as if his veins contained a spirit with whom he could commune, and he spoke aloud to the cavernous gold room filled with gods dead and living. As Chesmarul's voice had awed him in the cathedral-forest of her mind, so Cooper's voice thickened the air like soup, then honey, slowing down the apparent passage of time for the others. "I celebrate myself, and sing myself/And what I assume you shall assume/For every atom belonging to me as good belongs to you."

He stole the poetry that unfolded inside his memory, which he wielded like prophecy, and was glad the verses were Walter's. Not that the words themselves mattered, at all—what mattered was the intention to commune with the spirit of his blood, threaded through the ether from hand to finger and back again.

"Have you felt so proud to get at the meaning of poems?" Cooper called out like a braggart, and the Cicatrix froze with a look of horror as his intent caused her kernel to panic. "Stop this day and night with me and you shall possess the origin of all poems." Faerie logic cores began their infinite sum failures.

"You shall no longer take things at second or third hand, nor look through the eyes of the dead, nor feed on the spectres in books." Cooper healed Sesstri, who coughed in surprise, soaked through with blood that suddenly no longer seeped from the wound in her gut.

"You shall not look through my eyes either, nor take things from me." Lallowë wrinkled her brow in momentary confusion, as though she'd been smacked. His blood! Cooper's body felt filled with fire—Lallowë did not know it yet, but the link between them no longer flowed both ways. The blood flowed, but any attempt on her part to exploit the connection would be violently rejected.

"You shall listen to all sides and filter them from your self." Light danced across gold as Prama and Asher spread the finlike wing-things that sprouted from their shoulders and lower backs. Asher hung his head in shame; Prama lifted hers higher.

Cooper focused on his pounding heartbeat and the blood that had become so central to the fate of the metaverse. When he seized control of the Cicatrix's vivisistor network, his perception of time slowed as his mind expanded to apprehend the sudden vastness. Nearby, he felt the queen's vivisistors—a cluster of local stars in tight formation. But he felt others, too, far away from the City Unspoken. They pulled at him with enormous gravity, as old and distant as stars in the night sky, spangled across the metaverse. Were they *new*? Some seemed to flicker awake while he watched.

Cooper refocused on the Cicatrix and the stars comprising the constellation of vivisistors within the queen began to flare up, then fade away. Popping sounds like dying lightbulbs filled his ears, as some of the fey vivisistors began to crack open, incapacitating the Cicatrix's systems and disemboweling the wee faeries who powered them. They went too easily, Cooper thought, trying to remember the next line from "Song of Myself."

"You shall possess the good of the earth and sun, (there are millions of suns left.)" But her little suns were gone. Deprived of power, errors swamping her systems, the Cicatrix collapsed to the floor; the sound of her dry hip sockets splintering against the metal made Cooper wince, even in his trance. Lallowë had tears in her eyes, but did not move.

The length of golden lace that impaled Asher drooped toward the floor, and Prama pulled him down and began the painstaking task of removing the filaments woven through his alien body.

The Cicatrix's laughter sounded like a broken engine. She was running on reserves, dying and in pain. "You've won so many battles," she quavered. "Shattered so many *thoughtful* contingencies: banished my allies; defeated their host; murdered my daughter and, it seems, myself. You've rendered warheads useless and agitated vivisistors into sedition. So many weapons you've countered and disabled, but you have not yet met my weapon of choice." She twisted her face in pain and pushed herself up on her arms, pivoting from her shattered pelvis. "And then, of course, I cannot stop myself from wondering: what will you do when the *other* engines begin to wake?"

The lost queen began to laugh but choked on engine oil and, unable to breathe, clawed at her throat with one hand. The pressure valves beneath her diaphragm had failed, and as her atrophied lungs struggled to compensate, the queen pointed a broken finger and tried to curse her progeny. Denied voice, her lips fell off in a cloud of steam as the silver mouthplate fell off of her face and hit the floor with a clatter, trailing blood where it had dislodged from her upper jaw, its vocalization mechanism squawking wet static. The quicksilver lips stopped moving at last and lay still as a broken mask.

The Cicatrix tried to cover her disfigured mouth and throat with her good hand without falling over again, but there was too much exposed flesh—her tongue dangled, impotent amidst a clutch of sparking wires, and the skin of her lower face and neck had been peeled back from her palate to her collarbone, curtains of bloody meat hanging loose from beneath her upper lip.

"Mother?" Lallowë's hands shook—her face brimmed with conflicting emotions. "What do I do? Mama?" She looked up at Cooper, pleading.

Sesstri lurched to her feet with a groan, stepped forward, and reached into the exposed throat of the mortally wounded queen. She grabbed her mother's windpipe and yanked, crushing it and withdrawing a fistful of dripping tubes. The queen's eyes rolled back and she flopped to the ground, dead.

Lallowë looked at Sesstri with a helplessness that seemed full of questions.

"That"—Sesstri turned to shake her bloodied fist at her sister—"is called mercy, bitch." Then she stumbled into Asher's arms and buried her face in his chest, hiding her tears in the blinding light of his body.

Lolly knelt by her mother's head, huge in its deformity. She stroked the smooth black horns—recurved and massive—the sealed weapon ports and ventilation gills, the synthetic venom glands bulging beneath molded cheekbones. She ran her fingers through the cables behind the crown of horns, dark metal dreadlocks and plastic curls that had spilled down the dead queen's back but now spread their tendrils across the golden floor, seeking with the last of their energies the warmth of life that had fled their mistress.

Sesstri and Asher made their way down the stairs, leaning on each other for support. Purity and Prama drifted away, talking civic politics. Cooper and Lallowë shared the empty, blood-spattered engine room with the corpse of the unnamed First Person that Prama had called the mother of all aesr.

But the divine battery was not the only dead thing in the room.

Something stirred upon the corpse of the Cixatrix. The chassis shifted and began to reject her nonliving tissue, uncurling from the queen's body and exposing the barbed teeth that had pressed the inorganic components to the flesh of the queen. Lallowë, startled, hovered her hands palms-down over her mother's body, not knowing what to do. She felt a fleeting and horrifying urge to hold her mother's body together.

Her husband watched from the side, silent.

The marchioness nodded to herself, humming. She stroked the helm; it did look like an enormous beetle's carapace, horns curved and flared like a dung beetle—but from another angle it was the skull of a dragon, and from another a praetor's helm, black and pronged instead of platinum and single-crested. There were vivisistors inside that she could repair, if she cared to. What kind of code had her mother written? She shuddered— it would be all that was left of her mother. That poetry . . . verses of faerie logic that would chase electrons through the circuits like moonlight on ash-wood, pale and perfect. The colors of leaf and twilight, emerald and lilac . . . like her beautiful jewelry.

She tugged at the helm and it slid off her mother's head easily, eager to be free of the dead flesh. Beneath lay the sweat-streaked, pale face of a woman, pretty but not beautiful, with a nub of a nose and soft brown eyes. Short-cropped ginger hair covered her scalp in patches—she looked as if she had been ill for a long time. Lallowë closed her mother's eyes and felt a moment of peace.

Lallowë's eyes were huge, the past touching the present. Was this what victory felt like? She supposed that despite her healthy self-confidence, she hadn't ever really *won* before. Just moved pieces across the board. Taking a bishop, marrying a knight, obliterating pawns. And now, a queen.

A deformed, mostly inorganic, nightmare queen with the head of a polyvinyl dung beetle for a helm. Well, it was more of a mask, she supposed, or maybe a headdress. Her mother had worn it as a crown. Yes, that was the appropriate point of view—the crown Lallowë had *earned*, whether it disgusted her or not. She cradled the smooth thing in her lap, stroking it with turquoise-tipped fingers.

In the corner of Lallowë's vision an indicator began to pulse with the colors of pale sapphires and deep forest cover; leaf and twilight. She did not find them unpleasant colors, nor was she surprised by their appearance, though she thought perhaps . . . perhaps she ought to have been alarmed. Maybe she would use those colors in the redesign of the bower, *her* bower, when she returned to rule the Seven Silvers. When she razed the ruined land and restored the proper Court of Scars that she knew from child-hood.

It is time to retreat into the Ruby Naught, she decided, and felt at her waist for the jewel box tucked away there.

She had business to attend to now and did not care to tarry. Lallowë felt herself seized by the desire for efficiency, for using her resources as surgically as possible. The Seven Silvers were hers. The Court of Scars was hers. She held up the crown—*it* was hers, this trophy, this magnifi-cent and possibly functional war-helm. *Hers.* It should have been enough to make her cry.

Looking at the marchioness, Cooper saw her namesign shimmer: on the face of the green serpent, a lilac eye winked in time to his own heart-beat. One-two, one-two, one-two.

He saw the way she clutched the Cicatrix's headgear and felt the blood in his pinky finger begin to hum a playfully odd little tune, and Cooper knew. This was how it would begin, for Lallowë—how she would come to share her mother's addiction. The shaman senses uncoiled in his chest, not to exert themselves but to get out of the way, to clear his thoughts of any influence so that Cooper could realize it was only his natural instinct, his lifetime of stories and fantasies and observations he had thought use-less, that *knew.*

"Lallowë, don't. Please."

She met his gaze and shook her head. A corner of her small mouth twitched, half-smile, half-sneer. "Too late." Lallowë lifted the crown upon which she had wasted so much effort; it no longer felt heavy in her hand. In her other hand she revealed a beveled box of red metal.

The marquis let out a long sigh. "I had hoped you didn't have it, song of my song." His voice was full of heartache. "But of course you are who you are. I do love you for that, you know."

If the marchioness heard her husband it did not show. She held the box level with her face and locked eyes with Cooper. *You are a part of this now,* she thought to him. *You are a part of me, and I of you. Who laughs loudest at that, furry man? Who predicted this? Not you, not me. The worlds surprise, Cooper. They surprise and surprise and surprise.* Lallowë Thyu triggered something inside the box and with a sucking twist of space, she and the looted war-helm evaporated. Green stars glittered for a moment in the empty air, a snake's head and searching tongue, a winking lilac eye.

EPILOGUE

The next day dawned red and smoggy, streaking the sky with heavy cloud cover and scenting the air strongly with ammonia. Through the tyranny of the methane sunrise, a small procession followed a redheaded woman in an old purple robe—*unbelievably* old, if she cared to brag about it—down the nearly deserted Boulevard of Metal Mornings and around the Garrison of First Wakings. Garlands of marigolds appeared as she passed, draping themselves over gaslights and rain gutters, and cherry blossom petals fell at her feet. Where she walked, the madness cleared.

The gathering was small but solemn: masons walked with Winnowed, intermingling, their eyes hollow with fatigue and shame; a smattering of plumbics and canalworkers followed behind, regarding their masonic brothers with uncertainty; a cortège of the Dying followed too, bleached of color and tremulous—the Dying, who were once the lifeblood of the City Unspoken, but who had retreated of late to abandoned districts, huddling over trash-can fires and waiting for the absolution that would dissolve their selves into the nothingness from which they had, so long ago, been born. Behind and amidst the Dying walked a handful of ordinary citizens, curious and aware that the past twenty-four hours had forever changed their city—the Dome opened like a shy flower, the Undertow scattered, and True Death, the cash crop of the City Unspoken, broken like a clock. As if to confirm that truth, a group of nobles brought up the rear, steely-eyed and determined to make the proper impression as they returned to the city from which they had been sequestered for five long years.

All twenty-three noble families were represented, surrounded by a platinum ring of praetors, and every single member of House Kloo had turned out to support their daughter, sister, and cousin, Purity. Even NiNi came, alone, to represent her house, though she clung to the periphery and looked lost in a sea of black tulle. For once, her face remained uncovered, her hawkish nose and high forehead facing the day, whatever it brought. Also to the side walked Oxnard, unaccompanied, still wearing the red jacket and high boots of the admiralty.

At the head of the procession, Cooper followed just behind Alouette, and beside him Kaien and Purity held hands and kept their heads bowed. Cooper wished Asher or Sesstri were with him, and his eyes watered a little at the thought of Nixon, who was beyond them now.

The route they followed was old and unused, the highway merely one of dozens of abandoned thoroughfares in the City Unspoken. Beneath the curling crust of Amelia Heights, the highway that a crowd of citizens now followed was too old to sport a half-forgotten name or purpose; it was just a straight line of pylon-suspended concrete that followed itself down farther than anyone had a good reason to walk, and passed into Winnowed territory as well. Too bare to be of use even to thieves and their ilk, the way had been truly and thoroughly ignored until this morning.

Now, Alouette led a procession of citizens, guildsfolk, noble families, Winnowed, interlopers, and visiting powers down the thoroughfare that ran beneath the crust of the city to emerge on the far side of the rind of the world. They didn't know it, but she led them to the neck of the beast who bore the city upon his back, where she would bury her mother at sea, in the Sea of Remembered Skies.

She looked wee and frail as a human, though Cooper knew better. It amused and confused him to see her in her mortal body, now. He didn't like Alouette as much as he liked Chesmarul—whether or not she called herself the caretaker of the lost and abused. At least the route she took was marvelous—Alouette intended to impress, in her way: after the red morning light faded, scarlet witchlights appeared at her shoulders, sentinels of bloody light that soon spawned satellite lights that drifted behind her, floating overhead to light the way for those who followed.

For a long time they walked in the ruddy darkness, silent save for the sound of their feet against concrete, the dancing red sparks of Alouette's witchlights the only light to see. When the pavement ended, they carried on across smooth, quarried granite. When the quarry-scraped granite gave way to natural rock, the procession did not falter.

A sound like breathing wound through the tunnel, which seemed odd until all of a sudden the tunnel opened into a cavern lit by a faraway source of light, and the cavern gave way to a great hall filled with birdsong and mist and a deep pounding reverberation that shook the bedrock on all sides. Still-distant light glimmered from across the enormous space, obscured by pillars nearly as thick as city blocks supporting an unseen ceiling that disappeared overhead, hidden by clouds of the mist that poured in from the far end of the hall. Nobody in the gathered assembly had ever seen a cavern so vast and so alive, not even the Winnowed—this was an ancient way, isolated by geography and subtle enchantments placed aeons ago. The vanishing distance consumed the walls, most of the ceiling, and the source of both the light and the bass-thumping noise, which lay at the far end of the habitat like a curtain of rainstorm on the horizon.

Birds spiraled and bats bobbed, betraying the size of the cavern-hall, and ferns sprouted in clusters poised to gather the light. Where visible, walls of natural rock joined with the crumbled, candlewax billionstone of the aesr from the post-Anvitine era; the First People had stopped here before they conquered the surface, carving their perches into rock walls that still scrolled with their ancient, oddly organic stone. This was their first bulwark, and Cooper saw their ghosts arriving on the world that would one day sprout the City Unspoken; they flew/swam through the Sea of Remembered Skies and founded a rookery here, to collect themselves and explore the forested world beyond.

As they progressed through the mile-long chamber, Cooper saw shafts of sunlight stream sideways through a haze of waterfall spray—the falls still lay half a mile or more distant but they must be massive to generate such seismic noise and volume of fog. What would it feel like to march out from beneath Niagara? He'd seen those falls and felt their pounding— this was more intense by far. Or was there a second sound, a titanic breath, that underlay the merely breath*like* pounding of the water? The world was a beast, after all, Prama had revealed that much, and beasts must breathe.

And there she waited, before the wall of water, a column of winged light that outshone even the brilliant sunlight refracted in all directions by a billion-billion droplets of mist. She stood beside her father, who draped his restored incandescence in layers of cloth, and who clung to Sesstri, red-faced and pink-haired, tightly bandaged about her middle but standing with the support of her lover, the disgraced prince.

Alouette greeted Prama with a bow, which surprised everyone except for Prama; Asher's heir had stepped into her role seamlessly, rising above her mortal subjects with the inhuman grace and remoteness that her father had long ago abandoned, unwilling or unable to remain detached from the worlds. Prince Prama Ramay showed no such weakness.

Together, Alouette and Prama turned and led the funeral procession through the thundering mist and out into the world.

After such a trek beneath the ground, stepping through the curtain of parted water into the light was a shock. The suns branded his eyes, and Cooper experienced the last leg of the trip as a blear of overexposed still frames: the masons and the Winnowed and the switchback trail down to the horn of the beast, where the water falls into the sea; a longboat with the head of a beluga, tied all 'round with red ribbons and floating in mid-air above a sheer drop off the edge of everything; Alouette in her purple gown and petals filling the air overhead and brass bowls pouring milk and saltwater into the spray; an isthmus neck leading out to a spur of rock—or was it bone, or chitin, or shell?—jutting out into the day, while the crowd clung to the steep gradient of the makeshift amphitheater afforded by the densely packed switchback route; no horizon, just cloud and sky, a hundred skies, above and below, a sea of them, drifting by.

Out past the improvised cairn altar where Alouette stood, the neck continued, swallowed by fog and miles of clouds, bearing the continental head and mouth of the beast who was the world. Cooper could only imagine what the world-beast looked like, and was too full of vertigo and awe to dare try and send his vision out there into the skyborne depths. Alouette came to a stop before the longboat, made of dark wood and floating in the air but tethered to the makeshift cairn of piled stones and shale. Within the vessel lay the red-draped corpse of the nameless First Person who had powered the engine of Death since before the advent of humankind. She looked enormous here beneath the tidal infinities of the Sea of Remembered Skies, larger than she had seemed in the engine.

Prama stood on a rocky prominence surrounded by praetors in their platinum kit, a semicircle of metal that could almost be light. The prince herself was dimmed by the day, and the brightness of the suns would have revealed her hide had her praetors not covered her with layers of white linen, draping over her wing-fins and blowing in the gusty wind. Her hands and head were bare, and the people could not help from staring at her head, so similar in shape to the helms of her guardsmen. She made for a living reliquary, and to walk with her was to travel back in time by millions of years.

The man who approached Cooper seemed diminished by the environment, so essential was domesticity to Tam's vitality. In the sun his face looked lovely rather than dodgy, his tawny hair and prominent nose seemed more fox-like than ever. He wore a trim gray suit and light brown tie, and he looked at Cooper expectantly.

"What next, Young Tam Lin?" Cooper asked, shading his face to look Tam in the eyes.

"I'm free, fuck you." Tam's tone was snappy but he smiled.

"Aren't you worried Lallowë will come back for you?" Cooper couldn't help but project his own fears—although Tam should share them, he thought.

"No. I'm not important enough." He tossed his hair out of his eyes. "You are, though."

"Yeah. I can still feel my finger inside her body, wherever that is. It's beyond disgusting."

Tam held up his own pinky and looked at it as if it were a talisman of doom. "Cooper, one way or another, she's going to . . ."

"Yeah, I know. I'm dead meat."

Tam made a face. "I'd suggest killing yourself to break the connection and kill the finger, but the Sixth Silver will keep your finger safe for her no matter what. I'm sorry."

Cooper agreed, and nodded at Asher and Sesstri, at Alouette, and Prama beside her, waved to Purity and Kaien with a so-so gesture, and shrugged toward Oxnard, who looked lost. "But I've got backup. And bigger problems."

Tam looked doubtful. "What can you possibly do about the end of Death, Cooper?"

What *could* he do? Watch the worlds turn into a madhouse? Cooper pulled a wry face. "I meant my back. Have you seen it? I'm hideous."

Something dry and warm squeezed his hand. He looked down and saw that it was Tam's hand inside his own.

"I'm used to hideous."

Cooper grunted. Tam laid his tawny head on Cooper's shoulder.

"You should probably stay away from me, Tam."

"I know. Fuck you."

"I'd rather have coffee." Cooper squeezed the warm dry hand, thankful for it.

"How about both?"

Cooper smiled, then frowned—feeling his phantom finger twitch, somewhere amidst the worlds. He thought of the vivisistors that linked him to the new queen of the Seven Silvers. *It doesn't stop, does it?*

As if to prove his point, Alouette stepped forward and expanded into something bigger than herself. In one stride she opened up the kernel of herself and regrew whole branches of awareness, thought, and ability that had been denied her embodied consciousness. Looking at her directly, Cooper felt the change wash out from her body like a wave of ice water, as a woman exploded with the energy of herself, only to be replaced with a woman-shaped being. For a moment, as she grew in what Cooper could only identify as *presence,* her clouds of red hair began to burn the space they occupied with the fullness of her being, and he knew she wore her real name, Chesmarul. So many selves, for one meddling creature—were all the First People that complicated? Asher did not seem so, but how could Cooper tell?

But it was not Chesmarul the Red Ribbon who spoke. The invocation came from Prama, assuming her place as prince.

"These are inauspicious days. The Dying do not Die. The bile of the worlds rises in all our throats, but for this day, even here at the edge of all things, we share a moment of peace. In the years to come we may all need the memory of today, so open your minds to the taste of tears and milk, to the smell of petals on the wind, the sound of the water that spills into the sea of skies."

She paused. The spray from the falls cooled Cooper's face. Marigolds and cherry blossoms filled the air.

"Some of you feared, these past few days, that you faced the end of the worlds. You face something far worse than that. Still, if one thing can be said of our trials it is that life goes on, and so do we—in fact, we have no other choice. Now that *she* is dead."

Prama waited, and Chesmarul nodded her head at the funeral bier. Red curls licked through the air around the pyre like stylized winds, tendrils of the attention of Chesmarul. The caudal polyps still smoldered within the unrecognizable remains—so vast in age and size that her death took days—but the light was feeble. What had flickered like tea lights before now winked red and weak.

She must once have been spectacular.

"Rare in the worlds is a final funeral, but today we send to sea the remains of one of the savants-of-being, the very earliest First People, older than almost any before her, whose brood gave birth to the aesr race who founded the City Unspoken. Also the mother of Death, and perhaps even of sacrifice, who gave her flesh to become a battery for peace.

"Before the Third People, perhaps before even the lost Second, this nameless hero became bound beneath the earth within a sarcophagus of gold and light, and with her life the ancients pierced the gourd of *is* and opened up the Last Gate, the threshold to *is not*. With her Death that threshold is barred to us all, and consciousness returns to the mercy of the curse of *is*."

Prama kept speaking to a rapt assembly, but Cooper broke away from the crowd and found the edge of the nearest cliff—Tam was so focused on the immortal's words that he let Cooper walk away—and looked out over the emptiness, so full of sky. Far off, hundreds of miles away in every direction, he saw other skies, green firmaments and orange and black, lit by a vagary of stars. It really was a sea of skies wasn't it?—wrapping sky within sky within sky.

Why had Chesmarul stolen him away from his life? What had he *done*? He hadn't conquered the Undertow, or opened the Dome, or killed the Cicatrix. Not really. Was he just a witness, or was there more?

Behind him, Prama deferred to Chesmarul, who turned to face the crowd. More accurately, *part* of her spun toward the assembly—her eyes were portals to a plane of red electricity, a vital energy that was her true self. They brimmed with her.

"She was my mother too, you know. Before my little cousins became the aesr, she was *my* mother. I do not know who or what gave birth to the worlds, you gathered People of Remembered Skies, only who gave birth to me. We swam down the waters of the river Sataswarhi in the red-shifted dawn of things, my mother and me. Long before the worlds knew the counting of time, I swam out with my mother through a sea of light and music, and we were whole."

The crowd was frozen, the birds hung still in midair, and the waterfalls had become sculptures of broken glass. Cooper stood alone in a spot of shadow with Chesmarul, and he felt the tendrils that were her true self drawing a circle of stillness around them; he reached out with his own self and felt the boundaries of her spell—a simple thing, now that he noticed it, that didn't so much stop time for the rest of the worlds as speed up its passing within the circle she inscribed.

It struck him. "Oh, it must be Tuesday. For a whole week I didn't need to know what days were. Isn't that strange? Do you know about Tuesdays, or is that like me knowing what ants call the increment of time it takes for crumbs of my cake to fall from the table to the floor?"

"I know Tuesdays, and this a Tuesday." Her dress faded in and out of existence, showing the ruby lights crawling up the sides of her body. Lining her flat stomach. Coiling around her small but perfect breasts. Portals, just like her eyes. "Another fucking Tuesday."

"We're stuck in a loop, aren't we?" He looked at his hand. "It used to be that I was caught in a world of weekdays, and Tuesdays were my worst enemy—the second day, not as universally dismal as Mondays, but a depressing reminder of the rest of the week and month and year ahead. Now I've whole *lives* to contend with. Endless fucking lives, not to mention a seemingly endless number of overpowered beings who like to give me new powers that don't quite stop other overpowered beings from cutting bits of me off." Cooper nodded to himself and looked out into the vastness. "We are well and truly stuck."

Chesmarul shook her head; her pure red eye-holes left streaks trailing to either side like afterimages. "We're the opposite of stuck, now, Cooper. In fact, you might consider the thought that travel is the closest thing left to oblivion. You cannot cease to be, but you can cease to be *here*. Now that we cannot Die, we can only learn. Only voyage."

He made a noise that was half laugh and half sigh, and looked at her with a flat expression. "What the fuck are you doing with me, Chesmarul?

I have a little experience now, a few tricks up my sleeve. But I'm still nothing compared to you, or even compared to Asher. Christ, Sesstri can outfight me and outsmart me, and now she's a half-elf. I know I'm not here just to stand up to monsters in a rising gold bubble, or give Lallowë Thyu a little finger. What are you up to with me?"

She reached out with one hand to stroke his cheek, running her knuckles down the week-long growth of beard. Her skin felt like paper fire. She looked at him sorrowfully with her arm still outstretched; he smiled.

Chesmarul seemed to hesitate, then she commanded, "Cooper: *voyage.*" And in one deft motion she snapped his neck.

The waking current swept him away. Somebody who feels just like him smells menthol cigarettes and opens his eyes to a brand new sky.